BLUE

LISE GOLD

Edited by Claire Jarrett

Cover design by Neil Irvine Design

Unable are the loved to die. For love is immortality.

— EMILY DICKINSON

1

The preparations for the night ahead were in full swing as Celia roamed the dark corridors of the medieval Krügerner Castle in search of someone who could lend her a blow-dryer. All doors were open, airing the spacious guestrooms that were decorated with lavish fabrics and wallpapers, and filled with antique furniture. Maids in traditional black and white uniforms were rushing in and out with towels and linens, preparing the rooms for the annual summer ball.

Coming here was like going back in time. Celia liked the smell of damp in the old walls, and the sound of the floorboards creaking under her feet when it was quiet at night. Many would find it creepy, but this place was her home away from home, and she was genuinely excited to be back again. Although the winters here were spectacular, with snow-covered mountains and crisp air, summer was her favorite time of the year in Switzerland. It smelled fresh and green, and the lake that stretched along the back yard lay still, shimmering in the sun. The white roses that grew up against the walls gave the castle a romantic touch, and especially at night, it looked spectacular when the facade was lit up by spotlights.

The impressive property in Lucerne, Switzerland, was owned by her uncle, an eccentric aristocrat who despite being semi-retired, also happened to be one of the biggest art dealers in the world. Since Celia was family, she was one of the lucky few who always had a room waiting for her, and after visiting since her childhood, she knew the castle inside out. The interior hadn't changed much over the past twenty years, as Dieter Krügerner liked everything to be original, down to the smallest details. Sometimes that meant comfort had to give a little. There was no central heating in the hallways or corridors, and it was cool inside, even in the midst of summer.

Celia buried her hands deep in the pockets of the black velvet robe, her family crest embroidered in a dazzling gold thread over the left side of her chest. Her hair was wrapped in a towel as she'd just come out of the shower, and she was barefoot, allowing the deep red nail polish on her toes to dry. She was still recovering from jet lag, after arriving from New York yesterday, but the two-hour nap had perked her up a little, and she was excited for the night ahead and keen to get ready.

"Can I help you, Frau Krügerner?" One of the maids asked her.

Celia pointed to the trolley that the maid was pushing toward the next room, holding appliances and a variety of toiletries. "Yes please, Lina. Can I take one of those blow-dryers?"

"Of course." Lina handed her one. "Do you need anything else?"

"No, thank you, I have everything in my room." Celia smiled at her. "Have any of the other guests arrived yet?"

"Not yet." It wasn't the maid who answered, but her uncle who had snuck up on them. He was wearing a velvet robe too; his, a deep green that matched his padded slippers.

"Uncle Dieter!" Celia flew around his neck and gave him a long hug. "It's so good to see you again. Sorry I missed you last night; my flight was delayed."

"Good to see you too, kiddo." He squeezed Celia so hard that she could barely breathe. "You should have come a couple of days earlier like I asked you to. Her ladyship will be here soon, so the peace will be short-lived." The cheeky undertone in his voice as he referred to his sister-in-law— Celia's mother—hadn't gone unnoticed, and they both laughed.

"Believe me, I wanted to, but I had a problem with one of my shipments and I wanted to solve the issue so I could relax while I was here." Celia only saw her mother a couple of times a year, and the summer ball was one of the occasions she had to put up with her demanding and irrational behavior. The woman was simply impossible, and so was her brother, who was always at her heel. "I heard she's bringing a date," she said, rolling her eyes. "Poor man. Or perhaps I should say poor boy, as I doubt he's a day older than twenty-five; that seems to be her limit these days."

"I'm sure the poor boy knows what he's getting himself into." Her uncle narrowed his eyes as he looked at her. "But speaking of dates, I see you've come alone this year, and that's a first."

"I didn't feel like company."

"Or maybe you were hoping to reacquaint yourself with someone here?" He paused. "Erin, perhaps? She's confirmed her attendance."

Heat rose to Celia's cheeks just at the mention of Erin.

Her uncle was right; the woman she'd met here last year had been on her mind ever since, and Celia was secretly hoping she'd see her again. Nothing had happened between them, as they'd both brought a date, but that one dance they'd shared had stayed with her like it was yesterday. The way Erin had held her; tight and possessively... She'd never been held like that. Even after the song had finished, they'd lingered in the middle of the dance floor until Erin's girl-friend had pulled her away for the next dance. Celia suspected she'd spotted the instant attraction that had sparked between them that night, no doubt aware of the way Erin's fingers were caressing her back, and how her hands had lowered to pull her in closer.

"No. I'm genuinely happy with my own company," Celia lied after a passing maid pulled her out of her thoughts, and she chuckled when her uncle's lips stretch into a knowing smile. "Besides, the last time I saw Erin she had a girlfriend. A very beautiful girlfriend," she added, thinking of the cute blonde who had been on Erin's arm. Not only was she tall and stunning, Celia had also learned that she was a civil rights lawyer in the brief conversation they'd had, and there was no way she could compete with that.

"I don't think it was very serious between them," her uncle said casually.

"Really?" Celia nervously fiddled with the buttons on the blow-dryer. "Do you mean she's single now?"

"I knew it. You were smitten then and you still are; I can see it all over your face. You never could hide anything from me." Her uncle laughed, holding onto his belly. Extravert, overweight, bald, and with a rugged, white beard, he was larger than life in all senses, but for the first time in decades, he was looking slimmer and his face even looked a little gaunt. "I'm not sure about her current status. I guess you'll just have to wait and find out." He scratched his shiny scalp and shot her a challenging grin, knowing he was driving her crazy with his relentless teasing. Erin and her uncle were good friends, and there was no way he wasn't informed about her dating life.

"Okay, I confess, I might have found her somewhat attractive," Celia admitted with a smirk. She looked him up and down, now noticing he really did look significantly different. "Have you lost weight?"

"I have, can you tell? I stopped dieting altogether and guess what? The weight just started dropping off." He spread his arms and shrugged. "Anyway, it's a beautiful day, so let's not linger here in the dark. Care to join me for breakfast by the lake?"

2

Erin dropped her weekend bag on the floor and hung up her suit before she opened a beer from the minibar in her hotel room, tired after the journey. An eleven-day journey, to be precise. But it had been a fabulous eleven days on her yacht, and she'd gotten a lot of work done while sitting at the covered seating area on the upper deck, enjoying the view over the Atlantic. Her tan was deep now, and even with her short hair, she looked like her mother, she thought as she stared at her reflection in the mirror.

Sipping her beer, Erin took in the room. It was a little over the top and she didn't like the design, but it was practical for a couple of nights until she headed back to France, where her yacht was moored. The view from her corner suite, however, was exquisite. Endless green mountains with grazing cows dotted around stretched out in front of her. The charming old city of Lucerne lay below stretching along the large lake. She could see Krügerner Castle, her destination, on the other side of the lake, and the sight sent a flutter to her belly.

It would be her second year attending Dieter Krügerner's summer ball—a widely anticipated event held in June—with invitations so sought after, they were like gold dust. She'd met Dieter a couple of years back through mutual friends when she was in California visiting her parents, and a wonderful, tight friendship had developed, despite their age-gap and their backgrounds that couldn't have been more different.

Erin was looking forward to seeing her lovely, fun friend again, but the main reason she'd been a little nervous over the course of her journey, was the thought of seeing Dieter's niece, Celia. They'd only shared one dance last year, nothing more, but she remembered every moment of those brief five minutes. The way Celia smelled as she held her; fruity and sweet. Her long, dark hair that tempted her to run her fingers through it, her big, brown eyes and her beautiful smile... Her voice and her enchanting laugh, so delicate in her ear. Erin could still recall how her hand felt in hers, how they'd moved, like they'd danced together for years. But even after replaying that dance over and over, there wasn't one specific thing she could pinpoint that had drawn her in the minute they'd been introduced to each other. What had slayed her was the invisible force that seemed to radiate around them; one she couldn't name or explain it if she tried. Chemistry just wasn't a strong enough word.

The instant attraction had come as a shock to her because frankly, it was unheard of for her to fall for someone she didn't know. Just one glance was all it had taken, one second of eye contact and she'd wanted Celia like she'd never wanted anyone before. She'd seen a twinkle in Celia's eyes too, and looking back, that made sense because something as powerful as the pull she'd felt couldn't be entirely one-sided.

Of course, it wasn't that simple. She'd brought a date to the ball last year, and Celia had brought her girlfriend, Darcy. Darcy was the polar opposite to Erin; feminine, elegant, sophisticated, and frankly, she'd been surprised when Celia had asked her to dance while Darcy was distracted.

Her own date had been nothing but a brief affair. The woman was stunning, intelligent and sweet. Erin had even entertained the idea that it could grow into something more serious, but after meeting Celia, she just wasn't feeling it anymore, and she'd been comparing women to her ever since.

It was only ever one dance and Erin had told herself many times to forget about it, to put the woman out of her mind. Celia came from aristocracy. It wasn't just the gold signet ring she wore with the family's crest that gave that away; it was apparent in her poise and the way she moved and spoke, the way she held herself in conversations; polite but with a certain distance. She belonged in a whole different league, quite possibly darting through life like a princess and no doubt running in high circles. Erin herself was wealthy, but she was self-made and came from a working-class background. Having worked her ass off for everything she owned, the last thing she needed was a high-maintenance woman by her side who took everything in life for granted.

Still, Erin longed to kiss her, even a year later, and that was the reason she'd come alone tonight. She wasn't short of women in her life—in fact, she was very, very popular with the ladies in Bermuda—but she knew it wouldn't be fair to bring a date to the ball if her focus was on someone else. Women sensed things like that, just like they always sensed Erin wasn't long-term relationship material.

She zipped open the bag she'd hung on one of the clothes hooks, her mouth tugging into a smile as she studied the custom-made tuxedo. Just like last year, she'd certainly stand out as the only woman wearing a tux, but Erin hadn't worn a dress since she'd last visited her grandmother in Morocco at the age of fifteen, and anything other than a suit simply wasn't an option. Attending a ball solo was kind of frowned upon too, but Dieter was a good friend, and she knew he didn't care about etiquette and appearances like the rest of his family. Besides, she was donating a significant lot to the charity auction that would be held over dinner, so that should impress his guests.

Stripping off her clothes and grabbing a towel, another rush of excitement coursed through her at the hope of seeing Celia in a couple of hours. It was likely she'd bring a date, or perhaps she was still with the same woman. Erin had tried to find out, but Celia's social profiles were set to private, and she knew Dieter and Celia were close, so she hadn't dared to ask him about her love life either.

Erin finished her beer and headed for the shower. Date or no date, she was planning on making a lasting impression on the woman who had been on her mind since last summer. And if for some serendipitous reason Celia came alone, well, then she'd do everything in her ability to charm the hell out of her. If there was something Erin wasn't short of, it was confidence.

3

Celia let the satin fabric of her red gown fall down over her stiletto heels, then adjusted her thin shoulder straps in the mirror. It fitted her like a glove and was the perfect dress for the occasion; elegant and sexy but not revealing enough to be considered vulgar. The bias-cut fabric emphasized her slim waist, modest curves and full breasts, and although the low back didn't allow for a bra, she could still get away with not wearing one at thirty-eight. Besides, she was in the mood to seduce tonight and showing a little skin would only help in that department. Her long, brown hair fell over her shoulders in loose waves, and apart from mascara and the bright-red kiss-proof lipstick that claimed not to smudge or wear off, she was wearing little makeup. She smiled at herself in the mirror, feeling satisfied with how she looked.

An unexpected knock on the door made her jump, and she rushed over to open it. Letting out a dramatic cry, she gave her mother a hug and told her all the things she wanted to hear; that it was great to see her again, that she'd missed her, and that she looked beautiful and ten years younger than the last time she'd seen her.

"Thank you, dear. I paid Dr. Sebastian a visit last week, and he agrees that I look ten years younger, too." Her mother stroked the fabric of her silver ballgown, then looked Celia over while she pointed at her dress. "It's red," was all she said before her big lips pulled into a straight line of disappointment.

"Yes, it is." Celia raised her brows questioningly and waited for her to elaborate, but she didn't. Her mother never let a chance pass to take a compliment whilst subtly offending another woman over her appearance, and that included her own daughter. It didn't sting; Celia was used to it and she'd decided a long time ago that she couldn't care less what her mother thought of her. "Where is your chaperone?"

"Leopold is coming." Her mother looked over her shoulder. "Leopold, hurry up for God's sake! I need my purse."

Celia's heart went out to the man who joined her mother in the doorway and handed her a silver pouch. He was older than she'd expected; probably her age, which was an improvement from the last string of boyfriends, and he shot her a sweet smile as he held out his hand to shake hers. "Leo. Nice to meet you."

"Leopold," her mother corrected him. "He goes by Leopold." Celia doubted anyone of his age still went by that name, and the absurd idea of her mother insisting he presented himself as such, almost made her laugh.

"Hi. I'm Celia. It's really nice to meet you too." She was about to engage in small talk with him, but her mother interrupted them.

"Have you seen the table plan, dear? They've just put the board with the table plan up by the ballroom entrance and I saw that you're not even seated at the family table. It's simply unheard of; I'm going to speak to your uncle about it right away."

That news was like music to Celia's ears and she swiftly put a hand on her mother's arm and smiled in an attempt to calm her down. Apart from her uncle, there were very few relatives she enjoyed spending time with, so she'd be the last person to feel insulted or complain about not sitting with them. "It's fine, Mom. Please don't bother him right now, he's a little stressed today." Another lie had slipped from her tongue. Uncle Dieter was rarely stressed, and he'd been nothing but chirpy since breakfast. Her mother was right though; it was unusual, and it might even spark rumors about a family feud, but she was sure he'd done it for a reason. A tingling sensation spread through her core as she speculated what the reason for the curious arrangements might be. "It's okay, really. We'll have plenty of time to catch up tomorrow."

'Her ladyship' looked bitter at being thwarted and drew in her lips as if she'd sucked on a very sour lemon. "All right. But he has to know that it is unacceptable. I don't even know the people you're sitting next to. Brian Prendergast and Erik something..."

"Erin?" Celia asked hopefully.

"Could be. I didn't pay attention as the surname didn't ring a bell. Something foreign." Her mother let out a deep sigh. "Basically a nobody."

Celia's face flushed, and her pulse started racing. *Good old Uncle Dieter. He's made me a very happy woman.* "I really don't care, so let's not make a fuss. Please," she begged, until she finally saw her mother relax a little. "How about we have an aperitive together? I'd love to get to know Leo better." She turned to him and winked. "Apologies, I meant Leopold."

"Fine." Her mother turned on her heel. "We'll see you in the entrance hall in ten minutes. Your brother and his girl-friend should be there, too."

"Wait... Girlfriend?" Celia was talking to herself now as her mother had already disappeared. She let out a silent groan as she closed the door. Her pompous brother Fabian was quite possibly her least favorite member of the family but luckily, he had just as little interest in her. He had her mother wrapped around his little finger, leeched off her, and he hadn't worked a day in his life. Frankly, she had zero respect for him.

Coming from old money in a long bloodline of Swiss bankers, of which most moved to the US two generations back and started investing there, the small fortune Celia had inherited from her father was enough for her to do the same. She liked to work though, and she felt good about herself when she accomplished things on her own.

Unlike her relatives, she lived in a modest three-bedroom apartment that she'd bought a couple of years back, and she didn't waste money on expensive cars, women or drugs. Instead, she ran a compact business that exported organic baby food to China because she'd seen an opportunity there seven years ago. It had become very successful and what she liked about it was the simplicity. Apart from one middleman in Beijing and an assistant and an accountant in New York, she had no staff, and that gave her the freedom to take time off, or to go away whenever she wanted.

Despite her easy lifestyle, Celia didn't date much. Burned by numerous women in the past—who turned out to be more interested in Celia's family fortune than in her—relationships had taken a backseat, but the lack of intimacy didn't bother her. She liked her own company, she was popular in the casual dating department and all in all, she was comfortable in her life. Sometimes, she longed for something more, but it was hard to find a woman she both trusted and liked, especially if she took the very important factor of chemistry into account. Chemistry was rare, at least for her, and as much as she'd like to lose herself in passion, that wasn't in the cards for her right now. *Or maybe it is*, the little voice in the back of her mind told her as she grabbed her purse and headed out the door. Her head was spinning just at the thought of seeing Erin again.

4

_____

"**G**ood to see you again, my friend." Erin gave Dieter a hug and a pat on his back. "You're looking very trim." Most people had already arrived, she noticed, the valets busy parking cars in the last few spots on the premises. Dieter was smoking a cigar in front of the main entrance and he seemed relaxed and happy while he welcomed his guests.

"Thank you. Lost some weight so I can keep up with my young Andy."

"You're still seeing him?" Erin asked. "I'd love to meet him."

"Yes, he's inside, mingling like a queen. I'll introduce you to him later." Dieter eyed Erin's tux and gave her an approving grin. "I'm terribly sorry I couldn't put you up here tonight. Turning down family causes more drama than I'm willing to deal with and I only have eleven bedrooms, so I hope I didn't cause offense."

Erin chuckled at his 'only eleven bedrooms' remark and shook her head. "Don't worry about it, the hotel is just fine."

"No, it's not fine. I'd much rather have you here than

those terrible gold-diggers, but if I did that, they might start asking questions and..."

"I know." Erin lowered her voice. "And really, you don't need to apologize. I'm just happy to see you." She looked through the enormous double doors and heard music and laughter coming from the entrance hall. A red carpet ran from the parking lot to the entrance, where guests' eyes were drawn upward to a canopy of white string lights that hung down from the castle's ceiling like a sparkling shower of rain. Underneath it, butlers ushered people inside to take their coats. "This looks spectacular yet again. I don't know how you do it."

"Trust me, none of this is my doing, but we have gone all out this year." Dieter took a long drag from his cigar and smiled at one of the maids, who came out to empty the standing ashtray. "As you know, my staff is fantastic." He regarded Erin, who narrowed her eyes as she continued to glance into the hall.

"Looking for anyone in particular?"

"No." Erin flinched at how quick and loud her answer left her lips.

"Okay." Holding up both hands in defense at her unexpectedly sharp tone, Dieter laughed. "Just asking. How was the journey by the way? I can't thank you enough for your generosity in donating a vacation on your yacht for the charity auction. Some of the guests already have their bags packed and their minds set on placing the highest bid so I have high hopes we'll raise a lot of money."

"That's fantastic. What charity are you supporting this year?"

"Actually I decided on two. Half of the proceeds will go to an LGBTQ refugee and asylum seekers charity, and the other half will go to my foundation that gives money to the arts, which includes providing college grants to talented kids from impoverished backgrounds." Dieter stubbed out his cigar and gave her another big smile. "It's the biggest auction I've organized so far."

"Yes, I had a look through the auction catalog online and can see you're selling off some impressive pieces yourself." Erin wanted to ask him about his health, but this was not the right time to discuss such serious topics. "Well, fingers crossed your guests will be digging deep into their pockets tonight. I'd better go inside," she said, gesturing to a couple that was walking up to Dieter to say hello. "I'll see you later. Enjoy the party."

Her pulse started racing as she entered the grand hallway where guests were being welcomed. Now crossed off the guestlist, she handed her phone to one of the security guards, who marked it with her name and placed it in a safe. Phones or cameras were off-limits at Dieter's summer ball. Besides the fact that he preferred people interacting with each other instead of with their phones, this was a night for the rich and famous to party without the risk of being exposed. According to Dieter, there was rarely a serious scandal, but his guests drank a lot, and sometimes people got caught cavorting with ones they shouldn't be cavorting with.

Taking a glass of champagne off a tray, Erin thanked the waitress. She was just about to cross the room and greet her and Dieter's mutual friends from L.A., when her eye caught the board with the table plan in front of the doors to the ballroom. She scanned the list for her name, then felt a wave of excitement as she saw who she would be sitting next to. There was no way this could be a coincidence as Celia would normally be at the family table, and she silently thanked Dieter, who had obviously been a lot more observant last year than she'd realized.

"Erin!"

Erin turned to find her friends had already spotted her. "Mark, Dunja," she said, walking over to them. "It's lovely to see you both again." She gave them a hug and held up her glass in a toast.

"You're looking very tanned. Have you been out on the water much?" Dunja asked.

"I have, actually. I..." Erin stopped mid-sentence as she caught sight of Celia, standing with her mother. For a moment, she felt paralyzed and could do nothing but stare. There was another man with them, whom she recognized to be Celia's brother, but apart from him, there was no one by her side. It was as if Celia could feel Erin's eyes on her, the way she suddenly looked around the room, distracted while her mother was talking to her. The long, red dress with its low-cut back looked gorgeous on her, and Erin could already imagine her hand on her bare skin while they danced. Everything about her was still as captivating as last year, and when a hint of insecurity flashed over Celia's features as she scanned the entrance hall once again, Erin knew she'd been looking for her too. "I'm terribly sorry," she said, excusing herself. "I'll be right back to catch up with you guys but there's something I need to do first."

Just as she was about to approach her, Celia turned and started walking down the passageway where the ground-floor restrooms were situated. Erin picked up her pace, and she could feel the pull getting stronger while she closed the distance between them, as if Celia was magnetic and drawing her in. Normally, she would have waited until they were seated before speaking to her. Erin was patient by nature and lived by the motto that all good things came to those who waited, but now, another hour without even saying 'hi' to Celia suddenly seemed like a lifetime away. She looked so damn hot swaying her hips while she walked, her hair dancing over her back in long waves.

Unaware of Erin behind her, Celia gasped when she said her name and took hold of her wrist. Erin hadn't meant to touch her; she'd acted on impulse, but now that it was too late, she figured she might as well go with it. Seeing Celia shiver and noticing the goose bumps that appeared on her arms, she moved closer as her object of desire froze to the ground.

5

Celia liked the anticipation, the waiting game, and she felt good about how she looked as she joined her mother, brother and a handful of distant family members at one of the standing tables in the entrance hall where champagne and finger food was being served. Even if nothing happened tonight, she would make sure Erin noticed her.

She could have looked her up on social media, or asked her uncle for Erin's number, but she'd been worried that that rare sense of attraction and mystery surrounding her would fade if she gave into the temptation. And so, she still knew nothing more about Erin than she'd learned last year, which was very little. She was American, she lived in Bermuda and she did something with boats.

Keeping half an eye on the door while she engaged in meaningless conversation with her brother, she adjusted her red dress that was as dramatic as the castle in full decor. Hundreds of candles were lit, and a large classical orchestra was playing a waltz on the wide staircase. The absence of artificial light and electronic music was unique in this day and age, and she heard gasps of delight each time new guests arrived.

"May I check your purse, please?" a member of staff asked her. "I've noticed you haven't been through security yet and you need to store your phone, if you have one on you."

"I'm so sorry. I forgot to leave my phone in my room and have my name ticked off the list. I'm in the red room," Celia clarified, noticing the woman was not one of Dieter's full-time staff members. She shot her an apologetic look as she handed over her mobile.

"No problem. I'll make sure it gets returned to your room." The woman marked it with Celia's name and put it in a velvet pouch. The only proof that tonight had ever taken place would be in her memory.

As always, it felt strange to be without her phone, but Dieter Krügerner never did things the traditional way which was exactly the reason why this ball was so popular.

Celia and her family weren't the only people who had flown over from abroad. Out of the four hundred guests attending the ball, at least three hundred had travelled extensively to get here, knowing it would be worth their time and effort. The room dripped money. Artists, actors and other people from the creative industry, celebrities, aristocrats, business moguls and family members like herself were dressed up to the nines; the women in fabulous dresses, the men in exclusive designer suits.

When Celia spotted the only woman in a suit walking through the doors, she took in a quick breath, because although she was standing across the other side of the room, there was no mistaking her identity. Erin's tailor-made tuxedo was cut to perfection, and she wore it like no woman ever could. Her posture and the way she carried herself was that of someone entirely at ease in her body, and Celia loved the longer locks of her pixie cut black hair that fell casually over one eyebrow, the way she imagined her to wear it every day. Just like last year, Celia could feel the pull from afar as Erin entered the room, unaware of her eyes on her.

The way she smiled as she handed over her phone had a purity to it that was incredibly sexy. Celia remembered that smile all too well. Alluring, determined, and a little dangerous. But what she like most about her appearance was the absence of a woman on her arm. Erin grabbed a glass of champagne and greeted a couple of people while her eyes scanned the crowd. *Is she looking for me?* When she walked over to the table plan next to the ballroom entrance, Celia saw her smile widen, and she knew Erin had come here with the same intention.

"Celia?" Her mother raised her voice. "Celia, your brother just asked you a question." Again, she glared at Celia's dress as if it was the most hideous thing she'd ever seen.

"Sorry, Fabian. What were you saying?" She tried not to sound irritated, but she was, because now she'd lost sight of Erin.

"I asked why you haven't brought a plus one." Fabian raised a brow. "Was it that hard for you to find a date? Did that last woman dump you too?"

Rolling her eyes at him, Celia shook her head. "You're an asshole, you know that? It was never serious in the first place and I'm not seeing anyone right now. Unlike you, I don't pay for my dates."

"Hey, Mira's not an escort." Fabian's eyes shifted nervously from their mother to Mira, his supposed girlfriend, who was already rubbing herself up against another man in the far corner of the hall. It had only taken her ten minutes to find someone who was richer and more successful than her brother, and that amused Celia.

"Of course she isn't. It was a tasteless joke," she said with a sweet smile while she squeezed his arm. "If you'll excuse me, I need the bathroom." Walking off, her eyes darted across the hall, but she couldn't see Erin anywhere. When she turned the corner and headed into the dark corridor, she felt an electric presence behind her.

"Celia." Someone grabbed her wrist from behind, and she immediately knew it was Erin. Her heart was pounding hard in her chest as she stopped, but she didn't turn around. Feeling Erin's body against her back and the sensation of warm breath against her ear instantly turned Celia on, and she was relieved that the powerful attraction toward her hadn't faded. If anything, it had grown way stronger, because she was pretty sure the way her body was now reacting wasn't normal.

"Do you remember me, Celia?" Erin asked.

Celia shivered at the sound of her low and sultry voice. "How could I forget?" she said with a tremble. She wasn't a shy person, but the way Erin approached her made her feel vulnerable, and it rang through in her voice. Although she'd imagined this moment many times since her uncle had hinted that Erin would be here, she'd never felt so unprepared in her life. "Erin," she added, then finally turned around to meet the woman's dark, intense gaze. She was still holding her wrist, which, in any other situation would be highly inappropriate, but with Erin, it set her on fire.

Erin smiled as she unashamedly looked her up and down. "It's good to see you again." She bit her lip and hesitated. "I'm sorry to corner you here, but I saw you from the other end of the room and after our dance last year, I just wanted to say hi before dinner. I see we've been seated at the same table." She paused as her eyes raked over Celia again. "I hope you don't mind me being so direct, but that dress looks stunning on you and I've really been looking forward to seeing you again." Her gaze lowered to Celia's left shoulder. "I remember that birthmark; it looks like a half-moon. It's cute."

"You're observant," Celia said, and swallowed hard.

Erin reached out to circle the dark mark, and Celia was aware she could see what her touch did to her as her breath hitched and the hairs on her arms rose. "I hope you will give me the pleasure of a dance again." She smiled. "That's if your date doesn't object."

"I came alone." As soon as the words were out, the electricity between them sparked to alarming levels. "Where's *your* date?" Celia asked innocently, because Erin didn't need to know that she'd been watching her.

"I came alone too." Erin finally let go of her and took a step back, burying her hands deep in her pockets, as if she feared doing something she'd regret. Immense sexual tension flowed between them as they took each other in. "Well, now we have that straightened out, I'll let you do your thing. I'll see you at the table."

6

_____

The doors to the ballroom opened, revealing long rows of tables to either side of the polished dance floor where a coat-tailed pianist was playing classical tunes behind a grand piano. The tables were laid out with white linen, delicate china and silverware, crystal glasses, long white candles in silver candlesticks and large centerpieces made of white lilies. It was elegant and spectacular, and when the beautifully dressed guests wandered around the room to find their seats, Celia really felt like she'd gone back in time.

Erin joined her at their table and pulled out her chair before taking a seat herself. "So, you're not sitting with your family this year," she said with an amused smile.

Celia chuckled and looked over at her mother, who was already taking over the conversation at her table, clearly getting worked up over something insignificant as usual. "Can't say I mind."

"Good. Then I guess their loss is my gain." Erin turned to the man sitting next to her and introduced herself and Celia did the same. Her manners were impeccable, and

Celia liked that. Erin didn't seem like she came from old money like her own family, though. She was too real to have been brought up with a silver spoon dangling from her mouth, and the ruggedness she had about her was insanely attractive.

"We never got the chance to talk much last year, so I didn't ask you what you did for a living," she said when the formal introductions were out of the way. "My uncle told me you did something with boats and that he was invited onto your yacht last summer. He said he had an amazing time with you."

"Yes, Dieter is a good friend. We met through mutual friends at a dinner party. Mark and Dunja are here too." Erin took a sip of her wine and licked her lips as her gaze lowered to Celia's mouth. "And to answer your question, my company designs and builds yachts, and we specialize in building customized superyachts. I still do most of the design work myself."

"Interesting," Celia said, even more intrigued by her now. "Did you design your own yacht?" Again, Erin looked at her mouth, and Celia wanted her to kiss her so badly that she subconsciously inched a little closer.

"I did. It's currently moored in Antibes, in the South of France. It took me a while, but I managed to get there all the way from Bermuda, then got on a flight to Zurich and took a cab here."

Celia's eyes widened. "My God, did you really sail all the way from Bermuda?"

"Yes. It took me eleven days to get here; I didn't rush. The weather was great, and I've always wanted to see the French coast, so it was worth it."

"Then you'll have to take it back too, I assume?"

"Not personally. I've donated the return journey to the

auction. I have a fantastic crew; a great captain and it's run like a five-star hotel so I'd be surprised if no one bids for it." She paused for a moment then draped her arm over the backrest of Celia's chair. "The starting bid is thirty-thousand dollars, which is a bargain since chartering it costs ten-thousand a day. Maybe you should consider bidding on it?"

Celia laughed at that and shook her head. "As amazing as that sounds, the idea of being out on the open sea terrifies me."

"If that's all that's stopping you, how about I come along to keep you safe?" Erin raised a brow as her fingers played with a strand of Celia's hair.

The featherlight touch sent a bolt of arousal through Celia's core, making her gasp softly, and she noticed Erin's expression darken at her reaction. "I'm not so sure I'd feel safe with you. There's something about you that makes me a little nervous."

"Hmm..." Erin tilted her head and inched closer. "Are you afraid of me?"

"Should I be?" Celia asked in a whisper. The tension between them was electric and she had a feeling Erin was about to kiss her any minute. Erin didn't answer her question, and that turned her on even more. Instead, she pushed Celia's hair to the side and ran a finger down the back of her neck, causing her to shiver.

"Enough about me. Tell me about yourself," she said, changing the subject. "What do you do?"

"It's boring compared to your superyacht design business."

Erin shook her head. "Nothing you do could ever be boring. Come on, I want to know. I've only met you once before and these circumstances aren't exactly normal. Unless you're always dressed like this and spend every night at amazing parties as the most beautiful woman at the ball. Being a member of the Krügerner family, it's certainly a possibility, but now that we're talking, I don't get that vibe from you."

Her words made Celia blush, and she was grateful for the dim light in the room. "I export organic baby food to China," she said. "It's a lucrative business for me, and it brings a healthy and balanced diet to babies there, so everyone wins."

"I don't think that's boring. Do you like babies?"

"Not necessarily." Celia laughed and shook her head. "Sorry, that came out wrong. I just meant that I have no children myself and not much affinity with babies. I just spotted an opportunity in the market. Do you have children?"

"No." Erin seemed amused by her question. "I enjoy my freedom too much and I wouldn't be a great mother, with all the traveling I do." She paused. "But I do make a great lover."

"I have no doubt about that." Erin's confidence was thrilling, and for a moment, Celia had no idea what to do with herself. She turned slightly, so their table companions wouldn't notice Erin's hand in her hair. "Where are you staying tonight?"

"In your room, of course." Erin's eyes caressed her cleavage, her breasts now straining in the low-cut red dress.

"Is that so?" Her bold answer sent a twitch between Celia's legs and she swallowed hard. "I don't recall anything about room sharing arrangements."

"Oh, you haven't heard?" Erin sat back and twirled her wine around in her glass with an air of total nonchalance. "Apparently, I'm supposed to sleep in your bed... and you're supposed to be naked."

Celia got all fired up as she quietly processed Erin's indecent proposal. No one had ever been so direct with her, and the way this was heading, she was going to get more than she'd hoped for tonight. "And are you supposed to be naked too?" she finally asked, meeting Erin's eyes.

Their moment was interrupted when the tuna tartare appetizers arrived and reluctantly, they took that as a cue to pick up conversation with the people to the other side of them. Celia didn't normally mind the etiquette of a formal dinner but right now, she regretted having to pause their flirty back-and-forth. "Brian," she said, forcing a smile while she tried to remember if she'd met the man next to her before. "How was your journey?"

7

After the main course and an hour of relentless flirting, four violinists gathered around the pianist who had replaced the orchestra with subtle background entertainment, and as they joined in, the music grew louder and more dramatic. Strips of white aerial silk that formed a triangle in the high ceiling were released over the dance floor, and Erin watched as three women in white leotards walked onto the floor and took hold of one each.

Conversations halted as all eyes were on the acrobats who made their way up to the ceiling while wrapping themselves in the cloth. It was a beautiful sight, the way they climbed and swung around each other with immense control and grace. Erin was having a hard time focusing though, and she shifted closer to Celia, craving her nearness. Celia's family was sitting at a table nearby and her mother occasionally shot them disapproving looks, but Celia seemed more than happy with the situation.

She hadn't been taken aback by her straightforward approach. In fact, she'd played along and by now, there was no question she felt the same physical craving as Erin did.

Fueled by a desire to feel her arousal, Erin reached under the table and placed her hand on Celia's thigh, never taking her eyes off the show. She wasn't normally this bold, but the woman next to her was simply so irresistible that she couldn't help herself. Many, many fantasies involving Celia had taken control of her mind over the past year and none of them involved holding hands or candlelit dinners. No, her fantasies were purely physical, and if it was up to her, she would make each and every one of them come true as she longed to rake her hands and her mouth over that delicious body.

Celia's gaze was directed toward the ceiling too, but Erin heard her take in a quick breath at her touch, and she felt her muscles tense under her exploring hand. Glancing sideways, she saw Celia's lips were parted, and her chest was heaving up and down fast. Knowing she was turning her on made Erin crave her even more, and she left her hand there. When she made no effort to remove it, Erin squeezed her thigh softly, causing Celia to shift in her seat.

Making sure no one was watching them, Erin moved her hand to the inside of Celia's thigh and she slowly started gathering the fabric of the long dress, hiking up the hem little by little. Turning to look at her, she saw Celia's eyes flutter closed, the anticipation clearly getting the better of her. When she opened them again, she glanced at Erin for a split second, and the desire in her expression was clear; Celia wanted her just as much, and Erin wasn't sure how she was going to make it through the long night ahead without tearing her dress off.

Erin felt hot, so she removed her bow tie and unbuttoned the top two buttons of her dress shirt while her other hand continued to hike up Celia's dress. She froze when she heard gasps around her, thinking they'd been busted, then realized the audience was reacting to the acrobats, who had spiraled down the strips of silk and wrapped themselves in a foothold just before they were about to hit the floor upside down. Hoping this wasn't the end of their performance, she continued, her fingers finally reaching the hem of the red gown. She slipped her hand underneath it, stroking her fingers over Celia's bare knee. Her skin felt delicious; soft, smooth and warm, but what made her heart race even more was the intense tremble in her thigh.

What they were doing felt terribly dangerous, but Celia didn't stop her. Unable to control her desire, her gaze was hazy now, a soft moan escaped her mouth when Erin started stroking her skin.

Applause broke out, and Erin retracted her hand, then clapped along as if nothing had happened. While the applause continued, she leaned into Celia and brushed her lips against her ear. "It's a shame the show is over. Another ten minutes and I'd have made sure you were seeing stars instead of dancers before your eyes."

Celia's cheeks flushed again, and she stared at her as if she was some rare species she'd never seen before. Her reaction didn't surprise Erin; she didn't imagine Celia engaging in naughty games in public on a regular basis, and she could tell she was wondering why the hell she was going along with it.

"Are you warm, Erin?" the man next to her asked. He gestured to her bow tie on the table, pulling them out of the moment.

"Yeah, it suddenly feels boiling in here." Erin opened another button, then shot Celia a flirty smile.

"Good idea, I don't know why I'm torturing myself." Her neighbor followed suit and took off his own bow tie, then stuffed it in his pocket. "Formal wear... Why people bother in this day and age?"

Polite exchanges flowed back and forth, but Erin had trouble concentrating on what her neighbor was saying as the sensation of touching Celia's skin had left an agonizing tingle between her legs. All she could think of now was taking her to bed, and she muttered a quiet curse when the entrée arrived, knowing she'd need both hands to eat.

"Perfect," she said, turning to Celia when the waiter put down a plate with sole à la meunière in front of her. Now that she was completely in thrall of her, there was no way she was going to let her lose interest, even though that seemed an unlikely prospect at this point. She lowered her voice to a near whisper and locked her eyes with Celia's, losing herself in their brown depths. "I've been looking forward to my meal tonight and I'm very, very hungry."

8

Celia sat through dinner, only half listening to the conversations. She'd never been so distracted in her life and her mind was consumed with fantasies of being intimate with Erin and more to come. Yes, she'd hoped Erin would come alone to the ball this year, but nothing could have prepared her for Erin's unapologetic and predatory attitude in expressing and taking what she wanted. She wasn't used to women like that, but she'd loved every second of sitting next to her and was still shaking from Erin's wandering hand that had left her so aroused that the last few hours had passed in a blur.

While dessert was served, an old-fashioned canvas screen was lowered over the back wall, and a lectern was set up on the dance floor, replacing the musicians. Instead of a laptop, an old projector was used, its first images sharing information on the charities her uncle was raising money for.

"Are you bidding on anything? Apart from the yacht vacation, of course," Erin joked.

"I'm not sure. I kind of splurged on a painting last year, so I might be sensible and just give a donation. You?"

Erin shook her head and lowered her voice as the auctioneer did his introduction speech, then started with a vintage diamond and ruby ring that had belonged to the Norwegian royal family. "I didn't see anything I really wanted but I'm hoping the vacation will raise some funds."

"I'm sure it will." Now that everyone was focused on the auction, Celia was hoping Erin would continue what she'd started, but disappointingly she kept her hands to herself. Several pieces of jewelry, paintings and sculptures were sold successfully before a picture of Erin's yacht filled the screen.

"And now for the more adventurous among you," the auctioneer said. "A two-week vacation on *The Barracuda*, sailing from Antibes to Bermuda, return plane tickets included. Twenty-four-hour service, fine dining food cooked to order, access to snorkeling and diving equipment, a pool and a jacuzzi, and let's not forget about the spectacular views as you cruise the Mediterranean and African coastline. Starting bid thirty thousand dollars. Ladies and gentlemen, this once in a lifetime trip comes courtesy of Erin Nour, CEO of *Barracuda Designs*. Let's all give her a round of applause for donating this amazing lot."

Celia raised a brow as she studied the pictures of the vessel. This wasn't just any yacht, and the whole experience sounded like indulgence of the highest level. "Nice boat," she whispered.

"It's not a boat, it's a yacht," Erin said as she shot her an incredulous look, pretending to be insulted. "Still not tempted?"

"No. I'll admit that it looks amazing, but I'm busy at work, I don't like being on the open water and—"

"I'll start. Thirty thousand." Celia turned in surprise

when she heard the first bid coming from her uncle. As he had already donated a small fortune in art, he didn't usually bid during his own auctions.

"I didn't know he was interested," she said, turning to Erin.

"I didn't either. He's probably just pretending in order to drive the bid up."

"Thirty-five thousand," a woman in a black gown said. Then, another five people joined in, driving the bid up to sixty thousand dollars.

Celia chuckled, suspecting Erin was right. Her uncle was sitting back now, watching the last two people standing until only the woman in black was left with a sixty-five thousand bid.

"Sixty-five thousand for this lady here. Anyone else?"

"Seventy thousand." Gasps and murmurs filled the room as her uncle stood again.

"What the hell?" Erin looked just as surprised as Celia felt, and she frowned when Dieter finally won the bidding war, the room erupting with cheers and applause as the auctioneer slammed the gavel down on his final bid of ninety-five thousand dollars. "I know this is for charity but still; he doesn't need to pay for that. He could have just asked me."

"I don't get it either; he doesn't usually splurge on vacations." Her uncle pointed at Erin and shot her a cheeky smile, looking genuinely happy with his purchase. A shorter, much younger man in a white suit hugged him, then jumped up and down in excitement after her uncle whispered something in his ear.

"Is that the mysterious Andy?" Celia asked. "I know Uncle Dieter's been seeing someone on and off for a while now, but he arrived late, so I never got the chance to introduce myself."

"Highly likely. From the way he's gloating, I'd say he's just been told he's going on a romantic vacation."

"Hmm..." Celia regarded the man with interest. Although she'd heard about Andy, he was never around when she visited, and her uncle hadn't formally brought anyone to the ball for years. "He looks a lot younger, doesn't he?"

Erin followed her gaze. "Does that bother you?"

"No, not at all. He's just very different from his ex-partner and I suppose I expected he had a type or something, but that's clearly not the case."

"I must admit, they're an unusual pair." Erin turned to the screen where the next item—a gold watch—was being showcased. "How much longer do you think this will go on?"

"Maybe another forty minutes. Why?" Celia's eyes met Erin's and she shivered at the intense pull between them.

"Because I can't wait to dance with you again."

"Oh, you want to dance with me, do you?" Celia asked in a teasing tone.

Erin nodded slowly as her lips pulled into a seductive smile. "I want more than that, but let's start with a dance."

9

The dessert plates were removed, and the table was cleared from clutter as the first guests headed for the dance floor. The orchestra—now at full capacity again—started playing a slow version of 'Moondance'.

"May I have this dance?" Erin asked. She stood up, gallantly took Celia's hand and kissed it.

"I thought you'd never ask." Celia let Erin guide her to the middle of the dance floor and sighed in delight when she pulled her close against her, one hand pressed firmly on the small of her back, the other holding her hand. Her backless dress felt like a blessing, as it allowed Erin to caress her skin while they danced. Had she bought it with that in mind? Celia wasn't sure of anything anymore apart from one thing; she wanted this woman.

Erin's thumb stroked her softly, then harder, before she shifted her arm and took hold of her waist. She led, and soon they flew across the floor so naturally that Celia couldn't help but wonder if they'd be just as attuned in bed.

"You smell great," Erin said, inhaling against her neck.

"So do you." Celia rested her head against Erin's

shoulder and ran her fingers through the short hair at the back of her neck. "Did you look me up?" she asked.

"Kind of." Erin pulled back a little to face her and dipped her head. "I tried the easy way, using social media." Her mouth was almost on Celia's as she continued. "But you're a private person and although that made me even more curious, I decided to leave it at that. I'm very patient; I chose to wait a whole year to learn more about you."

"You didn't seem so patient at the table," Celia joked. A smile played around her lips and she fought the urge to press her mouth against Erin's.

"You're right. I seem to have run out of patience, now that you're near. Does my boldness bother you?"

"No." Celia felt breathless and leaned in further to kiss her, but instead, Erin turned her head away and pressed her cheek against hers while she spun them around.

"Did you look me up?" Erin asked.

"I did," Celia said honestly. "But I didn't find much either." She paused. "It didn't bother me though; I'm a very patient person too."

"We'll see about that." When Erin pulled her in and pressed their hips together, Celia had to admit that her patience was crumbling. She was moving, but she had no idea what she was doing as her mind was spinning, filled with so many fantasies that there was no space left for coordination. It didn't matter; Erin's dancing skills were strong and Celia hardly needed to put any effort in at all as she effortlessly guided them around the floor in perfect synchronicity. She imagined they looked like they'd danced together for years, but their obvious chemistry told a whole different story. Between them hung the tension of two people who were only just getting to know each other, two people who were hungry to explore, and Celia was aware of her mother staring them down. She ignored her, and let Erin spin them around once again, basking in the blissful glory of their closeness. "So... would you like to see my room later?" she asked, locking her eyes with Erin's.

"I would love to see your room." Erin tightened her grip, and Celia let out a quiet moan.

The band switched to playing a tango, and she saw a spark ignite in Erin's eyes. Couples left the dance floor for a breather, or because they weren't familiar with the complicated steps, and soon there weren't many guests dancing. Dancing the tango wasn't Celia's strong point either, but Erin's smile told her they'd be okay. "You're a good dancer."

"Thank you. So are you."

"I'm hardly doing anything," Celia retorted with a chuckle. "I like how strong you are; it's easy with you."

Their postures shifted passionately with the music, and Erin moved her hand between her shoulder blades, facing her while they continued to glide. Their interaction was controlled as well as sensual and dramatic, a push and pull of longing and desire. Celia seduced her and Erin reacted. Erin led and she responded. They were connected on all levels, their movements hot and fiery as Celia's feet slid neatly between Erin's in short, smooth strides.

Erin dipped her and Celia arched her back to the point that her hair reached the floor. One hand held her firmly behind her back while Erin's other hand let go of her and traced her neck, then continued down between her breasts while she leaned over her. For a moment, Celia thought she might bury her face between her breasts, but she suddenly straightened herself, pulling them back into an upright position. She doubted this was part of the dance, but Celia let her and noted her skin was tingling everywhere Erin had touched her.

All eyes were on them now, intense stares telling her the audience was fascinated by the mysterious Erin and their fiery connection. She wasn't sure if their sensual interaction was appropriate; they were at a formal ball after all, full of people her family wanted to impress. It had taken them long enough to accept that she was gay, and they'd only mellowed when her uncle, who was gay himself, had begged them to stop being so dramatic and get over it.

They were both out of breath when the song came to an end, but that had nothing to do with the physical workout and everything to do with the fact that they were turned on beyond imagination. Celia grinned when she realized Erin's hand was on her ass instead of on her back, where it should be, and she quickly pulled out of her grip, creating some distance between them.

"Hey, I might not be an expert on dancing the tango, but I'm pretty sure ass-groping is not one of the moves," she whispered with a smile. The struggle was real—she was having trouble controlling herself too—and she decided that perhaps it was best if they sat back down, at least for a while.

Erin laughed and took her hand. "I guess I'm busted. You're just too hard to resist." She led them back to the table, then shot Celia a wicked smile. "Come on, let's have a drink. But you're not off the hook yet. I want another dance before the night is over."

10

———

The tension between them grew when the band stopped playing and the first guests started to leave. Erin knew Celia would have invited her to her room hours ago, if it wasn't for the fact that she was expected to be here until the end. Being a Krügerner, she had a duty to represent the family, yet she hadn't left Erin's side once. Both so aroused after hours of dancing and sitting close together, she suspected they might break things once they were alone.

"Do you need to say goodbye to people?" she asked as they walked back to the table to grab Celia's purse.

Celia shook her head and lowered her voice. "No, let's just leave quietly. Everyone is tipsy; they won't notice I'm gone."

"Whatever you say, sexy." Erin snuck her hand into the side of Celia's dress as they rushed through the long passageways and took the staff staircase so they didn't have to use the main staircase in the entrance hall.

She looked around the room while Celia lit the candles on the antique oak nightstands, then some in the ornate silver candlesticks on either side of a vase of red roses in the middle of the vanity table. It was a beautiful room, and it was clear that this had always been hers, as there were framed pictures of Celia and her family on the bookshelf and the walls. The biggest picture was of Celia as a child and she was posing with a handsome, dark-haired man which Erin suspected was her father. She sat on his lap in a frilly yellow dress with a cute matching bow in her hair. The antique furniture was more feminine here than in the rest of the castle, and it blended in so well with the luxurious cream and gold wallpaper and the silk drapes that she wondered if Celia had decorated it herself. It smelled of old books and conjured up a sense of history; a scent Erin loved, and mixed in with Celia's light perfume, it evoked a dreamy sensation in her.

Celia turned to her, leaning against one of the bed posts. Erin sensed she was waiting for her to make the first move, as from the first moment they had met again, there had been a silent understanding that she would be in charge tonight. Seeing Celia standing there in the shimmering candlelight took her breath away—she looked resplendent in her red dress and the shadowy light in the room was giving her an almost angelic appearance—so much so, that she almost forgot to keep up the air of confidence she'd worked so hard to maintain all night.

"God, you're beautiful." Erin licked her lips and closed the distance between them. Now that the moment had come, it felt surreal to be alone with her. She felt hot breath against her lips when she leaned into her, tilted her head and closed her eyes, finally brushing her lips delicately over Celia's. After so much teasing they both let out a quiet moan at the physical tension their kiss released, and Erin was startled at how the light touch awoke all her senses at once. As she pressed into her, Erin felt Celia's chest rise and fall fast, and soon she was enveloped in a heated glow. She laced her fingers through her long hair, then cupped her neck and pulled her tighter against her.

Celia moaned again and parted her lips to let her in, then hungrily pushed into her. Colliding into a passionate embrace, they gave into the delicious sensation of claiming each other and neither of them held back. Soft, then firmer and more determined, moist, breathy and full of longing, the kiss couldn't have been more perfect in Erin's wildest dreams. Celia's lips felt delicious and cushiony, the velvet touch of her tongue just like she'd imagined, and she tasted of the whiskey they'd had after dinner. Her insistent mouth sent a wild tremor through Erin as she answered her call for more, wedging her hands inside her tuxedo jacket to run them over her back. In return, Erin's hands explored the curves of Celia's hips and her behind until they both pulled away as they were out of breath and about to lose all control.

Bringing two fingers to her sensitive lips, Celia stared at her, wide-eyed. "I don't know what I expected," she whispered. "But it wasn't this."

"Me either." Erin's gaze fell on Celia's shoulders, and unable to resist, she pulled her hair to the side and pressed her hips into her. Pleased to feel Celia tense up with anticipation as murmurs of pleasure escaped her, Erin leaned in and kissed her neck while she slowly pulled down the zipper on her left side. Just that simple action made her heart jump as it caused the fabric to part, inviting her in. Exploring Celia's smooth curves, she ran her hand inside the dress, tracing her aroused flesh. Her hair and her neck smelled delicious, and each time she moved her mouth farther down, Celia's breath quickened. Bringing her mouth back to Celia's, she took her into a tight hold and pressed their lips together once again. She wasn't careful or tender, but kissed her fiercely, grabbing her hair to pull her head back. When she let go of her hair and pulled away, resting her forehead against Celia's, she couldn't remember the last time she'd made out with someone like this, so all-consuming and explosive.

"I want you," Celia said, running a hand over Erin's cheek before she brought it down to the lapel of her tuxedo jacket. "These clothes need to come off. Way too many layers."

"Not yet." Erin shook her head and caught her wrists when she started unbuttoning her shirt further. "Soon. But not yet." A mischievous smile played around her mouth, and she could tell by her reaction—her flushed face and the fire burning in her eyes—that Celia was enjoying this cat and mouse game. The stunning belle of the ball would be hers tonight and if she could manage to pace herself, she was going to take her sweet time.

Her fingers moved up to skim Celia's shoulders and worked their way under the thin straps, pulling them down her arms so the garment was barely covering her. She could hardly believe she was here in Celia's room, undressing her, because although she'd fantasized about it many times, there had always been a little voice in the back of her mind telling her it was never going to happen. That it was too good to be true.

"I want to make sure you never forget this." Erin's voice was raspy from talking over the loud music all night and when she met Celia's eyes again, she could see a hint of inse-curity in them. Or maybe it was fear; she didn't know her well enough yet to be sure. Whatever it was, it was mixed with an immense desire that told her Celia was hers and only hers tonight.

Welcoming her touch, as if she'd been starved for her, Celia had no idea Erin had thought of little else in the past weeks either. "I love how you take control," she whispered through moans. "The way you held me and pushed your hips into mine on the dance floor earlier... It drove me insane."

"Yeah? You liked that?" Erin loved knowing that she had an effect on her, because if there was something she craved right now, it was making this captivating woman surrender to her sexual fantasies. She moaned too, as Celia's hand glided through her hair, then over her shoulders and back down to her chest.

A sudden knock on the door tore them out of the moment. Celia jumped away from her, swiftly secured her straps and zipped up her dress. "Who's there?"

"Celia! It's Fabian. Mom's had an accident."

"What?" Celia opened the door to meet her brother's bloodshot eyes. "What happened? Is she okay?"

"More or less." Fabian was slurring his words. "I think she hurt her leg and her back. And she wants you to go to the hospital with her." He shrugged. "I'd go myself but I'm not exactly in a state to do that right now, and Leo walked out after she blamed him for the accident." He leaned heavily against the doorframe as Erin came up behind Celia and for a moment, Erin thought he might fall asleep standing.

"Have you called an ambulance?" she asked.

Fabian's eyebrows shot up as he shifted his attention to Erin. He clearly hadn't expected to see her there. "No, it didn't seem serious enough. She's by the front door with like a million people fussing over her, but she insists that Celia takes her."

"Okay, I'm coming." Celia shot Erin a regretful look as

she turned to her. "I'm sorry, I have no idea how long it's going to take."

"Don't worry about it. Do you want me to come along?"

"Probably better if you don't." Celia gave her hand a squeeze before she grabbed her trench coat and her purse. "Make yourself at home, I'll see you later."

11

_____

By six a.m., Erin regretted not going back to her hotel. Celia had gotten hold of her number and sent her a message a couple of hours ago. Apart from a bruise, everything seemed to be fine with her mother's leg, but as she kept insisting that she couldn't walk, they were still performing tests. She figured Celia wouldn't be in the mood for company by the time she got back from the hospital, and frankly, the last message she'd received was the only reason she'd stayed. _'Please don't leave. I hope it won't take much longer.'_ That had been two hours ago and now that it was starting to get light, she felt like she was overstaying her welcome. The taste of Celia still lingered on her lips, and she could hear her soft moans when she closed her eyes and recalled that magical kiss. Perhaps it was best to leave it with that, to let it simmer as her most recent memory until someday, hopefully, they'd meet again.

Erin had a shower and decided to leave, but not before she'd checked the backyard to see if Dieter was there. He was an early riser, and even though it had been a late night for him, she suspected that wouldn't stop him from reading the morning papers over his first coffee while the sun came up.

'Dear Celia, I hope your mother will be okay. Thank you for an unforgettable evening and call me if you'd like to meet up again,' she wrote on a slip of paper, then placed it on Celia's pillow. Looking at the red roses on the vanity table, she hesitated for a moment, contemplating if it was too much, then grabbed one and placed it next to the note. God, she was seriously pining over this woman, but there was no point playing it cool. She really liked Celia and she wanted her to know that.

Taking the staircase at the back of the castle and following the ground-floor corridor to the kitchen, she said good morning to the staff, who were already busy preparing breakfast, then went into the backyard through the staff entrance. She flinched as she realized she'd fallen back into old habits. Over the winter months she'd spent a substantial amount of time here, so she knew the castle inside out. The family was not supposed to know that though, and neither was Celia, so she'd have to be more discreet, even if everyone was still asleep.

She smiled when she saw Dieter in his chair, looking out over the lake while sipping his coffee, and he turned when he heard her approach. "Sorry, I should have come out the main door. I wasn't thinking."

"No worries. Good morning, my friend. I'm glad to see you're still here. Are Celia and Babette back yet?"

"No, they're still at the hospital. I thought I'd better get back to the hotel to freshen up." Erin patted his shoulder. "Congratulations with your winning bid. I must admit; I was more than a little surprised."

"Thank you. I'm looking forward to my vacation." Dieter narrowed his eyes at her as if he knew something she didn't.

"No newspaper today? What's up with that?"

Dieter shook his head and beckoned to a chair, then poured her a coffee from the pot on the table. "No, no newspaper. I stopped reading them. Please, sit down with me."

Erin frowned as a knot formed in the pit of her stomach. She took the coffee, then regarded him. He looked sleepy, but overall happy and content. "You always said you couldn't live without your newspaper."

Dieter shrugged, pulled another chair out and propped his feet up on it. "Well, things change."

"How are you feeling?"

"Hungover," he joked.

Erin chuckled and poured some milk into her coffee. "You know what I mean."

"Yes." Dieter was silent for a long moment as he stared out over the lake that was so still it was hard to tell the mountains and their reflection apart. "I need you to keep what I'm about to tell you very quiet for a while. Can you do that?"

"Of course." Erin swallowed hard. This was not what she'd expected. "I haven't told anyone about last year; I'd never do that."

"I know." Dieter looked over his shoulder to make sure no one was listening in before he turned to her. "I'm dying, Erin."

"What?" Although she'd expected bad news after the newspaper comment, she had not seen this coming, and his words made her stomach clench and her heart rate shoot up. "Prostate cancer again?"

"No, liver cancer, HCC. Totally unrelated and just bad luck, really. It's spread and it's too late for chemotherapy so there's not much they can do. I didn't catch the symptoms in time; thought they were side effects from my treatment last year and you know me; I don't like hospitals, so I kept putting off making an appointment."

"Is there nothing they can do?"

"No." Dieter shrugged. "To be honest with you, even if they could, I wouldn't put myself through aggressive treatments at my age. I've already lost my sex drive and my appetite from the chemo."

Erin nodded. "I know it's been hard for you." She tried her best not to get emotional, because Dieter seemed fine talking about it. Over the past two years, she'd grown to love him like family. It felt like part of her heart had just been ripped out, but she didn't want to upset him. "How long have you known?"

"Three months. The first month was very hard. There was this constant panic that threatened to choke me every time I thought about how much time I had left. It was like I had an ever-present, ever ticking countdown clock in the back of my mind." Dieter paused. "The panic wasn't that bad the first time around, because I had hope. But there's no hope now, and I've had to come to terms with that."

"Dieter, I'm so sorry."

"Yeah, me too." Dieter let out a deep sigh before he continued. "Then there were all the questions about life and death and religion—you name it—constantly bugging me. I've always been a hedonist at heart, never taken the time to explore spirituality or anything like that, and I felt this inexplicable need to make up for it, like I could find answers somewhere if only I looked hard enough. I tried attending church a while ago, then went to Thailand to immerse myself in Buddhism for two weeks." He rolled his eyes. "Of course, I came to my senses. There are no answers out there, and I don't believe in anything, so I've managed to make peace with the fact that soon, I simply won't exist anymore."

"How long do you have left?" Erin's eyes met his, and for a split second, she saw his fear. "And why didn't you tell me sooner?"

"Three months, optimistically four. Pessimistically... well, who knows? It's spreading fast." Dieter took a slow sip of his coffee and went back to contemplating the serenity of the lake. "It was something I had to go through on my own; that's why I kept it quiet for so long. It's impossible for others to know what it's like when you know you're going to die, and I needed to make peace with it myself before I told anyone apart from my therapist. But I'm telling you now, because you're the only one who knows everything about me and you've been a very, very special friend to me throughout my treatments last year." He turned his head and shaded his eyes from the upcoming sun. "But you have to promise me you won't tell anyone."

"So, you don't want anyone to know you're dying?"

"No." Dieter's tone indicated there was no discussion to be had. "I want to tell a handful of people eventually, but only because I want to spend time with them or make amends before I die."

"What about Celia and Andy?"

"Not yet. But I want them to come along on the vacation I bought last night."

"Are you even healthy enough to embark on a journey like that?" Erin asked.

"Yes, I have medication and I need this now more than ever. Now that I can still travel... There's no need for Andy to know just yet. Andy is..." He frowned, searching for the right words. "Andy is wonderful, but I suspect my wealth might be one of the main reasons he's with me. I think he's hoping to settle into a comfortable life with me at some point. I'm pretty sure he likes me, and I genuinely don't think he's repulsed by me in the bedroom, even if I'm double his age and have trouble performing," he added with a hint of amusement. "But my wealth most certainly plays a role in his interest toward me, so that only leaves two people who I trust with my life—quite literally now—I suppose. You and Celia."

"Then you should tell her."

Dieter shook his head. "I don't want to upset Celia. I'd like to spend some time with her without her knowing, so we can just have fun and enjoy those precious last moments." He paused. "As you know, I love her like a daughter, so it's important to me to have her in my life during my last months. And Erin, I'd like you to come along too. Will you please come?"

"If you want me to, I'll come." Despite the gloomy conversation, Erin's heart skipped a beat at the thought of being on her yacht with Celia. She'd suggested it during the auction, but it had been a flirtatious joke rather than a serious proposal. "But how are you going to get Celia onboard without telling her? She made it very clear last night that open sea wasn't her thing and she has her job and—"

"I'll think of something," Dieter interrupted her. "And if I don't succeed, maybe you could help me? She clearly likes you very much."

"She does?"

"You're still here, aren't you?" Dieter laughed. "You should have seen her face when I told her you might be coming to the ball alone. Such a shame Babette had to pull that attention-grabbing stunt."

"What do you mean?"

"You'll come to learn that there is nothing wrong with

her leg or her ankle, nor with her back. She just does that sometimes and it's always Celia who has to save the day."

"Right." Erin pondered over that for a moment but didn't enquire further. "Even if Celia does like me, that doesn't mean I'll be able to get her to change her mind. I'm still practically a stranger to her."

"But I'm not, and Andy will be there so it's a group vacation, not a romantic getaway." Dieter took a sip of his coffee. "Don't worry. I'm pretty sure I'll manage to persuade her one way or another, and as long as you don't tell her about my illness, we can all have a wonderful time together."

Erin felt conflicted, but seeing the desperation in her friend's eyes, she found herself nodding in agreement. "Okay."

"Thank you. Can I ask you for another big favor?"

"Anything." Erin meant it. The shock of his news was only starting to settle in now, and she swallowed down the lump in her throat before taking deep breaths.

"Do you mind if we make a couple of detours? There are some places I'd like to visit, people I'd like to see. A pilgrimage, if you will. But that means it might take a little longer for you to get back to Bermuda. I know you're busy and—"

"Hey, I don't mind at all," Erin interrupted him. "Anything you want, seriously. Just give me a list of where you'd like to go, and I'll send it through to my captain so the crew can prepare. I'll check if their schedule is free, and if not, I can hire some freelancers."

"Thank you, you're the best friend anyone could wish for." Dieter gave her a grateful smile. "And I might be pushing it now, but I need one more favor." His eyes narrowed in amusement when he added, "But I'm a dying man, so I'm allowed to push it."

Erin managed a chuckle. "Of course. What is it?"

"I don't want you to be sad or feel sorry for me. I've had a good life—a great life—and I would love for us to have a fun trip together without thinking about the fact that it will be our last. I'm okay. I'm physically not in bad pain as my doctor gave me a whole arsenal of goodies, and I need you to be okay too."

"You know I can't promise you that," Erin said, knowing there was no way she could just switch off her emotions. "But I can promise you I'll try."

"Thank you, that's all I want." Dieter put a hand on hers, a rare sign of sincere affection from his side. Although he loved to hug and kiss people, he didn't often open up. "Why don't you pick up your things from the hotel and come back here? My guests will be leaving today so there are plenty of free rooms and our adventure starts tomorrow, so you might as well stay over."

"Really?" Erin hesitated. "According to the auction itinerary, *The Barracuda* is departing tomorrow, but this is not a standard situation and we can wait a couple of days if you'd prefer?"

"No, tomorrow is perfect," Dieter replied.

Erin nodded, then stood and lingered on the spot. "I don't like the thought of lying to Celia, it doesn't sit well with me, Dieter."

"I know, but it's not technically lying. You're just keeping my secret safe for a little while longer, and once I do tell her, she'll understand."

"Okay. I won't say a word." Remembering Dieter wanted life to carry on as normal, Erin forced a smile before she called a cab and walked around the estate to the drive.

12

C elia clenched her jaw as she saw a cab passing their car, going in the other direction. As it came directly from the castle, she suspected it might be Erin. *Damn it. I've just missed her.*

She'd been worried about her mother at first, but after the third doctor had assured her that she was perfectly fine, she'd started to get irritated as this wasn't the first time she'd fallen for this particular trick. And in the meantime, Erin had been waiting for her all night, until she'd finally given up and left. Although it was frustrating, Celia tried not to take it out on her mother. Yes, it had most likely been a stunt to gain sympathy or attention, but that also meant there had to be a reason for her strange actions. While her mother was going through tests, Leo had messaged to let her know that he'd booked an earlier flight and would be leaving without her. She didn't blame him; there was only so much criticism a person could take, and her mother was very generous when it came to handing out that.

"There you are. How are you feeling, Babette?" Her uncle came walking toward them as they got out of the cab.

"I'm tired, Dieter. Very tired and in a lot of pain. I might take a nap; Celia and I are having tea before Fabian and I leave for the airport, but that gives me a couple of hours to rest." She walked toward the door slowly, hunched like an old lady.

"Do you need help getting to your bedroom, Mom?" Celia asked, although she knew no help was required.

"No, I'll be fine, dear. Thank you for coming with me."

Celia followed her mother with her eyes and noticed she walked straighter the moment she disappeared into the hallway. Turning to her uncle, she let out a long sigh. "Why does she keep doing that? Last year at her sixtieth birthday party, she fainted when I was about to leave and as soon as we got to the hospital, she was fine. No headache, nothing. In my opinion, that's just not possible."

"Only God knows why Babette does what she does. That woman is as unpredictable as the weather. But in the end, she's family, and I'm glad you've forgiven her for what she did to you after your—"

"Please, let's not talk about that," Celia said, stopping him. "Mom and I have managed to maintain a degree of civility over these past years but that's about as far as our relationship goes."

"Of course." Her uncle buried his hands in his pockets and nodded toward the table. "Coffee?"

"God yes, I'm in serious need of a decent coffee. That hospital brew tastes like crap." Celia followed her uncle to his breakfast table and helped herself to a cup. "By the way, I think I just saw Erin leave," she said as she sat down. "I wish I could have at least said goodbye before she left."

"No worries, you'll have plenty of opportunity. Erin went back to the hotel to pick up her things because she's coming with me tomorrow."

Celia almost choked on her coffee and needed a beat to get her coughing fit under control. "What do you mean? Where are you going?"

"*The Barracuda.* The auction, remember? We're taking a trip."

"Oh, of course. I totally forgot about that with everything that's been going on." Celia frowned as she met his eyes. "So, you're telling me you've invited Erin onto her own yacht? That's kind of funny."

Dieter laughed. "Yes, precisely. Andy is coming too. He's gone home to pack his things and he's meeting us here tomorrow. Erin will be back later and she's staying the night."

A flutter ran through Celia at his words. Being given a second chance of a night with Erin was more than she could have hoped for, and this time it would be without interruptions. "That's great, I'm glad I get to see her again," she said, trying to sound casual. "We were kinda in the middle of something when I had to leave last night, but I couldn't exactly ignore Mom when she was sitting on the floor in floods of tears, could I?"

"No, you did the right thing." Her uncle smiled. "Anyway, I was wondering if you'd like to come along. Join us on our adventure. The yacht sleeps eight, we're only three so far and honestly, there's no one I'd rather have with me than you. I think the four of us would have fun."

Celia stared at him, wide-eyed. "Me? Tomorrow?" She chuckled. "That's a bit last minute, don't you think?"

"Yes, it is last minute, but I bought the package, the vacation is mine and *The Barracuda* is departing tomorrow." He winked. "And you could be on it. Imagine beautiful shores, white beaches, sunset cocktails, open water swimming, visiting the most amazing places, exotic food, the smell of the ocean..."

"You're really selling it, but as lovely as the auction pictures looked, I have no desire to be stuck on a boat for days on end." As Celia said it, she wasn't entirely sure about that because the idea of being stuck anywhere with Erin was rather appealing, and she shivered, remembering their moment in the bedroom. She'd relived that moment over and over while waiting at the hospital, suffering through the uncontrollable twitch between her thighs that still showed no signs of abating.

"A yacht," Dieter corrected her. "There's a big difference."

"Sure." Celia threw her head back as she laughed. "Yacht, boat, plane, car... It's a confined space; it's all the same."

"Come on, honey. When was the last time you did something truly spontaneous?"

Celia pursed her lips as she pondered over that. "You're right; it's been a while since I did something out of my comfort zone but even if I wanted to come, I have to work."

"You work from home, don't you? The yacht has high-speed Wi-Fi and you'll have plenty of private space, not to forget full-time service, so you'll have more time on your hands than you would at home."

"Hmm..." Celia tilted her head and smiled. The idea had seemed preposterous yesterday when Erin had joked about it, but it didn't seem so crazy anymore. "I'll think about it."

13

"You must know she's only after our family money, Celia." Babette Krügerner took a sip of her coffee and winced. "God, the Swiss really don't know how to make a decent brew."

"Please, Mom. We were just having fun, at least until I had to leave for the hospital with you and trust me; Erin doesn't care about my money." Celia let out a deep sigh and glanced at her watch. Only an hour had passed but it felt like a lifetime. Her mother had been banging on about Erin ever since Fabian had let it slip that she'd been in her room last night. She was still walking with a limp that magically disappeared when no one was looking. 'A severely sprained ankle,' she'd told anyone who was willing to listen.

They were sitting in the 'parlor', as her mother called it. The room she'd chosen for their family catch-up was one of the social rooms in the castle that was originally built to receive guests of lower class, but Celia didn't tell her that as she had no intention of moving somewhere else. Frankly, it was exhausting enough as it was, and she just wanted to do her duty—to be a good daughter and sister—then disappear as soon as she could and get into bed with Erin, once she returned from the hotel.

Memories of their fiery make-out session flooded her mind once again and she hadn't felt this happy and alive in a long time. It made it much easier to handle her family duties because she simply didn't care that much about the ridiculous conversations that were going on.

Her brother and mother were sitting opposite her on a Victorian two-seater, and she herself was perched on the edge of a chair after getting changed into a white summer dress that was so virginal in its simplicity that she couldn't imagine even her highly critical mother could find anything bad to say about it.

Poor Lina was searching her mother's room for her sleeping pill that she desperately needed for her flight back. She claimed it had fallen out of her purse, but Celia wouldn't be surprised if she'd already taken it and had forgotten all about it. Her brother was looking a little rough, and she looked him up and down, seeing an opportunity to move the conversation away from Erin. "Are you okay, Fabian? What happened to your date?"

"She had to fly back," Fabian grunted, before clearing his throat. "She had some business in Texas to take care of."

"Mira is a busy little bee," their mother added.

"Right, what a shame. I would have loved to have gotten to know her better." Failing to sound sincere, Celia painted on a smile. She didn't mention that the gossipy maid had also told her his 'girlfriend', who he'd undoubtedly paid a lot of money to accompany him, had taken off with another man last night.

"Yes, well, perhaps next time." Fabian added a splash of whiskey to his coffee while their mother pretended it was milk. "I'm sorry I interrupted your rendezvous with that woman wearing a tux."

"I'm sure you've gathered from Mom's monologue that her name is Erin." Celia left it at that, as she had no intention of defending what she'd done, or rather what she'd been desperate to do. "What time is your flight?" She knew it sounded like a stab, and honestly, it was. Just like every time they met up, she was looking forward to seeing them go again. Her mother had been sweet and needy last night, but now she was back to her acerbic self.

"Five p.m. The driver is taking us to the airport at three." Fabian glanced at his ostentatious gold watch, looking just as frustrated as Celia at the realization that they still had a good fifteen minutes left.

It hadn't been that bad when her father was still alive; Celia vividly remembered those family vacations and celebrations during which everything seemed fairly normal and fun. Perhaps they had been a normal family once, but sadly, since her father had passed away, everything had changed. After suddenly coming into a lot of money, her brother had become a total asshole, and her mother... well, her mother was just her mother. These days, her uncle was the only person left that Celia trusted. Their opinions were aligned when it came to most things, and it didn't surprise her that he hadn't joined them as he'd already had to endure her mother and brother last night over dinner.

"We thought we'd try ANB Airlines for our journey back," her mother said. "I wasn't happy with our inbound flight on American, but apparently ANB's first class cabins are exquisite."

"So I've heard." Celia took a sip of her coffee while she calculated they must have spent a sickening twenty-two thousand dollars between them just on flights. "Uncle

Dieter will be leaving for his yacht vacation tomorrow, and Erin and Andy are joining him."

Babette's eyes widened as she clearly hadn't expected her brother-in-law and Erin to be such good friends. "That was just a ridiculous stunt he pulled. I'm sure he gives enough to charity." She huffed. "Why would he spend God knows how long at sea when he can simply fly? And why bring that strange little man Andy, and why bring Erin?"

"Because they're fun?" Celia suggested, and just to wind her up, she added: "Erin and Uncle Dieter are really close, you know. Plus it's her yacht, don't forget she donated the trip." She toyed with the idea of telling them she might join too, then decided against it. Threatening to go was one thing but embarking on a journey for several weeks was another.

"Well, she's clearly after poor Dieter's money too."

Again, her mother had beaten her, and Celia shook her head and held her tongue as she got up, swiftly followed by her brother, who downed his 'coffee' in one go, making sure no hard liquor went to waste.

"Celia, honey, we have to go. It was really lovely to see you again. Please come and visit us soon, we don't see nearly enough of you these days." Her mother held her arms out in a dramatic Mother Theresa-like gesture.

"I will," Celia promised, and gave her a hug. Then she received two air kisses, the way Babette imagined chic people in London did, even though she'd never been there. Fabian gave her a stiff hug too, their heads almost colliding in the awkward farewell.

Her mother turned at the door and pointed at Celia's outfit. "You really should reconsider that dress. It looks way too conservative on you and it does nothing for your figure."

"Are you serious?" Celia was speechless and even a little amused at her ability to come up with something to put down her appearance, even though she'd tried her hardest to dress for her mother's approval.

"Yes. You have my genes; you should be proud and show off your curves," her mother said, then blew her a kiss.

With that, they disappeared out of sight and Celia let out a long breath, relieved to be alone again.

14

"**Y**ou're back."

"I'm back." Erin's heart skipped a beat as Celia opened her bedroom door for her. They lingered there for long moments, staring at each other, until Erin finally stepped closer and kissed her softly. The moan that escaped Celia's lips told her she hadn't changed her mind about them yet, and that was a relief. After what they'd started last night, she'd imagined their reunion to be passionate beyond belief, but with the news she'd received this morning, it was hard to think of anything else than the fact that her best friend was dying. "And so are you, I see. How is your mother?"

"Fine." Celia smiled, brushing her lips against Erin's. "She and my brother also left an hour ago, so no one will disturb us this time."

Erin reached out to run her fingers through Celia's hair, loving the feel of her silky locks. If anything, she looked even more stunning than last night without the makeup, wearing a simple white dress that looked super cute on her.

She wanted nothing more than to take off that dress, but at the same time, she also felt like crying, and that wasn't a healthy combination.

"Are you okay?" Celia asked when Erin remained silent. "It's okay if you've changed your mind..."

"No, I haven't changed my mind. Trust me, I want you." Erin let out a long sigh. "But as much as I've been fantasizing about you, I've just had some bad news, so I'm not in the right frame of mind, I'm afraid."

"Oh. I'm so sorry to hear that." Celia's soft expression was nothing but genuine, and as she wrapped her arms around Erin's neck and pulled her in, Erin felt tears rolling down her cheeks.

"Fuck," she said through sniffs. "I didn't want to cry, it's just that..." Falling silent, she held Celia in return as she couldn't explain why she was upset. Although they were practically strangers, this was exactly what she needed. Celia's warmth comforted her, and the sweet smell of her shampoo distracted her from gloomy thoughts, relaxing her a little. She hadn't cried in her hotel room; she'd just slept in the silent hope she might feel better when she woke up. But she hadn't felt better, because Dieter's cancer wouldn't just go away, and she realized that now. "Fuck," she said again, wiping her eyes as she stepped back. "This isn't exactly the best way to woo a woman."

"Hey, it's okay." Celia took her hand, got on the bed and gestured for Erin to lie down next to her. When they were face to face, she ran a hand over Erin's cheek, then pulled her in and kissed her forehead. "If you want to talk about it, I'm here. And if you don't, that's fine too. We still have two hours before dinner, so let's just lie here unless you prefer to be alone."

Erin nodded and buried her face in Celia's neck. It was a

strange sensation as she never allowed herself to be vulnerable around others. If she was sad, she usually retreated and avoided people until she felt better. But she was going away with Dieter tomorrow, and there was no escaping the outside world this time. Somehow, she would have to find the strength to make the journey enjoyable for him and not only that, it would have to be the trip of a lifetime. Not because she prided herself in providing one of the best yacht charter experiences in the world, but because it would be his last.

"Thank you," Erin whispered, inhaling deeply once more. Honey; she recognized the scent from last night when Celia's lips had sent her flying. Her mouth that she'd been longing for like nothing else. God, it had been heavenly and so sexy. She could still feel the softness of Celia's skin on her fingertips, still taste her on her tongue. "I'm sorry we have to say goodbye tomorrow. This isn't what I had in mind."

"Me going off to the hospital with my mother wasn't what I had in mind either," Celia joked in an attempt to cheer her up. "But sometimes things just happen. Are you still traveling with Uncle Dieter tomorrow, or are you cancelling? If you're not in a good place you shouldn't feel like you have to go just for him."

"No, I'm still going." Erin managed a smile. "I'll feel better in the morning, I'm sure."

"Then I'm coming too."

Erin narrowed her eyes as she studied Celia. She looked surprised herself, as if she couldn't quite believe what she'd just said. "Really?"

"Yeah. If that's okay with you..."

"You don't have to ask me; it's Dieter's gig." Erin smiled, and this time it was genuine as a flash of happiness coursed through her for the first time since that morning. "But I'll be delighted with your company."

"Good. And if I change my mind, I can always disembark somewhere while we're still along the coast, right?"

"Anytime you want."

"Okay." Celia bit her lip and hesitated. "I'll go and buy some stuff in town tomorrow morning. I only packed for a week and I'll need to get a couple of things."

"No need. Just give me a list and I'll send it through to the crew. Clothes, shoes, underwear, swimwear... anything."

"Surely they don't have time for that? And I don't want you to stress about anything either. You're clearly upset and—"

"And you're the best distraction for me," Erin interrupted her. "Besides, the crew are in Antibes and they're very resourceful. It's much easier to get stuff in a French hypermarket than it is here, and we can shop on our stop offs too."

Celia smiled. "Okay," she said, draping an arm around Erin's waist. "I'll write you a shopping list. I'm going to need at least a couple of bikinis if I'm going to vacation on a yacht."

Erin's mood lifted a little, knowing she'd have Celia with her, and the thought of seeing her in a bikini did intense things to her already anxiety ridden core. She'd have to be strong and wake up every day with the mindset that this was Dieter's dying wish. That the whole point of this trip was to have fun together. To spend quality time with Dieter and create some amazing memories. Lowering her gaze to Celia's irresistible full lips, she felt a deep physical urge to drown herself in her body, but she refrained. This was not the right moment, not when she was so overwhelmed with emotions.

"You can stay in my room tonight," Celia whispered. "We can just sleep. Or you can take the room next door, it's free."

"Thank you. I'd like to stay with you, but I think it might be best if I take some time to myself. It's not you, it's me."

"I understand." Celia pulled her in once again and held her close. "You don't need to explain."

15

"There you are!" Dieter looked pleased as Celia and Erin joined him for dinner in the back yard. Apart from the staff, it was just the three of them left in the castle, and Celia loved the tranquility that came with having so much private space. "I was worried you'd sailed into the sunset without me." He gave Erin a wink as he unfolded his napkin and placed it on his lap.

"Still here," Erin said. "It's your vacation, we're just tagging along."

"We?" Dieter asked.

"Yes. Celia and myself."

"Excellent!" Dieter clapped his hands together. "That makes me a very happy man." He nodded at his butler when he held up a bottle of white wine, then waited for him to pour it. "Can't say I've ever crossed the Atlantic before. It feels like a big adventure."

"It does." Celia smiled at him. "I can't promise you I'll stay for the entire journey, but I'm sure it will be a lot of fun." She realized how surreal it was to sit here in the yard with her uncle and his friend, whom she was crushing on like a teenager. Apart from the annual summer vacations in her youth, her recent visits had always been short; a quick hello and goodbye, and that was a shame really, because it was so peaceful here. They were sitting right near the lake's edge, and it was lovely at this time of day with the low sun reflected in the ripples on the water. "Are we stopping off anywhere on our journey?" She asked.

"Yes. At your uncle's request, we're doing a couple of additional stops." Erin took a sip of her wine and smiled, seemingly a little better after her short nap. She'd fallen asleep in her arms and Celia had loved the closeness and the soothing sound of her breathing. If anything, she wanted her even more now. "We'll be mooring in Tarragona, Menorca and Casablanca, and in Dakar and Cape Verde." She gave Celia an infectious smile that made her stomach flip. "And the final stop is Bermuda, of course. I have to return to work again at some point, but we're not in a rush as I can work remotely."

"That sounds like one hell of a trip, and a lot longer than the initial auction vacation."

"Yes, Erin very kindly agreed to change the itinerary." Dieter shot Erin a wink. "I'm looking forward to introducing you to my friend Andy. I think you'll like him. He was here last night but you two were so busy getting reacquainted with one another that I didn't get the chance to introduce him."

"I can't wait to meet him." Celia arched a brow at him. "But come on, Uncle Dieter, there's no need to call him a 'friend'. Everyone in the family knows a 'friend' is code for boyfriend, which you seem to have no shortage of." Her uncle didn't hide the fact that he was gay, but ever since his life partner died in an accident many years ago, he'd had no interest in committing and many men in his life had come and gone over the years.

Dieter chuckled. "Friend, boyfriend, lover, whatever you want to call it. But Andy and I are a little different because above all, we really are good friends and whatever happens, I know we'll remain close."

"Then he must be very special," Celia said, shifting to the side when a member of staff put a beautifully presented but terribly complicated salad in front of her. "I haven't heard you speak so fondly of someone since Roderick."

"Yes, Roderick..." Dieter had a faraway look in his eyes as he turned his attention to the lake for a moment. "I still miss him every day."

"I miss him too. You were good together," Celia said. "You're one of the most positive people I know, but you had a twinkle in your eyes back then that I haven't seen since."

"Yes, when you know you've met your soulmate, you just know." Dieter snapped back to the present and took a bite of his salad, clearly confused himself as to what was on his plate. "You'll have to excuse me; I have no idea what this is. I have a new chef and he's showing off. I told him I like simple food but instead of just cooking schnitzel and sauerkraut like my old chef, he makes these visual masterpieces that I don't understand." He attempted another bite and furrowed his brows, then laughed. "Tastes pretty damn good, though."

"It's really good," Celia agreed, trying a bite of pickled radish and haloumi. "So, you're all ready to go?"

"Always." Dieter patted his blazer pocket. "My passport is on me at all times and I don't need much else."

"Are you planning on buying some art on the way?" Erin asked.

"As a matter of fact, yes. I'm meeting with an artist in

Tarragona. She's not really recognized yet, but I love her style and I'll be picking up a painting."

"Nice. You'll have to show me some of her work online later," Celia said.

"Of course." Dieter smiled and turned to Erin. "Celia's got a keen eye for art too. She's accompanied me on some of my trips and I always value her opinion."

"An eye for art?" Erin narrowed her eyes at Celia.

"An eye, no. I think Uncle Dieter is being kind and over-selling my talents. But I am passionate about art, and I even studied art history for a couple of years." Celia shrugged. "I never intended to work in the field, it was more out of interest as I don't have the passion, intuition and vision to make it in the art world like my uncle."

"Not true," Dieter protested. "Celia's taste is just more classical. I took her to Rome for her twelfth birthday and she cried when she saw the three Caravaggio's in the Basilica of St. Augustine. That, for a twelve-year old is very unusual."

"I was overwhelmed," Celia admitted. "We were walking into this small church and I hadn't expected them to be there." She paused. "Recognizing pure, classical beauty is easy; there's a reason why millions of people cry in front of great works. Equally, recognizing something radical is easy too; you either love it or hate it. But it's the gray area where my uncle truly knows how to play. The works that are challenging and open to personal interpretation. Endless presentations or predictions on rising value are redundant in his opinion. If it sets off a spark in him, he'll buy it, if it doesn't, he won't, whether it will make him a fortune or not. He always goes with his gut and overall, Uncle Dieter's intuition has made for a very lucrative business over the past forty years."

"Yes, I've been fortunate to have had an amazing run as a dealer in the art world." Dieter pointed in the direction of the helipad at the far corner of the property, where his helicopter stood. "If you don't mind me veering off topic here for a moment, I thought it might be fun to take the old chopper out for a ride and make our own way to France. It's been a while since I've flown."

"That would be cool." Celia twirled the wine around in her glass and sniffed it before she took a sip. "I used to love flying over the lake with you when I was younger."

"You were always a brave little girl. Never afraid to try something new."

Celia smiled at him but couldn't help but wonder if there was more to his words than he was letting on. He was right though; she'd always been up for an adventure, but lately, she'd become a little complacent. Content might be the right word, and although there was nothing wrong with that—in fact, it was said to be the formula for long-term mediocre happiness—there wasn't much excitement in her life either. Sure, she lived comfortably, and had fun friends. She got invited to a lot of parties, and in general, she enjoyed her job. But she couldn't remember the last time she'd felt truly excited, apart from last night, with Erin. "Things change," she said, and turned her attention back to her food.

16

———

"Would you like to see the library before you go to bed?" Celia asked as they were about to go into their separate rooms.

"The library? That's where Dieter keeps his most valuable pieces of art, right?" Erin knew the castle very well; she'd been in the library and Dieter's office many times, but she couldn't tell Celia any of that. It would only lead to questions she wouldn't be able to answer. Dieter didn't want anyone to know she'd spent three weeks at the castle to help him through his chemo, and he certainly didn't want anyone to know he was dying. That thought brought another wave of sadness to her stomach, but she tried to block those thoughts out as best as she could. She'd been up and down all day, and although she felt a little better than this morning, tears still threatened to fall.

"Yes. He's got quite the collection, if you're interested?"

"Sure, I'd be delighted." Erin didn't know much about art, but she loved being in Celia's company, and she sensed Celia felt the same, as she didn't seem ready to say goodnight yet either.

Dieter hadn't been any different from his normal self over dinner. He'd been upbeat, outgoing and he'd laughed a lot. Perhaps that was a front, she thought, because how could he be so at ease when he knew he was going to die? How could he pretend like everything was fine? Wouldn't it be easier to see out his last days with emotional support from his friends and family? There was no point trying to place herself in his situation, because she knew it would be impossible to grasp how he felt. For now, she had to stay strong for him, and being in Celia's presence strengthened her resolve.

Celia took her hand as they walked through the long, dark passageway. The spiraling staff staircase they'd used on their first night was deserted and knowing everyone was asleep or in their rooms, she placed her index finger over her lips, beckoning Erin to be quiet. They went up another flight of stairs to the second floor, where the library, a couple of staff rooms and her uncle's office were situated.

Despite having been here before, Erin's excited expression was genuine when Celia typed in the security code and opened the doors to the library that was still partially used for storing books. In fact, there were thousands of books here, but it had also been turned into a makeshift personal gallery for the art Dieter collected. The room was installed with a state-of-the-art security system and the temperature in the room was climate controlled to ensure the various eye-wateringly expensive works of art were kept in perfect, ambient conditions. Paintings, sculptures and obscure installations were carefully placed or hung in the high space that was almost as big as the ballroom; some waiting for a potential buyer and some of his favorites for him to take to his grave. The paintings—a mixture of classical and modern, including those of famous artists from impressionism, abstract expressionism, cubism, modernism and even classicism and baroque—were hung among new names she'd never heard of.

"I always love to browse the library to see what he's recently acquired," Celia said as she switched on all the lights. "As you know, my uncle isn't too keen on technology, but this room has museum-worthy lighting, and even its own generator in case the electricity fails."

The windowless space was impressive with the high ceiling that was emphasized by the tall rows of bookcases and the smooth, white walls that were a stark contrast to the bare brick walls in the rest of the castle. They wandered among the bookshelves and stared in rapture at the array of art on the walls, and Celia talked her through the rare books on display in various glass cabinets, whilst at the same time sharing her knowledge of the artworks she was familiar with.

"You're very sexy when you talk art," Erin said, sliding her arm around her waist. She didn't mean to flirt—in her present state of mind she wasn't in the mood for it—but she just couldn't help herself. Celia's passion for the subject was incredibly attractive.

Celia blushed and shook her head. "You'd be better off with my uncle giving you the tour but tonight, you'll just have to do with me." She shrugged as they passed a plinth with an old tire placed on top of a pile of recycled plastic bottles. "Because this, for example, is not my area of expertise. I kind of get it, but I don't like it."

"If it makes you feel better, I don't get it at all." Erin frowned as she studied the pile of stuff and decided that abstract installations were beyond her comprehension.

"Good, then let's move on." Celia pointed to a photograph of a woman with a baby in her arms. The sepia colors and the woman's long, straight, mid-parted dark hair and eyeliner hinted that it was taken in the seventies. It was a simple image like a classical Madonna; just her face, torso and the child wrapped in cloth in front of her chest against a cream background, but the woman's gaze was immensely intense as she stared into the lens. It felt sad and lonely, even though the baby in her arms looked healthy. "This is my favorite piece. It's called 'Girl in Dorm Room' by American photographer Seth Gary, and it's been here for years. I suspect my uncle never sold it on because I love it so much. The woman is unknown. I've tried to track her down to find out more about her, but her identity was protected."

"It's beautiful. Very powerful." Erin glanced at Celia sideways and saw that she was genuinely touched. Her eyes were glistening as she stared up at the photograph, like she was hypnotized by it. Suddenly, she snapped out of her state and gave Erin an apologetic shrug. "Sorry, I tend to get carried away when I look at it. Come with me. There's a sculpture I want to show you."

17

"Thank you for that. It was fascinating to see your favorite pieces through your eyes." Erin was still holding Celia's hand as they wandered into the yard for a midnight stroll after visiting the library. What had started as the most exciting night of her life had ended in pain, and they were in a strange place, somewhere between lovers and new friends. Both craving constant physical contact, they hadn't left each other's side since Erin had returned, but they'd refrained from anything more intimate.

Celia hadn't asked questions, and Erin was grateful for that. Soon, they'd have more than enough time to get to know each other, and more than enough time to get physically close. Perhaps that was the best way; one-night stands had never turned into something lasting for her, and with Celia, she really wanted to do this the right way.

"You're most welcome. I'm glad I didn't bore you."

The front of the castle was spectacularly lit from underneath, its illuminated facade making for an impressive and enchanting sight but on the lakeside, there wasn't as much as a small security light. It took a while to get used to the dark as they followed the moonlit path that led to the dock. Although the yard was maintained on a weekly basis, Dieter liked a little overgrowth along the edge of the lake and Erin loved the scent of elderflower as they stepped onto the wooden dock.

"It smells lovely here."

"It does. And I like the soft sound of the water lapping against the timber," Celia said. "I haven't been for a swim here in years."

"You used to swim here?" Erin's mind wandered to a vision of Celia naked in the lake, but she shook it off as it was too much to handle. "It looks cold." Again, the image of Celia with hard nipples hit her, and she cursed herself for having such a one-track mind.

"Yeah. I used to play in the lake for hours on end with my cousins and later when I was a teenager, I spent my days sunbathing and dreaming about girls on the dock."

"That's cute." Erin squeezed her hand and got a goofy grin in return that made her smile as she looked over the water. On the other side of the large lake, the old city of Lucerne's lights shone bright, and the ethereal Mount Pilatus rose from behind it, its imposing form lording over the city.

"The mountain is home to dragons, or so the legends say," Celia continued, looking up at its peak that was partially covered by mist. "Kids used to scare each other with stories about them." She walked to the edge of the dock and ran her hand through the water to check the temperature. "Coming here always inspires nostalgia in me and tonight is no exception. Every time I come back, I feel like I never left."

They both stood there in silence, gazing at the view, no doubt both thinking this was an awfully romantic thing to do for two people who had only just met. It was so quiet, Erin could hear the wood creaking under her feet, and the stars and the moon were bright against the endless midnight blue of the sky.

"Dragons or no dragons, it's pretty spectacular," she whispered.

"Yes." Celia turned to her. "Do you want to go for a swim?" She held up a hand and chuckled. "I promise I'm not trying to seduce you; I just thought it might help you sleep better if you've got a lot on your mind. There's nothing better than crawling into bed after a swim in the lake and the water is so clean that you can drink it, so you won't even need a shower."

The corners of Erin's mouth pulled into a smile. Right now, the idea of Celia seducing her was rather enticing, but she kept that to herself. "Okay. After you." Her breath hitched as she watched Celia strip off to her underwear. She was gorgeous, and she allowed herself to indulge in the curve of her waist, her long, lithe legs and her full breasts in her pale pink satin bra. Celia shot her a cheeky look over her shoulder before she dove in and resurfaced a little father out.

"Come on."

Erin shook her head as she snapped out of her dreamy state and swiftly stripped down too, following her in. She knew it wouldn't be that cold, but it was still far from warm, and her teeth were chattering as she swam toward Celia. It felt strange to be near-naked in the lake, surrounded by pure, inky blackness.

"You look like you're freezing." Celia's laugh cut through the silence, full and lovely, and Erin was so enchanted that she instinctively wrapped her arms around her, causing ripples that distorted the glistening moonlight.

The past days had been so unexpectedly intense that it hardly felt real. The castle and its breathtaking surroundings, the soothing water, Celia's skin against hers, their intense attraction, the sounds and smells of nature around them, the silver moon and the stars, and the trip that lay ahead of them, promising more time with Celia than she could have hoped for. If it wasn't for the sad secret between them, this night would have been perfect.

"I'm torn," she whispered, brushing her lips against Celia's. "I want you so badly, but I just can't right now."

"That's okay." Celia closed her eyes as she kissed her softly, then smiled against her mouth and kissed her. "We have time."

The weightless sensation of being in the water together and Celia's lips on hers filled Erin with passion, but there was also a tenderness in their kiss that told her there could be more than just lust between them. From the way Celia looked at her, she knew she felt it too.

"Yes," she whispered, running a hand through Celia's wet hair as she watched droplets trickle down her gorgeous face. "We have time."

18

Captain Eddie welcomed Erin, Celia, Dieter and Andy at the helipad in the harbor of Antibes, along with three of his staff members who helped them out of the helicopter and gathered their luggage.

Excitement tugged at Erin when she saw *The Barracuda* moored between two other enormous yachts, polished to perfection. With its stunning location along the Côte d'Azur, nineteen berths for superyachts and an on-site team that provided a wide range of services, Port Vauban was an institution in the luxury yachting industry, and she was yet again stunned by the long rows of white monster vessels shimmering in the sun. She recognized one of them; a seventy-two-meter hybrid storm breaker she'd designed for a Frenchman five years ago. It had been one of the biggest projects of her career and it felt incredible to see it moored here. Feeling the pull to inspect her own work, Erin contemplated going over to say hello, then remembered she really didn't like him. That was the thing with people who had more money than they were able to spend; many of them turned out to be narcissistic, selfish and even unethical.

Still, she took a moment to reflect her contribution and allowed herself to be proud. It wasn't every day that she had the opportunity to see her own work 'out in the wild', and she knew just how lucky she was to be able to do what she did for a living.

Erin felt a little more in control today after the initial shock of Dieter's news, and the fact that Dieter seemed genuinely happy made all the difference. Celia had been right; she'd slept like a log after their swim and had only woken up when Celia knocked on her door late this morning.

The weather in the South of France was on their side, the soft wind warm and balmy, and she knew it would be a perfect evening to be at sea. She turned to Celia, who seemed equally elated by the prospect of setting off as she took her hand and gave it a squeeze.

"Jesus," she muttered, casting her eyes over the long rows of impressive yachts. "Even to me this is a little extravagant."

"Just wait until you see my pride and joy in its full glory," Erin said. "Hang on a minute while I catch up with my staff."

Dieter also needed a moment to talk to the freelance pilot who would fly his helicopter back to Switzerland for him. They could have just gotten on a commercial flight here—it certainly would have been easier logistically—but Erin knew he loved flying himself. She felt a stab at the thought that it might have been his last flight, but she tried not to think of that as she left Celia and Andy with him and walked over to her crew.

"Eddie, it's good to see you again." She lowered her voice to a whisper. "Is all the paperwork for Dieter's medication in order?"

"All arranged." Eddie gave her a friendly nod. "I also booked the moorings for those extra stops you requested. We can be flexible though. We're not in high season yet and they're not the most popular yachting destinations. The crew is happy to stay on longer, but it's Ming's birthday on the Fourth of July, so she might want a day or two off."

"Of course, no problem." Erin turned to Ming, her head of housekeeping. "Your birthday...."

"Uh-huh. Big 3-0. It seems like only yesterday that I graduated." Ming chuckled and added: "In computer science."

Erin laughed too as she knew about Ming's background. Each year she vowed it would be her last year sailing around the world. That she'd start living a grown-up life with a real home and maybe even that husband she'd threatened to find. But every time her contract appeared to be coming to an end, she got nervous at the idea of spending the rest of her life in an office, or worse—in the suburbs—and so here she was still free and single. "Well, that calls for a celebration. Where will we be that day?" she asked Eddie.

"If everything goes according to plan, we'll be somewhere along the African coast or near Cape Verde, so we can plan it accordingly."

"Fantastic, then Ming and the crew can have some time off."

"Really?" Ming, who was always nothing but professional could not help but do a little jump of joy before she gave Erin a hug. "I'm sorry. I know this is out of line but I'm super excited. Thank you," she said sincerely.

"No, thank *you*. I'm happy you were willing to stay on longer. I wouldn't have asked if it wasn't hugely important to one of my guests." Erin shot her a wink and opened her phone to go through her checklist with them before they were ready to board. "So, did you manage to get everything from the request list I sent through for Miss Krügerner?"

"Yes, it's all in the master stateroom," Ming said. "We've prepared the *Dolphin* stateroom for Mister Krügerner and his companion, and the *Wahoo* stateroom is also ready in case Miss Krügerner prefers to have her own private cabin." Her tone was neutral and all business again, but the curiosity in her eyes was obvious as she glanced in Celia's direction for a split second.

"Excellent." Erin pretended she hadn't noticed. She'd sailed with this crew for years and she knew them really well, but not once had she brought a love interest on a long-haul trip. She imagined they'd speculated before they'd arrived, and even though they would never comment on anything, the line between employer and friend had also become increasingly blurred over the past years, especially with Eddie and Ming. "I'll ask her what she wants," she said with a humorous twinkle in her smile. "She might not want to put up with me for that long."

"Exactly." Ming laughed and gestured to *The Barracuda*. "We're all stocked up on food and beverages, and we've arranged deliveries at our stops. No specific diets were mentioned in your brief, so Marcus suggested we'll just play it by ear and see what you all feel like. Is that okay?"

"That sounds good to me." Erin turned to Eddie. "How about the weather?"

"It's looking pretty smooth over the next five days; I'll let you know if anything changes. I thought it would be best to set off right away if that suits you and your guests. The stretch along the French coastline is beautiful at night and we could anchor somewhere for an evening swim."

Erin nodded in agreement. "You know me so well. Sounds like everything is ready. I'll go get the gang."

19

As they waited at the dock, Celia watched Erin interact with the captain and a female member of her crew. She was amicable with them, even hugged them, and it made her like her even more. She was casually dressed in white slacks and a light blue shirt, her sleeves rolled up and the top three buttons were undone. Her look matched that of other people heading for their yachts; simple, crisp and clean, like there were unspoken rules about how to dress for sailing. Although Celia had quite a few wealthy friends, she'd never been on a yacht. The concept had simply never appealed to her that much, and the thought of not being able to see land made her feel uncomfortable in general. Now that she was looking up at *The Barracuda* though, she was more than willing to reconsider her opinion.

She was glad she hadn't gone overboard with her own outfit and the light-yellow sundress she'd slipped on before they left seemed appropriate. It was clear that Erin liked it, as she'd been shamelessly glancing at her legs non-stop during their flight here.

"Fuck me, this is amazing," Andy said, staring over the

harbor. Celia had learned that their travel companion was thirty-four, which was significantly younger than Dieter, but he was sweet and witty, and they seemed to have a lot of fun together. "I was prepared for a yacht, but I didn't expect *this* kind of yacht. It looks so much bigger than in the pictures." He shot Celia a smirk as he playfully slapped her behind. "You should seriously consider holding onto this woman."

"Let's see what more than two weeks in a confined space does to my opinion about this woman first," Celia joked, then put on her shades and started walking as Erin beckoned them to follow her onto the yacht.

Her mouth fell open in shock as she stepped onto the red carpet that had been rolled out for them on the gangway. The yacht was beautiful in its simplicity with a striking streamlined design and plenty of outdoor space.

"Welcome to *The Barracuda*." Erin was beaming as she took Celia's hand to help her onto the vessel where cocktails were waiting for them in the luxurious lounge space on the lower deck. "From now on, no shoes until we get to land. Deck shoes in your size have been left in your rooms, but barefoot is very comfortable here too." She waited for everyone to remove their shoes and place them in a box on the deck, then introduced them to the crew. "This is Captain Eddie. You're in good hands with him." She smiled at Eddie and gave his shoulder a squeeze. "I'll take over from him from time to time, but he's the main man here. He's also a damn good barracuda diver, so if we're lucky we might get to throw one on the grill."

"I'm looking forward to that." Celia shook Eddie's hand and immediately felt at ease with him. He was of Asian descent, short and muscular with a friendly smile and scruffy dark hair sticking out from underneath his captain's hat. His uniform was white and crisp, just like the uniforms of the rest of the crewmembers who were handing out drinks and serving finger food on the big coffee table. Around the table were built-in couches with white leather cushions that looked stylish against the timber decking.

Erin put an arm around Celia and pulled her in. "And this is the rest of the crew; Ming, head of housekeeping, and her team, Desirée and Josh, and this is Donald, our engineer. Our chef Marcus and his sous-chef Louise are currently busy in the galley, so I'll introduce you to them later. These lovely people have worked for me for six years, so we know each other pretty well. Anything you need, just give them a shout." She waited while everyone introduced themselves and put on the wristbands that Ming was handing out. "Believe it or not, these simple bands work wonderfully against sea sickness," she continued, putting one on herself. "So I'd advise you keep it on at all times. I'm not sure how they work exactly, but it's got something to do with the two little knobs on the inside and a pressure point on your wrist."

"Thank you." Celia allowed Erin to slide it onto her wrist, then chuckled when she lifted her hand and kissed it. Erin was a charmer, but she liked that about her, and she seemed in a much better place mentally today. Whatever was going on with her, Celia suspected she was going to be okay. "Your yacht is incredible," she said, still taking everything in while her uncle and Andy wandered around, discussing the impeccable craftsmanship.

"I'm glad you like it." Erin pulled her along with cocktail in hand. "Come on, let me show you the rest of the vessel. She looked over her shoulder at Ming. "Ming, will you please show Dieter and Andy to their room? I'll show Celia around."

The automatic sliding glass doors opened, revealing a

spacious living and dining area that was modern, simple and tastefully decorated. The furniture was white with brown leather accents, and the feeling of the thick, white carpet felt heavenly under Celia's feet as they sank into it. At the back was an Art Deco inspired cocktail bar and a dining table that seated eight, with a huge, fresh flower arrangement in the middle.

"It must cost a fortune to run this vessel," Celia said, taking a sip from her mint cocktail that was beautifully presented in a sugar-rimmed martini glass and topped with fine lime shavings. Everything about the service was nothing but perfection.

"It's not cheap, but I charter *The Barracuda* most of the year. That way, it pays for itself and it enables me to keep the staff on full-time." Erin leaned in to smell the flowers. "I'm really pleased with how well the crew has prepped this time. I'm not usually that bothered when it's just me, but I want my guests to have the best experience possible." She walked ahead through a long, narrow corridor and showed Celia a beautiful cabin with a large bed before they continued to a reading room with shelves full of books and two chesterfield couches next to a big window and a working fireplace.

"You designed all this?" Celia asked incredulously.

Erin nodded. "Exterior and interior. Most yachts I design are way swankier, as my clients like to show off, but I personally like things simple and slick."

"You're clearly very, very talented." Celia felt over-whelmed as she took everything in. "This yacht is possibly the most striking thing I've ever seen."

"I'm glad it's to your taste because it's going to be your home for the coming weeks." Erin opened the door to the yacht's bridge that was furnished in mahogany and fitted with an innovative dashboard with advanced touchscreen monitoring systems and soft leather chairs, each facing a row of windows that wrapped around the vessel. Among the rich décor was a fully working classic wood and brass ship's wheel, its shiny rounded handles and copper detailing in stark contrast to the futuristic scene. The modern cockpit instruments were finished with copper too, the detail and craftsmanship so intricate that it looked like a work of art. As she looked out over the Mediterranean Sea where their adventure would begin, the sight of the unknown sent a flutter through Celia.

"So you operate the yacht, too?" she asked.

"Yes. I have a master's license, which requires regular health and criminal checks. In general, you need one for any vessel over fifty feet, but it depends on the international waters you're in."

"A woman of many talents..." Celia shot her a flirty glance. Despite holding off on sleeping together, they'd never stopped flirting and she felt permanently aroused whenever she was near Erin. "Do you wear a captain's hat when you're onboard?"

"I do." Erin grinned. "You'll see it soon enough." She turned and beckoned Celia to follow her down a short flight of stairs, to her cabin. "I won't show you the mess—it's what we call the staff quarters—or the galley, as that's the crew's space and they're probably busy preparing dinner right now, but this is my cabin and you're welcome to stay here too, if you want. They've prepared one of the staterooms for you upstairs as I didn't want to be presumptuous, and I thought it might be a little weird since we haven't even..." Her voice trailed off, and she shrugged. "Well, you know."

Celia chuckled. "Yeah. It's an unusual situation, isn't it?" She glanced around the beautiful room before she looked down at the immaculately made bed, and imagining them in that bed together brought butterflies to her stomach. Still, after Erin's emotional outburst yesterday, she wanted to give her space. "I'll go upstairs, for now. Let's see how it goes, shall we?" She narrowed her eyes as she stared at the *Picasso* hanging over Erin's bed. "Nice. Is it real?" The small drawing was protected by thick glass and surrounded by an antique, gilded frame. Apart from the bed that was made up with white linen, there were only two nightstands, a closet, a chest of drawers, a minibar and a leather chair in the corner of the room, next to a coffee table with a huge bunch of white roses.

"It is. Dieter helped me acquire it. There's a *Magritte* in your room but it's a bit grim; I'm not sure it will help you sleep better," Erin joked.

"I can't wait to see it." Celia laughed and gestured to the adjacent door. "What's through there?"

"That's the bathroom. All rooms have en suites, so you won't have to share. I put the two biggest staterooms down here as it's the most stable part of the boat; less prone to the rolling and swaying should we get into some wild waters."

"I'll come and find you down here if I need rescuing." Celia's heart pounded wildly when Erin pulled her closer and licked her lips as if she was looking at her last meal.

"Is it wrong that I'll be hoping for a storm?"

Celia shook her head slowly, drowning in Erin's dark, lust-filled eyes. It was the same look she'd seen at the summer ball, and she shivered when Erin pushed her against the door. "We don't have to wait for a storm..." Her resolve was already crumbling, but she didn't care. As long as Erin was okay, she'd take whatever she was willing to give her, because she'd never felt this attracted to anyone before.

"Then maybe you should reconsider sleeping upstairs tonight," Erin whispered, her hot breath tickling Celia's lips.

"I would love to have my way with you right now, but we have guests and it wouldn't be very nice of me to leave them on their own just yet."

"I can wait," Celia said, although her body language told a whole different story. Her chest was heaving fast and she felt her cheeks flush as Erin pressed her body harder against hers. "I have a feeling it will be worth it."

20

D inner was served on the upper deck, where the dining table had been laid out meticulously with white linen and a delicious selection of miniature desserts. They'd enjoyed a wonderful meal of fresh mussels in white wine, triple-cooked chunky fries and a tarragon sauce, prepared by Erin's chef, who had talked to everyone about their food preferences. Between courses, they'd gone for a swim and now Celia felt entirely relaxed after a shower and delicious food and wine. She helped herself to another petit four and marveled at how gorgeous the vessel looked in the dim lighting.

Besides the central dining table, there was also a built-in seating area, various lounge chairs, a jacuzzi and a small swimming pool. The whole experience was indulgence of the highest level, and she seriously wondered why she'd ever doubted coming along.

It was dark now, and they were anchored in the Bay of Cannes, where they would stay for the night as Erin had ensured them the Mediterranean coastline was stunning and should be enjoyed in daylight, as well as in the dark.

The city shone brightly under the black sky, and higher up, built against the mountains behind Cannes were smaller villages, their clustered lights twinkling like stars. The candles flickering on the table and the music in the background enhanced the romantic atmosphere, and although Celia secretly looked forward to some alone time with Erin, it was great to catch up with her uncle and get to know Andy better. He was very funny; she hadn't laughed this much in a long time and she totally understood why her uncle was so charmed by him.

"Celia always loved the ladies," her uncle teased, after telling a slew of terribly embarrassing stories about Celia when she was younger. "I knew she was gay before she knew it herself. Do you remember that girl who was over at the castle with her parents one summer?" He furrowed his brows while he dug through his memory. "Rizzo, was it?"

Celia smiled and shook her head as she thought back to her first crush. "No, I think her name was Rizza, with an 'a'. Strange name, right?"

"Yes, her parents were quite eccentric. Art dealers, like myself." Dieter turned back to Erin. "Anyway, Celia was smitten with this Rizza girl, and she followed her around like a little lost puppy. One day, Celia's mother and I found them kissing on the dock, and you should have seen Babette's face." He burst out in laughter. "She obviously had no idea Celia liked girls and I was worried her eyes might pop out of her sockets."

"I think I have an idea." Erin laughed too. "Babette didn't seem like a big fan of me either, the way she kept glaring at me when I was dancing with Celia. Her eyebrows went up so high I was worried they'd disappear into her hairline." She put a hand on Celia's thigh and bit her lip with a grimace. "I'm sorry, I shouldn't make fun of your mother, that wasn't nice."

"No need to apologize. Making fun of my mother is our favorite pastime, right Uncle Dieter?"

"Most certainly." Dieter sat back and put his arm over the back of Andy's chair. "Oh, Andy, you've heard so many stories about my sister-in-law by now that I suspect I'm starting to bore you with them."

"Yes, I've heard many, darling, but they never fail to amuse me." Andy smiled sweetly at him. "*You* never fail to amuse me, you fascinating man."

"Well, I'm glad this old goat is able to hold your attention." Dieter chuckled and finished his rosé. "How about we try out that wonderful bed in our cabin?"

"I like your thinking." Andy stood up and blew kisses in Celia and Erin's direction. "Thank you so much for dinner, Erin. This was really, really amazing. It's all amazing." He gestured to the yacht and the coast, still overwhelmed.

Celia felt overwhelmed too, but for different reasons. Erin's hand resting on her thigh had set off a spark in her, and she was having trouble hiding how turned on she was.

"So, you were always a big fan of the ladies, huh?" Erin said with a smirk when they were alone. The staff had cleared the table after Dieter and Andy had left. There was half a bottle of rosé left in front of them and the candles were still burning, but Erin had switched off the music so Dieter and Andy could sleep in peace. Celia doubted that was what they were doing though, as she'd seen them exchange flirty looks throughout the day.

"I guess I was." A little tipsy from the wine, Celia moved

onto Erin's lap and wrapped an arm around her shoulder. "I still am. One in particular, actually."

"That's good news for me." Erin raised a brow and her eyes darkened. "Because I'd like to finish what we started the other night."

Her words drew a soft gasp from Celia's lips, and when Erin's hand slipped under her dress and up her thigh, she squirmed in her lap. Celia couldn't quite understand how someone could have such a dramatic physical effect on her, but it didn't matter. This felt good and that was all that mattered. The coming weeks wouldn't just be a break from her life; it would be a break from her old habits too. And those bad old habits included overthinking her decisions and weighing up every action until, without even realizing it, she had managed to suck all the excitement from her life. She generally didn't have crushes anymore, and she hadn't been on a spontaneous trip in years but in the past days, all of that had changed. Erin drove her wild with the things she did and said, and especially with the way she looked at her. It felt so good to be desired again, to know someone longed for her.

Erin's hand moved over her body, exploring her curves before it disappeared into the cleavage of her dress, and leaning back against her, Celia moaned softly as her fingers slipped into her bra. A fleeting thought about the crew and her uncle and Andy possibly still wandering around somewhere crossed her mind, but all thoughts faded when Erin caressed her nipples and kissed her way down the side of her neck.

"Fuck... how do you do this to me?" she whispered through ragged breaths, her chest shooting up to meet Erin's touch.

"I don't think you have any idea what you're doing to *me*

right now." Erin's voice was low and sultry, her lips and warm breath tickling Celia's ear.

Celia turned, taking Erin's face in her hands to kiss her fiercely, and when Erin parted her lips and deepened their kiss, she let herself be carried away on a wave of endless pleasure that reached every part of her body. Hands roamed freely and soft moans rang through the night air as they consumed each other like hungry wolves. Kissing Erin was a revelation; she invaded all her senses, aroused her beyond reason, and Celia felt sure then, that she was the only thing on Erin's mind too. Her hair felt silky soft as it slipped through her fingers, her lips soft, moist and alluring, and then she remembered joking about being afraid of her. There was more truth to it than she'd realized because this woman had the ability to touch her in deeper places; to dive under the surface, to probe inside her mind and to tap into her darkest fantasies.

She pulled out of the kiss and touched her lips as she studied Erin's handsome face. "Is this normal? To feel so much?" she whispered.

Erin chuckled and shook her head. "I'm shaking all over, so no, I don't think it is." She bit her lip as she lowered her gaze to Celia's mouth again. "Come to my room. It's soundproof."

21

———

"Are you sure you're okay about this?" Celia asked as she closed the door behind her and leaned back against it.

"Yes. I'm fine." As Erin said it, she knew it was true, at least for now. All day, she'd been undressing Celia with her eyes, and it had distracted her from the dark cloud hanging over them. She was shaking on her legs, all too aware of the scorching heat between them. She studied Celia, taking in her smoldering expression and her trembling limbs as she traced a finger over the crescent-shaped birthmark on her shoulder.

Celia reached out to unbutton her shirt, and in return, Erin slid the straps of Celia's dress off her shoulders and inched the garment down her body, leaving her in a white, lacy lingerie set.

"You're my ultimate fantasy," she confessed, running a hand through her short hair. Adrenaline was pumping through her veins as she watched Celia's nipples harden through the thin fabric of her bra. When Celia was about to take off her shirt, Erin caught her hands and held them above her head against the door as she kissed her neck and ran her tongue over her earlobe. Celia's reaction spoke volumes; shivers, goose bumps, moans, so sweet and pure...

"I sense you like to be in charge," Celia whispered through ragged breaths, tilting her head as Erin continued down to the nape of her neck.

"I do. Are you okay with that?" There was no question about it; Celia looked more than on board, but Erin still wanted to hear her say it.

"Uh-huh." Celia hesitated before she continued. "It's been a while since I've had sex, and a very long time since I've had good sex, but I have the feeling that's about to change." Their chemistry was through the roof, their bodies inexplicably drawn to one another, and they were both aware they were about to do something very memorable.

Erin let go of her, and her stomach did a flip when Celia dropped her hands and leaned back against the door, waiting for whatever came next. She stared her up and down like a dog in front of a big, juicy bone, and for the first time in her life she didn't know where to start.

"Jesus, Erin. You're killing me with that look," Celia finally said after a long silence. She smiled. "It's a little frightening but I like it."

"Don't be afraid. Can I take this off?" Erin hooked her arms around Celia, finding the clasp on her bra. When Celia nodded, she unclasped it and slowly pulled off the bra. Her lips parted as she took in the full breasts before her, and as she reached out to trace her fingers over her full curves and her hard, pink nipples, Celia's lashes fluttered, and she took in a quick breath.

"Kiss me again," she begged, pressing Erin's hands firmly against her chest.

Erin pushed herself against her and kissed her hard and

deep, wedging her thigh between Celia's legs while she claimed her mouth and her breasts. Celia Krügerner had been on her mind for over twelve months and now that she had been given a second chance, she was not going to let her go again. Erin was out of breath when she gestured to the bed, her bewildered expression no doubt giving away how badly she wanted her. "Lie down."

While Celia got on the bed, she grabbed a bottle of massage oil from her nightstand drawer and held it up as she straddled her. Celia's gaze turned hazy as she looked at the oil, her eyes meeting Erin's in a loaded exchange.

"What are you going to do with that?"

"Do you like massages?"

"I do. I especially like the idea of your hands all over me." She chuckled when Erin took her wrists and pinned them above her head on the pillow. "And they're strong hands," she continued, shooting Erin a playful smile as she wiggled in her grip.

"They are. Now keep your hands there," Erin said. "Unless you want me to tie you up?" That thought sent a spasm between her legs, but even when Celia remained silent, confirming her suspicion that she was down with that idea, she refrained from looking for ties. "Good." When Celia stopped resisting, she moved down her body and kissed her breasts, finally running her tongue over the pink pebbles she'd been longing to taste. Her breasts felt so perfect in her hands, and her nipples reacted to her touch with such sensitivity. Celia was squirming underneath her, jerking her hips up, and she chuckled occasionally when she reached out and got pinned down again.

Erin ran her mouth back up, along her neck and her cheek, then moved to Celia's ear to bite her earlobe just hard enough to make her gasp in delight "I'm going to fuck you senseless," she whispered. "But first, I'm going to cover you in oil so you're nice and slippery."

At that, Celia crumbled, and by now, she seemed so aroused that Erin was afraid she might come right away. Her own clit was throbbing, her body held hostage by an impatient need that consumed all of her. When she reached between them, squeezing Celia's center hard without warning, Celia gasped and threw her head back.

"Oh God, Erin..."

Even through her panties, Erin's fingers were coated by her wetness as she curled them repeatedly, making Celia moan loudly. She looked into her dark eyes while she did this, enjoying her fierce reaction to the sexy torture. Then she let go and opened the bottle. "Not yet."

Celia watched Erin's eyes rake over her body as if she was her favorite treat in the whole world. Her weight on top of her felt delicious and she bucked her hips, knowing she was in for a long and teasing ride as she remembered to keep her hands in place.

Erin was the first woman to literally drive her crazy with desire, and she could only hope she had the same effect on Erin because whatever was going on here was beyond her wildest dreams.

"Hmm... orange blossom," Erin said, sniffing the bottle. "Natural and harmless ingredients only." She winked. "May I?"

"Please." Celia was desperate for her touch or anything else she was willing to give her, and when Erin dripped a little of the oil over her oversensitive breasts and started rubbing it in with slow symmetrical circles, it felt so good that she never wanted her to stop. She arched her back, her chest rising to meet Erin's hands as her eyes fluttered shut. Both her hands were doing the same delicious thing, one on each side. Erin teased around her nipples, and her chest shot up again when she suddenly pinched them.

Celia expected her to let go but instead, she pinched harder, watching her closely as a guttural groan escaped her. It hurt, but she liked it. There was pain, but the pleasure was so much greater. While she attempted to analyze these newfound insights, Erin continued her firm but slow massage, moving to the sides of her breasts, then down to her waist, covering her in the scented oil that turned warm under her touch.

Erin knew what she was doing and had clearly done this before. She was intensely focused on her, but she was also enjoying this herself; Celia could tell by her aroused expression and the way she kept shifting on top of her. She reached her belly, and the lower her hands travelled, the more trouble Celia had lying still. Making sure not to miss a single inch of her skin, Erin treated her body like a canvas, taking in every part of her as she familiarized herself with Celia's erogenous zones. It wasn't that hard to figure out as her reaction to Erin's continual caresses was out of this world. By the time her fingers skimmed the edge of her panties, Celia had reached a state of complete and utter delirium, lifting her hips off the mattress to chase her touch. Her body was covered in a thin sheen of liquid heat, her skin lustrous and hot from the oil, her nipples sore and swollen.

"Can I take this off?" Erin asked, hooking her thumbs under the fragile lace edge of her panties that lay over her hipbones.

"Yes." Celia almost laughed, because there was nothing

she wanted more. Erin's hungry gaze sent a shudder of arousal through her, making her yearn for her even more. It was obvious she liked her submissive and, curiously, Celia liked it too. She was by no means a pillow princess and she loved to pleasure women, but someone taking their time with her the way Erin was doing now, was incredibly sexy.

Slowly, Erin pulled down her panties, making her tingle all over. "I like your style," she said with a smirk, licking her lips as she admired Celia's freshly waxed center before bending over and blowing warm breath between her legs.

Celia's first reaction was to pull her face down against her throbbing flesh, but Erin took hold of her wrists again and placed her hands back over her head on the pillow. "Keep them there, Celia."

She complied with her command without even thinking, moaning when Erin moved back down and spread her legs apart. "Delicious," she said, staring at her most intimate parts. Celia was hoping she'd devour her with her mouth, but she didn't. Instead, Erin concentrated on her thighs, covering them in oil too, before moving inward and working her way up, again with the same symmetrical movements that had almost made her lose her sanity only moments ago.

"You're so good at this," she mumbled, her center dripping wet and throbbing for Erin's touch. She bucked her hips again, seeking contact, and when Erin finally slipped a hand between her legs and dragged her oily fingers through her folds, Celia cried out in ecstasy. "Oh my God, please don't stop whatever it is you're doing," she said through ragged breaths. She could feel a climax building and it promised to be a shattering one. "Fuck!"

"Fuck?" Erin grinned and continued to drag her fingers up and down while Celia's head frantically moved from side to side. "Is that what you want?" She kissed the inside of her thigh, then retracted her hand.

"Yes. I want you to fuck me."

Erin leaned over her and bit her earlobe before she whispered: "Do you mind if I use a strap-on?"

It was just a simple question, but Erin's words made her pulse race as she stared up at her. "You've got toys here?"

"I ordered a couple ahead of the trip." Erin shrugged, and her boyish grin was so sexy that Celia would have let her do anything she wanted to her. "I hope you don't think this was too presumptuous, if it's not something you're into I'll never mention it again, but—"

"Yes." Celia's cheeks flushed as she interrupted her. "I do like toys... I mean, I think I do." She shook her head at her inability to form a decent sentence. Erin seemed to have that effect on her, because she barely knew up from down right now.

"You think?" Erin reached over to her nightstand and opened the drawer again, pulling out a black harness with a matching dildo. "Then let's find out."

Celia's trembling limbs felt weak as she waited for Erin to undress and put it on. She watched her take off her jeans and her shirt, and finally her sports bra and her boxers. Raking her eyes over Erin's athletic body, all her nerve endings were zinging with anticipation, her patience reduced to zero. "Come here," she whispered, struggling to keep her hands to herself as she fixed her eyes on Erin's full breasts, then on the harness that covered the strip of dark hair between her thighs as she fastened it on.

Erin lowered herself on top of her and they sighed in unison at the warm contact. Her weight felt perfect, her skin smooth and slippery from the oil on Celia's own body, and when they fell into a heated kiss, she felt so connected that she never wanted the moment to end.

Erin moved the shaft between her legs while they consumed each other, and Celia wrapped her legs around her hips as her hands moved into Erin's hair, needing her as close as she possibly could.

"You feel incredible," Erin whispered, carefully pushing into her as she took her hands and laced their fingers together.

Jolts of pleasure shot through Celia's core when she entered her. It felt so good to finally be taken, to feel the satisfaction of being filled after the massage that had aroused her beyond imagination. All of Erin covered all of her and closing her eyes, she moaned when Erin penetrated her deeper and started moving in and out of her slowly, squeezing her hands.

"Is this good?" she asked, her voice trembling with arousal.

Celia knew she was pacing herself, wanting to make her feel as stimulated as she possibly could. "So good," she murmured, tightening her grip on Erin's hands as she looked into her eyes. Their shared breath was flowing rapidly between them, their movements perfectly attuned, and she didn't understand how they could have such synergy their first time together. "More. I want more."

Lifting her chin, she kissed Erin, and Erin kissed her back as she continued to move into her, deeper and harder. She wanted all of her; her body, her mouth, her hands, her emotions, and in that moment, she even wanted her thoughts. The muffled moans against her mouth and the deep frown between Erin's brows told her she was close too, and Celia nodded, letting her know she wanted her to let go.

Erin picked up her pace, filling her over and over, and

Celia moved with her as they chased release, causing the bed to rock and shake. The storm in her core drew louder moans from her mouth as it culminated into a hurricane inside her. Soon, the deliciously slow and controlled game from before turned animalistic and they were crying out, losing all control.

Erin crashed on top of her, and Celia felt her relax as she let out a deep sigh. She pulled Celia's hair to the side and kissed her cheek, then softly ran her hand through her hair while she pulled out of her.

Celia shivered and wallowed in satisfaction. Their breathing was in sync as they lay there silently, slowly coming back to reality, and she felt a strange sense of closeness to this woman she barely knew.

"You're amazing," Erin whispered, then rolled away before turning on her side.

Celia chuckled. "I didn't do anything, *you're* amazing..." She felt her smile widen as she locked her eyes with Erin's. She was gorgeous in every way. Fine lines of the laughter kind gave even more character to her sculpted features. Her eyebrows were full and dark, her skin a dark tan, and it was only then that she wondered where Erin's roots lay. "Erin Nour," she whispered, just because she liked saying her name. "Did I pronounce that right?"

"You did." Erin stroked her cheek, and as if reading her mind, she added, "My parents are Moroccan. They moved to L.A. forty-five years ago. My birth name is Ezahra, but some of my American friends started calling me Erin for some reason, so I just stuck with it. Anyway, it suits me better."

"It does suit you." Celia closed her eyes as Erin kissed her softly and pulled her in. "Your parents made one hell of a specimen," she mumbled against her lips.

At that, Erin laughed, and Celia loved that she could see

her personality shining through. Her wide smile combined with the lyrical sound of her deep laugh were a beautiful combination, and that brief moment—with Erin relaxed entirely—was precious to her and one she would never forget. She knew she'd always remember the way they were lying there, staring into each other's eyes.

"Do you mind if I stay here tonight," she asked.

"Celia..." Erin sighed and the way she said her name made Celia swoon. "You're mine tonight and you're not going anywhere." She paused and ran a hand between Celia's thighs. "I haven't even tasted you yet."

Celia's cheeks burned at the thought of Erin's tongue on her. "I like that but I want to taste you too," she whispered. "It's my turn now."

22

Now that she was awake, she took the opportunity to indulge in the sexy woman beside her, who was lying on her side with her arm draped over her. Celia turned toward Erin so she could look at her handsome face in the morning light. Her lashes were long and dark, her tousled hair sticking out on all sides, and her full lips looked so kissable that she could barely resist leaning in and tracing her tongue over them. Those lips had been everywhere.

Contrary to her dominant demeanor last night, Erin looked so innocent now, so unaware that she was being watched in her vulnerable state. Thinking back to their steamy night made her insides flutter, and Celia scooted a little closer, craving Erin's body heat. Just her presence was enough to arouse her beyond comprehension.

They smelled of sex, Celia was sore in all the right places, and there was something very satisfying about that. Knowing they were both naked, and that what they'd started last night would most likely be continued when Erin woke up made her want to touch herself. When she reached between her legs, Erin grabbed her hand and opened her eyes with a mischievous grin that told her she wasn't sleeping at all.

"Good morning, princess." She placed Celia's hand over her head on the pillow and rolled on top of her, her full breasts covering Celia's as she wedged her leg between her thighs, grinding into her sensitive center. "Were you about to touch yourself?"

"No," Celia lied, then chuckled, shifting underneath her. "Were you pretending to be asleep?"

"Uh-huh." Erin's smile widened, and it sent all sorts of wonderful sensations to Celia's core. Whatever this woman had done to her, she was truly enraptured. "I watched you wake up. It was cute." Her voice sounded different from last night, her eyes had lost their sharpness and were filled with something else. Something softer. Or was it sadness? Celia wasn't sure so she let it go. Erin was probably just sleepy, but the difference was still significant.

"You're pretty cute this morning too," she said, stroking Erin's cheek. "You're like a different person. Not that you weren't adorable last night," she added in a flirty tone. "But... I don't know, you're just different."

Erin leaned in to kiss her. "Not afraid anymore?"

"I never was." Celia tilted her head and looked into her dark eyes. "You seem kind of innocent."

Erin laughed and surprised her by lowering her hand between them and cupping her center. Celia gasped and threw her head back at the unexpected jolt of arousal that sent her insane with lust. "Are you sure about that?" She raised a brow and watched Celia squirm. "God, you're wet already."

The dangerous look in her eyes was back again when she entered Celia with two fingers, never taking her eyes off her as she started fucking her like it was the last thing she'd ever do. Hard, fast, deep, with purpose, reacting to her needs with effortless instinct.

Celia moaned at the delicious feeling of her filling her up, their bodies rhythmically in sync, their hips meeting each other's thrusts. Celia freed her hand and wrapped her arms around her, her nails digging into the soft skin of Erin's back as she brought her to the brink of an orgasm.

Erin looked determined, the frown between her brows deep as she bit her bottom lip. It was sexy as hell and there was nothing romantic about this; it was carnal and greedy, and all the things Celia didn't know she loved. She had trouble keeping quiet and was worried about waking people up, but the pleasure was too much and she moaned louder, wrapping her legs around Erin as she climaxed with a force that surprised them both. As her walls squeezed around Erin's fingers, she took an even tighter hold of her, meeting her eyes for as long as she could hold them open. Everything turned white as an ocean of pleasure washed over her. She didn't remember sex ever feeling so good, and it was like Erin knew her body better than she knew it herself. Trembling all over, she stared up at her in a state of total bliss.

"I think you enjoyed that," Erin whispered against her ear and retracted her fingers so slowly that Celia squeezed her thighs together, wanting to hold onto their connection for as long as she could.

"You know I did." When their eyes met, Celia frowned as she traced her cheek. She expected to see that smug and carefree look Erin had shot her so many times last night, but there was no mistake about the sadness this time. "Hey, are you okay?"

"Yeah."

"You don't look okay," Celia said when she noticed tears welling in the corners of Erin's eyes.

"Really, I'm fine. I don't want to talk about it." Erin turned on her side and pulled Celia in, holding her as she buried her face in her neck like she needed her for comfort.

Celia stopped enquiring and wrapped her arms around her in return, placing soft kisses on the top of her head. She didn't ask questions. If Erin wanted to tell her something, she would. If she didn't, this was all she could do. They didn't know each other after all, and Celia had no business pushing her at this moment in time. She expected tears to trickle down her shoulder, but after a while, Erin composed herself and shook her head as she looked up at her again.

"I'm sorry, I didn't mean to be so dramatic."

"It's fine." Celia laced her fingers through Erin's hair. She wanted to tell her she could trust her, that she could talk to her, but that made no sense. One night didn't make them close, and the fact that Erin was emotional didn't make this any more than it was. Not yet, anyway. "Do you want to be alone?"

"No. I want to be right here, with you. You make me feel better." Erin kissed her fiercely then, and although Celia suspected she was drowning herself in their shared passion as a means of distraction from whatever was hurting her, her arousal was real.

"Then tell me more about yourself," she said, sliding under the covers and aligning herself with Erin's body.

Erin's nipples hardened as Celia ran her hand over her breasts, then down to her stomach, and she shivered at the soothing sensation of her touch. "It's a little hard to talk when you're doing that," she said with a grin, catching Celia's hand and keeping it on her stomach just before she was about to slide it farther down. "What do you want to know?"

"Well, for starters... what about your love life? Have you been married, or in a serious relationship?"

Erin shook her head. "No. Nothing serious."

"But you've had girlfriends, right?" Celia asked. "You brought a date to the ball last year. Weren't you guys dating?"

"Kind of. We dated for three weeks but it didn't work out." Erin paused for a moment, stroking Celia's hand. "Three weeks to a month is the longest I've dated someone and I'm not going to lie; I've been with many women. I love them in every way, and I especially love to please them in bed."

"I know that." Celia gave her a lazy smile. "I've been lucky to experience that first-hand."

"I'm glad you enjoyed it." Erin returned her smile. There was so much fire between them that Celia had trouble keeping her hands to herself. "But to answer your question, no, I haven't been in a real relationship at all, ever. I think it's because I've never felt that real spark that everyone talks about. A special connection or even just the feeling of wanting to stay. With you, it's..." She shook her head and muttered a silent curse. "Never mind."

Celia's heart raced as she studied Erin. Their connection after only one night was beyond anything she'd ever experienced; not only were they sexually compatible but their chemistry was through the roof, and if Erin also recognized how rare that was she wanted to hear her say it. "With me it's what?"

"Nothing, I shouldn't have said anything." Erin swallowed hard, avoiding her gaze.

"Okay, then I'll tell you something," Celia said. "Last

year, something happened to me during our dance. I was a little shocked by my instant attraction to you, and I never understood how that feeling stayed with me for a whole year without ever seeing you again. That's why I came alone this time, hoping you would do the same."

"Really?"

Celia nodded. "I swear."

"I felt it too," Erin admitted as relief washed over her features. "It was very, very strong."

"Yes. There was something about you that drove me insane with desire that night. Maybe it was your smell, or your voice, or the way you held me while we danced. Whatever it was, it made a lasting impact on me, and I remember every second of that dance."

"Me too. I remember everything and I've longed for you ever since." Erin ran her hands through Celia's hair, pulled her face closer and kissed her.

Celia's insides turned to mush as she melted into the embrace, the slow and sensual make-out session so deep and demanding that she almost lost her breath. When they broke apart, they were both shaking with need. It was crazy how good it was to kiss her.

Erin moaned and shifted on the bed, spreading her legs a little when Celia's finger skimmed her thighs, and Celia sensed she didn't mind giving up control right now. Wanting to make her forget whatever was bothering her, she moved over Erin's body like a tigress, kissing her way down her breasts and her stomach while she teased her with her fingers.

"I want you," she whispered, and Erin closed her eyes and surrendered to her touch.

23

When Celia and Erin arrived at the lower deck where breakfast was set up, Dieter and Andy were already having coffee in their swimming trunks, both sitting back with their feet up, covered in white smudges of sunblock. Andy was in his element, sporting aviators and a captain's hat, his voice high-pitched with excitement.

"Morning, ladies," he said. "Looking very chic, the two of you in matching robes."

"Good morning." Celia walked over to them and gave her uncle a kiss on his cheek and Andy a pat on his shoulder.

"Good morning, sweetheart. Don't ask where he got the hat," her uncle said.

"I won't." Celia laughed and shielded her eyes from the sun while she glanced over the Bay of Cannes and the city. She could see the marina, filled with luxury yachts, the iconic beachfront promenade with Belle Epoque hotels, the *Palais des Festivals* where the annual film festival was held, long sandy beaches and the sun-bleached buildings in the old city center, built up against a hill with a medieval castle perched on top. Palm trees and umbrella pines rose from what she imagined to be small parks in between the densely built areas. "Such a mesmerizing view," she said softly, leaning against Erin who wrapped an arm around her waist. "It's dreamy."

The sandy seashores stretched out for miles to either side of the city, with smaller beach towns dotted along the coast for as far as she could see. The color palette before her was vibrant in its natural shades; from the tree-covered hills and the azure coastline, to the subdued tones of the buildings that matched the color of the beaches in cream, terracotta and light-yellow variations.

"The French Riviera is famous for its morning light," Erin said. "I'd like to come back here one day, to explore. But for now, our first stop will be Tarragona so Dieter can go and visit that artist he was talking about."

"You're certainly very generous with your time when it comes to Uncle Dieter," Celia joked. "I don't think many people would do what you're doing for him. And by that, I mean all the stops he's been so adamant about. It's almost bordering on diva behavior and it's very unlike him."

"Well, he's a good friend and he also paid a bundle of money for the trip at the auction," Erin said.

"But still..." Celia was sure she detected a hint of sadness in Erin's voice, but she quickly composed herself and her carefree smile returned, putting her at ease.

"I'd do it for you too, you know. Just tell me where you want to go, and we'll go."

Celia chuckled. "You're such a charmer."

"Hey, it's true. I really would." Erin let go of her, walked over to the seating area and pressed a button, causing a flap to open at the end of the deck. A stepladder folded out and lowered itself into the sea. She turned to Dieter and Andy, raising her voice. "Gentlemen, would you like to have a swim before breakfast? We're setting off in an hour."

"Are you going in?" Celia asked, taking off her robe. She'd already put on a bikini, figuring she wouldn't need to wear much more today.

"Yeah, the water's great here. Clear and warm." Erin gave Celia a thorough appraisal, clearly liking the red triangle bikini. "I loved you in a bikini last night, but I think I prefer the daylight, so I can see you better." She grinned. "So, red's your color, huh?"

"What about red?" Celia shot her a flirty look in return, taking in Erin's body in the black sports bikini. She looked strong and sexy with very little on, and she had to remind herself that there were other people present as it was hard to keep her hands off that body.

"Your favorite color? You were wearing a red dress at the ball, and now a red bikini..." Erin lowered her voice. "A very small red bikini I might add."

Celia laughed. "I'll have you know, red is not my favorite color, but I do generally like red lipstick, red roses, Louboutins, red dresses..." She paused. "And red wine. Let's not forget about that."

"Oh, you like red wine, do you?" Erin narrowed her eyes at her. "There's so much I don't know about you. We have an assortment of great vintages below, but maybe we could stop off at a vineyard somewhere, to get you some really special bottles."

"No need, I'm not picky. And I'm certainly not high maintenance, if that's what you think," Celia added, inching back as Andy and Dieter caused a huge splash by jumping in simultaneously. "I'm no food or wine snob, or any kind of snob for that matter, even though most people expect me to be because of…" She sighed and shrugged. "Well, because of my background."

"You don't strike me as a snob," Erin said. "And I'm a pleaser so if you like red wine, I'll make sure you'll have the best." She paused and took Celia's hands. "Look, we'll have a lot of time to get to know each other—unless you decide you've had enough half-way and I promise you; I will not be offended if you leave us. But assuming you do decide to stay, and I'm pretty positive you will, I think we should do this thing where we ask each other three questions a day and both answer honestly. Just think of it as a really long date."

"What if I give you the wrong answer?"

Erin threw her head back and laughed. "There is no wrong answer, we're just getting to know each other."

Celia laughed too as she walked over to the edge of the platform and dipped a toe in the clear water that invited her in. "Okay. So, what's *your* favorite color?" she asked, lowering herself into the Mediterranean. The saltwater caressed her skin and cooled her as she immersed herself and floated away from *The Barracuda.* Being in open water so far from the coast frightened her a little but it was also exciting and liberating to feel so at one with nature. The waves were gentle, and the sun was shining on her face as she turned on her back and let herself float. Although it was a Tuesday and she would have to get online at some point today to check her orders and catch up on work, she felt like everything could wait right now. She'd never experience a day like this again—a day that started with a morning swim in the sea before setting off and exploring the world from the luxury of a superyacht.

"Going back to your question, personally I don't have a favorite color." Erin followed her out and paddled next to her. "But from a design perspective, it's white, without a doubt. I know it's technically not a color, but it's clean, the perfect starting point to build around and it's got more depth than people realize. It's forever contemporary, it creates a sense of space, it balances warm wood and goes well with glass. In feng shui it's linked to harmony, in marketing it's linked to freshness, in some religions it's linked to purity, and all of that makes perfect sense. The color white is both light and loaded and there are lots of great shades of white—my current favorite is vintage cotton."

"Hmm... good answer. And a very thorough answer; I feel like I need to step up my game now." Celia stared at Erin as her long, dark lashes swept up and down, blinking away the water from her eyes. "Those white shirts you wear look great against your skin, by the way."

"Thank you." Erin licked her lips, her gaze lowering to Celia's mouth. "And you look..."

"Pink!" Andy yelled, interrupting their conversation as he swam away from the vessel with Dieter hot on his heel. "My absolute fave color is pink, all the way. Although I am partial to dramatic shades of yellow too, but they usually don't gel with my complexion." He spread out his arms and legs to demonstrate his lack of tan. "But that is about to change. Give me three days on the water and I'll be darker than you, Erin."

"Just be careful or you'll be fifty shades of red instead," Dieter said, grimacing as he touched Andy's shoulder. "You're already going pink. But I guess that's fine as it's your favorite color."

"Am I burning? Heavens above, I'm going to look like a grilled lobster if I stay out here any longer. Okay, I've had my morning swim. Been there, done that." Andy swam back to the ladder and climbed up. "Will you come with me and put some more sunblock on me, darling? By the way, you're starting to look like a lobster yourself. A very big, red lobster."

"I'm fine and I don't care if I burn. It's not like I need to keep my skin young."

"It's not just that. What about skin cancer?" Andy handed Dieter a towel as he joined him on the deck. "I suppose you're right," Dieter said with a sigh. "Will you do my back too, then?"

Celia and Erin laughed as Andy squirted a generous amount onto Dieter's big back, smeared it out and drew a phallic shape with his finger.

"There, all done!"

"God, Andy. I know exactly what you're doing. How old are you?" Dieter rolled his eyes as he turned back around and took the bottle from him.

"Much younger than you, that's for sure." Andy laughed and wiggled his butt. "So, no jokes on my back, Diets. It won't look good in those thousands of Insta shots of me living my best life."

Erin had laughed so hard while paddling that she was out of breath, so she swam to the steps and held onto them. Celia followed her and flung her arms around her, craving the contact. "Favorite ice cream flavor?" she asked, wanting to keep their questions and answers going.

"You still owe me your favorite color."

"Fair enough." Celia bit her lip as she thought about it. "I actually don't know. Can I have a couple of days to think about that?"

"Sure. It's not an interview." Erin shot her an amused look. "Anyway, my favorite ice cream flavor is mint chocolate chip."

"Gross." Celia grimaced. "I don't get the mint. As far as

I'm concerned, it should be used for toothpaste and cocktails only."

"Then what's yours?

"Vanilla."

"Okay, that's totally boring." Erin returned her grimace. "Now I'm undecided as to whether I should ask you to name your favorite food."

Celia laughed and wrapped her legs around Erin's hips, "That's a hard one. You mean a cuisine?"

"No, only one dish. If you could eat only one dish for the rest of your life, what would you choose?"

"Damn, that's hard, but I think I'd have to go with white truffle risotto." Celia brought a hand to her temple and groaned. "Okay, now I *do* sound like a snob."

"You kind of do," Erin said in an amused tone. "But it's definitely a more interesting answer than vanilla ice cream."

Celia's smile widened as she arched a brow at her. "Hey, I thought you said there were no wrong answers."

"I lied." Erin's hands lowered to Celia's behind and the corners of her mouth pulled up as Celia pushed her hips into her. "I'm not sure if I'll be able to behave down here."

Celia took her hand and lowered her voice when Erin was about to sneak it into the back of her bikini bottoms. "Stop it. Uncle Dieter and Andy are up there."

"Okay, okay, I'll be good." Erin raised her hand above the water then reached out to stroke Celia's face.

Celia closed her eyes as she leaned into her touch. "That's better," she whispered. "At least until we're alone again." She turned to kiss the palm of Erin's hand. "So, what about you? Favorite dish?"

"For me it would be my mom's tagine. Its taste brings back so many memories—it reminds me of my childhood. I may not have lived in Morocco, but I grew up with the culture, so the flavors of the country make me happy."

"That's sweet. I hardly dare say it, but I don't think I've ever had a real tagine before."

"Then I'll take you out for one, when we stop off in Casablanca."

"That's a deal." Celia held her gaze. "Next question, and this one's a bit more loaded. What character traits do you value most in people?"

Erin hesitated for a moment, then shook her head and grinned. "Sorry. The three questions of the day are up, so you're going to have to wait until tomorrow."

24

"Why do you want to go to Tarragona? It seems like a random place to stop off; I've never even heard of it." Celia took a sip of her lemonade and leaned back in her lounger on the upper sundeck. Erin and Andy were sitting in the jacuzzi, their animated chatter and laughter filling the air. Her uncle was lying on the lounger next to her, playing some silly game on his phone. "I mean, you told me you bought a painting, but isn't it easier if the artist just sends it to Switzerland?"

Dieter was silent for a long moment, then nodded. "Yes, it would be easier and it's what I usually do, but this painting is dear to me and I want to look at it over the course of my journey."

"*Your* journey?" Celia paused as something about the way he said it didn't gel with the way he normally spoke. "Forgive me, but that sounds awfully spiritual, coming from you."

"Well, maybe I'm getting a little spiritual in my old age," he joked.

"Okay." Celia shrugged, deciding that answer was good enough for her. "Anyway, I'm excited to visit Spain. I haven't been there since you took me to the Guggenheim in Bilbao for my sixteenth birthday." She regarded her uncle as his fingers moved over his phone, his shoulders shooting up every few seconds. "Also, why are you on your phone? I've never even seen you look at your phone until now. As far as I'm aware, you hate phones and you hate computer games even more."

"What's with all the questions? It's just this game Andy got me hooked on." Dieter held it up, showing a man fighting little green aliens. "Want to try?"

"No thanks. But I'm glad Andy's introduced you to the wonderful world of technology. I like Andy."

"I like him too," her uncle said absently as his body shook like he was physically fighting himself. "He's fun." He hesitated, then lowered his voice so Andy couldn't hear him. "But apart from the fact that we're good friends, it's not super serious."

"Do you want it to be serious?"

"I don't know. He's a lot younger than me." Dieter let out a curse, clearly losing the game, then put his phone away with a frustrated sigh. "I doubt he's serious about me either, but sometimes that's enough." His gaze shifted to Erin, who was topping up Andy's champagne. Andy loved bubbles and jumped at any opportunity or excuse to have a glass. "He's loving the perks of dating a rich man with rich friends, that's for sure."

Celia smiled. "Yeah, but money aside, I have a feeling he genuinely likes you. It's the way he looks at you."

"You mean the same way Erin looks at you?" Dieter put a hand on hers and smiled. "I'm really glad you came along, Celia. And I know she is too."

Celia had a feeling he was holding something back and if she wasn't mistaken, he sounded melancholic, but unable to come up with an explanation, she let it slide. "I'm having fun with her."

"I know you are. I haven't seen you this animated and relaxed in a long time." He smiled. "So, it's not so scary after all, this 'being stuck-on-a-boat' thing, huh?"

"Not yet," Celia joked. "At the moment I'm still seeing land every now and then." She passed him the jug of lemonade next to her to fill up his glass and noticed his hand was shaking. "Are you okay?"

Her uncle looked caught as he poured himself a glass so quickly that he spilled half of it over his wrist. "I'm fine," he said resolutely as he passed the jug back, put his glass down and buried his hands underneath his thighs, repeating his statement. "I'm fine." Shifting his gaze to the coastline, he changed the subject. "It's spectacular, isn't it? That must be Barcelona over there."

"Yes, that's Barcelona," Erin confirmed after overhearing their conversation. She stepped out of the jacuzzi and wrapped a towel around her waist, then sat down on Celia's lounger, pulling her legs up on her lap. "We'll be in Tarragona before dark, but we can't moor there as the waters are too shallow for *The Barracuda* to dock. We'll have to anchor farther out and take the tender to the harbor." She turned to Dieter as she started massaging Celia's feet. "Are you planning on spending the night there or do you want to go tomorrow morning?"

"Tomorrow is fine," Dieter said. "I just need to pick up the painting, then Andy and I will have lunch with the artist to celebrate the purchase. Just let us know when you want us back."

"Okay, I'll let Eddie know we need the tender after

breakfast." Erin lifted Celia's foot and kissed it. "Would you like to go and explore with me, or do you have to work?"

"Of course I want to explore." Celia smiled widely, already giddy at the treatment her feet were getting and now at the prospect of having a romantic day alone with Erin "I'll do some work tonight, and I can get up early tomorrow to get ahead of schedule."

"Great, it's a date."

Dieter groaned as he stood up, holding onto his chest. "I'm feeling a bit tired. I think I'm going to lie down for a bit, so I'll be on form for dinner."

"I knew something was wrong. You were shaking earlier." Celia stood, too, and placed a hand on his forehead. "Are you too warm? Do you feel dizzy or nauseous? Could it be your heart or sunstroke? Do you think you need a doctor?" She suddenly felt worried as her uncle never complained, and ever since she'd seen him in his swimming trunks, she'd noticed his weight loss was significant. His ever-present beer belly was still there, but his arms and legs looked a lot skinnier than before and his cheeks had lost their plumpness.

Dieter waved a hand dismissively. "It's okay, I'm fine, sweetheart. Just tired, that's all. I'm getting older; it's normal." Celia reached for his hand to help him down the steps, but he refused her assistance. "My legs work just fine. Stop worrying about me, go lie back down and enjoy yourself. I just need a nap, that's all."

Celia looked up at Erin and lowered her voice as she watched him descend the stairs to the lower deck. "I don't think he's well."

Erin frowned, following him with her eyes, then shook her head. "If he says he's fine, he's fine. Let me go check on him, though."

"He'll just get irritated; he's stubborn like that."

"That's okay, I can take it." Erin shot her a sweet smile. "Wait for me in the jacuzzi?"

25

Tarragona was still sleeping as Erin and Celia climbed the steep hill that led into town. They passed through an arboretum that looked out over an old Roman amphitheater, its weather-beaten structure rising from pale coastal rocks behind a long stretch of white beach. The colors here were different, more earthy compared to the pastel-colored buildings of the French Riviera, and with the beach being so quiet as it was a weekday morning, it felt incredibly peaceful. Big trees shaded the cobbled path that cut through thick lawns and flower beds with red carnations, purple bougainvillea and huge, juicy aloe vera plants.

Erin loved to explore new countries and places, but with work having been so busy in the past couple of years, she hadn't taken much time off, and she couldn't remember the last time she'd just been for a stroll. Today was a perfect day to do just that. Best of all though, was the captivating woman by her side, who seemed equally enchanted by the view.

Celia smiled at her and it made her heart race. Today she was wearing a simple, sleeveless navy and white striped jersey dress and white sneakers, and her long, dark ponytail was pulled through the back of her navy cap. Her casual look was perhaps even more attractive to Erin than the red dress she'd worn at the summer ball, because she had a feeling this was the real Celia. The woman she was when she was at home in New York. "You look happy."

"I am happy." Celia took her hand and looked down at their entwined fingers. "Sorry, is this okay?"

"Of course, why wouldn't it be?"

"Well just, you know..." Celia shrugged and took off her shades to meet Erin's eyes. "It's all a little strange. We ended up in bed, we haven't left each other's side, and that's unlikely to change while we're on this vacation."

"Too much?" Erin asked.

"No, it's not that..." Celia hesitated.

"Because if that's what you're thinking, I get it; I've been thinking the same. It's a lot to go from nothing to where we are now and I'm not used to this either, but I don't regret asking you to come along. I've enjoyed every moment so far."

"Me too." Celia relaxed a little, her shoulders dropping. "But you have to agree that it seems too good to be true. The amazing sex, the connection, this trip... it feels like a dream."

"Sometimes good things happen." Erin completely understood where Celia was coming from. It wasn't exactly a classic dating situation, and she'd wondered herself if they were heading for disaster by diving in so fast, but it wasn't like she had a choice. Celia drew her in, made her happy, made her feel high on life, and that feeling was addictive. "We don't need to give this a name; we've known each other for less than a week. But we do have an opportunity to get to know each other better, so why not do just that and take it from there? If it becomes too much, you can sleep in your own room, and I don't want you to feel like you have to hold hands with me either."

Celia chuckled and took a tighter grip of Erin's hand. "I know. But when you're near, I crave being physically close to you; I don't think I could manage a night in my own room, knowing you're naked in bed only a few feet away from me."

"I agree, that would be hard." Erin paused. "How about we take it one day at a time? We're not crossing the Atlantic yet, so you have plenty of opportunity to escape, should you change your mind."

"Okay, that sounds good." Celia's peachy lips stretched into a smile. "Although I doubt I'm going to need to plot my escape, considering how wonderful it's been." A yawn passed her lips, and she covered her mouth with her hand in a gesture so delicate that it made Erin ache with longing. Everything Celia did was attractive to her, even something as mundane as yawning or scratching her head. She realized then, she had it bad.

"Tired?"

"A little." Celia rolled her shoulders and rocked her head from side to side. "You kept me up all night for all the right reasons, but it's nothing another strong coffee won't fix."

Erin felt a stir at her words. Their night had been pleasurable indeed, and it seemed they were insatiable around each other.

They'd reached the top of the hill and walked past an old fort from which the remains of the old city walls stretched around them, embracing a network of narrow streets. The crooked three-story houses in various shades of yellow painted a beautiful picture against the blue sky, and the small bars, cafes and restaurants scattered in between boutiques and galleries were utterly charming. "Plenty of coffee here, it seems." Erin gestured to a table on a shaded terrace and they sat down and ordered espressos.

"In the spirit of taking it one day at a time and getting to know each other, can I have my three questions now?"

"Absolutely." Erin thanked the waitress and stirred a sachet of sugar through her espresso. "Shoot."

"What character traits do you value most in people you date?"

Erin arched a brow and laughed. "I see you haven't forgotten about that question."

"I'm like an elephant, I never forget anything." Celia returned her playful look as she sipped her coffee. "Well?"

"Okay, let's see. It's kind of a hard question to answer as I haven't been in any serious relationships, but I suppose I would want my girlfriend to be kind. I think kindness is the most beautiful and attractive character trait a person can have."

"Really?" Celia seemed surprised at Erin's straightfor-ward answer. Had she expected her to make a joke out of this game?

"What about you?" Erin asked.

"For me, it would be honesty," Celia said without hesita-tion. "Lying puts me off people. I've been lied to too many times in my life, even by my own family, so that's a big one for me. If you lie, you're out. It's as simple as that."

"Hmm..." Erin's eyes shot toward the breakfast menu before she turned it around to study the selection of coffees on offer. "Good answer," she finally said, avoiding Celia's gaze. "Would you like another coffee? They have iced cappuccinos."

Celia frowned at her shifty reaction, but she didn't comment. "Sure. Let's have one to go, I'd love to see the castle."

26

After a wonderful day of sightseeing and exploring, Erin, Celia and Andy sat down for dinner on the deck and waited for Dieter, who was in his room. They'd just set off again, and were heading for Menorca, where they'd arrive tomorrow morning and stay the night.

Erin was glowing from her day with Celia. They'd wandered through old streets and enjoyed a long lunch in a beautiful garden. Then they'd visited the castle and walked along the fort walls of the town, taking in the vibe while they talked. Her 'three questions a day' had come to bite her in the ass, as she'd been taken aback by Celia's comment about lying. Of course, it made perfect sense. No one wanted to be lied to, and as much as she'd tried to tell herself that she was doing the right thing—that she was only keeping information back because her dying friend had asked her to—the secret between them was beginning to haunt her.

"Here it is." Dieter came out with the painting he'd acquired. He carefully carried it to the table, then turned it around to show it to them. Apart from a sarcastic snort from

Andy, who had already seen it, everyone fell silent as he held it up. "What do you think? Isn't it powerful?"

Erin didn't know what to say as the image in front of her felt too close to home and her discomfort prevented her from making any positive comment. The dying man's face as he lay on the bed bore too much resemblance to Dieter's to be a coincidence. Lying on his back and wrapped in white sheets, Dieter's stricken features looked up at a black unicorn that was flying over him. The man was laughing as his spirit left his body, his translucent arms reaching for the unicorn's neck.

"I'm sorry to ruin your big reveal, Uncle Dieter, but it's a little grim," Celia said with a pensive stare. "That man looks like you; it's creepy."

"That's what I thought too," Andy said. "I guess it was meant to be."

Dieter laughed and shook his head. "I don't find it creepy at all. I find it hopeful. The artist is known for portraying death in different forms, using her delicate, almost photorealistic yet surreal painting style. Here, she has painted death as a black unicorn and the dying man is embracing him like a friend." He winked and pointed to the man's other hand, hanging over the edge of the bed. "All the while holding onto his bottle of wine for dear life. It's about letting go without regrets."

Celia was the first to speak after a long silence. "Is that you?"

"Yes," Dieter admitted. "The artist took the liberty to use my face. It's great, don't you think?"

"Honestly, it scares me." Celia continued to stare at the painting. "It's powerful—I have to agree with you there—and if it wasn't you, I would probably love it. But I don't like to think of you as a dying man."

"Like it or not, art should be challenging. That's something we've always agreed on."

"True." Celia shrugged. "Well, as long as you love looking at it, that's all that counts."

"Hey, what about me?" Andy shrieked. "Dieter wants to hang it above our bed."

Dieter laughed. "Oh, come on, Andy. It's a glorious piece of work." He turned the painting, held it up and looked at it once more before he turned. "I'll go put this under the bed for now, I won't be long."

"Isn't it awful?" Andy whispered as soon as Dieter had left.

"I wouldn't say it's awful. In fact, I think it's very good, but it's definitely a little sinister," Celia said, moving aside so Ming could put her starter in front of her. "Thank you, Ming." She smiled and waved a hand when Ming put down the next plate in Dieter's place at the table. "That must be for Erin, my uncle doesn't eat fatty foods anymore. He needs to watch his cholesterol."

"Oh." Ming looked puzzled. "But he told me this morning that he'd like to eat the same as everyone else."

"She's right," Dieter chipped in as he returned and sat down at the table. "I'm done with dieting. It's boring. Anyway, my appetite's been down lately, so I don't eat nearly as much as I used to."

Andy shook his head with a frown. "But you have a bad heart, and—"

"Yes, I have a bad heart but it's not like I'm going to drop dead after eating this." Dieter picked up his knife and fork, letting him know there was no discussion to be had. "Besides, I'm on vacation, so I'm allowed to indulge." He scooped a piece of burrata onto his pesto bruschetta, sprinkled it with sea salt, then drizzled a generous amount of olive oil on top.

"How about we all eat healthy then?" Celia suggested. "I'd be happy to do that."

"Me too," Andy agreed.

Erin didn't comment when Celia and Andy looked at her for support. She felt trapped, knowing Dieter wanted to live like a king during his last months, but going against them seemed like a bad idea too. "I'd be happy to do that," she carefully said. "But I think you're missing the point here. Dieter is a grown man and if that's what he wants…"

"How can you say that?" Celia shot her an annoyed look, and Erin felt like she was being stabbed. It was horrible to be in this position; she'd have to convince Dieter to tell them sooner rather than later. "His doctor told me he's high risk and he wasn't feeling well yesterday afternoon."

"Don't take this out on Erin; she's right." Dieter focused his attention on Celia. "I want to enjoy my vacation and eat whatever I want. A few weeks of eating like a normal person is not going to give me a heart attack." He held up his glass in a toast and painted on a smile. "Now let's drop the subject and catch up. I want to hear all about your day."

27

———

"I'm sorry I snapped at you earlier." Celia shot Erin a regretful glance. Dieter and Andy had gone to bed and they were enjoying the calm of the empty deck, listening to the sound of the waves.

"It's okay. I get it; you're worried about him."

"No, it's not okay. I know I need to stop mothering him, but I can't help but think something isn't right. He's different. Not in a bad way…" Celia paused. "In fact, he's more relaxed than ever, and he hasn't even thought about work. But still, he's not the same. Have you noticed that?"

Erin shrugged. "I haven't noticed a difference, but then I haven't known him for as long as you have." She smiled. "I'm sure he's fine. Do you want to come up to the bow with me, or are you tired?"

"No, I'd love to," Celia said, deciding to let it go. Maybe she was just being paranoid. She pointed to the bridge. "But Eddie is up there, and he can see us, so no funny business."

Erin laughed and shook her head. "No funny business. I was actually thinking of watching the stars with you. Out at sea there's no light pollution, so the stars are usually pretty spectacular and we should enjoy it."

Celia was a little unsteady on her feet as she got up. The difference in movement was significant, now that they were farther from the mainland. She veered toward the right when the vessel tilted and held onto Erin. "It's not the wine, I promise. It's just harder to walk," she joked, before she finally found her balance.

"Not feeling nauseous yet?"

"No, thankfully not." Celia let Erin help her toward the front of the yacht where a padded seat was hanging over the water. The railing around it ensured it was safe to sit down, but she was still a little apprehensive as she carefully climbed in. The double seat was snug, deep and tilted back slightly, so she felt comfortable when they were both settled. "This is incredible." Her legs were dangling over the edge, the sea water splashing up every so often as it cooled her bare feet.

"Wait, it gets better." Erin called a number on her phone. "Hey, Eddie. Is it safe to switch off the masthead light for five minutes? Great. Thank you." She settled back and put an arm around Celia as if they were in the cinema, waiting for a movie to start.

When the light went off, Celia's eyes needed a moment to adjust to the dark. There was no land in sight, and she'd lost all sense of direction since they'd left Spain behind. With the absence of her vision, her other senses came to life, sharpening as she adjusted to her surroundings. She listened to the sound of the water washing away from the hull, and she found herself moving along with the vessel each time they hit a wave. It felt like they were going faster, even though they were still sailing at the same speed, and the wind seemed to sweep through her hair with a more powerful force. There was nothing but the smell and the sound of the sea, and apart from the crescent moon above them, the sky was so dark it was hard to make out the horizon. After a few minutes of getting accustomed to the dark, she looked up to see the vast space above them was now filled with stars. It was so beautiful that she stared up in silence, in awe of how small it made her feel.

"Pretty cool, right?" Erin breathed in deeply as she took in the scene before them, and Celia could tell she loved being at sea. "I like to sit here at night and watch the stars. To see the universe laid out in front of me. It's so pure and simple. Sea, sky, moon, stars... Nothing else. It reduces life to its purest form."

"This must be the most romantic thing I've ever done," Celia said, turning in her seat so she could lift her legs onto Erin's lap. "It's quite a way to impress a woman." She steadied her elbow on the back of the seat, resting her cheek in the palm of her hand.

"Yeah, being at sea at night is very romantic." Erin reached out and ran a hand over Celia's cheek, then let her fingers slip through her hair. "You probably think I have women on my yacht all the time, but I've actually never taken a love interest on a trip."

"You haven't?" The statement came out of nowhere, as if Erin was dying to get it off her chest, and Celia frowned as she turned to her. "Why not?"

Erin shrugged. "The idea of being stuck at sea with someone I'm sleeping with freaks me out, so I prefer to sail with friends, or just by myself."

"Then why me?" Celia was sure her presence didn't make Erin feel nervous or trapped. She was intuitive and would have known if it did. "We're sleeping together, you barely know me, and yet I'm here. Unless my uncle put pressure on you?"

"No, it's nothing like that." Erin played with a lock of Celia's hair, twirling it around her finger. "Confession?"

"Go on."

"Promise me you won't freak out."

"I promise," Celia said, bracing herself as Erin seemed deadly serious all of a sudden.

"Our dance last year affected me more than you know. I love having you here because I've thought about you every day since, and that's unheard of for me." Erin hesitated. "I never actually thought you would join us, but I was secretly hoping you would. And while I arranged this trip for the auction, I had fantasies about you bidding on it. If you had bought the vacation, I would have given Eddie the time off and taken over as captain so I could be here with you."

Celia's stomach did somersaults at hearing her words. "Are you serious?"

"Yes." Erin gave her an adorable, shy smile. "Magically, it all worked out, and the result was even better than I'd imagined in my fantasies."

"That's so sweet. I'm not freaking out, by the way. It's refreshing to have someone simply tell me the truth."

"Good." Erin leaned in closer and lowered her voice. "Well, that's my confession." Their lips brushed, and Celia parted hers to claim Erin's mouth while she cupped her neck and pulled her in.

The kiss was electric and sent a surge of desire through every part of Celia's body. Frankly, there was nowhere she'd rather be, and she'd been basking in a heavenly haze since the ball. "Even if I did freak out, it's not like I can go anywhere," she whispered with a smile.

Erin chuckled. "Even if you decided to leave, I still might follow you."

28

Celia ventured outside with coffee in hand, dying to see what the morning was like now that they were anchored along the shore of Menorca. She was naked under her soft, fluffy white robe, her bare feet warmed by the clean and slick decking.

It was another sunny day and she inhaled deeply as she blinked against the bright sunlight, cherishing the scent of the sea. Every morning felt like a dream. Waking up like this was bliss, and knowing she'd get to spend the day with her new favorite person was even better.

The view that greeted her made her stop in her stride. She hadn't known what to expect from Menorca, but it certainly wasn't anything as pretty as this. Before her was an azure blue bay with a small harbor that moored no more than a dozen white fishing boats. The wall surrounding the small town behind the harbor was painted white, and behind that, everything else was whitewashed too; the houses—even their roofs—the church, the benches that stood in the shade of olive trees, the quiet restaurants and the parasols on the terraces. The sea of white against the blue sky was breathtakingly beautiful, so pure and clean and at the same time so charmingly authentic.

"Good morning, princess."

She turned around to find Erin, who was wearing a white robe too, and that seemed perfectly fitting, considering the view. Her hair was still wet from her recent shower —she smelled of coconut soap—and her eyes were sparkling in the sunshine.

"Hey." Celia's lips pulled into a smile at the sight of her, even though she'd just seen Erin less than five minutes ago in their room. Her presence was addictive, her touch all Celia needed, and when Erin placed a soft kiss on her cheek and took her hand, her insides turned to mush.

"This pretty little town is called Binibeca Vell," Erin said. "I'd never heard of it myself and wouldn't have come here if it wasn't for Dieter, so I'm very grateful to him. He and Andy left early this morning. They're staying with a friend of Dieter, and they'll be back tomorrow."

"Hmm... that means we have the day and night to ourselves." Celia turned and wrapped her arms around Erin's waist.

"We do." Erin licked her lips, unable to hide how much that thought turned her on. "And I've taken the liberty to book a place here, if you don't mind." She smiled and greeted Ming, who was setting up the breakfast table for them. "Shall we go and sit down?"

Binibeca Vell was a sweet town; quiet and quaint with cobbled streets that looked over the harbor. Shaded areas provided plenty of seating space; locals caught up on benches or on the edge of small fountains, and the little white village church they'd visited was more of a social club too. With only four restaurants and a couple of stores, Celia was impressed that Erin had managed to find a place to rent tonight as there didn't seem to be any other tourists around.

"I feel like I'm in a monochrome dream," she said as they were having dinner. They'd started their morning with a lazy breakfast and numerous coffees while cruising around the island. After that, they'd anchored back at the harbor and taken a refreshing dive in the Mediterranean. Now, they were at a romantic harborside restaurant where the food was delicious, the wine crisp and the view to die for. Their rickety table was filled with small dishes which neither of them had ever tasted; fresh bread and oliaigua, cod balls in a garlicky white wine sauce, eggplant salad, grilled octopus and lobster stew.

"If this is a dream, I'm not complaining." Erin took a sip of her wine and smiled at her. "You're more beautiful than the town and the view put together."

"So are you." Celia found it hard to draw her eyes away from Erin. She was casually dressed in a white shirt and jeans and her eyes were extraordinary in the fading light of dusk. Almost black. With her olive skin and laid-back attitude, she could have easily passed for a local.

It was hard to believe she had been in New York last week as that life seemed so far away now. Instead of her usual view that consisted of skyscrapers and smog, she gazed over the sea as the sun drew closer to its own reflection, turning the sky red.

"Can I ask you something?" she said. "Tell me if I'm getting too personal, but I figured I might as well as it's been bugging me."

"Sure." A hint of worry flashed over Erin's features, but she hid it behind her smile.

"You seem to have these almost unnoticeable mood shifts," Celia started carefully. "You're here one moment, and then the next, it's like you're somewhere else. I'm not saying I want to know what you're thinking; that would be intrusive. But I was just wondering if you're okay, or if there's something you'd like to talk about, since you told me you'd had bad news back at the castle..."

Erin looked down at her plate, avoiding Celia's eyes. She clearly had trouble answering the question, as she nervously fiddled with her napkin.

"I'm sorry, I shouldn't have brought it up." Celia regretted starting a serious conversation on such a beautiful night. They weren't close enough yet for her to ask questions like that, and this was a time to have fun with her new lover, not psychoanalyze her.

"No, it's fine." Erin looked up then and leaned in closer, lowering her voice. "Look, you're right. I'm not entirely okay." She hesitated. "But I can't talk about it and you have to believe me when I say that it has nothing to do with my love life. There's no other woman than you in my life right now. And yes, sometimes I get sad and that might not change for a while, but having you here makes all the difference. And I mean it when I say that I'm genuinely happy in this moment. I mean, how could I not be?"

Celia relaxed a little, returning her warm smile. "Okay. That's good to know." She pierced her fork through a piece of octopus and held it out for Erin, who took the bite. The way her lips folded around it made Celia's pulse race. Everything she did was seductive, and she didn't even know it. "Can I ask you something else?"

"Anything. And if I'm able to, I'll answer. That's all I can promise."

"You said your parents are Moroccan. Do they know you're gay?"

"They know. And they're not delighted with it, but we get along just fine." Erin angled her head and looked at her as if she already knew what the next question was going to be.

"Are they religious?"

"Yes, they're Muslim. And to answer the next question you undoubtedly want to ask, no, I'm not religious myself. Don't get me wrong; I don't dismiss Islam, but I didn't grow up like my parents did. Different generation and all that. Sometimes I go to the mosque when I visit them. I haven't blessed them with grandchildren or the life they envisioned for me, so it's the least I can do. They're good people and I love them, we're just very different."

Celia nodded. "Sorry, you must get these questions all the time, and I'm not against religion in any way, but it must have been difficult to come out to them."

"It was. I think my mom always knew; there's no way she could have missed it, the way I was only ever interested in girls and that I always insisted on dressing like a tomboy from the age of six or seven." Erin paused, and Celia followed her gaze toward the horizon. The last of the red glow was fading but the water was still brightly colored and purple at the edges of the sun's reflection. "It's been a very long time since I've really talked about myself," Erin continued. "So forgive me for being a little apprehensive."

"You don't need to talk about anything you don't want to," Celia said, reaching for her hand over the table.

"No, it's refreshing. Most of my dates only want to know about my yacht and they're generally just fishing for an invitation to go on vacation or to be taken on a lavish night out. But it's different with you, and I'm slowly getting used to that." Erin looked at her pensively. "Of course, you're wealthy yourself, but that's not even what distinguishes you. You're a genuinely kind person."

"Thank you." Celia smiled. "So are you. I like how you treat your crew with utmost respect. It says a lot about a person."

"I appreciate that you see that. They're hard workers and the most professional team I've ever had, so it's important to me that they're happy in their jobs." Erin squeezed her hand. "Anyway, about my parents... I told them I was gay when I was eighteen, on the day I moved out. I guess I'd expected them to kick me out of the house, so I'd found a small rental. They were upset, but looking back, I don't think they would have done that. My father blamed my mother at first, for raising me too liberal while he was away at work. But he's come around now, and he doesn't bring it up anymore. Or maybe he's just given up on the idea of me marrying a good Muslim man." She chuckled. "I'm forty-eight, so kids are out of the question too. I suppose that makes it easier; it certainly takes off the pressure."

"Forty-eight?" Celia frowned as she looked her up and down. "You look a lot younger. I thought you were in your late thirties."

"Thank you, I'll take that." Erin laughed. "Now that I've shocked you with my age, I hope you haven't changed your mind and want to go back home. I should have probably told you sooner and I can't believe we haven't had this conversation yet."

"No, not at all." Celia laughed too. "I just didn't expect a ten-year age-gap, but it makes no difference to me."

"Good. I'm glad you don't mind." The fire in Erin's eyes sent a flash of arousal through Celia, making her shift in her chair. She knew exactly what Erin was thinking. They'd had the most amazing nights since the summer ball, exploring each other's sexual desires for hours until they were too exhausted to move. A whole new world had opened up to her, and it was a world she wanted to explore so much more of.

"So, we're staying here tonight?" she asked.

"Yes. I've rented a place right up there; Ming picked up the key for me this morning." Erin pointed to the white houses built up against the hill above them. "I think you'll like it."

29

Narrow cobbled steps led up to *The Birdhouse*. The name was spelled out in gray pebbles, cemented into the white wall along the side. Erin opened the gate and followed the path that cut through the yard, her excitement growing at the sight of the cute house and the breathtaking view. It looked incredibly sweet, a world apart from her luxury yacht they'd just stepped off. The patio was filled with an abundance of flowers and dozens of bird feeders led to the entrance of the white house that had been built cave-like into the cliff, and at the edge of the patio was a small, shallow infinity pool with built-in benches that overlooked the sea.

"Erin, this is so unique." Celia's eyes twinkled as she admired the premises.

"Yeah, it's perfect." Erin herself had never seen anything like it either. They could see the white rooftops of the village below and the lights from the harbor. Stars were twinkling above them and the little lights along the edge of the pool lit up the water that looked incredibly inviting after their climb. The church tower rose from behind the house, its white cross and silver bell almost illuminous against the night sky, and she was pleased with her choice as she unlocked the door. "After you."

Celia stepped in and turned on the lights. The house really was a cave. The low, rounded ceiling shaped the rooms into domes, and the main features had been carved, rather than built or placed. Two benches and a table along the windows in the kitchen, the kitchen surface, the platform that served as a base for the double mattress and the sofa in the bedroom were all made of rock and painted a chalky white like the rest of the interior, and the shower was placed in an alcove. It felt organic, as if they'd been swallowed by a living and breathing creature, yet the small, dome-shaped windows stopped it from feeling claustrophobic.

Erin opened the fridge and took out the bottle of Xoriguer—a local gin—that their host had left for them, along with some lemonade, ice and two chilled glasses to prepare the local 'pomanda' cocktails. "Want to have a nightcap in the pool?"

"Yes. Give me a minute to get changed." Celia gestured to the weekend bag she'd brought with her.

"No need for a bikini." Erin shot her a mischievous smile. "It's super private; we're too high up for anyone to see us." She took the bottle and the glasses and walked back outside, where she placed them on the edge of the pool and took off her clothes.

Erin was aware of Celia watching her as she stepped into the pool, and her body was already on fire, knowing where their nightcap would lead. She immersed herself in the water, then draped her arms over the edge as she stared back at Celia. "Strip for me," she said in a low voice. "I want to see you naked in the moonlight."

The command made Celia shiver, and she slowly lifted her white summer dress over her head, then dropped it to the ground. She wasn't wearing a bra and her white, lace thong didn't cover much. The breeze was blowing loose strands of hair around her face and her skin looked almost illuminous in the light reflecting off the pool. There was no doubt about it; Celia was seduction personified as she pulled down her thong and stepped out of them, then walked to the edge of the pool and stared down at her with that sultry and longing look in her eyes that made her think she wanted to eat her alive and hold her forever all at once. Reaching for the band that held her ponytail together, she pulled her hair free, then shook out her long, dark hair, knowing Erin loved to see it down.

"You're so damn sexy." Erin took her time to appreciate Celia's naked form against the starry sky, her ravishingly attractive face and her full breasts that rose and fell in time with her soft breathing.

"And I think I'm obsessed with you." Celia stepped into the pool, straddled her on the bench seat and embraced her. They sighed at the sensation of finally coming together after a long afternoon of withholding on the island. Erin's whole body trembled as Celia brushed her lips against hers, the featherlight touch so electrifying it made every nerve ending zing with pleasure. "Are you going to pour me a drink?"

"Of course. Where are my manners?" The corners of Erin's mouth tugged up into a smile as she picked up the bottle and followed the handwritten instructions to make the drinks. "Gin with cloudy lemon," she said, preparing them both a glass. "Let's see how this local homebrew tastes."

Celia held up the yellow liquid and took a sip. "Mmm... it's good."

Erin took a small sip too, then set her glass to the side.

"Not drinking?" Celia asked.

Erin shook her head, her eyes darkening. "You're too distracting; I think I prefer to taste it from your lips." She cupped Celia's neck and pulled her closer, then ran her tongue over her bottom lip, drawing a quiet moan from Celia's mouth.

Celia put her glass down too as she ground her center into her lap, rocking her hips back and forth. Erin felt her desire as she tightened her grip and held her close.

"I've noticed there are two sides to you," Celia whispered against her mouth.

"Is that so?"

"Yes." Celia continued to grind her hips into her lap as she talked. "There's this Erin; the primal Erin who acts on her animalistic needs and gets a kick out of dominating me. This Erin has the ability to make me do whatever she wants because ultimately, her goal is to please me. And then there's the other Erin. The talented, vulnerable, fun and generous woman who's also surprisingly romantic."

Erin thought about that and realized she was right. She hadn't played games with Celia but she seemed to have fallen into a certain role with her because she'd sensed from the beginning Celia loved her natural dominance. "Which Erin do you prefer?" she asked, unsure if she wanted to know the answer.

Celia shrugged and gave her that incredible smile that took away all her sense of reason and logic. "I'm falling for both and I'm falling hard."

Her words flooded Erin with joy as she moved her hands to her behind, stood up and lifted her onto the edge of the pool. "I fell for you a long time ago," she whispered, stepping between her legs. She traced Celia's thighs before spreading them wide, and when she blew warm breath between her legs, Celia gasped and threw her head back, steadying herself on her hands behind her.

Erin kissed her way up her thighs, then moved her mouth to her center so soft that she barely touched her, but Celia levitated off the edge with a throaty groan as if she'd just put a vibrator against her clit. She was so sensitive that Erin was afraid she'd hurt her if she did anything more, but Celia's hips betrayed her as they bucked, begging her to continue. The taste of her was divine—her sweet and musky flavor arousing her so much that it made her throb—and Erin moaned as she dragged her tongue between Celia's folds.

Arching her back and wrapping her legs around Erin's neck, Celia cried out as she repeated the action over and over, lapping up her juices. When she started shaking heavily—her breathing telling Erin she was on the edge—Erin moved up to her clit and sucked it into her mouth. She held her firmly around her thighs until seconds later Celia covered her face in her hands to stifle her climactic cries.

"Yes! Oh God, yes..."

Erin closed her eyes and moaned while she felt her explode against her mouth. It was sensual and sexy and mind-blowingly beautiful, and she loved how Celia gave herself to her without hesitation. Her reaction was so pure and intense; she'd never witnessed that with another woman. Celia jerked her hips while she cried out in the silent night. Letting out a chuckle through her heavy breaths, she shook her head with a smile, meeting Erin's eyes as she pulled away from her.

"That was..." She lowered herself back into the water

and wrapped her arms around Erin's neck. "Fucking liberating..."

Erin exhaled deeply while she held her and as with every time she felt this immense closeness, conflict started brewing inside her again. Celia had no idea she was about to lose the most important person in her life.

"Are you okay?" Celia mumbled against her neck, clearly sensing her sudden shift in mood as she tensed up.

"Yeah." Erin squeezed her tighter, shook off the heart-breaking thoughts and forced herself to be in the moment. "I've never been better." She noted her voice was unsteady, and she kissed her so she wouldn't have to talk.

30

"Good, Marcus, this looks amazing." Erin gave her chef a big smile as she leaned back, so he could serve her moussaka. "I'm sorry we kept you waiting for so long; Dieter and Andy should be here any minute."

"No problem. It's my job to serve whenever you're ready and trust me; this is nothing. I worked for a guy once who once left me waiting for twelve hours." Marcus looked from Erin to Celia and back. "I got some nice ingredients on the island. Stop offs are fun for me; I love visiting markets in new places and you're always welcome to come along if you're interested."

"I would love that. Please let me know next time you go." Celia thanked him and helped herself to salad. They had just started sailing again and were cruising along the northern shoreline of Menorca, heading for the Strait of Gibraltar, which they would pass through to connect to the Atlantic Ocean. Dieter and Andy had boarded an hour ago and were in their room freshening up. Celia hadn't seen them yet as she'd been working in a covered area on deck while Erin caught up on work in her library. As much as she'd enjoyed her private time with Erin, she was also really looking forward to seeing them again.

"Hello, lovebirds!"

She glanced over her shoulder to find Andy, who was standing behind them, wearing a pink rhinestone covered cap that matched his pink shorts and polo shirt. "Sorry we're late. Dieter had a little trouble saying goodbye to his friends." He rolled his eyes. "Guess he's getting sentimental in his old age."

Celia laughed. "Hey, Andy. Good to have you back. You're looking very…"

"Spark-a-licious?" Andy fanned his face and chuckled. "I know. I'm fabulous."

"There's no doubt about that." Erin gave him a smirk and pulled out a chair for him. "Did you guys have a good time?"

"Totally. Dieter's never introduced me to any of his close friends before, so I wasn't sure what to expect, but these guys were mad as hatters. Total hippies, living off the grid in the mountains with their sheep, beehives and fruit trees." Andy beamed as he sat down. "But I can't say I mind being back here. As much as I loved sleeping in a yurt in their yard, I think I prefer this lifestyle. And you know what else I just realized? There are no mosquitos on the water, which means I can stop spraying myself with this horrible citronella stuff." He sniffed his arm and let out a deep sigh. "Oh, Erin, this is so magnificent, I feel like a prince. Ever thought of making the yacht your permanent home? Need an assistant by any chance?"

"I have a feeling you'd have me running around doing stuff for *you* if we worked together," Erin joked, looking him over in amusement. She turned to Dieter who looked exhausted as he joined them. "Hello, my friend. Are you okay?"

"Yes, just a little tired." Dieter winked at Andy. "Not sure if bringing my younger boyfriend on this trip was the best idea. He's worn me out already." He took a seat opposite Celia and waited for Marcus to put down his plate. "You look good, kiddo. Did you like the island?"

"Loved it," Celia said. "And you? Was it fun to see your old friends again? Andy told us you got a little emotional when you left."

"Oh yes, well what can I say." Dieter's eyes carried a hint of sadness before he looked down at his plate. "Roderick and I lived with them for a year, back in the late eighties. It was only meant to be a short visit—we'd met them on a vacation, and they'd invited us to their home—but we kept putting off our departure because we were having such a wonderful time. Finally, one day, my caretaker called me to tell me some urgent work needed to be done to the castle, so we flew back home to take care of things. It's strange how people come and go in your life, but you never forget them. I hadn't seen them since then, but it felt like only yesterday that I was sleeping in a hammock between their olive trees."

"You could have invited them onto the yacht, we have more cabins," Erin said. "And it's not too late; we can still turn around to pick them up."

Dieter placed a hand on Erin's forearm and gave her a warm smile. "That's very kind of you but I don't think they've left their home in the past fifteen years. They're older too now."

"That didn't stop them from drinking me under the table." Andy rubbed his temple. "One word. Gin. I was going to take a quick nap when we got back but then I noticed Dieter had replaced that lovely Reverón opposite our bed with that creepy painting he'd picked up in Tarragona, and I just couldn't."

"Come on, it's a beautiful painting," Dieter protested. "Just cover it up before you take a nap if it bothers you; as long as you're careful with it." He turned to Erin. "Don't worry; I gave the Reverón to Captain Eddie for safekeeping. I have no intention of stealing it," he joked.

"I don't think my modest collection has anything on yours, so I'm not worried about that." Erin thanked Ming, who came to fill their wineglasses, and they enjoyed dinner as they caught up on the happenings of the past two days.

"So, where exactly are we?" Andy asked. "Is this the Atlantic?"

Celia burst out in laughter, then held up a hand in apology. "I'm sorry, but that's just too funny." She studied Andy for a hint of a joke, but he seemed serious. "You really don't know where we are on the map of the world? Not even remotely?"

Andy shook his head. "I know I'm on a superyacht in fabulous company." He took a sip of his wine, lifting his pinkie in a dramatic manner. "But all joking aside. I would like to know where we're heading, so I can start planning my outfits. Where are we going next?"

Erin dabbed her mouth with her napkin and pointed in the direction they were heading. "We're currently sailing between Europe and Africa and tomorrow we may be able to see the Algerian coastline, depending on what route Eddie decides to take. We're heading for The Strait of Gibraltar, which will take us out to the Atlantic, and unless Dieter wants to stop off somewhere else, our next mooring will be Casablanca in four days. I'll take turns with Eddie up on the bridge, so Celia can finally get some work done," she joked. "We can spend the night in Casablanca so you guys can do some shopping after visiting your friends, if you want."

"Yay, shopping!" Andy clapped his hands in excitement, and Dieter planted a sweet kiss on his cheek.

"And if I may give you some advice on planning your outfits for Morocco, I think it might be best to tone it down on the pink," Erin joked.

"It's not even the pink I'm worried about. We need to tone down Andy," Dieter said with an endearing humorous smile. "Just kidding, handsome. I like you just the way you are."

"Good. Because I like me too, and I'll wear pink whenever and wherever the hell I please," Andy retorted, making them all laugh.

Celia put a hand on Erin's thigh and smiled. "And while the boys are out shopping, how about you show me around and teach me a little about your culture?"

Erin looked surprised at her suggestion. "Sure. Are you really interested?"

"Of course I am. Your parents are Moroccan; it's your heritage." Celia tilted her head and studied Erin. "Do you still have family there?"

"My grandmother lives there, about a three-hour drive inland from Casablanca, but I haven't seen her in over thirty years. She and my mother fell out when my parents refused to move back to Morocco. She wanted them to take over the family farm, after my grandfather died but by then my parents had their own life in LA, and they had no desire to do that. My grandmother refuses to move away from the farm, so she's still there. My parents send her money so she can afford staff to help her out, but other than that, she won't have anything to do with them."

"That's kind of harsh. But surely she'd want to see her granddaughter?"

Erin shrugged. "I don't know. I only saw her every couple of years when I was younger, so I'm not exactly close to her. I'm not sure if she cares."

"And you? Would you not want to see her?"

"Maybe." Erin felt her stomach sink at the thought of paying her grandmother a visit. Not because she didn't want to, but because she felt guilty for leaving it so long. She could have easily visited her; it wasn't like she was short of funds, but the family feud and the fact that her grandmother's world was so different to her own now made it daunting, so she'd kept putting it off until one day, she'd decided to stop worrying about it and just ignore the whole matter altogether.

"I'm sorry, I didn't mean to make you feel uncomfortable," Celia said.

"You're not making me uncomfortable." Erin hesitated. "It's just the guilt that's keeping me away. I've neglected her." She took another sip of her wine and ran her fork through the cheesy eggplant dish. Suddenly, she wasn't hungry anymore. "You know what? I'll think about it."

Celia nodded." Yeah, think about it; now's your chance. I can stay here if you want to go alone."

31

S itting on Erin's lap in the jacuzzi on the upper deck, Celia felt more relaxed than at any point in her life. She'd woken up fresh and caught up on work today, she'd had a great time with her uncle and Andy, and after dinner, she and Erin had headed up for some alone time. The Balearic Sea was a little rough tonight but sitting in the water stopped her from getting nauseous. Night sailing was beautiful, and she'd truly started to appreciate the total darkness that surrounded them.

Erin had switched the lights in the jacuzzi and the guiding lights along the deck and the stairs to red, so it wouldn't disturb Captain Eddie's vision, and it made the balmy night feel even more sensual.

She draped an arm around Erin's neck and shifted closer. "Three questions," she said, giving her a daring look. "We haven't done the three questions yet today."

Erin laughed. "Oh God, why do I have a feeling I'm going to regret ever starting this game?"

Celia batted her lashes innocently. "Just answer honestly and you'll be fine." She narrowed her eyes, digging through the questions she already had lined up. "What's your biggest regret?"

"Another serious one? What's with all the serious questions? Can't you just ask me about my favorite TV show or something?" Erin joked.

"We're supposed to get to know each other, aren't we?"

"True." Erin let out a sigh of defeat. "Okay, let's see, my biggest regret. I don't regret much, actually. I've lived life in a way that I can feel proud of, I think. But I do regret not staying in touch with my grandmother." She steadied her elbow on the edge of the jacuzzi, finger combing her hair. "I'd managed to put it out of my head, but our conversation last night brought it all back, and it's been bugging me."

"Then maybe it's time that you consider visiting her," Celia said softly. "Surely, she must be very old now."

"You're right." Erin paused, then turned the question back on her, deciding she was done talking about her grandmother. "What about you? What's your biggest regret?"

"Hmm... I don't know."

Erin laughed. "You asked the question."

"I know." Celia pursed her lips as she pondered over her answer. "I suppose I regret trusting certain people."

"The people who lied to you?" Erin asked, sinking lower into the warm water. It got chilly out on the open sea, especially at night.

"Yes."

"Want to tell me about it?"

Celia dipped her head back in the water and shook her hair out. "I guess the first person who did that to me was my mom. She's obsessed with money, always has been." She let out a sarcastic chuckle. "I believe that's why she married my father."

"I figured as much," Erin said. "Your mom doesn't strike me as the type to marry a working-class man."

"No, she's not. When my father was still alive, I just took my parents for what they were. My father was a kind and caring man. Strict, for sure, but fair. And my mother was just my mother; I didn't know any better." She paused. "But after his death, I seriously started to wonder what he ever saw in her. She's so greedy, it makes me sick sometimes."

"What did your father do for a living?"

"He was a private real estate investor, and a good one. Like Uncle Dieter, he had been blessed with the family fortune, and he was a hard worker." Celia forced herself to set her emotions aside and talk about this as if it was just another story. Thinking about her father's death was still too painful and she didn't want to burst into tears in front of Erin. "It wasn't until my father's will was read out that I realized how greedy and vicious my mother really was. Most of his money was left to me and my brother, and she was unable to accept that, even though he left her enough properties to live like a queen for the rest of her life. Now don't get me wrong; I don't really care about money and I would have quite happily given her half of what I inherited. She's my mother after all. But then she contested the will and claimed my father had changed his mind on his deathbed. My brother and I both knew that wasn't true and she lost, of course, as she had no proof. But knowing she was lying to rob her own children, well, that kind of rubbed me the wrong way."

"Understandably." Erin looked at her and gave her a sad smile. "Your brother and mother seem close, though. How did that happen?"

"They're not really close. They just pretend to be. My brother plays the perfect, supportive son because he's just like her and hopes to become the sole inheritor of her fortune one day. He's already frittered away most of his money, so he needs more, that's all."

"God, that's so sad."

"It is. Maybe now you understand why I don't jump for joy when I see them. But they're still my family, so I tend to make nice as our get-togethers never last very long." Celia managed a smile. "And then there was this woman, Marcy. I regret her too. We met in the line at the grocery store and got talking while we waited for a broken cash register to be repaired. We went on a couple of dates—just low-key ones, nothing fancy. I'd told her what I did for a living, but nothing about my background. I tend to keep my cards close to my chest until I get to know people better. Having a lot of money can often attract people for the wrong reasons as I'm sure you know."

Erin nodded. "I've had some experience with that."

"I thought you might. So, anyway, I was kind of smitten with Marcy. She was cute, smart, funny... and she seemed super interested in me. Asked me all kinds of questions about my family, which I tried to avoid where I could, but you know, I don't like to lie so I did open up a little. She was a veterinary surgeon, which I thought was interesting, and she lived in Brooklyn." Celia felt a lump forming in her throat but forced herself to continue. If they were going to get to know each other, it was important for her to tell Erin about her dating history. "One night, she stayed over, and the next morning, she forgot her phone at my apartment. I tried to find the surgery where she worked, to let her know I'd drop it off, but the name didn't come up in any searches. So, then I decided to look her up on social media so I could send her a message. Marcy had told me she didn't care for social media and that she didn't use her accounts much anymore, but I thought it would be worth a shot." She shrugged. "It suddenly seemed strange that I couldn't find a Marcy McCain listed as a veterinary surgeon anywhere in New York."

"Jesus, I don't like where this is going," Erin said.

"Can't say I liked it much either. After I'd given up on finding her, her phone rang, so I picked up. Figured the person ringing her could point me in the right direction, as by then, I was really curious about the whole situation. So, I said hi, and was about to explain I wasn't Marcy, when this loud woman's voice cut me off and said, 'Hey, babe, any progress with the rich woman?'" Celia shook her head. "I swear, I've never felt so stupid as in that moment. I asked the other person who she was, but she hung up. Marcy never came to pick up her phone, so I dropped it off at the police station and told them what had happened. I didn't think they'd be remotely interested in tracking down a gold-digger, but it turned out Marcy was a known con artist and I'd just about dodged a bullet."

"Jesus." Erin looked disgusted. "Did they ever arrest her?"

"I don't know. She hadn't robbed me or anything, so I didn't have a case against her, although I have no doubt that she was planning something before I found out. I don't think meeting her at the grocery store was a coincidence either. Thinking back, I'm pretty sure she targeted me. She was seriously charming, and most women just assume I'm straight—no one ever flirts with me. Who knows, maybe she got someone to mess with the cash register, set it all up. I guess I'll never know."

"That makes me so angry." Erin huffed. "Someone as lovely and sweet as you..." She cupped Celia's cheek. "But you're not stupid. This could have happened to anyone."

"I don't know about that, but anyway, there's your long answer. I know this was my idea, but let's make the next question a light one, shall we?"

"Absolutely. Shoot."

"Okay." Celia turned her gaze skyward while she thought about her next question. "What does a perfect day look like to you when you're at home?"

"Hmm..." Erin smiled as she thought about that. "When I'm not traveling for work or pleasure, I generally go into work five-and-a-half days a week, just because I enjoy what I do. But my perfect day would be a Sunday, when I have the whole day to myself. I'll start with making a coffee, and I'll drink that outside while I feed the chickens."

"You have chickens?" Celia laughed. "I'm sorry, I don't know why that's so funny."

Erin laughed too. "I never meant to have chickens. They're feral and Bermuda is overrun with them. We don't have stray dogs or cats, but we do have tens of thousands of chickens roaming the island and one day, this flock decided to make my yard their home." She shrugged. "It's a win-win. I get fresh eggs and they have a nice, quiet place to live."

"That's so lovely. So, you make yourself an omelet every morning?"

"Nene, my housekeeper does. I'm useless in the kitchen, so I'm grateful for her." Erin paused as she fell into thought. "Then, I'll go for a swim in the ocean. There's a beautiful little beach below my house and it's only accessible through my yard, so I always have it to myself."

"Perks of living in paradise," Celia said.

"True. There are huge bright blue and multicolored parrot fish and angelfish and I even occasionally see small sharks; not the dangerous kind," Erin added. "Then I'll catch up on the news while I dry in the sun and take my speedboat out to go fishing. If I catch something, I usually invite friends or my nearest neighbors over for a sunset barbecue and cocktails." She grinned. "So there's my perfect day. What about you?"

"That sounds amazing, and there's no way I want to tell you more about my dull life now." Celia chuckled. "So, let's move on to the next question."

32

Concentrating was hard. Celia stared at the email on the laptop in front of her and tried to formulate a reply, but knowing Erin was up on the bridge looking down at her, didn't make it easy. A message came in, and she took in a quick breath as she read it. *'You look so hot in that little black bikini. I can't wait to pull those strings and make it drop to the floor.'*

She glanced up for a moment, even though it was pointless; the darkened glass making it impossible to see through the window.

As Erin was on duty today, she was catching up on work. It wasn't overly busy as her assistant had proven to be highly efficient and assertive, taking over a lot of work from her while she'd been away. But some things needed her approval, so she'd been ploughing her way through a list of orders for the past two hours.

She shifted in her seat, arousal stirring as she felt Erin's eyes burning into her. They'd had the most amazing nights together; the sheets close to catching fire each time they were alone. Erin loved to be in charge, and Celia loved to be at her mercy. It was something she never knew about herself, and her newfound passion for sexual games only fueled her appetite for more. Another message came in and she picked up her phone to read it. *'Take off your top.'* It made her chuckle, and she looked up, seductively pulling at the string behind her neck only to stop and turn back around, pretending to focus on her screen again. Her phone lit up once more. *'Take off your top, Celia. I need something to look at other than the horizon.'*

'Why don't you come down and take it off yourself?' she replied, her eyes fixed on her keyboard as she fought back a smirk. Although she had considered taking it off for a moment, she'd changed her mind. It wasn't Dieter and Andy she was worried about. They were chilling under a canopy on the upper deck and going by the silence, she suspected they were asleep. But she liked to tease, to make Erin go crazy for her. Reading the next message, she suspected Erin was running out of patience. *'Don't make me call you up here.'*

This time, Celia was unable to suppress a giggle, and she demonstratively put her phone in her purse under the table and turned her back to focus on the view. The coastline was getting greener now and they weren't far from passing through the Strait of Gibraltar, which would take them into the wilder waters of the Atlantic Ocean. The narrowest point, where Morocco and Spain were connected by a ferry crossing, was already visible in the distance. It felt surreal to sail between continents—the colors of the land clearly showing two entirely different worlds—but her attention was yanked away from the gorgeous view when Erin's voice suddenly blasted through the yacht's speakers.

"This is Captain Nour speaking. Miss Celia, please make your way to the bridge. I repeat, Miss Celia, please make your way to the bridge. Thank you."

Laughing, Celia shook her head, knowing Erin would not give up until she gave in. When she didn't immediately get up from the table, Erin spoke again.

"This is an announcement for Miss Celia. Miss Celia, will you please make your way up to the bridge. Ignoring your captain's orders will result in an official warning."

Andy's loud and high-pitched laughter came from the upper deck, and Celia stood up, put on her sheer, black kaftan and raised both hands in defeat as she faced the window.

~

"You've been a bad girl, ignoring my direct orders," Erin joked as Celia joined her up on the bridge.

"And you're the worst, keeping me from my work like that..." Celia's breaths quickened, and her mouth pulled into a smile as she looked Erin up and down for the first time since she'd left their bedroom this morning. Erin was wearing black tailored slacks, a white shirt, and a captain's hat that looked incredibly sexy on her. "...Captain Nour."

Her desire was reflected in Erin's eyes as she stared back at her, clearly amused at her fascination with the hat. Deep down, Celia had always been a sucker for uniforms, and she assumed she wasn't the first woman to look at her like that.

"Lock the door," Erin said. "And come over here."

"Hmm..." Celia's lips curled into a smile as she leaned back against the door. "Why don't you come and lock it yourself?" She pulled out her ponytail and shook out her hair until it fell over her shoulders in long waves, then shot her a daring look.

Erin seemed to like this game, as she struggled to keep her stern expression while she closed the distance between them. "Are you arguing with the Captain, Miss Celia?" She yanked up Celia's kaftan and pressed her body against hers as she reached into Celia's bikini bottoms and ran her fingers through her heat, making her moan.

"You're aroused, Miss Celia. And you're not supposed to be aroused. You're supposed to be working. I've been watching you down there; you've barely typed a word all morning." Erin sounded all businesslike, but her eyes were full of fire and she gasped when she felt Celia's juices coat her fingers.

Celia chuckled through heavy breaths. "And how do you suggest I work when we're playing games like this?" she asked innocently. "You have to make me come, Captain, or I'll never be able to concentrate. It's..."

Her words were muffled by Erin's lips on hers, and she moaned louder, jerking her hips forward, needing more of her touch. Celia knew Erin hadn't planned on kissing her. She'd planned to tease her relentlessly, but Erin was clearly unable to resist and that pleased her. Weaving her fingers through Erin's hair, she kissed her back and let Erin push her against the door as their tongues collided in a wild dance.

Just as she was about to lose all control, Erin pulled away and pointed to the ship's wheel. "Go stand in front of the wheel and hold onto it. I'm going to have to multitask as we pass through the Strait."

With shaking legs, Celia crossed the floor and waited at the wheel. Anticipation coursed through her when Erin came up behind her and inhaled against her hair, then pulled it to one side to kiss her neck.

Celia's hands clamped around the handles on the wheel, groaning when Erin sucked at her skin so hard, she felt it sting. "What if I turn it by accident?" she asked in a whimper. The wheel was large and reached from her navel to her chin, and she was afraid she might cause an accident, knowing she'd be using it to steady herself.

"You won't. We're currently on cruise-control and even if we weren't, it's a big vessel, so it takes a lot of effort for it to turn." Celia felt Erin smile against her skin. "So, you need me to release you, huh?"

"Yes," Celia whispered. She was so aroused that it wouldn't take much to make her explode. She felt herself twitch uncontrollably and was unable to stand still.

"Yes, what?"

A chuckle escaped Celia as she corrected herself. "Yes, Captain. I..." Her voice trailed away as Erin hiked up her kaftan again and placed one hand over hers on the wheel.

"I'm going to give you your first orgasm in Africa," she said, looking over Celia's shoulder as she snaked her hand around her waist and lowered it into her panties. "And we'll be there in about ten..." She circled Celia's clit, then ran her fingers through her folds, making her moan loudly. "Nine, eight..." Her fingers moved lower. Two of them slipped inside her, and she exhaled deeply in Celia's ear as she pushed deeper.

"Don't stop, please." Celia had trouble keeping still as she felt a climax building. It wasn't strange, considering how turned on she'd been all morning, yet she still marveled at how skillful Erin was.

"Seven, six, five..." Erin kept one eye on the displays, where the navigation panel showed they were about to hit African territory as they veered slightly to the left. She curled her fingers, making Celia cry out as she rubbed a spot inside her that sent her to even greater heights. "Four, three, two..."

"Fuck!" Celia yelled, her knuckles turning white as she

clung onto the wheel, a series of vibrations now racing through her body. Erin stayed inside her and nuzzled her neck while she breathed fast between moans, her orgasm just not wanting to stop. "Erin..." She was still shaking after long moments had passed, and she opened her eyes, only then truly appreciating the view of the rocky coastlines to either side as they started sailing through the eight-mile wide strait.

Erin pulled out of her and turned Celia around, so her back was against the wheel. Pressing her lips to Celia's, she looked satisfied as a smirk painted her gorgeous lips. "Welcome to Africa, honey."

33

"How's the pink boy?"

"The pink boy's enjoying this slice of paradise, sweetie." Andy blew Celia a kiss and held up his freshly squeezed orange juice in a toast. He was wearing a pink satin robe and huge shades and was draped over the lounge chairs like a sultan in his palace. He pulled up his legs when Celia joined him and poured her a glass from the jug in front of him. "Cheers to the good life. You, my friend, have hit the jackpot with Erin."

Celia laughed and took a sip of her drink. "Nah," she joked. "Erin hit the jackpot with me."

"Well said." Andy straightened himself and scooted closer. "Have you seen Dieter?" he asked, lowering his voice.

"I think he's in the library with Erin." Celia noted Andy's worried expression and a wave of unease hit her core. She had a feeling something was wrong, but there was no evidence to back up her intuition. "Why are you asking?"

"I wanted to talk to you. In private," Andy said, casting shifty looks in the direction of the automatic glass doors. "You see, I think something's going on with Dieter." He paused and a deep frown appeared between his bleached brows. "He's being secretive about something but each time I ask him about it, he gets irritated and acts like I'm being paranoid."

"What makes you think something's going on?" Celia's sixth sense spiked as he confirmed her suspicions.

Andy shrugged and took a moment before he answered. "He's got something in the safe, in our room. He goes in there and shuts himself away twice a day and I know it's not necessarily my business, but it seems like something significant and the fact that he doesn't want to talk about it..." He sighed. "I know it's not money; we're at sea so it's not like he can spend it anywhere. And he goes through these mood swings and every time he's done this thing in the room, his mood lifts almost right away. I just wonder if he..."

Celia narrowed her eyes and lowered her voice too. "Are you saying you suspect he's taking drugs?"

"I think so." Andy sounded hesitant, as if he was scared of voicing his thoughts. "And if that's the case, he'd never admit it to me, so I thought maybe you could try and talk to him."

"I see." It was quite an accusation of course, but Celia couldn't deny that she'd noticed her uncle's mood swings too, not to mention his weight loss. She knew many people who dealt with addiction issues; it wasn't uncommon for wealthy people to turn to cocaine or prescription drugs or even heroine, purely because they were bored with their lives. But she knew her uncle, and he just wasn't the type. He was a wholesome man who had his head screwed on, and he'd always warned her about the dangers of drugs when she was younger. "I understand why you think he might be taking something," she said. "But I don't think he's an addict."

"Addicts tend to be good at hiding their addiction. Sometimes they're the people you least expect it from and if that's the case with Dieter, I want to help him." Andy paused. "He was also very tired in Menorca. We took a taxi to his friends and back and we only stayed at their house, so physically it shouldn't have been challenging for him, but I could see he was struggling. Maybe it was withdrawal, I don't know." He looked sincerely worried as he furrowed his brows. "I care about him very much."

"I know."

"No. I don't think you know how much I care about him. I think that deep down, you believe I'm with your uncle for his money. Perhaps he believes that too. I'm half his age and let's face it; I'm pretty handsome if I say so myself," Andy joked. "But you have to believe me when I say that I'm truly crazy about him. Hell, I love him." He fiddled with the stem of his glass, spinning it around absently. "He saved me from an abusive relationship and without him, I don't know where I'd be right now."

"Oh..." Celia met his eyes and saw the sincerity in them. "Do you mind if I ask what happened?"

Andy shot her a sweet smile. "Not at all. I was with this asshole called Erik. We'd travelled to Switzerland together because Erik is an art dealer and he had some business to take care of there. We were having lunch at this fancy restaurant overlooking Lake Lucerne. He was already grumpy with me, giving me sneer after sneer, but suddenly, he became aggressive after receiving a message that his meeting had been cancelled. He was very unpredictable like that and when something went wrong, he would usually take it out on me." He paused. "Being dependent on others is horrible; I've learned that over the years. When I was younger, I made the stupid mistake never to build something for myself. I always had wealthy boyfriends who treated me like shit, and instead of stepping out of the relationship and sorting my life out, I just hopped from one to the other. I should have studied or gotten a job; any job. But I was young and foolish, and I didn't have any self-respect. Anyway, Erik shouted at me as if it was all my fault and walked off. I didn't follow him because he frequently became physically abusive once we were alone, and I could feel it coming that day."

"I'm so sorry to hear that." Celia reached for his hand and squeezed it.

"Don't be sorry; It was the day my life changed for the better. Dieter stood up from the neighboring table and sat down with me. It turned out that he was the one Erik was supposed to meet with, but Dieter had been listening in on our conversations and didn't like the way Erik spoke to me. That's Dieter; he'll only do business with people he respects, so he'd come early to get a feel of Erik's personality. He asked me why I was with someone who treated me like that and when I was unable to give him an answer, he ordered a bottle of wine and we talked for hours. He wasn't hitting on me; he was just trying to help me. I found myself opening up to him, and he offered me a job and a room at the castle, so I didn't have to go back to someone who used me as a punch bag. Finally seeing a way out, I took your uncle up on his offer and broke off all contact with Erik, and I felt so free after that. It wasn't a fancy job and it wasn't full-time, but it was a job and it made me feel good about myself. I arranged the transportation and insurance for all the pieces Dieter sold or acquired, and after three months of saving up, I was able to rent a small apartment for myself. Nothing happened between us for at least a year, but our friendship grew, and I started feeling immensely attracted to Dieter. A psychologist might say it was some sort of savior complex, but I really don't think that was the case. I saw him for who he was; intelligent, fun, charismatic and caring, and I fell in love with him."

"My uncle never told me any of this," Celia said, touched by his story.

"Well, he doesn't brag. What he did for me was life-changing and he didn't even know me. That's the kind of person he is. He's been very clear about the fact that he doesn't want a traditional relationship though. We only see each other romantically about once a month, and over winter, we didn't see each other at all for about four months. He said he needed space. I respected that, so back then, we discussed everything regarding his art business over the phone."

"And you never went back to France?" Celia asked. "What about your family?"

"I'm not in contact with my family. They're farmers in Burgundy, and they didn't understand my sexuality. In fact, they kicked me out of the house, so I haven't seen them since I was seventeen." Andy held up a hand. "Please don't feel sorry for me. I'd rather be myself than stay in contact with my parents; I think I got my low self-esteem from them in the first place. It's not obvious to most people, as I tend to hide it with a fabulous layer of pink."

Celia shot him a sad look. Of course Andy's dramatic appearance and behavior were a little over the top, but she'd never guessed it was his way of hiding his insecurities. "You're a great guy and you have no reason to feel insecure. You're very funny. Did you know that?"

"I know." Andy laughed it off.

"Do you still work for my uncle?"

"Technically, yes, but lately Dieter's not been making

many purchases, apart from that creepy painting he bought in Tarragona. When we get back, he has a list of pieces that will go up for sale, so it will be busier then. I'm looking for a full-time job as I don't expect him to employ me forever. The art world suits me, and now that I have a little bit of experience, they might take me on in a gallery or in an auction house. I don't even think Dieter needs me; employing me is just his way of me helping out without making me feel like I'm leeching off him."

"Yes, it's important to him that people feel at ease around him; he's great like that." Celia straightened herself and cleared her throat when she heard Erin and Dieter approach, their laughter roaring as the glass doors opened. "Thank you for telling me," she whispered before giving Erin a wave. "There's not much I can do right now since we won't see each other for two days in Casablanca and I doubt I'll have him to myself tonight, but I'll keep an eye on him when we continue the journey, see if I can figure out what's going on."

34

"See you guys tomorrow," Celia yelled as her uncle and Andy disappeared into the private limousine they'd booked for the day. She and Erin lingered there for a while, amidst the bustle of in-and-outgoing yachts and commercial vessels. Tourists and locals were dodging the traffic as they tried to cross the road where cars, motorcycles and trucks were fighting over the two lanes leading into the city center. Erin looked around, mumbled something about a cab stand, then gave up and held up her hand, causing the first cab that drove by to stop so abruptly that he almost caused a collision.

It was strange to have her feet on steady ground again, and Celia wondered how her legs would feel after their long stretch, sailing from Cape Verde to Bermuda, as it felt as if she was still swaying. Still a little off-balance, she was glad to scoot next to Erin in the back of the cab.

"I speak a little French if you tell me where you want to go," she said when the driver turned to them. "If that helps."

"No, it's fine, I've got this."

Celia could hardly believe it when Erin started speaking

Arabic to him. She opened her mouth to say something, then closed it again, glancing at her incredulously. To her, it seemed like it came out fluently, the intonation and throaty sounds so different to how she was used to hearing Erin speak that it was difficult to grasp this was the same person talking. "What? How…"

"My parents raised me bilingual." Erin shrugged as if it was no big deal. "I still speak Arabic with them."

"Yeah, but you're American born and bred, so I just didn't expect it. I'm impressed."

"I'm not fluent anymore; I don't speak it enough to stay fluent, but it's actually really helpful in my job. I have a lot of Saudi clients, and they're always surprised when they hire my Bermuda-based company and find out that the CEO is an Arabic woman with short hair who speaks their language."

"I can only imagine." Celia smiled at Erin, seeing her in a different light. She kept learning new things about her, and she fascinated her more and more by the day. "So, where are we going? I obviously didn't get a word of what you just said."

"I thought we could do some sightseeing if you're okay with that…" Erin discussed something with the driver and showed him an address on her phone. Then there was more discussion before they shook hands. "We have him for two days, so he can take us up to visit my grandmother tomorrow; I've decided I want to go and see her. Just not today; I need some time to acclimatize here first."

"That's great." Celia rested her hand on Erin's, then slowly retracted it, remembering this was not a place for same sex couples to be exchanging PDAs.

"Would you like to come with me?"

"Do you want me to come? Wouldn't you rather go and

see her alone?" Celia asked. "I mean, I don't want to be in your way; I imagine it could be quite the reunion."

"No, I'd like you to come with me. It might be a bit of a culture shock for you, but we won't be staying the night, and I think you'll find it interesting," Erin said. "And if it's too late; if she doesn't want to see me, then it will be a consolation to have you there on the drive back."

After spending the day scanning various souks in the old Medina, they walked back to their driver with bags full of souvenirs, delicacies and spices Erin had bought for her mother. Celia had enthusiastically embraced the art of haggling, although she was pretty sure she'd been ripped off on a couple of occasions. The beautiful purse with ornamental leatherwork she'd bought was filled with trinkets for her friends and some argan oil and a set of small tea glasses for herself. They'd tried moreish pastries, drank strong, dark coffee and they'd even smoked an apple hookah together, simply because it felt fitting and she was curious to try it.

"How about dinner?" Erin said as she handed a card to the driver. "One of my clients recommended a restaurant here, it shouldn't be too far."

"Dinner sounds good." Celia rolled down the window to let in the dry, warm air and smiled as she glanced at the city. French Colonial architecture and even Art Deco style buildings were things she never expected to see here. Mixed in with the Moroccan artisanship that adorned the traditional buildings and mosques, it was a sight to behold. The streets were chaotic, and the central food market overflowing with people as they drove past. "I like this city. Do you mind if I book a place to stay for the night?"

"Go ahead. I thought about it, but I wasn't sure if you'd rather sleep on the yacht since it's quite noisy and hectic. Would you like me to arrange something?"

Celia shook her head. "No, I've got this; it's the least I can do." She scrolled through her saved hotels on her booking app and found the riad she'd been eyeing on the yacht yesterday. It still had a room available. "There's this place I think you'll love." She booked it and quickly put her phone away managing to avoid Erin's glance as she leaned in to look. "Not yet, it's a surprise."

"A surprise, huh?"

"Yes. Do you like surprises?"

"Is this part of the three questions?"

Celia laughed. "No, I still get my three questions later, this is just conversation."

"Okay..." Erin chuckled as she considered the question. "I don't think anyone's ever surprised me before."

"Really? That's so sad." Celia jutted out her bottom lip in a dramatic gesture. "Then I'll make it my mission to surprise you as much as I can, so you can decide whether you like surprises, or not. Deal?"

"Deal." Erin gave her a wink, then glanced out at the small carpet and fabric stores they passed. The merchandise was displayed outside, creating long rows of color along the terracotta buildings in the narrow street. When their driver decided to mount the pavement to get past a car coming toward them, she gripped onto the handle above the window, holding on tight.

Celia had noticed earlier that Erin had taken off her expensive watch, and she appreciated that she wasn't flaunting her wealth here. She'd dressed down in a gray T-shirt and jeans, and Celia had followed suit with jeans and a boatneck navy and white striped top as it felt appropriate to cover up a little more.

"Do you feel a connection to Morocco?" she asked.

Erin shook her head. "I haven't been here enough. My parents aren't wealthy, so we could only afford to travel and visit my grandparents every two or three years when I was younger. So, as much as I like Morocco, no, I can't say I feel a connection. Quite the opposite—I feel rather detached." She turned back to Celia and there was a hint of vulnerability in her eyes. "I'm nervous about seeing my own grandmother tomorrow; it's like I'm going to visit a stranger. A significant stranger, but a stranger, nevertheless."

"That's understandable." Celia gave her a reassuring smile. "But there's a big chance she'll be very happy to see you."

"She might not recognize me."

"I think she will." Celia turned to her, holding onto the driver's seat when the driver, who was a road maniac, took a sharp bend. "I wanted to ask you about something else."

"Shoot."

"It's about my uncle..." Celia met her eyes. "You would tell me if you knew something was wrong with him, right?"

Erin bit her bottom lip and took a moment to answer. "Of course."

"I was just wondering if you think there's a chance that he might have a drug problem."

"A drug problem?" Erin's eyes narrowed in confusion. "Why do you think that?"

"Just, you know... mood swings, weight loss, he looks like he's in pain from time to time, and according to Andy, he's being secretive and keeps going back to his room for something in the safe. And if that's the case..." A hint of worry flashed across Celia's face as she pursed her lips. "If he does have drugs in that safe, then I'm worried for all of us. It's not just him; it's your vessel sailing through international waters, and if we get searched…" As she voiced her worries, she suddenly felt very nervous about having the yacht on Moroccan territory. "Damn it. I should have discussed this with you sooner."

Erin nodded slowly, but she didn't seem particularly worried herself. "I'll talk to him, if that puts you at ease, and I'll ask Eddie to check the safe while they're away; he has the master code. I can't say I've noticed a difference in Dieter, but you're right; we have to make sure there's nothing illegal onboard and most of all, we have to make sure he's okay." She leaned forward when the driver asked her something and answered him, then sat back and shot Celia a reassuring smile. "But I'm sure it's nothing like that."

"Thank you. I appreciate you talking to him and calling Eddie, because he'd never tell me if he had a problem, and I doubt he'd tell Andy." Celia studied Erin with interest, noting she didn't seem one bit concerned after she'd raised her suspicions. "Promise me you'll tell me if you know what's going on?"

Erin avoided her gaze and opened her window wider. "Sure," she said casually. "Don't worry about it."

35

The driver dropped them off at a restaurant among the city's old fortifications on the edge of a cliff. A row of ancient cannons lined the long and narrow patio, facing the sea. In the middle of the outside dining space stood a fountain, and shaded tables were placed in rows on either side, beautifully decked out with ceramic tableware. Soft traditional music was playing in the background and there was a wonderful sense of calm in the air, with the sea breeze blowing underneath the canopies.

"What a lovely place," Celia said as she took a seat opposite Erin. Her core summersaulted as their eyes locked. There would be no opportunity to hold hands or kiss until they were in their room tonight, and she knew withholding from physical intimacy would only heighten the sexual tension between them.

"Yes, my client was right; this is really nice." Erin laughed when Celia looked down at the menu and shook her head as she was unable to work out what it said. "Want me to order? I don't read Arabic and my French isn't great either, but I can ask them what's good here."

Celia found herself swooning over Erin as she ordered tea and food, smiling sweetly at the waiter. She was always respectful, chivalrous and kind, and genuinely seemed like she was in a happy place in life. "I know I've already told you this, but I really like how you treat people," she said when their tea arrived. "Sadly, it's rare to see such manners from someone who runs in wealthy circles."

"Yeah well, I wasn't always wealthy, and I'll never forget where I came from. I couldn't afford to study after college and frankly, I wasn't clever enough for a scholarship, so instead, I applied for odd jobs in the marine industry as I'd always been obsessed with big ships. I was very lucky with my first boss, who took me under his wing as his protégée and taught me everything he knew about design and building. He didn't have to do that, but he saw the passion in me, and I'm forever grateful to him."

"Was he in the yacht business too?" Celia asked.

"Initially, no. He built commercial ships, and after eight years of working my ass off for him, he suggested I set up a separate department for private, customized vessels. Eventually, he let me buy myself into the company, and it went so well that I went independent after he retired. That's when the company really started to grow, and that's when I moved the business to Bermuda because I could afford it." Erin smiled. "I've worked very hard for almost thirty years, and now I'm taking it a little easier. I'm still busy, but I love what I do, so that's okay." She looked into Celia's eyes and smiled. "But I like that about you too," she continued. "That you're respectful. You're different from the rest of your family. The ones I've met anyway, Dieter aside."

"My family basically consists of a bunch of money grabbing snobs." Celia shrugged. "I was always closer to my father, and later, my uncle. They just seemed to make more sense to me as human beings, so I looked up to them." Another flutter ran through her when she saw Erin's expression softening as she looked her over once again. She could feel something very special growing between them. "Tell me about your job. What exactly do you do when you're not sailing and living like the queen of the ocean?"

Erin grinned and took a sip of her tea. "Believe me, daily life does not look like this for me, but living on a tropical island is nice, of course. I get up early in the morning, take my little speedboat to the shipyard and have my first coffee while I catch up with my small design team. Then I'll go and check on the building work with my senior engineer and meet with clients, my sourcing team or my design team before I focus on my own design work, which covers the bigger picture of a project rather than the details as I have experts for that. My workdays vary from seven to fourteen hours, depending on how busy we are. Sometimes I meet friends or my team for a beer after work. Nothing fancy, just a drink and a game of pool, and sometimes I take the boat out to enjoy the night on the water." She thanked the waiter, who brought over a deliciously smelling tagine, a bowl of couscous and a pomegranate salad for them to share. "What about you?"

"Nothing like this either," Celia said, helping herself to food. "I live in an apartment in Manhattan and in summer, I meet my yoga group in Central Park in the mornings for a bit of exercise. I work four to five days a week from home, and I occasionally go out for lunch or dinner with friends or with my assistant." The food was delicious, and she moaned as she took a bite of the lamb tagine. "And family commitments," she added. "I have those from time to time, but I try to keep them to a minimum, as you can imagine. But mostly, I just like to curl up on my couch and read at night."

"So you're not a jet-setter." Erin inhaled deeply above her plate before she took her first bite, her expression giving away her excitement. "I suspected you might be a princess before I got to know you, but I was wrong."

"A princess?" Celia laughed.

Erin shot her a comical grin. "Uh-huh. Demanding, spoilt and very high maintenance. But you're the opposite; you seem very down to earth and the fact that I want to make love to you twenty-four-seven aside, I also think you're a really great person."

"Thank you." Celia giggled, shifting in her seat at the 'making love' comment. "I really like you too." Erin had a way of turning her on in a matter of seconds, and she could only hope she'd be able to continue their conversation because her mind was starting to lead a life of its own.

"And because you're so amazing," Erin said as she reached into the back pocket of her jeans and handed her a small black velvet pouch, "I got you a little present while we were shopping in the souk."

"Oh, Erin..." Celia opened the gift and pulled out a silver necklace with a charm in the shape of an open hand. A small, dark semi-precious stone sat in the middle of a blue enamel eye mounted in the center of the palm. The crafts-manship was detailed, the silverwork intricate and refined. "It's beautiful."

"It's a Hamsa necklace," Erin explained. "It's an ancient symbol and talisman in Islam and Judaism, said to protect you from evil. I'm not superstitious, so I mainly bought it because I thought it would look pretty on you; the brown tourmaline is almost the same color as your gorgeous, dark eyes."

"Thank you, I love it." Celia put it on and ran a fingertip over the charm. "I ehm... I actually got you something too."

She'd been hesitant to buy something for Erin, afraid it might seem too much to give her a present already, but now she was glad she'd bought it. Rummaging through her bags, she found the box she was looking for and handed it to her.

Erin opened it and Celia loved how her smile lit up her whole face as she took out the vintage watch that was still working perfectly fine and strapped it around her wrist. "That's so thoughtful, I love it."

"I noticed you kept glancing down at your wrist but you're not wearing your watch today," Celia said. "So, I figured you needed a travel watch." She'd managed to buy it while Erin was distracted, wasting no time to haggle over the watch she'd no doubt paid way too much for. The brown leather strap was in good condition and the silver dial, which included a built-in compass, still seemed to work fine. "I'm glad you like it."

Emotion flashed in Erin's eyes, and it hit Celia deep in her core. It was incredible how they'd managed to find the perfect gift for each other when they'd only been dating for such a short time. There was a moment in which something hung between them, but Celia couldn't quite identify what was happening, so she gave Erin a shy smile and focused on her food instead.

"Is it better than your mom's?" she asked.

"What?" Erin didn't seem to know up from down right now, as she looked from the watch to Celia, then to her food and back.

"The tagine," Celia clarified. "Is it better than your mom's?"

"Oh that." Erin chuckled and took another bite, narrowing her eyes as she made up her mind.

"I hardly dare say it, but yes, it's better. But don't tell her that, if you ever meet her."

36

"I'm thoroughly impressed with your hotel hunting skills." Erin looked up at the grand, white riad that rose from behind tall palm trees. The striking Moroccan villa with classical features, green stained-glass windows and delicately carved pillars held six rooms, a spa and a restaurant that opened onto the plant-filled terrace in the courtyard. The main entrance was through the courtyard too; the huge doors were wide open behind a rectangular pond that took up half of the outside space. It was filled with water lilies and gold carp were swimming around underneath the blanket of green leaves and white flowers. The area around it was paved with green and white Moroccan tiles, the simple geometric pattern blending in seamlessly with its surroundings.

Considering they were in the middle of the city, this place felt like an unexpected oasis. The main building with a one-story arm on each side blocked out the noise from the traffic and instead, there was birdsong and the gentle sound of the water features that were dotted around.

"I'm impressed with myself too," Celia joked, handing her bags to a bellboy.

"Miss Krügerner?" A woman in a traditional Moroccan djellaba came out to meet them. "And Miss?" She turned to Erin when Celia nodded.

"Nour" Erin said, rolling her shoulders after ridding herself of her own bags.

"Welcome to Al Walid Riad, Miss Nour and Miss Krügerner. My name is Amira." Amira beckoned them to follow her inside and handed them a tasseled fob with a key attached. "Your room is on the second floor. We'll make sure your things are brought up there." She looked from Celia to Erin and back, perhaps speculating whether they were a couple, then simply said, "If you prefer another suite with two separate beds, let me know. If not, I hope you enjoy your stay. We've taken the liberty to run your bath and there is tea waiting for you on the balcony. Breakfast is cooked to order between seven and eleven, and if you need anything at all, please don't hesitate to call me, just dial one."

"Thank you so much, this looks incredible." Celia looked up at the high, green painted ceilings and the arch-ways, decorated in the same geometric tiles as the floor outside. Before heading up, they explored the big spacious rooms downstairs that were for communal use; one more opulent than the other. They passed through a suba, a reading room, a garden room with a small pool and two living rooms with luxurious carpets and lush couches in front of ornamental fireplaces, before they ended up back in the reception area from where a staircase led up to the next floor.

Erin's eyes were fixed on Celia's behind as they walked up, and her core tightened, knowing she could finally have her to herself again. One day may not have seemed that long this morning, but it had proven very, very hard to keep her hands off her.

As soon as Celia had closed the door behind her, Erin backed her up against it, smiling as she saw the same desire in her lover's eyes. She snaked her hand underneath Celia's top and ran it over her breast, wedging her thumb under the edge of her bra.

"What are you doing, Captain?" Celia joked in a husky voice that made Erin ache in all the right places.

"I'm claiming my prize for behaving myself today." Erin brushed her lips against Celia's and pushed her body into her, drawing a soft gasp from her lips. She was vaguely aware that she was in the most beautiful hotel room she'd ever found herself in after taking in the white drapes surrounding the bed, the white and gold rugs on the tiled floor and the tub in the corner of the room by a window that overlooked the garden behind the riad. But even with her design background and love for all things well-considered, she felt no desire to take her eyes off Celia for even a beat.

Celia's lashes swept up and she blinked seductively. "You're right; you have been good. I think you deserve your prize now." They fell into a slow and sensual kiss, their hands roaming over each other until Celia pulled away breathlessly. "Close the balcony doors," she whispered. "I want to take a bath with you."

Erin felt her stomach clench, her libido firing on all cylinders, and she walked over to the French doors to lock them, then closed the heavy, green silk drapes. When she turned around, Celia was naked next to the big, square mosaic tiled tub that looked more like a mini pool. The scent of rose oil was rising from the steaming water, and rose petals were floating on the surface. Pulling out her hair-clip, Celia shook out her hair in that seductive way that made her feel crazy inside before she stepped into the tub and lowered herself into the hot water with a long sigh.

"What are you waiting for?" She anchored her eyes on Erin and arched a brow, then swung one leg onto the edge of the tub as she sunk back and dipped her head back in the water.

"Are you trying to kill me?" For a beat, Erin stood as if nailed to the ground. Celia took her breath away each time she indulged in her without fail. Seeing her in that bathtub under the rose petals with her wet hair and water trickling down her face, waiting for her of all people, almost seemed too good to be true. Realizing she was staring, she shook her head with a grin, then undressed and joined her.

"Come here." Celia pulled her against her and ran her fingers through Erin's hair.

"God, that feels good." Erin moaned as she immersed herself, then ran her hands up and down Celia's thighs that were pressed against her hips. She was about to turn around and kiss Celia, but Celia stopped her.

"No. Stay there," Celia whispered in her ear, making her shiver all over.

Celia's hands roaming over her breasts made her ache for more, so she relaxed and settled back in her embrace, resting her cheek against Celia's chest. Her nipples hardened as Celia pinched them while she kissed her neck. Feeling her hand move between her thighs made her take in a quick breath, and she gasped when Celia's fingers skimmed her sensitive clit.

"You're the only woman who's ever turned me on like this," she whispered. "I swear, I didn't even like it when others touched me."

"Good," Celia whispered back, and Erin could feel her lips pull into a smile against her neck as she thrust her hips up, needing more. "Because I plan to make you scream... all night." Her fingers started circling Erin's clit faster and harder, drawing loud moans from her mouth.

Erin spread her legs and closed her eyes, the sensation almost too much. Leaning back against Celia's luscious body, she had trouble lying still, and her frantic movements made water splash over the bathtub's edge.

"Baby, you're making a mess," Celia said with a chuckle.

"I can't help it. This is just..." Erin stopped speaking as her climax washed over her. Her hands clamped around Celia's thighs as a throaty groan escaped her. It was much louder than she'd expected, and she was taken aback by the power of her own voice. Celia really could make her scream and best of all she could make her come so hard that she lost all control. She let go then and didn't care if the floor would be flooded. Without doubt, she'd found her perfect match.

37

"It's like another world out here," Celia mumbled as she gazed out of the window. They'd stopped opening them as dust kept blowing inside, and the heat was way more intense inland, without the coastal breeze. The landscape had been barren and rocky for the first half of their journey, and now the hills were getting greener again. The Atlas Mountains were just coming into sight and she gave Erin's hand a squeeze as she pointed to the snow-covered peaks.

Erin's heart started beating faster at the familiar sight she hadn't realized she'd missed until now, and a sense of nostalgia made her feel a little sad, then. They were heading toward her grandmother's farm in Asni, a small town in the foothills of the High Atlas, about an hour south from Marrakesh. The drive had been bumpy and rough, but Erin was relieved that Celia was enjoying herself. She hadn't complained about the heat or car sickness, and she'd dressed modestly and even bought a hijab to cover up her hair.

Erin herself had never worn a hijab; she'd blatantly refused when her mother had brought it up when she was eleven, and that had been the start of many fights and rebellious behavior from her side. Growing up in California, she'd had trouble embracing her parents' culture, and especially being a tomboy, it was simply out of the question. But today, she was wearing one that she'd bought in the souk yesterday. If she was visiting with the intention of rekindling her relationship with her grandmother, she felt she should wear one out of respect for her. There was that, and the fact that she had short hair and was bringing a female companion to a small village where her haircut was out of the question for most Moroccan women. It would only encourage others to draw conclusions.

"I'd forgotten how rural this province was," she said, staring at a lone farmer walking his goats along the dusty roadside. They passed a gas station of which the building's side wall had caved in, and a couple of old farmhouses that had seen better days. "They've built a new road since last time I was here, but it still feels like we're a thousand miles away from civilization."

"But you remember the area?" Celia asked.

"I remember everything." Erin pointed to a worn-out building with tapestries hanging down from the low roof. They were on display in front of the store too, and two little girls were playing on them. "Even this store. It must have been here for at least forty years."

The closer they came to the farm, the bigger the knot in Erin's stomach grew, and she took a couple of deep breaths in an attempt to calm herself. Her grandmother may take one look at her and send her back, and Erin was prepared for that. She had, after all, neglected her. She was deeply ashamed of that, but all she could do was show up, be kind and hope for the best.

Celia scooted closer to her and laced their fingers

together, and Erin tightened her grip. After hours in the car, their driver would have figured out they were together anyway, and it didn't seem to bother him. "Are you okay?"

"Yeah. I think so." Erin took another deep breath and nodded. "It's just been a long time since I've been here, that's all." She pointed to a tree just outside the village that had split during a storm when she was around ten years old. It had continued to grow at a low angle along the roadside. The tree had always been iconic to the area, and she supposed it still was. As expected, she saw little white patches between the branches. "I think you'll like this," she said, rolling down her window before they drove past.

Celia laughed when she saw at least a dozen white goats standing among the lower branches of the tree, bleating at them and following the car with their gaze. "What are they doing there?"

"I have no idea." Erin laughed too. "They've just always been there. I remember my mother specifically telling me to stay in the car as we sometimes stopped here to 'freshen up' before we arrived. Freshening up for her meant she would reapply her makeup and put on her best hijab, and for my father it was an opportunity to have a quick dry shave in the rearview mirror of our rental car. Anyway, I got out once, and I learned my lesson." She rolled her eyes humorously at the memory. "They'll attack anything that comes out of a vehicle and let's just say I arrived at my grandparent's house looking far from respectable."

The winding road became straighter as they drove through the village. A lot of stores that used to line the main street had closed, and many houses seemed uninhabited as they were boarded up or missing windows and parts of the facades. It was sad but not surprising. Unlike the previous generations, young people today had no desire to take over their family business anymore, and many would have moved to bigger cities where job prospects were promising and quality of life even more so.

Erin explained to the driver where to go, and he took a turn after the last house on the main street, then drove up a steep hill. The sandy road led past apple and olive orchards, and a little stream that ran down from the Atlas Mountains.

"Why didn't you call her to let her know you were coming?" Celia asked.

"I honestly don't think she has a phone. She never used to have one and the way she lives... well, let's just say, I hope you're prepared." Erin shrugged. "She might have a phone by now—things change of course—but my parents refuse to talk about her with me so I can't ask them. All I know is that they're still giving her money each month for help on the farm so that means she still lives there."

"How old is she?"

"Eighty-nine," Erin said with a deep sigh. They neared the farm, and she guided the driver, steering him toward the side of the house, then asked him to wait, promising to either bring him in for food once she'd spoken to her grandmother, or stop somewhere to buy him lunch if they'd have to make their way back.

"God, it's so different to what I'd expected," Celia said as she got out of the car "I mean, it's beautiful in the most rugged way. The mountains in the background, the fields of green farmland, and the goats in trees..." She gave Erin a sweet smile in an attempt to soothe her nerves. "It's unlike anything I've ever experienced, so authentic and untouched and..."

"Underdeveloped?" Erin suggested.

"Yes, that too." Celia glanced around the premises. The Berber house, made of rocks and clay bricks built into the mountain, looked tired and in need of renovation. Big cracks ran from the top to the bottom of the outside wall, and the gutters had fallen off. It wasn't a farm in the traditional sense of the word. Not what Celia was used to, anyway. There was no barn and there were no big farming machines. Next to the house stood an olive tree and underneath it was a chicken run. Around it, an assortment of pigs and goats roamed freely and in front of the house was a large apple orchard. A couple of men were roaming between the trees, watering them.

Erin followed her gaze and felt a stab at seeing two old pieces of rope hanging down from one of the trees, where her swing used to be. "Just so you're warned, I wouldn't be surprised if she still has an outdoor bathroom." She felt her legs shake as they walked up to the front door, and she took a moment to center herself, adjusting her hijab before she knocked.

38

The woman who opened the door did not come across as an eighty-nine-year-old. Her sun-damaged face, yes. Deep grooves between her brows and around her eyes showed her age but her posture was straight, like a healthy, strong woman. When she looked at Celia, then at Erin, her eyes narrowed in suspicion, and Celia was worried she might produce a baseball bat from behind the door and come after them. But then a beautiful thing happened. She took another look at Erin and her expression softened. She mumbled something in Arabic, and when Erin nodded, tears started trickling down her cheeks and she flew around Erin's neck, crying.

"Jedda..." Erin mumbled something else to her and held her tight for long moments, slowly swaying her from side to side.

Celia heard her sniff and it brought a lump to her throat. She felt like she was intruding in their private moment and was about to take a step back and explore the yard when Erin pulled out of the hug and gestured for her to come over. Erin's grandmother was cupping her face now;

pinching her cheeks and stroking her head with a big, toothless and emotional grin.

"Salam Alaikum." Celia repeated what Erin had taught her, locking her eyes with the old woman, and she got a warm smile and a hug in return. Then Erin's grandmother started rubbing their arms and shoulders in floods of tears before ushering them inside and leading the way down a worn clay-covered staircase.

"It's all good," Erin whispered over her shoulder while she wiped her eyes, relief written all over her face.

Celia took off her shoes, gave her a reassuring smile and followed them into the dark living room, where they sat down on battered cushions that lay on the floor surrounding a low table. "Should we help her with anything?" she asked, watching Erin's grandmother disappear into what she assumed to be the kitchen.

"No, not now." Erin gave her hand a quick squeeze. "I know it seems wrong to not help, but it's custom. She might be insulted if you tried to help her, considering we've just arrived."

"Okay, I won't, then." Celia was glad to see the anxiety had dropped from Erin's shoulders, the lightness of her grandmother welcoming her with open arms finally allowing her to relax.

"Thank you," she said. "I don't think I would have come here if you hadn't encouraged me. I'm glad you're with me."

"Me too." Celia shifted, crossed her legs and took in the basic room. A variety of worn rugs covered the bare clay floor, and apart from the big, square cushions they were sitting on and the low round table in front of them, there was no other furniture. A couple of faded photographs were stuck on the crumbled back wall, their corners curled and torn in places. Her lips pulled into a smile as she spotted a young girl who bore a close resemblance to Erin. "Is that you?"

Erin followed her gaze and chuckled. "Yeah, that's me. It was taken by my father, the last time I was here, I think."

"You look so different with long hair, but I can clearly tell it's you from your eyes and your smile."

"God, I did look different back then." Erin tilted her head, taking herself in at a young age. "I hated my long hair. I cut it the very day I moved out of my parents' house. My mother cried for a whole week; I still don't think she's over it."

Erin's grandmother came back with a tray full of dates, baklava and a pot of tea with three small tea glasses. She poured the tea, added honey and handed one to Celia while she mumbled something to Erin.

"Jedda is telling me you're very pretty, and I couldn't agree more."

"Thank you." Celia gave the woman a smile and bowed her head, then remembered the Arabic word for 'thanks'. "Shukran."

"Shukran," Erin's grandmother repeated with an approving grin. She gestured toward the tray with the dates and baklava, encouraging her to help herself.

Celia took one and turned to Erin. "What did you tell her about me?"

"I told her you're a friend," she said with a semi-apologetic tone to her voice. "Which, I suppose you are, so it's not exactly a lie."

"Okay." Celia smiled. "Well, please, don't mind me. Talk to her; I'm quite happy just sitting here listening to you. It's fascinating to hear you speak Arabic."

"Thank you." Erin started talking to her grandmother again. The passionate back-and-forth started off amicably with a chuckle here and there, but suddenly it seemed like the conversation was getting heated, with the old woman repeating the same sentence over and over.

Erin held up both hands, then rested them on her knees, shaking her head in frustration. "She wants to know why we're not staying the night," she said in a huff. "I explained that we have to get back to the yacht—that we have guests and an itinerary—but I guess since she hasn't seen me for so long, she thinks it's unacceptable that we'll be leaving so soon."

Celia raised a brow in surprise. She didn't get why Erin even had to think about that. "Then let's stay."

"You want to stay?"

"Why not? Just call Uncle Dieter and explain that the plan has changed. He and Andy are with friends; I'm sure he wouldn't mind staying there for another night, or alternatively, they can sleep on The Barracuda, which, let's face it, is probably better than any hotel in Casablanca."

Erin pursed her lips as she thought it over. "But we have places to visit and things to do. I can come back here next month if I want, and I might actually do that. Your uncle is on a schedule and I want to respect that."

Celia frowned in confusion. "What schedule? He's never been on a schedule in his entire life. I don't get why Uncle Dieter has the last say on this trip; he might have made the winning bid but it's your yacht after all. However, if that's what you really want, then we'll go back." She shifted her gaze to Erin's grandmother, who had now turned her attention to her, clearly trying to figure out if Celia was the cause of Erin's hesitation. And Celia certainly didn't want to be seen as the bad guy. "Seriously, Erin, look at this lovely old woman. She's so happy to see you; she's practically been crying non-stop since we arrived. It would just be wrong not to stay the night."

"Okay." Erin nodded and sighed in defeat. "You're right. I'll call Eddie and Dieter and let them know we'll be back tomorrow."

"Good." Celia gave Erin's grandmother a smile, letting her know everything was fine. "Shall I go tell the driver?"

"I'll go." Erin got up and rubbed her grandmother's shoulders as she walked past and said something in Arabic that made her cry with happiness once again. "I'll invite him in for lunch."

39

Surreal didn't even begin to describe the situation, Erin thought as they sat down for lunch. The driver had decided he'd rather sleep in his car than drive home and return the next day. She was paying him generously, so it wasn't like he was missing out on wages. She also had a feeling the smell coming from the clay pot over the fire in the kitchen might have something to do with him wanting to stay. The chicken tagine had been simmering since just after they'd arrived this morning, spreading a delicious aroma throughout the house.

Now she was here, in her grandmother's home where she hadn't been since she was a teenager, and she had Celia by her side. The driver seemed beyond confused as to why two wealthy looking Americans were sitting on the floor in a Berber house, but he was friendly and polite and joined in the conversation. Her grandmother had started complaining about her parents now, and although Erin had told her that was a no-go topic, she wouldn't stop, and even told the driver how she'd been betrayed by her own daughter, who refused to move back to Morocco to run the farm.

Erin let it slide. Her grandmother had never been interested in visiting them in the US either and having lived here her whole life, she couldn't possibly understand why her mother had no desire to move back. Although she seemed in good health, she looked so much older, and each time Erin looked at her, she felt a stab of pain for letting so much time pass. She'd become so used to the luxuries in her life that it was hard to imagine that she used to come here on vacation without thinking twice about the simplicity of the Berber lifestyle. The lack of furniture and electronics, the harsh weather conditions—the intense heat of the summer and the freezing winters, the absence of infrastructure, or even a bus route.

The pot with the tagine was placed between them on the floor. They used freshly baked bread to scoop up the sauce, vegetables and chicken and washed it down with tea. She still remembered the correct way to do it and was impressed by Celia, who watched her eat and mimicked her effortlessly, making sure only to use her right hand.

"This is an amazing experience," Celia said. "And the food is delicious." She turned to Erin's grandmother, pointing at the pot with a smile.

"It might sound strange, but people actually pay good money nowadays for a tour that includes lunch with a traditional Berber family," Erin joked. "I never realized how unusual my background was until now." Her heart warmed each time she looked at Celia. This incredible woman, who was wealthy and used to the daily comforts in her life, was willing to sleep on a dusty rug on the floor, just to make someone else's grandmother happy. She was courteous and polite and didn't seem taken aback by the state of the house or the lack of light or even the earthy smell; she was just her wonderful self, exactly as Erin had experienced during their time together. It touched her deep down in her core, and it was in that moment that her discernment of Celia changed dramatically. Her perception of their current relationship and their potential future. She'd never thought about her future when it came to women but now, she couldn't imagine not having Celia in her life.

Of course, it was way too early to think like that and she told herself not to get too carried away as she was constantly aware of the big secret that lay between them. She hated lying to Celia, and she was worried that if Celia found out, it might ruin her chances with her entirely. But she had to keep her promise to Dieter. He was having so much fun with his beloved niece, and if acting like nothing was going on would make the last months of his life happier, then that's what she would have to continue to do.

"You know, it's actually an amazing experience for me too, believe it or not," she said to Celia when her grandmother was talking to the driver, complaining about lack of loyalty in the family yet again. She knew it was only a matter of time before her grandmother asked her about moving here, and Erin was dreading having that conversation. "I forgot what it was like out here. And my grandmother aside, it's good to be back, even though I could never do this for very long."

"Do you feel like you're reconnecting with your roots?" Celia asked.

"In a way, yes. Apart from when I'm visiting my parents, I never eat Moroccan food, simply because there are no Moroccan restaurants in Bermuda and as I told you, I'm not much of a cook myself." Erin took a bite, savoring the moreish, comforting flavor of her childhood. "I never listen to Arabic music, and I don't have any Arabic friends, so it's easy to forget where I came from."

"Do you think you'll come back more often after this visit?" Celia took the bread being offered by Erin's grandmother, tore a piece off and passed it to her.

"I'd like to, but it depends on how it goes today." Erin shot a quick glance at her grandmother who was getting more worked up now, raising her voice at the driver and waving her hands around. She'd always been a feisty one. "Jedda was super happy to see me, but I'll bet you it won't be long before she starts scolding me for staying away all these years. I suppose she's in her right to do that, but she might even go as far as asking me to move in with her, since I'm not married." Erin chuckled. "I haven't been told off for wearing jeans yet, but that's just a matter of time too."

40

"Ouch." Erin sat up and rolled her shoulders.

"Sore back?" Celia asked, sitting up too. They'd slept on two mats in the living room, fully clothed as they'd figured it would be easier to wait with having a shower until they got back to The Barracuda. They'd woken up to the call for prayer coming from a nearby mosque, and the sound of it made Celia smile, as it announced another morning in another world. And it was a fascinating one. She never thought she'd be in this situation, but she was grateful for the experience. Yesterday had been a long and emotional day for Erin, and she felt like she understood her better now.

"A little sore, yes." Erin winced. "How's yours?"

"I'm fine, I think, but I'm much younger than you," Celia teased her while she stretched her arms above her head.

Erin's eyes widened, and she nudged her playfully in her ribs. "Hey, I'm not that old. But what I don't get is, how does a woman in her eighties sleep like this?"

"Are you saying your grandmother doesn't have a bed?"

"I'm not sure. I haven't seen her bedroom, but my guess

is that she sleeps on the floor too. She always did before, and she's not a woman who would change her ways for the sake of comfort."

"Maybe you should get her a bed," Celia suggested. She tried to imagine her mother's reaction at seeing her like this. Her hair was a mess, her face was unwashed, and the soles of her feet were a deep orange color from walking around on the clay floor. Then her lips pulled into an amused smile as she pictured the unthinkable: her mother in this situation.

"Nice thought, but Jedda is a woman of simplicity, just like most people who live around here. My parents tried to send her things when they first moved to the US, but she was having none of it and she gave it all away. Berbers originally moved around a lot, so they didn't have many things as it was impractical. Even though the ones who live in Asti now—including my grandmother—settled a long time ago, her mindset never changed." Erin shrugged. "She's just not interested. All she's ever accepted is a little bit of money to pay a couple of guys to help her harvest the apples. She still has a stall at the market twice a week. They drive her there in the morning and pick her up in the afternoon as she's adamant she wants to sell the produce herself."

"It sounds like such a hard life."

"It is a hard life," Erin agreed. "But she seems healthy and happy, overall. Even though she was a total nightmare last night, trying to match me up with the driver, I'll make sure to come back twice a year or so to check on her. When it comes to the point that she's unable to take care of herself, I'll have to discuss options with my parents."

"Hmm..." Celia paused for a moment. "Do they know you're here?"

"No, but I'll tell them next time I see them." Erin inhaled

deeply as the smell of freshly baked bread wafted through the living room. "Mmm... that smells good. I think Jedda's up. There's a well at the side of the house if you want to wash your face. Or I can get you a bowl of water?"

"Don't worry; the well is fine." Celia got up, brushed off her clothes and readjusted her hijab. Then she straightened Erin's T-shirt and pulled her hijab down over her forehead. "You look cute. I kind of want to kiss you."

Erin laughed. "I feel many things right now but cute is not one of them." She locked her eyes with Celia's and licked her lips. "You have no idea how much I want to kiss you too, but I'll be in deep trouble if she walks in."

"Let's wait until we're alone." Celia winked and switched on her phone to check the time. She'd turned it off last night to save the battery as there was nowhere to charge it. "Wow, six a.m." She chuckled. "That's why it's so nice and cool in here. Saying that, the temperature was quite comfortable last night too."

"These houses are designed to be cool in summer and warm in winter," Erin said. "Since it's partially built into the rocks and most rooms are underground, the insulation is great. I've never been here in winter myself though; I wouldn't dare."

"No, that sounds daunting, I suppose you'd be practically snowed in on bad days." Celia crossed the room to the staircase and put on her sandals. "Let me know if you need help, okay? It's not that I don't want to, but I assume she'll want some alone time with you." She blew Erin a kiss. "I'm going to freshen up and have a look around the orchard."

The sun almost blinded Celia as she stepped outside, and the dry heat hit her immediately, even though the sun was just rising. She looked up at the Atlas Mountains, their peaks glistening with snow while the call to prayer still echoed from its walls. Dirt roads snaked through the dry landscape that was filled with pines and cedar trees, and the colors of the landscape were spectacular, portraying earthy tones mixed with vibrant greens against the blue sky. There was nothing synthetic here; everything was authentic and just the way it was supposed to be. The wide mountain range made her feel small and insignificant and as she greeted the workers and walked to the well, she realized this was a very humbling experience. She was so lucky to be here, with Erin.

41

"You two smell nice," Celia said as she hugged Dieter and Andy upon returning to *The Barracuda*. She'd expected them to be here when she and Erin arrived, but they'd been doing some last-minute shopping, which Andy apparently couldn't get enough. Refreshed after a long shower and a change of clothes, she felt giddy with excitement. "What have you been up to?"

"Dieter's friend, Achmed, took us to a hammam this morning, and we got pampered!" Andy exclaimed before Dieter had a chance to answer. "Feel how soft my skin is. Seriously, feel it." He held out his arm and Celia shot him a bemused smile as she ran her hand up and down it.

"Wow. Your skin feels like a baby's. I've heard it hurts. Did it hurt?"

"Yes, it did," Dieter said. "Mine hurt anyway. I was like they were sanding me down, but I doubt Andy's was painful. He refused to have the scrub part of his treatment—which is the whole point of going to the hammam," he added with a chuckle. "He was terrified of losing his tan, so they just soaped him up and hosed him down instead."

"Hey, at least I've still got my gorgeous golden glow. You, on the other hand, are pink, my love." Andy gave Dieter a slap on his behind and turned his attention back to Celia. "We were supposed to go and see this belly dancing show last night, but daddy got tired," he joked.

"Gross, Andy, don't call me that." Dieter chuckled. "Tired or not, we were actually having a really great time, so it was nice that we could stay for another night." He pointed to a small bag dangling from Celia's wrist. "What did you get?"

"I got lots of stuff actually, but this one is for you." Celia handed him the gift bag that contained a silver cigar box. She'd had his initials engraved on the front, and on the back it said: 'To my favorite man in the whole world. Love, Celia.'

When her uncle took it and turned it around in his hands, his reaction shocked her. He was clearly trying to hide how much it touched him but was unable to stop tears from welling in his eyes.

"Thank you, sweetheart. You have no idea what this means to me," he said in a shaky voice, pulling her into a long hug.

"You're welcome." Celia didn't really know what to say as his behavior was so out of character. Usually he laughed things off, but lately, he'd been a little sentimental, and the conversations they'd had since boarding The Barracuda had been much more meaningful than before.

Dieter let go of her and shook his head as he stepped back. "I'm sorry, that made me all teary. It's just so thoughtful of you."

"It's true," Celia said. "You are the most important person in my life. You have been since Dad died."

Dieter nodded, his bottom lip trembling as he took her by the shoulders and looked at her. "And you've always been like a daughter to me. I hope you know that. Just like you, I miss your father very much."

"I know." Celia frowned as she caught Andy making a gagging gesture from the corner of her eye. "What?" she said, turning to him with a raised brow.

"What?" Andy repeated, rolling his eyes. "Enough with the sappiness, let's have some fun. I've known Dieter for four years and I've never seen him cry until we boarded this boat. Seriously, he hasn't stopped sobbing since we left Switzerland."

"Is that so?" Celia regarded her uncle, but he waved it off.

"Like I said before—I'm just getting older. Now, mister-it's-all-about-me, what kind of fun did you have in mind?" He put an arm around Andy and pulled him in.

"Well..." Andy placed a finger on his lips and raised his eyes skyward as if in deep thought. "How about you all sit down in the lounge and order me a Dirty Martini while I nip into our room. I'll be back in ten minutes to show you all the goodies I bought. Make sure my drink is extra dirty!"

Celia was amazed at how it really was always all about Andy, and he made no apologies for it. "Sure. If it makes you happy, I'd love to compliment you on your taste with each and every item you hold up or put on," she said with a hint of sarcasm.

"Great. I like you." Andy scanned the deck, then looked up at the top deck. "Where's Erin? She needs to join too; a one-person audience is not an audience."

"What about me?" Dieter asked.

"You don't count; you've already seen everything."

"And paid for it," Dieter added with a humorous grin.

Andy shrugged. "Okay, fair enough, honey. But don't forget that even though you paid, it will be your reward in the end. Just wait until you see me in those new tiny swimming trunks. You won't be able to keep your hands off me."

"That's one way of looking at it." Celia shot Andy a smile. "And to answer your question, Erin's with Eddie, planning the route. We'll be going into rougher waters after Dakar, so they're just discussing the weather forecast. I'm sure she'll be down soon."

"Excellent." Andy gave Dieter a peck on his cheek and turned on his heel. "Let's make it twenty then," he yelled over his shoulder.

"You've got your hands full with him," Celia joked as she followed her uncle toward the lounge on the lower deck, where the staff had prepared the bar for their arrival. She was ready for a drink after the past twenty-four hours, and she suspected Erin wouldn't mind a sundowner either.

"Hands full is an understatement." Dieter greeted Desirée, the bartender, and eyed the selection of bottles behind the bar. "Could I have a dirty martini for Andy please? Make it a weak one, he's a little hyper today," he added with a wink. "And I'll have a..." He turned to Celia and she smiled at the mischief in his eyes. "How about we start out with a shot?"

"A shot?" Celia burst out in laughter, then realized he was being serious. "Sure, I'll have a shot with you. But only tequila; I don't drink anything brightly colored or sweet."

"Tequila it is." Dieter leaned in over the bar and nodded to Desirée who had overheard their conversation. She was already on it, pouring top-shelf tequila into two frosted glasses with a salted rim, before adding a slice of lemon op top. "Thank you, Dessi. That is the prettiest shot I've ever seen."

"Have you ever even tried tequila?" Celia asked, clinking her glass against his. She licked the rim, bit into the slice of lemon without as much as a wince and downed her shot in one go.

"Of course I have. I was young once." Her uncle followed suit and tried to keep a straight face, too, but failed. "And God, I forgot how much I hate the taste of it." He closed his eyes and took a deep breath, then lowered his voice to a whisper. "But I do like the way it makes me feel, so let's have another one."

42

E rin heard music and laughter coming from the main deck, and she leaned over the railing to see what was going on below. Celia and Dieter were sitting on the corner couch, both with a glass of rosé and an empty shot glass in front of them, cracking up as they watched Andy put on some kind of fashion show. He was strutting up and down in a white and gold tunic, then paused in front of them, striking a pose before dramatically turning and walking back inside. Seeing how much fun Celia and Dieter were having together made her smile, and she made her way down to join them.

"What are we drinking?" she asked, eyeing the shot glasses.

"Rosé and tequila," Celia said with a grin. "Not necessarily a socially acceptable combination, but we felt like both, and it's surprisingly good when you drink them together."

"Right." Erin waved at Desirée and pointed to Celia and Dieter's glasses. "I'll have the same, please. And two more shots for these guys."

"Oh God, no more for me." Celia held up a hand. "I haven't had tequila for years and I'm feeling the effects already."

"Nonsense." Dieter stood up and took their glasses. "If I can drink it, so can you and tonight, we're going to get drunk together even if it's the last thing I do."

"Don't peek!" Andy yelled from behind the glass doors. "I'm still getting changed and I'm searching for the right tune to go with this outfit."

"I'm not looking, I'm just getting a drink!" Dieter yelled back. "You've missed Andy's first strut down the catwalk," he informed Erin. "But don't worry, there will be many, many more to come."

"Oh, I have no doubt about that." Erin glanced inside where Andy was barking instructions into her Alexa.

They took their beverages and joined Celia, who was wiping tears of laughter from her cheeks. She patted the space next to her and kissed Erin as she sat down. "Babe, you're going to love this."

Erin shot her an endearing smile and pulled her in. "You're cute when you're tipsy."

"Well, you'd better catch up because you're going to need tequila for the *Andy Show*." Celia held back a chuckle as she pointed to the automatic glass doors that opened, revealing Andy with hand on hip in another tunic—a pink one with gold embroidery this time. He wore matching pink babouche slippers and a golden fez hat, his blond hair carefully arranged around the edge. Truth be told, he didn't look bad in the outfit—in fact, it kind of suited him. But the way he walked out and posed to a *Pet Shop Boys* track, his face all serious and his mouth pouty was just too funny.

Andy's fabulous new wardrobe was impressive to say the least and he'd already planned his sailing outfits for the rest of the journey. More drinks were served and while the sun sunk into the horizon, they slowly started sailing farther along the African coast. They filled each other in on the happenings of the past couple of days, with especially Andy and Dieter wanting to know everything about the visit to Erin's grandmother.

Marcus, who had been to the market and loaded up on Moroccan ingredients and treats at Erin's request, brought out a selection of delicious snacks. Cheese and olive pastries, stuffed dates, omelet with saffron and cinnamon cut in wedges, dips and fresh breads, roasted almonds and a selection of mini kebabs were passed around.

"You really slept on the floor?" Andy asked incredulously for the fifth time. "You don't strike me as the kind of woman who comes from a poor family," he added, looking Erin over. "I just assumed your parents were rich Arabs or something."

"Well, I am from a poor family," Erin simply said with a shrug. "My parents paved the way for me of course. Growing up in L.A. gave me more opportunity to build something for myself than if I'd grown up in the Atlas Mountains but still, we struggled when I was younger, and I've had to fight for everything I have."

"But your grandmother still sleeps on the floor..." Andy looked emotional as he said it. "Why didn't you bring her back with you?"

"She doesn't want to leave her farm."

"The old woman is set in her ways and used to her lifestyle," Dieter said. "I totally understand she's not interested in change. Lots of people sleep on the floor; I've slept on the floor and it never bothered me."

"Exactly," Celia chipped in, then decided to change the subject as Andy looked like he was about to cry. "So, what's the route, where are we going next? Dakar and Cape Verde, right?"

"Yes. We'll be sailing along the African continent at a leisurely pace until we get to Dakar, where we'll top up on fuel as it's easier to do that there than in Cape Verde." Erin pointed to their left where they could see the wide and flat beaches of Morocco. "I've asked Eddie not to rush. The Western Saharan coastline is pretty spectacular." She smiled. "You'd better enjoy the tranquility of the coastline while you still can because it might get rough and rocky when we get out into the open sea."

"Then you and I can play *Titanic* during stormy weather," Andy joked, perching himself on Dieter's lap.

Erin laughed. "In case of a storm, everyone needs to stay inside so there will be no reenacting *Titanic*, but let's hope it doesn't get that bad."

43

"Celia… Wake up." Erin placed soft kisses on her forehead. "There's something I want to show you."

Celia brought a hand to her temple, noting she may have had too many tequila shots last night. "Ouch." After a fun-filled night, they'd tumbled into bed, tipsy and starved for each other. Both her relaxed state from their lovemaking and the soothing rocking of the yacht had sent her into a deep sleep, and she felt slightly confused as she sat up in bed. "What is it? What time is it?"

"Just come with me." Erin held out a robe for Celia to wrap herself in, then pulled her in and hugged her tightly. "You can go back to bed in a minute," she mumbled against her hair before breathing in her scent. "But I didn't want you to miss the sunrise."

Celia rubbed her sleepy eyes as she followed her. Either the ocean was unusually still, or they weren't moving, because she didn't feel like she was swaying as much this morning. "Are we anchored?" She winced against the bright light as the automatic glass doors opened and they stepped onto the deck.

"Yes. We're anchored, and what better way to start your day than with a view like this?"

As they walked to the aft of the yacht, Celia came face to face with so much red that she had to blink a couple of times to make sure it was real. Suddenly, all her senses were on high alert, the sheer beauty of the stunning shoreline making her gasp.

Dieter and Andy were already there, holding hands as they looked out over the resplendent desert landscape. The rising sun caused shadows to grow around oddly shaped red rock formations that rose from the equally red earth along the coast.

"Wow." Celia walked over to her uncle and hooked her arm through his as he straightened himself. "Is this Western Sahara?"

"Not quite; we're still technically in Moroccan territory, but we're close. It's quite magnificent, isn't it?" Dieter put his other arm around Andy and pulled them both against him.

"It's incredible," Andy agreed, taking pictures with his free hand.

Erin came up behind Celia. "It's called Legzira Beach. Worth getting up for, right?"

"Yes. Thank you for dragging me out of bed." Celia heard Ming's voice and as she looked over her shoulder, she saw the whole team on the upper deck, snapping pictures and taking in the view. She gave them a wave, and Ming smiled and made a 'perfect' ring gesture with her fingers.

"We'll be down with coffees in a minute!" she yelled.

"No need, I can make them," Erin said as she looked up too.

Celia let her head fall back against Erin's shoulder, amazed at how natural it felt to have her near. She was at ease around her, and with each day that passed, she could feel them growing closer. They'd both let their guards down, little by little, inviting each other in and that was a beautiful new sensation to her.

Stone arches reached into the North Atlantic like long arms in a deep, glowing red. Carved by the sea, for what Celia assumed must have been hundreds of years, the coastline looked like a dreamscape. There was an astronomical sandstone archway that framed the upcoming sun, creating a halo of light. "So pretty. It looks like a different planet."

It was quiet without the humming of the engines, and no one spoke for long moments while they enjoyed the tranquility and breathtaking beauty that stretched out before them. "Can we stay here for a couple of hours?" she asked.

"Yes, whatever you want," Erin said, wrapping her arms around her from behind. "We're not in a hurry."

"Okay..." Celia turned to her uncle who looked blissfully happy. She loved seeing him in his element, and she realized then how precious this time was, for both of them. They rarely took time to do fun things together, or to enjoy the wonders of life without having something urgent to get back to. "How about we have breakfast on the beach?" she suggested.

"Now that's an idea." Dieter raised a brow at Erin. "What do you say, boss?"

"I say let's do it." Erin placed a kiss on Celia's cheek and let go of her. "Let me get you all a coffee and speak to Eddie and Ming. They'll need some time to prepare."

"Want to go for a walk?"

"Sure." Celia regarded Andy. He didn't seem like the leisurely walking type, but she sensed he might want to talk, so she got up from the rock she was sitting on. Ming and Erin were setting up a folding table and chairs in the shade of the archway, while Marcus unpacked their breakfast consisting of coffee, fresh juice, croissants, tortilla wedges and a selection of condiments and fresh fruit. They'd turned her down when she'd offered to help, so she'd simply enjoyed the sun on her skin and the water splashing over her bare feet.

She didn't bother putting on her kaftan and smiled smugly, swaying her hips as she felt Erin's eyes burning into her when she walked past.

"I know what you're doing there waggling that sexy little ass," Andy said jokingly, slapping her behind. "You know very well she's looking."

"I do," Celia admitted. "But isn't that all part of the fun? A little seduction?"

"Absolutely. Andy wiggled his bum too, then blew a kiss at Dieter over his shoulder. "And you, princess, are a champion in seduction."

"Looks like you've had some practice yourself," Celia retorted when Dieter whistled through his teeth. She lowered her voice and turned to him. "About the drug thing... Erin asked Eddie to check his safe while we were in Casablanca. I know it's intrusive; I was going to talk to him first, but I had no idea how to start the conversation and I don't think he'd ever admit something like that to me either. Anyway, Erin assured me there's nothing illegal in the safe."

"Thank goodness." Andy let out a sigh of relief. "Did she say what *was* in there?"

"No... Come to think of it, she kind of just glossed over it." Celia shrugged, pushing the unease she felt to the back of her mind. "But I'm sure it's fine if she says so."

"Yeah." Andy didn't seem entirely satisfied either, but he

still looked significantly less worried now. "You know, I wanted to tell you that I've really enjoyed hanging out with you."

"Me too." Celia had really grown to like him over the past twelve days. He struck her as a lonely young man— someone not used to having genuine friends—and that wasn't unthinkable now that he'd told her about his background. "I'd love to keep in touch after we all return back home, and whatever happens between you and my uncle, I'm here for you, okay?" She meant it; Andy was fun to hang out with, and his desire to constantly be the center of attention, made her laugh every day.

Andy swallowed hard and instead of cracking a joke or laughing off her comment like she expected him to, he leaned into her and put his head on her shoulder. "Thank you, Celia. I really appreciate you saying that."

44

"How are you feeling, my friend?" Erin pulled out a chair for Dieter and sat down opposite him.

"Very tired but also very happy." He glanced at Andy and Celia, who were walking along the shore, away from them. "This was exactly what I needed and more. I've loved every moment with all of you and visiting my friends in Menorca and Casablanca was the right thing to do. I didn't realize how much I'd missed them until we saw each other again."

"Did you tell them about your—"

"No," Dieter said resolutely. "Andy was with me but even if he wasn't, I still don't think I would have told them. We had so much fun looking at old photographs and talking about our past adventures; I didn't want to put a dark cloud over our last meeting."

Erin followed his gaze and seeing Celia, the ball of guilt expanded in her stomach again. "I'm very glad this has been good for you and I love seeing you happy but..."

"But?"

Erin fell silent for a moment as Marcus put down plates and cutlery, then continued as he walked back to the tender.

"I hate keeping this from Celia. I know we've only just met but already, I feel we're growing close. I don't want to ruin it with her, but most of all, I think she deserves the truth. She's stronger than you think, Dieter."

"I know. And I understand." Dieter watched his niece and his lover turn into small colored specks in the far distance. "Just give me a couple more days, okay? After Cape Verde... I'm not ready yet."

Erin nodded slowly, realizing she didn't have much choice. "Okay. After Cape Verde."

"There's something else..." Dieter halted their conversation again as Marcus returned with coffee, and he raised his head skyward, pretending to enjoy the heat from the sun.

Marcus, who was highly intuitive after working on yachts his whole life, sensed they were having a private conversation, so he put down the coffee pot and immediately backed away. "Shall I leave you to take care of the rest?"

"Yes, we're fine. Thank you so much." Erin gave him a thumbs-up. "Take the morning off and tell the rest of the crew to do the same."

"Thanks, boss, will do."

"He's a lovely young man. And so talented." Dieter poured them coffee before he continued. "I'm having trouble with my energy levels. I'm tired all the time and walking is becoming harder than I thought it would be. I knew this would happen, I just didn't... well I guess I under-estimated how much this damn cancer would take out of me." He took a sip and winced, then added sugar. "I'm taking more pills and it's affecting my balance too. I might need a wheelchair in Cape Verde with the Fourth of July festival going on. There may not be anywhere to sit down in town as it will be so busy, and I won't be able to stand for very long." He let out a frustrated groan. "I certainly don't want to break up the fun because I'm in need of a rest."

"I understand," Erin said, trying to ignore the sting she felt, knowing he was getting worse. "We have a wheelchair onboard, but if you use it, you'll have to tell Celia and Andy."

Dieter shook his head. "Not yet. I want to spend the Fourth of July with them without any pain between us. I'll just say I hurt my knee or my ankle or something."

"More lies." Erin sat back with a sigh. Despite his cheery demeanor, he didn't look good today and soon, it would be much harder to hide what was going on.

"Yes, more lies but this experience means everything to me. I'll never get another Fourth of July." Dieter shrugged. "I know this sounds like emotional blackmail but it's not. I'm simply begging you."

"I know that."

"Then please just give me a couple more days and the wheelchair." As Dieter's pleading eyes bored into hers, Erin could almost feel his desperation. She wanted to give him anything she could, but she was so torn as she knew it was unfair to Celia.

"Okay. As I said, I hate lying to Celia, but your wellbeing is more important than my love life right now."

"Thank you." Relief flooded Dieter's features as he sat back and crossed his arms over his chest. "You really care about her, don't you?"

"I do." Erin paused as she added milk to her coffee. "I'm totally smitten with her, to be honest with you."

Dieter gave her a warm smile. "I can see that and trust me; Celia feels the same. I know you've only just met but I know that girl better than she knows herself and it brings me great joy to see her in love, especially with someone who

I know will be good to her." He tilted his head as he met Erin's gaze. "Do you see a future with Celia?"

Erin tensed up, firstly because Dieter had told her Celia was in love with her, and secondly because she suddenly felt like she was being subjected to some kind of father-in-law talk. That was understandable of course; he wanted to be sure that her intentions were sincere. After all, this concerned the person closest to him. "It's a bit early to answer that question, and it depends on how Celia feels too," she said honestly. "But I know there's something special between us. Something way bigger than anything I've experienced before." She shrugged. "Being together all the time is intense and my initial fear was that we didn't really know each other before we started this journey. It's not like we can escape from each other. But now, I'm not worried about that anymore because Celia makes my life rich and exciting every day and I believe she feels the same way about me."

"Then nothing is more important than that." Dieter's smile widened. "Not my wellbeing either. If you feel like you have no choice but to tell her, then tell her."

Erin shook her head as she returned his smile. "I don't want to make that decision for you. Tell her after Cape Verde. I'm already over my head dealing with this, so three or four more days won't make a difference."

45

The call to prayer told Erin they were nearing Dakar as she stepped out onto the deck, and the sound made her smile as it reminded her of Morocco. The crackling loudspeakers, the familiar lines... It was a different country, but her wake-up call was the same.

The outskirts of the city were already visible; small houses in yellow, brown and sandy tones were scattered around the dusty, flat desert terrain with only the movement of the odd buffalo here and there. It was warm, and the wind carried a dry heat that made her instantly thirsty. She made her way up to the bridge, already sweaty from the short walk. Summer had most definitely arrived, and she'd rarely felt a heat like this.

"Good morning, Eddie. Are we okay to moor?"

"Morning, Erin. Yes; I've been in contact with the station and we're scheduled to refuel in an hour. You'd better have your credit card at hand because we're running very low and we'll need about thirty-thousand liters," Eddie joked.

"Yes, it's been a while." Erin laughed and patted his shoulder. As her yacht was a well-engineered hybrid, filling up wasn't a regular reoccurrence and even though she'd designed it herself, she was amazed by how long she could sail on a full tank. "Celia, Andy and Dieter are ready to go. Marcus wants to visit the central market in Dakar and they're going to join him, so they won't have to wait on the dock until we're done. Desirée has been here before, so she's taking the rest of the crew out for a tour."

"Excellent. Shall we go through the checklist?" Eddie asked. Fueling was a strict procedure, during which all passengers had to disembark. Eddie would stay behind on the vessel, while Erin handled the fuel hose. "We'll be bunkering at around three-hundred liters per minute, so I'm expecting it to take around ninety minutes, and we have four hours of docking time."

"Great. That should give them enough time to do some shopping." Erin looked over the list. "No smoking signs?"

"Donald has hoisted them in the refueling area. Stoppers are blocked too."

"Great. Bravo flag?"

Eddie nodded. "Donald has hoisted it. I'll take care of the oil record book; I've already prepared the paperwork."

"Thank you." Erin refocused on the list. "Oil absorbers and snakes?"

"Donald has put them out on the deck. The fire extinguishers are there too."

Erin smiled. "Well you two have been efficient this morning. Do you even need me?"

"We're going to need your money," Eddie said with a chuckle.

"Of course." Erin joined in his laughter as she took her wallet out of the back pocket of her shorts and waved it at him. "I'll go kick everyone off the ship. I'll see you in the machine room for the final checks in ten minutes." She walked down to the lower deck where the crew and her guests were waiting to disembark. Andy had once again failed to dress down, sporting a white, silk Versace shirt over a pair of tiny, white denim shorts. The way he was drawing attention to himself, she could already foresee that he'd be overwhelmed by salesmen, but she didn't comment on it. "Are you guys ready to go?"

"All ready." Marcus held up his canvas shopping bags.

"Yes. We'll be back in three hours," Desirée said.

"No rush." Erin put a hand on Celia's back and kissed her. "If you happen to need more time, just give me a call. We'll anchor somewhere and I can pick you up in the tender." She pulled the handle to lower the gangway.

"Okay." Celia turned to her uncle, who had settled into a lightweight collapsible wheelchair Erin had found him onboard. "Are you sure you don't want to see a doctor while we're here? I feel like you should."

"I'm sure. It's nothing; I simply slipped in the shower." Dieter shrugged. "It's just a bruised knee and I can still walk fine, it just hurts a little, that's all." He stopped Andy when he was about to push him toward the ramp. "Thank you, darling, but I can do it myself. My arms work just fine."

"So stubborn," Celia mumbled. "It's a shame you can't come along. Want me to get you something?" she asked Erin while her gaze settled on her captain's hat. "Anything?"

Erin shook her head. "Not that I can think of." She pulled Celia in and kissed her once more, realizing she didn't like saying goodbye, even if it was just for a couple of hours. She'd become used to having her around all the time and they were so at ease in each other's company that she suddenly dreaded the moment Celia would return to New York. "Why don't you just surprise me?"

"Surprise you? So, you've decided you like surprises now?"

Erin shrugged and looked down to hide the blush on her cheeks. It was rare for her to blush, and she didn't understand how after all these years, someone was able to make her do that. "Yes. I'm pretty sure I'll like any surprise coming from you."

"Okay, I'm on it." Celia lingered before her, clearly not liking saying goodbye either. She laughed and rolled her eyes when Andy, who'd managed to flag down a cab, called her name and told her to hurry up. "Okay, I don't know what I'm still doing here; I'd better go." She blew Erin a kiss. "I'll see you later."

46

Andy, whose mother tongue was French, was in the front with the driver and Celia, Dieter and Marcus were squashed in the back, Dieter's wheelchair sticking up from the open trunk behind them.

"I've asked him to give us a tour before we go to the market," Andy said. "He's going to drive us through the Médina and through a working-class neighborhood just outside the Médina. Are you guys up for that?"

"Of course." Dieter fanned his face and opened the window. "Unless you're in a hurry, Marcus?"

"Absolutely not." Marcus checked his phone. "I have my shopping list on here, so I'll be pretty quick, and besides, it's nice to be on land for a while. Might as well see something while we're here, right?"

Celia opened her window too and absorbed Dakar's atmosphere. Women were cooking in groups, in the street in front of their homes; the smells from the big, clay pots meshing with the earthy scent of the city. Music was coming from most homes, stores and vehicles, their loudspeakers fighting as to who could play the loudest.

Dakar was a city full of surprises, extremes and contrasts, she noticed. Suit-clad businessmen dropped their cases to kneel down for prayer on a dirt road they passed. Behind them, in front of one-story homes, women with babies strapped to their backs were gathered in groups. Some were dressed conservatively in long black gowns and hijabs, some in colorful, printed dresses with matching headpieces, and some in tight jeans and crop tops. The main road that ran through the city was congested with not only cars, but also horse-drawn carts and other makeshift vehicles. Women somehow managed to conquer the dusty roads in stiletto heels, parading their impressive hair weaves, brightening up the streets that were lined with derelict concrete, graffiti-clad buildings.

It wasn't the architecture that made the city so vibrant, but rather the people. As they drove through the riot of noise, there was constant chatter and laughter everywhere she looked. People were catching up while hanging onto the back of trucks, others simply walked in the middle of the road as the traffic was so slow.

Driving into the Médina, the graffiti became more colorful and covered almost every home, like the neighborhood was one, big open gallery, the art ranging from black and white abstract patterns to impressive life-like illustrations of animals and people. Even the stores had art on their facades; illustrating their merchandise so there would be no mistake about what they sold. A haberdashery store had scissors, needle and thread painted around its windows, and a hairdresser had illustrations of intricate hairstyles covering the full front of the building. Between worn-out buildings were high-end fashion boutiques, fancy restaurants and nightclubs, and a limousine was parked next to a horse and carriage.

They stopped off for food as their driver had recommended a place he claimed sold the best traditional Senegalese breakfast, and they soon discovered it was his family joint, run by his wife. Sitting around one of the plastic tables on the pavement, shaded under a canopy made of old jeans, cars drove right past them as they ate ndambé, which consisted of beans cooked in a spicy tomato paste, served with fresh flat bread and a cold Coke.

To Andy, who hadn't travelled much, it was another world, and he was completely fascinated by everything he saw. To Marcus, it was food heaven, a portal where he could discover new ingredients and flavors, and to Celia, it was the most fun she'd ever had with her uncle, who embraced every experience with an almost childlike enthusiasm, as if it would be his last. No one would have ever guessed he was incredibly wealthy. Today he'd dressed down in shorts that were torn at the hem and his blue T-shirt was faded, a throwback to it having lived through the seventies.

"We should do this more often," she said, passing him another piece of bread. "I don't mean on a yacht," she added. "Although that would be fantastic too, of course. But just this is fun too. Seeing new things and experiencing new cultures together... The last time we travelled together must have been ten years ago?"

"Eleven," her uncle corrected her. "We went to Mexico City together eleven years ago, to see that Mayan exhibition. That was a good trip, I have amazing pictures and memories." He paused for a moment, lost in thought. "And yes, we should do this more often, my dear. I'm enjoying it very much." He helped himself to more beans and laughed as they overheard Andy talking to their driver, discussing the best places to shop for clothes. "My French may not be that good, but I've heard Andy say 'shopping' more times than I could ever count so I know exactly what he's planning."

"I'm worried *The Barracuda* might sink, from all the shopping he did in Marrakesh," Celia added.

"Hey, there's still space in the closet," Andy said defensively. "And there are two other staterooms, so once ours is full, I can start stocking up in there."

"You do realize everything will have to be brought back to Switzerland, don't you?"

Andy stopped chewing as he thought about that for a moment. Then he turned to the driver again to discuss something in French. "No worries. He knows a place that sells large suitcases," he said with a beaming grin. "I wonder if they sell ones with African prints..."

"How do you know what to buy?" Celia asked Marcus as they were strolling through the market. "There's so much here, I wouldn't know where to start..." She gazed across the large hall, where booths selling an assortment of fresh fish, meat, fruit and vegetables were mixed in with fabric and clothes stands and smaller tables selling anything from tech gadgets to souvenirs. It was a cheerful, chaotic bustle, and her first impression of Senegalese people was that they were happy people with a no-nonsense 'life is what you make-it' attitude.

"I do online research before I disembark," Marcus said. "I'll look up local dishes and the ingredients and things I want to try or experiment with. Even after being a chef for twelve years, I still find fruit and vegetables I've never seen before. I'm lucky with Erin because she loves to try new things and you guys are very easy too, so it makes my job fun." He scrolled through the list on his phone. "Let's see, we've got okra, cassava roots, eggplants, tomatoes, cowpeas, guava, plantains and avocados. Now we just need to get some sole, monkfish and tuna for the freezer. They sell barracuda here too, but Eddie wants to go diving when we anchor in Cape Verde, so he'll take care of that."

"Isn't that dangerous?" Celia asked. "It's done with a spear, right?"

Marcus nodded. "Yeah. Eddie's a brave man. I've seen him in action, and he may be small, but I would never pick a fight with him."

"I can see that." Celia shifted the strap of her purse farther up her shoulder. "So, what will you be making with all this stuff?" She was helping Marcus carry the groceries and the five bags on her arms were getting heavy.

"Tonight, I thought I'd make thieboudienne. It's the national dish of Senegal and the main ingredients are fish, rice, lots of green herbs and cassava root." Marcus leaned in to smell the fish at one of the stalls. "Senegalese is one of the richest cuisines in West Africa." He pointed to the whole tuna and gave the stallholder a thumbs-up before handing him the money. "But it's not widely known across the globe."

"Any other cuisines you haven't attempted to cook yet?" Celia asked. They passed a stall that sold some types of fruit that were entirely alien to her, and she picked up one of each to take back with her.

"Oh God, so many. Ethiopian, Nigerian, Nepalese... I've travelled the world a lot, thanks to my job, but the list with countries I haven't been to is much, much longer." Marcus took the bag with fish and thanked the smiling man, then pointed to the next table. "We should bring some of these deep-fried pastry pockets back for everyone. They're filled with fish and spices."

"Sounds good. And what's this?" Celia asked, gesturing to a juice booth.

"Well spotted." Marcus smiled. "This is…" He looked at the bearded man. "Bissap?" When he nodded, Marcus ordered four cups. "It's a blend of hibiscus flower, mint, water, sugar and orange blossom. It's supposed to be delicious." He handed a cup to Celia and took a sip. "God, this is great. Where are Andy and Dieter?"

Celia laughed when she heard Andy's voice in the distance. It was clear Marcus wasn't the only one who got excited about the market. She couldn't actually see Andy, as he was surrounded by salespeople who were trying to sell him fake watches, purses and phone gadgets. Apparently, word had gotten around that the blond man in the silk shirt loved to shop, and when she saw her uncle shaking his head in frustration behind them, she laughed even harder. "You know what? I'll happily drink two. I think Andy is busy right now."

47

"I just got your message that you had a surprise for me, so Eddie's taken over for an hour," Erin said, holding up her phone as she entered the room. She let her eyes get used to the dim lighting, then stalled when she saw Celia standing there in towering stilettos and a black, satin kimono robe with lace edges. "Jesus, that's hot. Where did you get that?"

"A store we passed in Dakar." Celia shot her a mischievous smile. "I promised you a surprise, didn't I?" She took Erin's captain's hat and put it on her own head.

Erin licked her lips as she stared at her. "I think I like surprises. And I like those heels too."

"Excellent. Now that you've made up your mind, let's take this off, shall we?" Celia said in a teasing tone. She unbuttoned Erin's shirt, inched her hands inside and roamed them over her breasts while she kissed her so seductively that Erin had trouble staying upright. Her legs were trembling as Celia's tongue traced her bottom lip, then sucked it into her mouth.

"What are you doing?" Erin noted she sounded breathless and unsure.

Celia smiled as she slipped the shirt off her shoulders. "It's a surprise, remember?"

Too overwhelmed to protest and too turned on to think straight, Erin complied, lifting her arms so Celia could take off her sports bra. Before she knew it, she was half-naked before her and she had no idea how that had happened. Her breath hitched as Celia went down on her knees and unbuttoned her white uniform slacks. "These will need to come off too, I'm afraid." She arched a brow as she looked up at Erin and started pulling them down, along with her boxers.

Erin let her take off her deck shoes and step out of her last garments, her mind spinning at not knowing what was going to happen. She liked it very much though, and when Celia took hold of her thighs and brought her mouth between her legs, all the while keeping her eyes fixed on hers, she threw her head back and moaned loudly. Celia's tongue slipping through her folds awoke an immense sense of arousal in her, and she pulled her closer and laced her fingers through her hair, needing more than she could handle in an upright position.

Erin wasn't used to being pleasured by other women. It was something she'd never cared about that much before, but with Celia, she was able to let go entirely. A groan of frustration escaped her when Celia stopped that delicious thing she was doing, stood up and licked her lips. The captain's hat looked cute on her, but there was nothing cute about her expression. Here was a woman on a mission and Erin had no idea what that mission was.

"Lie down," Celia said, pointing to the bed.

"Turning the tables on me, are you?" Celia didn't answer, so Erin walked over to the bed and lay down, her core fluttering with anticipation when Celia pulled a remote from her robe pocket and turned on the speaker. She immediately recognized the ancient big band song as a striptease tune, and her lips parted as Celia started swaying her hips to the music as a seductive smile painted her lips. Her movements were slow and sensual, and she seemed entirely at ease with her body as she pulled at the tie of her silky robe, causing it to fall open. "Fuck…"

"Do you like it?"

Erin nodded as she took in the black lingerie set. The hold-ups with black, lace edges, the black corset and the black, lace thong were so sexy that she felt an uncontrollable throb between her thighs. "You look incredible."

Celia played with her own hair, then traced her curves as she rolled her hips and her shoulders to the music. Moving toward the bed, she slid the robe off her shoulders and took a wide stance next to Erin, never taking her eyes off her as she leaned over and bit her lip seductively, giving her an amazing view of her cleavage.

Erin had witnessed a professional striptease on a handful of occasions, but those dancers had nothing on Celia and what her performance was doing to her. Her full breasts in the corset were calling to her but when she reached out to touch her, Celia stepped back and continued to dance, torturing her by forcing her to be patient. It was the sexiest display Erin had ever witnessed, and she shifted on the bed, dying to have Celia all over her. The visual stimulation drove her wild and feeling her burning eyes on her breasts, Celia ran her fingertips over them and massaged them before sliding her hands down as she circled her hips.

"You're killing me," Erin murmured, her pulse racing and her clit throbbing. "I so want to touch you."

"Do you now?" Celia wedged her fingers between her

hipbones and her thong, then played with the fragile fabric as she danced, pulling it away from her hips before she let it snap back. Chuckling at Erin's groans of frustration, she took her hand and placed it over her breast, then stepped away again when Erin squeezed it hard, leaving her outstretched arm to fall down. "Not so greedy, I'm captaining this vessel now. You'll have to be patient."

Swaying to the music, she reached behind her and started undoing the hooks of her corset, leaving Erin to wait for agonizingly long moments before the last one snapped open. Celia held it against her chest, grinning at Erin's pleading expression until finally, she gave in and let it fall down.

"You're amazing," Erin said, staring up at the curves of Celia's breasts that were beckoning her. Her irresistible nipples were hard and pink, and she fantasized about taking them into her mouth and sucking on them. Sitting up, she was about to get off the bed, but Celia shook her head and waved a finger dismissively, then beckoned her to lie back down. Erin was pretty sure she was getting back at her for all the times she'd teased her relentlessly, but if this was revenge it was revenge of the sweetest kind, and she didn't mind it one bit.

"No touching until I say so."

Erin chuckled as she rested her hands to each side of her head on her pillow, open palmed. She watched Celia hook her fingers under her panties again, and this time, she pushed them down and smiled as she stepped out of them. By now, Erin didn't know what to do with herself anymore, and she balled her hands into fists, fighting the urge to take charge.

Celia got on the bed and spread her legs, then crawled toward her on hands and knees. Erin knew she could see how wet she was, how desperate she was for her touch. Sensing her body was screaming out for more, Celia straddled her, coating her belly with her wetness and she leant forward until her hands were resting on Erin's breasts. Erin was throbbing as her hands reach for her ass and squeezed her cheeks hard.

"What do you want?" Celia asked, her eyes sparkling with mischief as she moved back, spread Erin's legs apart and started grinding into her throbbing clit.

"Jesus, Celia..." Erin groaned and closed her eyes, bucking underneath her. The friction was making her dizzy and delirious, and she could already feel the tension building in her core.

"Do you like that?" Celia spread her legs wider, arching her back each time she thrust forward. Her long hair was swaying around her shoulders, her eyes fluttering as she rolled her hips and Erin was sure she'd never seen anything as sensual in her life. The swell of her breasts, so bouncy and inviting, her tongue that kept flicking over her lips...

"God, yes." Erin grabbed her hips and changed her pace, pulling her in faster and harder. Celia's expression, the guttural sounds coming from deep within and her frantic movements told her that she was about to let go too.

"Come with me." Celia leaned back, steadied herself on Erin's thighs behind her and continued to grind into her.

It didn't take much for Erin to explode and when she did, she could feel it right down to her toes as her loud groan echoed through the room. She shook underneath her, and Celia didn't stop until she lay completely still. Quiet whimpers of release continued to pass from Erin's lips, even when Celia lowered herself on top of her, covering her body in warm bliss. Staring up at the ceiling, she needed a moment before she could speak. "I don't normally give myself to others like this but you're an exception, apparently."

"Apparently. I like that." Celia slowly stroked her face and her hair, tracing her fingers along every feature as if touching her was all she wanted to do. "You haven't seemed particularly apprehensive since we set sail, so I find that almost hard to believe." She smiled sweetly. "But thank you, for trusting me. It means a lot to me."

"It's true," Erin whispered. It was a new experience, a whole new dimension in lovemaking, and she knew by the way Celia looked at her that she wasn't used to this either. She seemed surprised and equally fascinated by their chemistry, as if she'd never considered having something like this. And now they'd have many more nights of drowning in each other's bodies.

"We still have many more nights," Celia said as if reading her mind. "This is going to be so good."

Erin nodded and managed a smile. She wanted to say so much in that moment, but most of all, she wanted to tell Celia the truth. Of course, they would have an amazing time together. It would be a journey of a lifetime, something they'd never, ever forget, but all that would eventually be polluted by grief and anger. Maybe she'd made a mistake in promising Dieter to keep his secret, but she couldn't see any other way than to carry on the way they were. Having Celia now was better than not having her at all and when the time came, she'd deal with it.

48

Celia patted the space next to her in bed, but Erin was already up. She sighed, wishing she could hug her good morning, or even better, make her feel really, really great before they had breakfast. The marine clock on the wall indicated it was only seven a.m., but instead of going back to sleep, she decided to get up, in search of coffee. The journey had been incredible so far and she didn't want to miss out on the time they had left sailing along the beautiful African coastline. Eddie had planned to continue their journey toward The Gambia first, then anchor there for a night as the landscape was meant to be spectacular.

"Good morning," she said as she spotted Ming, then greeted the rest of the staff who were already busy preparing the vessel for the day. Pillows were placed on the lounge chairs, tables were decked out, and the drinks cabinets that stayed closed overnight were open, and the glassware polished.

"Good Morning Miss Krügerner. Here you go." Ming handed her a cappuccino with almond milk before she'd even asked for it, and it was prepared just how she liked it.

"Would you like some freshly squeezed blood orange juice too?"

"Thank you, I won't say no to that." Celia had asked them if they needed help with anything on a couple of occasions, feeling guilty that she wasn't doing much apart from a few hours of work every day, but they'd kindly declined and told her that her only job was to enjoy herself.

Truth be told, she'd gotten used to doing less and had learned that she could easily run her business from anywhere, as long as she had her assistant help her out. It was quite a revelation and it was starting to change the way she looked at her life. Although she loved New York, there was really no need for her to be there all the time, and maybe now was the time to make a change in her lifestyle; travel and see more of the world. This trip had certainly awakened her sense of wanderlust and her curiosity for new destinations had been sparked.

Sipping her coffee, she ventured outside and gazed over the African shoreline. Yesterday, they'd sailed along stretches of golden dunes, perfectly wedged between the blue shore and the equally blue sky. A place on earth where the sun was cruel and the land so dry that no living creature would consider going there without a good reason. But today's view in Gambian territory was green and lush. Tropical hills stretched far and wide, their tips covered in a thick layer of morning mist.

Wondering why Erin hadn't woken her up earlier to see the morning view, she walked around to the front of the main deck. Her lips pulled into a smile when she saw Erin and Dieter, both in their robes, discussing something while rummaging through a pile of paperwork. Celia leaned against the vessel's body and watched them for a while, enjoying the sight of Erin's bare legs resting on another chair. She had her laptop open in front of her and was pointing to one of the pages on the table as they mumbled, keeping their voices down.

Suddenly, Celia heard Erin say her name, and her curiosity spiked. "You need to tell Celia," she whispered. "I thought I could do this, but I can't."

Celia narrowed her eyes and stayed still. She wasn't exactly hiding, but they were so engaged in the serious conversation—that clearly wasn't meant for her ears—that they didn't notice her.

"Not yet," Dieter replied, keeping his voice down. "I'm just not ready, Erin; I'm having such a great time with her."

A feeling of betrayal settled in the pit of Celia's stomach but deciding this was her favorite uncle and that she really had to stop being so mistrustful, she stopped eavesdropping and walked up to them. "Good morning. Whatever it is you can't tell me, I'm here now, so just spit it out." She looked from one to the other as she sat down while her uncle swiftly cleared the files from the table. Within a matter of seconds, he'd slipped them into his leather satchel before shooting her a smile that could only be described as utterly shifty. He looked caught out. They both did.

"Good morning, Celia."

"Morning, babe." Erin studied her, clearly trying to work out how much she'd heard.

Celia felt her face go pale and the knot in her stomach tighten. This was something serious, something they were desperate to keep quiet from her. And they were both in on it. "I don't like what's happening here." She paused when no reply came. "Seriously, Uncle Dieter. I totally understand there are things that don't concern me, but you just said my name, so I want to know what this is about. Being at sea with two people who are keeping secrets from me is not an option. Especially when one of those people is someone very, very close to me and the other someone I'm dating."

Dieter looked defeated as he held his breath for long moments, then let out a sigh, shaking his head. "Damn it," he muttered, then glanced at Erin as if looking for help.

"Shall I leave you two alone to talk?" Erin asked. Sweat was pearling on her brow while she nervously picked at her fingernails.

"No, it's fine, please stay. I need you here." Dieter was silent for what seemed like an eternity, and the tension between the three of them spread like a fog. "Celia, I didn't want to tell you this yet."

"You didn't want to tell me what?" When Celia's sensed his distress, her expression softened.

"I'm dying, honey."

She heard the words, but they didn't register, even though it wasn't the first time someone had said that to her. In fact, her father had used the exact same words, six months before he passed away. But this couldn't possibly be happening again. *Not again.* "No. You're not dying, you seem fine." Celia stared at him, hoping this was a tasteless joke, but deep down she knew it wasn't. The signs had been there, they just hadn't clicked into place.

"It's the medication. It makes me feel great, but it doesn't change the fact that I have cancer and it's spreading too fast to treat. It's why I've lost weight, and it's why I get really tired sometimes, when the meds wear off. There's nothing wrong with my knee, I just can't walk for very long."

"Cancer..."

"Yes. I beat prostate cancer last year, but now I have HCC."

Celia felt tears stinging her eyes as she covered her

mouth with her hands. "Last year? How long were you sick?"

Dieter shrugged, avoiding her gaze. "Almost two years."

"And you knew?" Celia glanced at Erin, betrayal stabbing her in the gut.

"Yes, Erin was the only one who knew," Dieter said when Erin didn't answer. "I let it slip when I was drunk over dinner one night, and I made her promise to keep it to herself."

"But why? How could you keep something so big to yourself? Were you ever going to tell me?" Tears started trickling down Celia's cheeks, and she suddenly felt nauseous. "And you? How could you keep this from me?" she asked Erin. "I trusted you."

"As I said, I made her promise not to tell anyone." Dieter's shoulders dropped. "Don't blame her, please. I was going to tell you, I really was. But I wanted to spend some quality time with you, without the sadness and without having to discuss the fact that I won't be around much longer. I just wanted us to be happy for a couple of weeks."

Celia nodded, and she swallowed hard as she looked at him through tear-glazed eyes. "How long..." Her voice trailed away, and she could hardly finish her sentence. "How long do you have left?"

"About three months. Certainly no longer," he added.

"Three months? Is there really nothing they can do?"

"No." Dieter shook his head. "It's too late. I have a whole arsenal of medication in the safe in my room and I intend to live my last months to the fullest." He stood up, took her hand and squeezed it. "I promise you that I've made peace with it. It's taken me a while but I'm fine now. And I need you to be fine too, or at least try to be."

Celia turned to Erin. "Promise or not, I can't believe you kept this from me. It's…"

"I didn't want anyone to know. It only makes it worse when people feel sorry for me," Dieter interrupted her. "Erin's been amazing. She cheered me up and made me laugh throughout my chemo last year." He shot Erin a grateful smile. "That's why we're so close, and I couldn't think of anything better than taking this trip with her, you and Andy while visiting dear friends who have been important to me during my life. You're the closest family I have, and if you hadn't agreed to come with us, I might have told you about my cancer and begged you to come along anyway." He sighed. "I just wanted a fun trip. No pity, no tears. Just fun."

Celia took a couple of deep breaths as she could feel herself on the edge of bursting into floods of tears. She could do that in the room later, but for now, she tried to stay strong for him. "Okay. I'll try." She wiped her cheeks and somehow found the strength to smile for a beat, then cracked anyway. She fell around his neck and cried. "This can't be happening," she said through sniffs. "You need to give me some time." As soon as the words were out, she realized how redundant that request was, as time was the only thing they didn't have.

"I know. I wish my situation was different too." Dieter got to his feet and held her tight for long moments, then stepped back, wiping his own tears away. "But it is what it is." He closed his eyes and when he opened them again, he'd stopped crying, as if he'd gained the ability to switch off his emotions in an instant.

"What about Andy?" Celia asked, scanning the premises.

"I'll tell him." Dieter kept his voice down. "I didn't want

him to know at first, but I see now that it wouldn't be fair to keep it from him. The time we've spent together on this journey has brought us very close, and I never meant for that to happen."

"Yes, you need to tell him. He loves you."

"I know. It was never that serious between us, but we've never spent this amount of time together and things have changed. I genuinely care about him too."

Celia sat down as her legs were shaking so badly, she didn't think she'd be able to keep upright. She recognized the signs of shock; shortness of breath, her racing pulse, the feeling of being choked and the pain that felt so physical that she had to hold onto her stomach. It was only starting to sink in now. Her eyes shifted to the satchel resting on the chair next to her uncle. "What was that?"

"I was just going through some paperwork with Erin. She's in charge of my will."

"Erin?" Celia frowned in surprise.

"Yes, I don't really trust anyone in the family, and as you're my sole heir I can't ask you."

"I'm what?"

Dieter took one of the files back out of his satchel. It was a copy of his will, Celia saw as he pushed it toward her over the table. "Now that you know, we might as well talk about it. Get all the grim stuff out of the way so we can carry on and enjoy our days on the water." He cleared his throat and shrugged. "That may sound naïve but it's what I want; for things to go back to normal."

"But things are far from—"

"I don't want a discussion about this, Celia. That's how it's going to be," Dieter interrupted her. "Anyway, as I said, you're my main benefactor although I'm leaving a little to Andy too. He's the only one I know who could really do with the money, and I worry about what will happen to him when I'm not around anymore."

Celia sniffed, unable to process the stream of information. "I don't want to talk about money, I just want you to get better."

"But I won't get better, and you need to accept that."

Celia picked up the file and flipped through the pages, more in need of a distraction than any genuine interest. "Why me? I certainly don't need the money."

"Because I love you more than anything in the world. And because I trust you with my estate and my art."

His words set Celia off again, and before she knew it, she was in tears once more. "I love you too. I love you so much and I don't want you to die." She knew she sounded immature, but she felt like a child all over again, remembering all the times she'd cried in her uncle's arms during her summer visits. Only this time, she hadn't bruised her knee, there was no girlfriend drama, and there were no fights with her mother. This was death they were talking about. Death was lurking around the corner again, and she wasn't sure if she could handle it. Taking deep breaths, she tried to compose herself as the knot in her stomach tightened. "I'm sorry, I'll try not to cry anymore."

"Please, sweetheart. Don't cry for me because I'm okay." Dieter reached out over the table and lifted her chin, forcing her to look at him. "And I want you to listen to what I have to say because it's important."

"Okay," Celia said softly.

"Good. Try to breathe." Her uncle flipped through the pages of the file in front of her and pointed to a list. "Everything will be yours. My castle, the part of my fortune that won't go to charities—except for the bequest that will go to Andy—but most of all, my art. I'd like most of it to stay where it belongs, in the castle's library, and I know the other members of the family would sell it off. I know it's ridiculous to worry about something like that." He shrugged. "I'll be dead after all, but I still want my favorite pieces to stay on display in Krügerner Castle. I also want my staff to stay employed for at least another year, so they'll have enough time to find a new job if you decide not to keep them. They're important to me." He paused. "I'm not asking you to move in, but if it's possible in any way, please keep my home alive. I know it's an expensive place to keep up, but I've taken care of that."

Andy appeared, and he swiftly put the file away and lowered his voice. "We'll go over the finer details later, when we're alone."

Celia nodded and forced herself to smile at Andy. Then she got up, desperate to be alone. There was no way she could pretend everything was fine.

"Wait, I'll come with you." Erin followed her, but Celia stopped her. "Don't come near me right now," she whispered. "Just give me some space."

49

E rin knocked on the door to their room, balancing a breakfast tray in her other hand. "Can I come in?" When she got no answer, she opened the door to find Celia on the bed with her legs pulled up, hugging her knees while she cried.

Her heart broke at seeing her pain. The moment she'd been dreading had come, and Erin was well aware that they'd left it way too long. It would have been better if Dieter had just told her upfront. Now that she'd found out about Dieter's secret, Celia felt betrayed and rightly so. Erin could only hope she hadn't ruined it with her. That thought made her nauseous, as she couldn't imagine losing the one person she'd ever felt such a close connection to.

"I brought you breakfast. Can I talk to you?" she asked, sitting down on the edge of the bed. Celia was staring right ahead of her, not even acknowledging Erin's presence. "We never meant for you to find out like this," she continued. "He was going to tell you."

"When?" Celia turned to her, her sharp glare cutting through Erin like a knife.

"When he was ready." Erin had never seen Celia angry before and she was taken aback by how cold she'd suddenly turned. Gone was the sweetness and affection that always sparkled in her eyes, and now there was only fury and pain left.

"And what if he didn't? Were *you* ever going to tell me? Or were you just going to keep me in the dark until he died?" Celia lifted her chin and studied Erin like she was seeing her for the first time. "Of course you weren't going to tell me," she mumbled, covering her face with her hands. "Oh my God, I feel so stupid right now."

"What? I don't understand what you mean. I—"

"All of this was just a game to get me on the yacht, wasn't it?" Celia cut her off. "Because my uncle needed your help to get me onboard. Am I right? You quite literally seduced me to get me onboard. Was that auction a setup? Did you plan this all along?"

"No!" Erin flinched and shook her head. She felt like she'd just been punched in the gut. Anger was growing inside her, but she told herself that Celia was terribly upset and that this was not a time to argue with her. She took a couple of deep breaths and lowered her voice. "I didn't lie when I told you I'd thought about you every day for a whole year. And tell me something; have we or have we not just had an amazing two weeks together? How could any of that possibly be a lie?"

Celia ignored her comment and averted her gaze. "I don't know what to think anymore."

"I was crushing on you like mad and I didn't even know Dieter was terminally sick until I spoke to him the morning after the party." Erin's voice went up a notch when frustration finally got the better of her. "*After* the ball. After the auction. I swear, that's why I was upset the next morning. He'd only just told me then."

Celia looked up at her and although Erin could see in her eyes that she believed her, it didn't soften her features. "You still lied to me. His medication, his weight loss, the wheelchair…"

"I had no choice," Erin tried again in defense, but it was pointless. There was no way she could get through to her right now.

"I'm moving to the other room," Celia said. Her voice was void of emotion as she got up and wiped her cheeks. "I want to spend the rest of this trip with my uncle, but I'd like to keep our interaction to a minimum."

"Please Celia…" When Erin reached for her arm, Celia pulled away and moved across the room.

"I want you to leave me alone."

Erin nodded, wringing her hands. "Okay." She'd lied to her and she knew that was a big issue for Celia, who had been betrayed in the past. She felt bad about it and wished she'd handled the situation differently, but what else could she have done? She'd been stuck between a rock and a hard place. "I'll ask Ming to move your stuff. Don't worry; I'll stay out of your way."

She watched Celia slip out the door and fell back on the bed. Celia was in shock and she was angry; that was understandable. Grinding her teeth, she tried to let go of the panic that was threatening to get the better of her. She couldn't lose her. Not now.

No one had made her feel as desired as Celia had, and no one had made her smile this much. She'd let her into her life, into her most private thoughts. Hopefully Celia would come to her senses and realize that she never had a choice. Surely what they'd talked about and had experienced together proved that this was way more than something she was doing for Dieter? There was no way she could have betrayed his trust but in keeping her promise, she'd betrayed the woman who was most dear to her.

Desperate for distraction, she picked up the sailing schedule on her nightstand and studied it. She'd take over from Eddie to captain the yacht, keep to herself and give Celia the space she needed. Hopefully she would come around.

50

After a second night in her new stateroom, Celia knew she had another sleepless night ahead of her. She kept thinking of her uncle and the fact that soon, he wouldn't be in her life anymore. She wouldn't be able to call him, see him, hear his laughter or ask him for advice and that was an unbearable thought.

Since Andy didn't know he was sick yet, it had taken all her strength to keep it together during the day, and every time she'd snuck back to her cabin in need of a breather, she'd lost it. Erin had given Eddie two days off and taken over from him, so Celia hadn't seen her at all and that was for the best.

Pretending was hard, and having been in Andy's shoes, she wasn't sure how much longer she could keep this up. Wouldn't it be much better for her uncle to just get it out in the open? To have honest conversations instead of pretending everything was fine? She didn't understand how that could possibly be enough for him. And poor Andy. He didn't deserve to be kept in the dark. He was a good man, and she'd grown to like him very much.

Frustrated after tossing and turning for hours, she got out of bed and put on her robe. Tiptoeing as to not wake anyone up, she left her room and went outside, pulling her robe tighter around her. It was chillier than yesterday, and the wind was strong tonight. She stalled for a moment, thinking the silhouette of a figure sitting in the bow was Erin, but then she saw the clouds of smoke coming from her uncle's cigar and walked over to him, relieved to finally catch him alone.

"Can I join you?"

Dieter looked up, smiled and scooted over. "Please do." He refilled his glass with red wine from the bottle next to him and offered her a drink.

"Thank you." Celia took a sip, then sat back to gaze over the water. Behind them were faint lights from resorts along The Gambia's coastline, but in front of them, beyond *The Barracuda's* lights, everything was dark, as if they were staring into nothing. Somehow, it felt that way. Her uncle's death was looming before them like a black hole and there was nothing she could do to stop the inevitable. She felt numb inside.

"Are you okay?" He asked her, putting his hand on her arm.

"I feel like I should be asking you that." Celia was lost for words. Anything cheerful would be fooling them both, anything too serious was off limits.

"Do you understand now why I didn't want you to know just yet?" Dieter asked.

"I think so." She gave him a small smile. "I'm trying, Uncle Dieter. I really am trying to be strong so you can enjoy..." she swallowed hard. "So you can enjoy the time you have left." Her hair kept blowing in her face, and she secured the loose strands behind her ears.

"I know, and I'm grateful that you're trying. It makes me happy." He paused. "Do you know what would make me even happier?"

Celia sighed deeply because she couldn't imagine her uncle being capable of feeling happiness at all, right now. "What?"

"If you stopped being so angry at Erin. This isn't her fault."

"She lied to me," Celia argued.

"I know you've had some bad experiences, but try not to see the worst in people." Dieter took the glass from her and finished the wine, then poured them more. "You'll have to excuse my excessive drinking; I have no idea if there will be Barolo in the afterlife, so I'm enjoying it while I can."

Celia managed a small smile at his gallows humor, grabbed the bottle and took a swig from it, then wiped her mouth. "I get that. I'm partial to Barolo too."

Her uncle's eyes were a little glazy, but he didn't seem drunk. "Look, the only thing you really need to know is that Erin is crazy about you. She has been for a long time. Last year, when she was keeping me company during my recovery, her whole face lit up every time I mentioned your name. She never enquired further about you; I guess she wasn't sure how I'd feel about the two of you together, considering I'm... Well, let's face it, I'm your father figure. But I know she's mad about you, Celia, and really, that's all that matters."

Celia nodded, remembering their dance last year. "Is it true that you didn't tell her you were dying until the morning after the party?"

"That's true. The auction, that was all my doing in case you thought she had any part in that. You see, there were a few things I wanted to take care of before I go. One of those things was seeing old friends who I've lost contact with over the years. True friendships never fade, even if you don't see each other for years, and I feel blessed to have the opportunity to do that now." Dieter cleared his throat. "The next point on my bucket list, if you will, was to spend quality time with the people closest to me, to experience extraordinary things together that you, Andy and Erin will never forget. Good memories are invaluable and who knows? Maybe I'll even remember this amazing vacation, wherever I'll be." He turned to Celia and smiled. "And the third point on my list, my dear, was to help you find true happiness, and I genuinely believe you will find that with Erin. I saw your chemistry from the get-go, and if I get to make one wish before I die, it's that I see you find happiness in love."

"How can you be so sure about me and Erin?" Celia felt the ball of nausea tighten in her stomach. There had been plenty of opportunity for Erin to come clean, but she hadn't.

"How do you feel about her?" He asked in return, then added, "Aside from the fact that you're angry with her right now."

Celia was silent for long moments, as she tried to push away her anger in order to answer honestly. "I have feelings for her," she finally said in a near whisper. "Big feelings."

"There you go." Dieter chuckled and held up his glass in a toast. "Once I know you've found love, I'll die a happy man. Because love, my sweet, sweet girl, is the most beautiful thing that life has to offer. I've been very blessed in the sixty-eight years I've been on this wonderful planet." He had a faraway look in his eyes as he averted his gaze and stared into the night. "I've travelled extensively, seen the most beautiful things, I've been touched by art, music, nature, and I've known love—love of the deepest kind. Some people are afraid to love because it hurts too much when you lose it. But I'm grateful for the years I had with Roderick. They were my best years."

Celia reached for his glass, needing the liquid courage to ask him the question that had been on her mind since she'd found out he was dying. "Are you scared?"

"A little. Not so much as when I first found out. I don't know what will happen when I die. I'm not religious and honestly, it's very scary to think about nothingness, so I try not to. But then again, I don't really believe in nothingness either." Dieter put an arm around her and pulled her in. "Look at all the beauty surrounding us. Smell the ocean, listen to the powerful waves crashing against the bow. Think of everything we've seen and experienced together." He squeezed Celia's shoulder and placed a kiss on her temple. "And look at the stars. Isn't the sky incredible? Wouldn't it be madness to think there's nothing after death, when there's an endless universe out there? There must be a point to all this, right? To life?"

"Yeah, there must be." Celia looked up, following his gaze toward the darkness above them, stretching onwards, endlessly. It wasn't something she wondered about very often but in the past days, she'd thought about nothing else. "Will you please tell Andy very soon?"

"I promise I will."

"Thank you. He deserves to know, and I can't keep pretending around him."

"I understand." Dieter paused. "You know, I tried to take my own life after Roderick died." The heavy statement came with such casualty, as if he was simply referring to a minor hiccup in his past.

"Oh God..." Celia's lips parted as she narrowed her eyes at him. "I didn't know that."

"No, your mother knew, and some other people, but you were only fifteen then and you'd just lost your father. You saw me as a strong person, so I didn't want you to know I'd taken a handful of pills."

"I knew you were devastated by Roderick's death, but I never knew that you felt you couldn't live without him. I'm so sorry to hear that."

"Yes, well, it took a while, but I found my happiness again, eventually. Life goes on, the sharp edge of the pain softens, and it becomes bearable. Then, after a while, you feel like life is worth living again and you carry on. You start looking ahead instead of back." Dieter gave her a sad smile. "I shouldn't have done what I did, and I'm glad I survived because even without Roderick, I had many great years by myself." He paused. "But there's one hope that gives me strength to enjoy my last months to the fullest."

"What's that?"

"I'm hoping to see Roderick again."

51

After an eight-hour shift navigating *The Barracuda*, Erin stepped out of the shower. Her eyes were tired, but she was too restless to lie down. Wrapping her bath towel tighter around her, she sunk into the armchair in the corner of her room. Celia hadn't reached out to her yet, and she was starting to wonder if it was time that she went to look for her. She'd seen her from the bridge, playing games at the dining table, and although she'd smiled and laughed, it was clear that she was just trying to stay strong for her uncle and Andy, who was still blissfully ignorant of what lay ahead. It hurt her to see Celia suffer, and even if there was nothing Erin could do to make it better, she was hoping she'd be able to comfort her just a little. If only Celia would let her.

Erin couldn't keep avoiding her; Andy would start to wonder why she wasn't showing up for dinner or coming down on her breaks anymore. While she contemplated that, her eyes fell on Celia's watch that she'd left behind. She picked it up and studied it. It looked expensive, but Erin didn't recognize the brand. She turned it around and read the inscription. *February 12th, 1996. Happy Birthday, honey. Love Dad.*

Erin had been lucky enough never to lose someone close to her, and she couldn't begin to imagine how Celia felt, now that she was about to lose the second most important person in her life.

A knock on her door made her jump, and she almost dropped the watch as she rushed to open it.

"Hey." Celia looked tired as she crossed her arms in front of her chest and leaned against the door, rubbing one bare foot over the other. Her normally vibrant eyes were red-rimmed and flat, and she was already dressed for bed in a semi-transparent, black negligée. "Is my watch here?"

"Yes." Erin felt caught as she was already holding it. "I didn't see it until a minute ago, otherwise I would have brought it to your room."

"Thank you." Celia put it on and ran her hand over her wrist, as if she'd missed wearing it. "I owe you an apology," she said then, looking up to meet Erin's eyes. "What I said to you, that wasn't fair. I was angry and..."

"Hey, it's okay." Erin reached for Celia's hand, pulled her into a hug and held her tightly when she suddenly started crying. "You don't need to explain."

Celia held her in return, her warm tears trickling down Erin's collarbone as she buried her face in her neck. "He's dying," she said through sniffs. "And he won't consider any further treatments and he refuses to go to hospital. Even just to prolong his life..."

"It's his choice," Erin whispered, weaving her fingers through Celia's hair. "You should have seen him last year. He was only a shadow of the man he is now, and he doesn't want to go back to that if there's only a tiny chance he'll gain a couple of miserable months. He wants to feel good in the time he's got left." She flinched as she said it, immediately regretting bringing up the looming timeline. It was so strange to think doctors could predict a time limit to someone's life and she felt her own stomach clench at the thought of losing her good friend. Stepping back, she took Celia's face in her hands and looked at her intently. "I'm sorry I didn't tell you, but I couldn't. He didn't want anyone to know in the first place, including me; it just slipped out one night when he was drunk." Celia's breath smelled of red wine, and Erin suspected she was a little tipsy.

"I understand. Uncle Dieter is so stubborn. He'll never let people see his weaknesses." Letting out a deep sigh, Celia leaned into her touch and closed her eyes, then lifted her chin and brushed her lips over Erin's.

Erin shivered at the contact and kissed her softly, then wiped her thumb over Celia's cheek. "Do you want to stay here tonight? I just want to hold you."

"I'd like that." Celia lowered her voice to a whisper. "But I don't want you to hold me. I want you to make me forget. Just for now."

Erin stared at her as she watched Celia's expression darken. "What do you mean by that?"

"You know very well what I mean." Celia took her hand and pressed it against her breast.

"I'm not sure if that's a good idea right now..." Considering the circumstances, it didn't feel right to make love to Celia, yet it was impossible to ignore the arousal between her legs and the desire that pulled Erin toward her, no matter what. Feeling her nipple harden under her touch and hearing her breath hitch only made her crave her more, and she knew she wouldn't be able to say no to her.

"Please," Celia repeated, desperation seeping through

her gaze. "Don't hold back. Make me feel good. Make me forget."

Erin felt her pulse race at Celia's plea and truthfully, she wanted to forget too. Celia was about to get on the bed, but she pulled her back, then turned them around and backed her up against the wall. The quick intake of breath told Erin she liked it, so she continued her quest, hiking up the silky negligée while she pressed her body into Celia's. She could feel her need by the tremble in her legs and the way Celia's arms clamped around her, her hands fisting her towel. "I'll make you forget like you have no idea," she whispered against her ear, then ran her tongue along the side of Celia's neck and sucked in her flesh, knowing she was causing her skin to bruise.

Her hand made its way between Celia's legs and she could feel her wetness against her fingertips as she rubbed them over the fabric. Celia's hips jerked forward, her arousal turning Erin on even more. She had to pace herself—to go against her natural instincts—and she took a moment to compose herself as Celia squirmed against her and let out a quiet moan. If she was going to take her pain away, she had to make it last.

"Let me tie you up," she said in a ragged voice. "I think you want that."

Celia's lust-fueled gaze confirmed her desire with a subtle nod.

Erin looked around the room, searching for something she could use, then opened the small chest of drawers beside them and pulled out a slim Armani tie. She slowly removed the negligée, and looked her over as she dropped the garment on the floor. Celia was so ravishingly beautiful that Erin almost forgot she was supposed to be in control. Her curves were smooth and inviting, her face both angelic and devilishly seductive. She was a woman of fascinating contrasts; respectable, kind and innocent at first sight, but when her clothes came off, the animal within her came out to play. "Lie down on your back," she said, gesturing toward the bed.

Celia did so, and Erin's lips parted as she approached, transfixed by her heaving chest. The full breasts and perky nipples, her lips, especially the juicy bottom lip she kept biting each time they had sex. Her beautiful hair that Erin loved to run her hands through, and her slim waist, curvy hips and long legs that were now tanned from the sun. She really was Erin's ultimate fantasy.

She took Celia's wrists and tied them together, then her eyes fell on the metal ring on the wall above the bed. It was just a marine detail, and she'd never considered using it for this purpose. Or had she? She'd always wondered why she'd put it right there, above the bed, as she hadn't applied such details anywhere else and wasn't into gimmicky interiors. Perhaps the desire to tie a woman to it had been there all along.

"There," she said, tying her wrists to the ring. "Now you're mine."

"Looks like it," Celia whispered. There was no sign of the flirty, mischievous smile that usually played around her lips. Instead, there was a pained yearning in her expression, a longing for Erin to distract her and take her away.

Erin stared down at her, filled with a mixture of sadness and desire herself. The conflict was real but maybe this was exactly what they both needed, because God, she really wanted to escape too. She licked her lips as she spread Celia's legs apart and sat down on her knees in between them. Splaying her fingers wide, she trailed her hands up Celia's legs while she looked at her. "Now, what am I going to do to you?" she mumbled, more to herself, although she wasn't exactly short of ideas. She cocked her head and arched a brow with a small smile as she met Celia's gaze.

"I'm all yours." Celia tugged at her restraints, and something flashed across her features when she realized she couldn't free herself. Was it fear? Erin was about to ask if she was okay, but as if reading her mind, Celia nodded, offering herself up. "I'm fine."

"Are you sure?"

"Yes."

Perhaps Celia was beyond caring as she had bigger things on her mind. Erin imagined the news about Dieter had destroyed her to the point that nothing else really mattered right now. It couldn't be worse, so why be afraid?

Erin hooked her fingers under the sides of Celia's panties and pulled them down, then lowered herself on top of her.

"I've missed you," she whispered, and kissed her softly. She'd missed the body contact and holding her at night. She'd missed the closeness.

"I've missed you too," Celia muttered. Her lashes fluttered and the ring on the wall rattled when Erin wedged her thigh between her legs, pushing into her aching wetness.

Although she felt far from patient right now, Erin kissed her until she was out of breath and then some more. Celia was a really, really good kisser; slow and sensual, fueling her screaming hunger to the point where her brain threatened to shut down. Her lips were sore when she pulled away and looked down at Celia, their burning need reflected in each other's eyes.

Erin teased the inside of Celia's thighs with her fingertips, then moved her mouth to her ear. She bit her earlobe, gently at first, then harder until Celia gasped and wiggled underneath her. "I want you so badly..." She rubbed over her swollen lips, hard and teasingly slow, and she sighed at the pool of desire she felt as her fingers slipped lower and lower until she entered her.

"Yes!" Celia threw her head back and bucked her hips against Erin's hand, sucking in a quick breath. Her movements became needier then, her body language desperate as she swayed her head from side to side and tugged at her restraints. "Please..."

Erin teased her until Celia groaned in frustration, then kissed her again as she started penetrating her, marveling at the sounds of pleasure that escaped Celia's lips. She loved being inside her, feeling her walls clench around her fingers, feeling her need as she brought her to the edge.

"What are you doing?" Celia whispered when she pulled out of her, just as she was about to explode.

"I'm making you wait." Erin smiled as her eyes fell on her nightstand drawer, and Celia followed her gaze, her lips parting when she took out the strap-on.

"Put it on," she whispered, and Erin complied as Celia's impatient body language and short answer told her not to linger any longer.

Erin kissed her hard while she entered her, moaning as Celia wrapped her legs around her hips. The ring above them rattled louder, and although Erin knew she desperately wanted to use her arms to pull her closer, Celia didn't ask her to undo the tie. "You're mine," she murmured, tugging Celia's bottom lip between her teeth while she pushed deeper inside her. "Mine."

They moved together rhythmically, faster, harder, and Erin felt an orgasm building from the friction between them. Celia was close too, her loud moans echoing through the cabin as Erin tumbled over the edge. Seconds later,

Celia followed, the spasms making her chest and hips shoot up fast and intense. Erin's mouth was on hers while they rode out every last wave, basking in the escape from reality.

Erin lifted her head and softly ran a hand over Celia's cheek. "Do you want me to untie you?"

Celia looked at her for a moment, her sad gaze returning as she shook her head. "No. Do it again."

52

"So, do we have a verdict yet? Is she a keeper?" Andy asked.

He'd perched onto Celia's lounge chair as she was sunbathing, taking a break from work. Not that she'd done much work; she'd mainly been staring at her screen, pretending to be busy so she could dodge Andy. The day had been a struggle so far, but she'd felt a renewed sense of tranquility after waking up in Erin's arms this morning and that had given her strength.

Celia managed a smile and a chuckle. "Are you going to keep asking me that?"

"Yes. I want to know if I'll be seeing you both again, after Dieter's gone. I don't really have any close friends apart from him, so I'd really like to stay in contact." He paused. "You and Erin are my only tie to him, and I want to remember him as vividly as I can with other people who cared for him."

Celia turned to him, her eyes narrowing. "You know?"

"Yeah." Andy let out a long sigh and shrugged. "Pretty fucked-up, huh?"

Celia nodded and swallowed hard. "Did he tell you?"

"Last night. He woke me up, a little buzzed after hitting the red wine with you, apparently. He told me you'd only just found out too. I'm sorry; it must be hard for you."

"It is." Celia sat up and took Andy's hand in her own. "I'm glad he told you." They were quiet as they stared out over the clear blue ocean and the equally blue sky. It was hard to tell the two apart; they simply blended into one. *'Just blue,'* she thought. *'Nothing but blue.'* Apart from *The Barracuda*, there was no other sign of life, and it felt immensely lonely as she stared at the horizon. Normally, this would be the time for her to start feeling uncomfortable, perhaps even panic at not seeing land. But it seemed fitting, and she didn't care about the lack of security because her greatest security in life was about to be taken away from her. "How are you feeling?"

"Sad and angry, but I'm trying not to drown in it. And frustrated, of course." Andy took in a deep breath as his eyes welled up. "I wish I'd known sooner. If I had, I would have cherished every single second so much more. I wouldn't have argued with him over stupid things like the mess he makes in our cabin, and the constant crunching from the peanuts he always eats in bed. I wouldn't have complained about the terrible movies he likes to watch, or the classical music that does my head in. I would have embraced it all, because I know that soon, I'd give anything to hear him hum along to Chopin or laugh at some stupid seventies comedy."

"I get that."

"And pictures." Andy had a tremble to his voice as he leaned into Celia. "Why do I always take these stupid selfies? I hardly have any pictures of Dieter and I together because I only ever think about myself, my outfits and how I hate that they don't match with his. It's just so selfish and—"

"Hey, you can't beat yourself up about stuff like that," Celia interrupted him. "There are many things I regret too, but that's not how it works. Last year, when he was sick the first time around, I didn't wonder why I hadn't heard from him, and I didn't bother calling him either. No one ever fully appreciates people until they're about to lose them, or until they're gone. Unfortunately, it's how life works."

"I suppose you're right." Andy put on his shades, hiding his tears. "I knew something was wrong, but I never expected it to be so bad. So final."

"I still can't believe it either," Celia said, shaking her head. "Do you think you can do it? Enjoy our time here with him?"

Andy shrugged. "It's going to be hard. He seems so detached from his fate, as if he's made total peace with it. That's crazy if you ask me. I would say that he's either still in denial, or he's had so much time to let the prospect of death sink in—especially because it's not the first time he's been sick—that he's managed to find some solace in something..."

"Maybe," Celia whispered, her uncle's comment about Roderick lingering in the back of her mind. "You're right; he seems to have made peace with it."

Andy nodded. "And I'm..." He rested his elbows on his knees and dropped his head into the palms of his hands. "I'm still processing the news. So, no, I have no idea how I can go through the rest of the trip, pretending everything is fine and fun and hunky-dory. We'll see."

"But you'll try, right?"

"Yes, I'll try," Andy said through sniffs. "I'm going to try very hard to live every moment I have with him to the fullest, no matter how I feel. I'm going to remember every second, every word spoken from now on." He slumped farther down, losing himself as he let go and started to cry. "Every look, every smile, every comment, every minute of interaction... I'm going to cherish it all like it's a fucking Madonna concert."

Celia scooted closer and took Andy in her arms. He was sobbing uncontrollably now, his tears streaming down her shoulder. She cried with him because she finally could and that felt good. It was okay to let go with Andy, to be sad with him, and it had been okay to let go in Erin's arms too. They were all in the same boat, quite literally speaking, and together they would be strong and make sure her uncle had the best time in his precious months left.

Every moment counted.

53

"Do we have a birthday cake for Ming?" Celia asked as they all sat in the jacuzzi, contemplating their first day of abnormal normality. She noted that she felt a little better than yesterday, and she was hopeful that she'd get through the rest of the day without breaking down. Now that the harsh truth was out, all she could do was try to keep it together while she tried to have fun. "It will be her thirtieth, right?"

"Yes, Marcus said he's taking care of it." Erin sunk farther down into the warm water and moved her shades up to her forehead. The sun seemed to be going down much faster at sea, and within the span of twenty minutes, the top deck had gone from scorching hot to mildly chilly. "Come to think of it, he did seem overly keen and prepared. He even knew what her favorite flavors were."

"That's not so strange, is it?" Andy said. "They've been working together for years."

"True." Celia kept one eye on the stairs, making sure Ming wasn't on her way up here. Not that she had any reason to; their second bottle was full, and the plate of hors d'oeuvres equally so, but Ming was nothing but efficient. "But I think they like each other," she said, lowering her voice.

"You think so?" Erin pulled her in, and Celia felt warm at the contact.

"I do but don't mention it. It's clear they want to keep it quiet, whatever's going on."

"That makes sense," Erin said. "Their contract states that the crew is not allowed to have intimate relations while on the vessel. People pay ten to twelve thousand dollars a day to charter *The Barracuda* and I can't risk my staff being caught out cavorting. I don't care as much now, of course, as it's just us." She shrugged. "But I get that they're hiding it."

"I never actually saw anything to indicate they were together," Celia was quick to say. "Just looks. I had no idea they weren't—"

"Hey, it's fine. They're not going to get in trouble for it." Erin shot her a reassuring smile. "So anyway, yes, we have a birthday cake for Ming. We'll be in Boa Vista tonight, but Dieter's friend isn't expecting us until tomorrow morning, so I suggest we stay onboard until then if you're all okay with that?"

"Sure." Celia frowned and looked up at the bridge as the speakers crackled—usually a sign that an announcement was about to be made.

"Look northeast, people." Eddie's loud voice sounded like a strict command. "That means your front right," he clarified with a chuckle when Andy turned the opposite way. Then he turned off the speakers, finally releasing them from listening to Andy's party playlist that Dieter had been complaining about.

Celia stood up in the jacuzzi, shielded her eyes from the low sun, and listened to a noise in the distance. "What's that?" The tip of an enormous tail disappeared into the water, causing a huge splash. When the creature reappeared, she gasped, and Andy, Dieter and Erin swiftly stood too.

"It's a whale..." Erin followed her gaze and stared at the enormous beast.

"A pod of whales," Dieter corrected her when two more jumped up. "How extraordinary." He let out a long sigh and rubbed his beard. "I'd never imagined I'd see something so..."

"Majestic," Andy said, finishing his sentence. "Wow, just the privilege to see them in the wild." He immediately reached for his phone on the edge of the jacuzzi, but as he held it up, he seemed to change his mind as he put it back down and put his arm around Dieter instead.

Dieter clapped his hands and let out excited cries as the whales came so close that the splashing water reached them. He looked genuinely happy, blissful even, and Celia understood then how important this was to him. To have these magical moments with his closest and dearest.

She put an arm around him and squeezed Andy's hand behind his back as she took in the horizon, straight and pure like a drawn line, shielding the mystery behind it. The sinking sun and its reflection turned everything golden before twilight, its vanishing glow, resulting in a surreal play of light over the water. The smell of the ocean and its movement—rhythmic as if breathing—was soothing, and witnessing the rare sight of whales swimming along with them filled her with wonder. They'd had special times together, but she'd never allowed herself to feel it with every fiber in her being, so determined to remember every second.

Having Erin, her new friend Andy and her uncle by her side while they watched humpback whales escort them through the endless blue, made for such a blissful memory that it moved her to tears. She wanted him to be happy, and this was a moment to embrace with all her senses.

54

"Happy birthday too you…" The terrible off-key singing resulted in laughter after a failed attempt from Celia to harmonize the song. The crew and the guests were gathered around the big table on the deck, drinking mimosas.

"And happy Fourth of July everyone," Andy yelled, holding up his glass in a toast. "You may not see any fireworks on your birthday this year, but that doesn't mean it's going to be any less fun."

"Thanks, guys. This is so lovely of you." Ming blew out the thirty candles on the white chocolate matcha birthday cake that Marcus had made with great care. "My mother actually told me fireworks went off the very moment I was born. I guess that's why I'm so fabulous," she joked, batting her lashes. "Seriously though, having my birthday off and getting to spend it on Boa Vista with my whole crew is a dream come true."

"The shore looks stunning," Celia said, pointing ahead. They were anchored far out, but she could see the very tip of the most eastern island in the distance; the white and green coastline promising white beaches and tropical vegetation.

Despite the circumstances, their trip still felt like an adventure, and one she didn't want to end for two reasons. Firstly, it would be the last time she did something fun with her uncle and secondly, her feelings for Erin were growing stronger every day. By now she was starting to wonder what would lie ahead of them, after they both returned home. Out here, New York seemed like a distant memory, and the only thing reminding her of the life she'd have to return to was her assistant who called her a handful of times a day.

"Yeah. I just checked in with Eddie; we'll be boarding the tender in about forty minutes." Erin put an arm around her and pulled her closer by her waist.

Erin's nearness was delightful and with every touch, she craved her more. Having these big feelings was a little frightening, but due to her current circumstances, she couldn't just go home and take some time to herself, so she decided it was best to just go with it. If she crashed and burned, then at least it had been worth it, and she would always cherish the memories they'd made together. Besides that, she really needed Erin, because the situation wasn't easy. Never had she felt such a jumble of emotions all at once. Although she felt like bursting into tears each time she looked at her uncle, she tried to focus on the good. And the one good thing they had was the here and now.

Erin placed a kiss on her temple and turned to her crew. "You guys can go explore, chill out on the beach or use the tender for snorkeling while we're meeting up with Dieter's friend."

"And my friend Joana knows the best places to celebrate Santa Isabel," Dieter added. "The Fourth of July is a big deal in Cape Verde, so our visit is perfect timing. She recommended we meet up here for dinner and drinks later." He handed Ming a slip of paper with an address on it. "It's on the beach and she told me they have a carnival celebration with live music and dancing so it should be good. That is, if you want to celebrate your birthday with a bunch of old farts."

"Hey, speak for yourself," Andy said, nudging him. "There are no old farts here apart from you."

Ming laughed. "I would absolutely love that. It's always best to go on locals' recommendations and music and dancing are my favorite things in the world." She shot Dieter a wink. "And you're no old fart. You seem very chipper and I'm sure you have many good years ahead of you."

Celia froze at the comment, and it happened every time she was reminded of her uncle's terminal cancer. It wasn't Ming's fault; she didn't know, and as far as Celia was aware, none of the other crew members apart from Eddie knew either. Yesterday, there had been moments when she'd been able to switch off those thoughts, and she tried once again to push them to the background as a sudden silence followed. Andy and Erin shot awkward glances at Dieter, but he burst out in laughter, easing the uncomfortable moment.

"Live for today, is my motto." He took a bite of the cake, his eyes widening in surprise as he turned to Marcus. "Well I must say, my dear man; I never thought I'd enjoy cake made of green tea powder, but this is pretty damn good."

"It's great," Andy agreed. "So, the big 3-0, huh?" He shot Ming a grin. "Let me guess. Are your parents pressuring you to get married?"

"Of course they are." Ming laughed it off. "Chinese parents are the worst; I don't think I'll ever hear the end of it. My mother has a candidate lined up for me every time I come home but they're all so boring..." She shrugged. "It's not easy to meet someone when you're always at sea but I'll take this life anytime over a life in suburbia."

Celia caught another subtle glance between Ming and Marcus. He'd clearly put a lot of effort into the cake, and with white chocolate dripping down the side, white tempered chocolate flowers and green macarons on top, it really was a work of art.

"Well, I for one, am very glad that you're still up for long-haul, and I'll have you onboard for as long as you can stand me." Erin patted Ming's shoulder. "Seriously, I hope you know how much I appreciate you." She raised her glass with a smile. "Here's to Ming!"

55

B oa Vista felt like a secret, Erin thought. They'd been driving over the moonlike volcanic landscape that covered most of the island in a 4x4 and were now heading for Sal Rei to partake in the Santa Isabel celebrations. Dieter was sitting next to Joana in the passenger's seat and Erin, Andy and Celia were in the back of the open vehicle that bounced over the bumpy roads.

Stretches of golden sand lay out to either side of them, only broken up by barren rock-filled vistas, date trees and abandoned villages. Unlike the lush seashore, Boa Vista's inland terrain was earthy and dry. It was equally beautiful though; untouched and quiet. In the two hours they'd been shown around, they hadn't seen a single tourist.

Dieter and Joana had been delighted to be reunited again and Joana was eager to show them around. Beeping the horn and waving animatedly, she greeted every single person they passed with an enthusiasm Erin had rarely witnessed, and she'd immediately warmed to the woman. Being an interna-tionally celebrated artist, Erin imagined Joana was a figure of high standing on the island and her looks were equally impressive. Long dreads with bright green fabric woven through, formed a huge doughnut on the top of her head and she was wearing a matching green flamenco-style dress. Her perfectly manicured hands were covered in traces of gray clay that carried up both her arms, and Erin suspected she'd been sculpting before she came to pick them up.

"Santa Isabel is the patron of Boa Vista, so it will be a lot busier here this afternoon as the festival attracts people from all the other islands." Joana nearly drove into the roadside as she looked over her shoulder while talking to them. Luckily, there was very little traffic as her driving skills were beyond poor. She quickly corrected the car and laughed as she concentrated on the road again. "Forgive me, I only just got my license. I sold a couple of my pieces to a private dealer, so I thought it was about time I treated myself to a nice car. At fifty-eight," she added with a grin.

"Don't worry, you're doing fine," Erin lied. She shot Joana a smile through the rearview mirror and clung onto Celia when they made a sudden, sharp turn onto a cobbled road that led into town. Celia looked beautiful in casual white palazzo pants, a white tank top and her dark hair blowing in the wind. The sadness in her eyes had lifted a little after seeing Dieter and Joana joking around together like they'd never been apart, and the carefree banter had done Erin good too.

"I saw your yacht in the distance," Joana said. "It's very impressive, but I have to warn you; there is no luxury on Boa Vista, so don't expect fancy restaurants and champagne. There is one four-star hotel on the island, but it's..." She shrugged, turning around once more. "Well, it's boring, let's just leave it at that."

Erin shook her head and chuckled. "I can't see any of Dieter's friends doing boring."

"Exactly." Joana patted Dieter's leg. "No one is rich here. Well, apart from me right now, since I sold those pieces last week," she joked. "But everyone is happy, and we celebrate life every day."

With only a handful of restaurants and the stores being more like open markets, the town was clearly not built for tourism and that made it all the more charming. Red, green and yellow one-story buildings and chunky palm trees lined the main street, where the locals had come together to enjoy food and drinks sold from the pop-up street carts.

"Here will do." Joana parked off the main square. A big stage had been set up there and the singer of the band who was doing his soundcheck yelled something at Joana in Creole as she got out.

"He's asking me who I picked up this time," she said, before yelling back at him. "I'm the only one here who gets visitors from outside Cabo Verde from time to time. Having outsiders here is quite the happening and at least ten people have insisted we should come to their neighborhood street party tonight."

"That's so nice," Celia said, waving at the singer.

"Yes, they're all are very welcoming." Joana moved a couple of pins in her hair, adjusting the enormous do. "But tonight, I thought it would be fun to have dinner and drinks at my local beach place as they have the best music and amazing caipirinha cocktails."

As she immersed herself in the crowds, pushing Dieter's wheelchair, Erin felt the pull of the music. Live musicians were playing and singing on every corner, reacting to each other as if it was some kind of play-off. A woman with a speaker on a wheelie cart shouted something through her microphone and the crowd cheered. Suddenly, every musician started playing the same song and children, parents and teenagers, as well as the elderly, filled the streets, moving as one to the rhythmic drumbeat.

Soon enough, Erin and Celia were pulled into the group to join in with the coordinated mass dance. Andy and Joana joined in too, with Joana showing them the steps, jumps and turns, and even Dieter got up from his wheelchair, unable to resist joining in with the fun.

"That was great," Celia said as they sat down on a brick wall to catch their breath, many songs later. She had her shoes in one hand and a plastic cup containing a cocktail someone had poured for her in the other.

"In Cabo Verde, music is woven into every aspect of life," Joana said, equally out of breath. "If you haven't danced, you haven't lived." She paused for a moment as a boy with a whistle directed the crowd to open up when twelve female drummers took center stage in the middle of the street, fanning out in a semi-circle. "Ah. They're doing batuko."

"Batuko?" Erin repeated, observing the female dancers who joined the musicians in the semi-circle. They were barefoot, dressed in short, frilly skirts and colorful T-shirts, and they all had the same white scarf tied around their hips that accentuated their movements.

"It's a form of dancing that follows complex drum patterns, also known as the original forbidden dance," Joana explained. "It was banned by the Portuguese colonialists, but the slaves kept the tradition alive. The drummers are always female and they're able to induce a trancelike state."

The drummers started playing and a call and response

began between the drummers and one of the dancers, who was shaking her hips wildly while yelling through the microphone she was holding. The rhythm was fast and feeling the vibrations from the beating drums, Erin found it hard to keep still. Once she reached the crescendo on their beat, the dancer was replaced by the next, who took the microphone from her and continued the back and forth.

"You've certainly made friends in the most amazing places," Celia said to her uncle, taking a sip of her drink.

"Yes, I've been lucky like that." Dieter shrugged. "I met most of my friends through work. People in the art business often have a significant amount of money and they like to live in special places. So do artists, as they need to feel inspired. And if you can live anywhere, why not move somewhere magical?" He patted Joana's shoulder. "This lady here is an exception, because she already grew up in paradise."

"True," Joana agreed. "I'm proud to be a Cabo Verdean and I'm not ashamed to say I've never left the archipelago."

"You've never left?" Erin's eyes widened in surprise.

"No. When I was younger, I didn't have the money to travel and when I became successful as an artist, the urge to escape simply faded. I think that because I could, I wasn't interested anymore. We always want what we can't have; it's human nature." She put an arm around Dieter. "You know I have this man to thank for my success, right?"

"I didn't know that," Andy said, turning to Dieter.

"Dieter visited Boa Vista around twenty years ago and bought all of my sculptures. After he got back and sold them on, I suddenly got orders from all over the world."

"Uncle Dieter is too modest to brag about something like that," Celia said.

Dieter shook his head. "Nonsense. Joana is very talented; someone would have picked up on that sooner or later. You know that big sculpture in the ballroom? The one with the twelve horizontal female figures, piled on top of each other?"

"Yes, I know which one you mean." Celia turned to Joana. "Is that one of yours?"

Joana nodded. "It's my very first. Do you really still have that, Dieter?"

"Of course. It's part of my precious private collection." He smiled. "I've written you into my will, so you'll get it back one day."

"What?" Joana seemed confused as she studied him. "But that's crazy, it should go to your family or—"

"Absolutely not," Dieter argued. "It was your first sculpture, so I figured it might have sentimental value to you."

"That's very sweet. But I'm positive you'll still be around for a very long time to come." Joana gave him a kiss on his cheek. "So, no talk about death, okay? We're here to celebrate life."

Neither Celia, Andy or Erin commented on it, and they were relieved that the conversation was interrupted by a local coming over to offer them a refill.

56

Tall flames rose up from the bonfire they were gathered around on the beach. The flickering light danced across Celia's face, highlighting her delicate features. Erin had fallen for her hard and deep, and she never wanted this trip to end. She'd sail five times around the world with her, if only circumstances would permit. A wink from Celia made her realize she was staring, and she smiled and tore her eyes away from her, reminding herself they weren't the only two people here. Celia seemed more relaxed today, as if she'd decided to take a break from thinking in general. She'd danced and drank a lot, and now she was talking animatedly, occasionally singing along to the music that blasted through the speakers.

After getting tipsy on caipirinhas, Joana had said her goodbyes and left with a man she sometimes hooked up with. The band had stopped playing but laughter was still coming from the bar, where Ming was partying with the crew and a couple of locals they'd met.

"Who is going to carry Ming back to the tender?" Andy joked, glancing at her. "She just fell over three times." He snickered as Ming held up her glass in a toast, cheered and tripped in the process. "Oops, there she goes again. Good thing it's just sand or she'd be covered in bruises tomorrow."

Erin regarded her, too, and laughed. "It's her birthday and she works incredibly hard, so she deserves a break. I've already told the crew I'll take care of breakfast tomorrow; Marcus looks worse for wear too."

Ming got up as if nothing had happened, yelled that she'd spilled her drink and rang the bell above the bar. "It's my birthday! Drinks on me!" Then she waltzed over to Erin, accompanied by the bartender, who had his arm hooked through hers to steady her.

"Last round on the birthday girl," he said, pointing to Ming. "Would you like another drink?"

"Sure, why not. You guys okay with that?" Erin looked at Dieter specifically, trying to work out if he was fine or just pretending. When he smiled and gave her a thumbs-up, she turned back to the bartender. "It's on me, though. I hope you put everything on my tab?"

"I sure did."

Ming grinned, then flew around Erin's neck. "You're the best boss ever. If I were into women..." She slammed a hand in front of her mouth and chuckled. "Oops. That was inappropriate, wasn't it? Please, please, please forget I said that."

"It's fine, already forgotten." Erin gently nudged her back up and turned to Celia, Andy and Dieter. "Caipirinhas everyone?"

"Caipirinhas coming up," Ming said when they nodded, slurring her words. "Are you guys telling scary stories around the bonfire?"

"We're not, but maybe we should." Dieter shot an amused glance at the bartender, who was helping Ming back to the bar. She'd already zoned out of the conversation and was yelling at Marcus that she wanted to dance with him.

"She's right, I think we should tell scary stories." Andy took Dieter's hand and placed a peck on his cheek. "Why don't you tell us about the hauntings of Krügerner Castle?"

"The castle isn't haunted," Celia said, arching a brow at him. "Come on, Andy. Do you really believe that?"

"Yeah. I do, actually. My car keys went missing a couple of times." Andy placed his hands on his chest. "I'm not a messy person; I know exactly where I leave my stuff. But I swear to God, one minute they were there on the table in the hallway, and the other—"

"Your car keys?" Celia laughed. "You know that's just Uncle Dieter, right?" She glanced at her uncle, who shook his head and subtly hushed her.

"I have no idea what you're talking about," he said.

"Come on, don't deny it. You used to hide people's car keys all the time. I remember one day specifically, when my parents were arguing. We were spending the summer at the castle and they disagreed on something silly and insignificant. I don't even remember what it was, but my mother got really worked up over it. When she was about to drive off, she couldn't find her car keys." Celia paused for dramatic effect before she continued. "I saw you take them. I saw it with my own eyes."

"What?" Dieter studied her, looking for signs of bluff. "That's nonsense."

"No. I was playing hide and seek with one of my cousins and I was hiding behind the drapes in the hallway. I saw you take them and when Mom was looking for them, you blamed it on the castle ghost."

Dieter threw his head back with a roaring laugh and

slammed a hand on his knee. "You really saw that? Why did you never say anything?"

"Because I knew you'd done it for the right reasons. They had no choice but to stay at the castle together as it was too far to walk into town, and you pretended that your own car was in for repairs. Eventually, they talked and made up."

"Wait... are you telling me that..." Andy frowned as he looked from Dieter to Celia and back. "Come to think of it; every time my keys went missing was after we'd had a fight." Rolling his eyes, he gave Dieter a nudge. "And here was me thinking the castle was haunted. God, Diets, you're the worst!"

"I always wondered why no one ever suspected me," Dieter said with a mischievous smile.

"And what about my car keys?" Erin asked. "I remember the keys to my rental went missing the first time I visited you. I didn't know you that well back then; it must have been well over two years ago. I was meeting a client in Zurich, remember? We met up for a drink in town afterward and you offered me a room at the castle." Erin looked mystified as she paused. "But there was no fight. In fact, we've never had a fight."

"That's true." Dieter shrugged. "We didn't have a fight, but I wanted you to stay for another night because Celia was due to arrive the next day."

"What?" Now it was Celia's turn to be stunned. "But Erin and I hadn't even met back then."

"Exactly. I just had this feeling about the two of you." Dieter held out his plastic cup when the bartender came over with a big jug to refill it. "Anyway, it never worked out because Erin was too damn stubborn and adamant that she had to get back home to finalize this project she was working on." He turned his attention back to Erin. "I think you caught a cab and left the rental at the castle for the agency to pick up or something."

"I did. That little stunt you pulled cost me five hundred euros," Erin said incredulously.

"Yes, I should probably pay you back for that." Dieter laughed even harder now.

Celia took a moment to process what he'd just told them and glanced at Erin. "We could have met two years ago. We just missed each other by a day." It was a strange thought.

Erin met her eyes, equally fascinated by the idea. "What do you think would have happened, babe?"

"Exactly the same," Dieter said before Celia had the chance to answer. "There are many roads that lead to Rome and the journey might be different but, in the end, the destination is the same. So, I tried again last year, inviting you both to the summer ball. I was hoping you'd come alone as neither of you were in a serious relationship, but you didn't, and my plan fell to the wayside again." He paused. "I was pleased to see you shared a dance, though. That dance was enough for me to know I was right."

"My God, Diets. You've wasted your talents being an art dealer. You should have gone into matchmaking instead," Andy joked.

"You've been planning this all along..." Celia's voice trailed off as she let his confession sink in.

"Hey, I didn't plan anything. I just wanted you to meet." Dieter held his hands up in defense. "I never made you fall in love; I don't have that power, although it would be pretty great if I did." He hesitated while he glanced at his friends. "Talking about ghosts... Now that I have your full attention, there's something I'd like to discuss."

"Please, no death talk," Andy begged. "We're just having

a fun night and I finally managed not to think about it for all of about..." He glanced at his watch. "Fifty minutes."

"It's nothing serious, Andy. But it is important. I need to know that things will be taken care of after I'm gone."

"What is it?" Celia asked. She felt strong and could handle it tonight. They'd had fun, everyone was in a great mood and the thought of helping her uncle actually lifted her spirits a little.

Dieter shot her a grateful glance. "Today I received an email confirmation with permission to be buried in my own grounds, and I've therefore arranged for work to start on building a mausoleum at the castle tomorrow. I'd like you to arrange for Roderick's remains to be moved there after my funeral. His family have given me their blessing; I've already spoken to them." He shrugged. "If there's any chance I'll still be around in some form or other, I want to be at home. I know this sounds like a strange request, and maybe I am a little crazy; I've had more pills than I can count today, but it's something I feel strongly about."

"No, it's not crazy," Celia said. "I like the idea of you being buried in the castle grounds." She could hardly believe she was going along with it because she didn't believe in ghosts, but tonight, she desperately wanted to believe in something. "Will you give me a sign if you're there?"

Dieter let out a roaring laugh. "I promise, and if I can, I might even scare you a little. You know I've always liked pranks."

57

E ddie, who wasn't much of a drinker and the only fresh-faced person onboard this morning, was sailing them along the tropical shores of the Cape Verde archipelago, passing the islands, each one more beautiful than the next.

"Thanks for your help, babe." Erin put the jug of fresh orange juice on the table and sat down next to Dieter.

"No problem, I like making breakfast with you." Celia held out the tray with cappuccinos so everyone could help themselves to one, then joined them. "And I think we did a pretty good job."

"I like making breakfast with you," Andy repeated in a squeaky, teasing tone while he glanced at Celia and Erin. "Would you like to swap seats? I feel like you guys won't be able to handle sitting apart."

"Ha ha, very funny." Celia rolled her eyes at him. Since their visit to Boa Vista, the mood had lifted and somehow, they'd been able to set aside their sadness. It was nice to be in each other's company without secrets. Today, she realized, she wasn't pretending. Seeing her uncle happy made it easier, and she was glad that he was attacking the croissants after having had little appetite for a couple of days. "Anyone got aspirin?" she asked. "My head hurts from the rum."

"No kidding; mine too." Andy produced a strip of pills from his man bag, took two out and passed them to Celia. "I can't imagine how Ming is feeling. She was—"

"Ming is feeling awful," Ming interrupted him as she appeared in the doorway, rubbing her temple. She was dressed in her uniform, but her hair was a mess and she had dark circles under her eyes. Glancing at the breakfast display, she shook her head in dismay. "Oh my God, is the rest of the crew still sleeping too? I'm so embarrassed; I know I had coffee duty." She turned to Erin. "Do we still have a job?"

"Of course, silly. I told everyone, including you, to stay in bed today. Don't you remember?"

Ming winced. "I don't remember much after my fourth cocktail I'm afraid, but I did have an amazing night."

Erin chuckled and pointed to a free chair. "Glad you enjoyed your birthday. Here, come and join us for breakfast. You need some carbs to soak up the alcohol. After all, you're not in your twenties anymore."

"Thank you, but I can't do that. I've managed to stay professional for ten years and I'm not going to break that rule now."

"Nonsense, this is not a normal sailing trip," Dieter protested. "In fact, this trip is about as unique as it gets, so sit your cute little ass down and enjoy the food."

Ming hesitated but eventually sat down and let Erin plate breakfast for her. "What's so special about this trip?" she asked Dieter, then shook her head. "I mean, it's special, I get that. We've been to amazing places, but the way you said it..."

"It's a pilgrimage." Dieter's tone was chirpy as he buttered his croissant, topped it with strawberry jelly and took a big bite. "A trip dedicated to seeing old friends and making memories with loved ones. On this journey, I'm remembering the best times of my life and it's made me realize how incredibly blessed I've been." He swallowed down the bite before he continued. "And the final stop, of course, will be Erin's wonderful home in Bermuda. Have you been to her home? Erin told me you live in California."

"Yes, I've been to Bermuda a handful of times," Ming said. "Erin sometimes organizes crew parties after a long journey, and I have a good friend who lives there."

"Maybe it's time for another crew party again." Dieter cringed as he turned to Erin. "I apologize, I shouldn't have said that. I know I've been terribly demanding already."

Erin chuckled as she helped herself to scrambled eggs. "Hey, I know you like a party and I think it's a great idea to finish this fabulous trip with a barbecue. And speaking of holding a barbecue, Eddie wants to anchor at São Vicente later today. He's hoping to catch a barracuda before we head into the great blue, so it would be the perfect opportunity for us to do some snorkeling if you'd like? That includes the crew too, of course," she added, turning back to Ming. "We have plenty of gear onboard."

"That sounds fun, I'll let them know." Ming closed her eyes and moaned as she took a bite of her buttered toast with scrambled eggs. "Mmm... these are tasty but Marcus makes the most delicious eggs. Yours are seasoned nicely but not nearly as good," she joked.

"Not nearly?" Erin's eyes widened. "Hey, I put blood, sweat and tears into those eggs so I think I deserve a little more credit than 'my eggs are not nearly as good'." She laughed when Ming refused to give in. "I even added some of those green sprigs he grows. The ones that look like grass."

"You mean chives?" Celia asked, fishing a stem out of her eggs that was about as long as her index finger. "I think you're supposed to chop them finely before you throw them in, but kudos for trying." She tore it up and sprinkled it back over her plate. "I did offer to help, but Erin didn't know how to work the oven, so I had to take care of the toast and pastries," she explained with a humorous smile.

Dieter laughed. "Well, I wouldn't have been of much help either, I'm afraid. It's been years since I've even set foot in my own kitchen."

"Me either," Andy chipped in. "But I'm an expert when it comes to eating."

58

"Are you ready, babe?"

"Not sure." Celia tightened her hold on Erin's hand as she looked into the water from the edge of the tender. The big flippers felt impossible to maneuver and her snorkeling mask was already fogging up. "We're really far from the island and there seems to be so much going on down there." She pursed her lips at the constant movement below her, unsure if the movement came from fish or coral.

Erin laughed. "That's the point. The coral reefs are beautiful here, but I get that it's daunting. You'll feel better when you're in, though. Once you can see what's going on around you, you won't be so nervous."

Celia wasn't convinced as she glanced at her. "Promise me I won't get killed by a shark?"

"I promise. It's not deep enough for sharks here." Erin gave her an endearing smile and joined her on the edge. "Just hold my hand and squeeze it any time you change your mind. I'll make sure you'll be back in the tender in no time." She pointed to Marcus and Ming, whose snorkels were sticking out of the water in the distance. "See? They're fine and they've been in the water for at least twenty minutes."

"Okay, you're right. Let's go." Celia took a couple of deep breaths, annoyed with herself for being afraid. For some reason, she'd become hesitant of taking risks and trying new things, but her journey on *The Barracuda* had made her feel braver, and it was about time that she acted on it. Nodding briefly, she let Erin know she was ready to jump in.

The water felt refreshing as she immersed herself, and knowing Erin was by her side calmed her. She adjusted her mask and breathed out through the tube as instructed, then lowered her face into the water.

Nothing could have prepared her for the tropical wonderland below her, and just like Erin had predicted, her nerves were gone. It wasn't as deep as she'd expected, and the reefs were easy to maneuver through, now that she could see clearly. Everything was breathtaking, from the flowing bright orange, red and yellow coral to the variety of tropical fish that were huge and colorful. They swam around them calmly, some of the smaller ones nipping at her legs and the bigger ones curiously checking them out from behind the coral. It was a different world, and one she wished she'd discovered sooner.

Celia held her breath when a turtle the size of a dinner plate swam past them and she looked at Erin, excited to share this moment with her. She'd never seen one in the wild, and she certainly hadn't expected to be so lucky to see one now. It was elegant in its movements, effortlessly gliding through the water, circling them once before it picked up pace and disappeared into the distance.

Erin turned to check if she was okay and entirely at ease now, Celia let go of her hand and gave her a thumbs up, letting Erin know she'd follow her. Feeling weightless and peaceful, she took her time and tried not to get too distracted by Erin's bikini clad body in front of her.

The variety of colors and sea life swimming around them was mesmerizing. Seagrass meadows moved with the tide in slow-motion, opening up in places to give her a glimpse of huge purple starfish, orange crabs with intricate patterns on their backs, and even seahorses. Clown fish and shrimp shot out from between the coral in quick, sudden movements and random directions. There was so much to see that she kept stalling and drifting to take everything in.

Time was a blur down there, and Celia emptied her mind as she glided through the reefs, tapping Erin's arm now and then to attend her of something in the magnificent seabed. After a while they took off their snorkels and dove down holding their breath instead, so they could explore deeper, until the sound of loud cheering drew them to the surface. Eddie was standing in the tender next to Ming and Marcus, holding up a silver fish that was at least four feet long. In the far distance, Dieter was clapping from the deck of *The Barracuda* while Andy took pictures.

"That's a bad boy you've caught there." Erin climbed back in the tender and helped Celia in. "A torpedo of muscle and teeth, but so are you, Eddie," she joked, pinching his bicep.

"He's so brave." Ming sat down on the other end, clearly uncomfortable being so near to the giant fish with shark-like eyes and razor-sharp teeth, even though it was dead now.

"I agree," Celia said, moving away from it too. "If I'd seen one down there, I think I would have panicked."

"You wouldn't have seen one." Erin started the engine to take them back to the yacht. "Just like sharks, they live much deeper, but Eddie can hold his breath for almost two minutes. No diving gear, nothing. Just a spear and sheer determination."

Eddie was beaming with pride as he posed for pictures, holding the fish in his arms like a newborn. He turned to Marcus, who was also staring at the fish, no doubt wondering how on earth to prepare something he'd never seen before. "Don't worry, I'll clean it for you."

"Thank goodness." Marcus let out a sigh of relief. "I'm all for a challenge but I've never fileted anything as big as that. I'll make some salads though, and anything you'd like to go with it."

"Great." Erin smiled as she steered the tender toward the yacht. "Then I'll get the barbecue going."

59

Blinking against the sun, Celia sat up and looked around, instinctively searching for land as she always did, but there was nothing in sight. She figured she must have been sleeping for hours, making up for the long nights in bed with Erin, as the sun was much lower now. The lounge chair was incredibly comfortable, like a bed, and warmed by the heat of the sun and the soothing breeze, it was pure heaven up here on the upper deck. There wasn't a cloud in the sky either and she sighed at the striking view that was so powerful in its simplicity. Ocean, sky, sun. Blue water and blue sky, that was all. The only evidence of the horizon was a large cargo ship in the distance.

Below, she heard Dieter and Andy bicker over a game of Scrabble, and it made her chuckle, knowing her uncle was most certainly cheating. It wasn't because he was a poor loser; he just loved to prank people, and he'd always done this, even when she'd played it with him as a kid. Whenever she'd questioned a word, he'd been so convincing that she'd fallen for it every time without fail. She knew better now, and so did Andy, apparently.

"'Daverick' is not a word, Diets," she heard him say. "You think you can fool me but you're not in the eighties anymore. I've just checked the dictionary on my phone and 'daverick' is not in it."

"There must be a mistake," her uncle replied in an amused tone. "Have you never heard of the expression 'dancing like a daverick'? Everyone uses it."

"Don't fall for it, he's cheating!" Celia yelled, loud enough for Andy to hear. The comment resulted in laughter, and she shook her head with a smile. Twirling the silver chain of her necklace Erin had given her around her finger, someone blocked her sun.

"What's on your mind?" Erin put down the tanning oil she was holding and joined her on the wide lounge chair in a crop top and a pair of shorts.

Celia scooted over and turned, so she could rest her cheek on Erin's chest. "Blue," she whispered. "You asked me about my favorite color a while back but I don't think I ever gave you my answer. I think it's blue. It seems like a sad color, but there's also peacefulness and calm to it. Something endless, infinite like the ocean."

"I like that," Erin said, pulling her closer. "Are you okay?"

"Yes. I think so. It's good to hear him laugh." Celia looked up and smiled at Erin while she ran a hand over her abs. "It feels weird to be drifting in nothingness. Don't you think?"

"It may feel like we're drifting, but we're actually going about twenty-five knots." Erin kissed her forehead, and Celia let out a deep sigh of contentment. "No panic yet?"

"No, I'm fine. It helps that you're here, of course. You make me feel safe." Celia's eyes darted to Erin's wrist and she noticed she was still wearing the watch she'd given her, rather than her gold Rolex. "At first, it seemed like a ridiculous idea. Then, once we'd boarded, I felt free and alive and happier than ever. And when I learned about my uncle being terminally ill, well, I guess I wished I could escape." She paused. "But now it makes more sense than anything." Unsure if her comment was too much, she averted her gaze, but Erin lifted her chin to meet her eyes.

"I'm so glad you said that, because it makes a lot of sense to me too." There was tenderness in Erin's eyes, and the sweet caress of her hand on her cheek brought a lump to Celia's throat. "I've never been so head over heels about anyone, Celia." Reaching around her, she pulled at the string of Celia's bikini top, releasing it. "And you're simply irresistible in that little bikini," she joked, lightening the mood. "Are you wearing that just to tease me?"

"Yes, Captain." Celia giggled and slapped Erin's hand away when she reached for her breast. "Don't. My uncle and Andy are down there."

"They're too busy arguing," Erin said, painting on a cheeky smile. "Your uncle just claimed that 'starling' is a type of cigar, and that a 'bentinck' is a part of a car engine."

"I know, I can hear him cheating." Celia chuckled and stopped resisting when Erin's hand sneaked back. She shivered as her thumb skimmed her nipple and let out a quiet moan.

"I give up," they heard Andy say. "Come on, let's go take a nap in our room. At least you won't be able to cheat me out of sleeping."

Erin's brow shot up at that. She picked up the tanning oil and dangled it in front of Celia. "I think you need some more factor thirty, just to be on the safe side."

"I think you're right. I think my ass got sunburned," Celia said, playing along as she turned onto her front. Her core tightened when Erin squirted some oil into the palm of her hand and gestured for her to turn around.

"Then your ass will get extra attention." Erin's hands started massaging in the oil, working Celia's behind like a pro. "But let's not forget the rest. It is after all, best to cover every inch of skin under this unforgiving cloudless sky." Slowly, her fingers moved to the inside of Celia's thighs, slipping up and then back down just before she reached her center. "Oh my, you're burning here too."

Celia gasped as Erin hooked a finger under the edge of her bikini bottoms. She was most certainly burning but it wasn't from the sun. Teasing her, Erin pulled back and started working her shoulders instead, chuckling at the groan that escaped her lips.

"If your plan was to drive me wild with lust, you've succeeded," Celia murmured into the mattress.

"Good. because I plan to drive you even wilder," Erin whispered in her ear. She nibbled at her earlobe and tugged at it, then moved her mouth to Celia's neck, dragging her tongue down to her shoulder. "And I plan to take my time."

"Maybe you should hurry up instead," Celia retorted with a hint of humor, wiggling her hips when Erin straddled her. Erin's weight felt incredible and she was so aroused that every nerve in her body was tingling with anticipation. "Aren't you supposed to be on the bridge?"

"I don't see any traffic. Do you?"

Celia chuckled "No... is it safe, though?"

"I'm only joking; I asked Donald to keep an eye out for an hour." Erin traced Celia's back up and down. "I was going to ask you to come up to the bridge earlier, but then I envisioned you lying up here in a bikini and I was all worried that you might get a sunburn." She wedged her hands underneath Celia's chest to massage her breasts while she kissed her shoulders and her neck.

"Sure you were." Celia's eyes fluttered closed at the delicious sensation of her hands and mouth all over her. "Well, you'd better get started if you only have an hour."

60

"How's work? Do you have a lot to catch up on?" Erin joined Celia at the table where she was sitting behind her laptop after spending the morning playing Scrabble with her uncle.

"It's fine, actually." Celia shrugged. "It seems like Anna can handle it fine without me as I haven't had to step in once. I'm starting to wonder if she needs me at all anymore."

"Then you're lucky to have her."

"I know. I should probably give her a big raise. Just the fact that I've been able to let go of work to spend time with Uncle Dieter is priceless. But you've been quite busy, right?"

"Yeah, it's quite hectic at the moment; we've just secured a commission for a huge hybrid." Erin sat back and ran a hand through her hair. "But it's nice that I can work while I'm on the bridge. That's the upside of being at open sea, I don't need to concentrate as much, so I can multitask."

"Who's the commission for?"

"It's for an Indian prince." Erin grinned. "Big money but also big expectations so I've already started drafting up the first designs. It's hard because I need to build in space for the security detail as well as the staff, and they want a helipad on the top deck too. So far, it's going great though; I can't wait to discuss the plans with his team."

"Jesus…" Celia noticed the twinkle in Erin's eyes as she talked, and she was impressed by how unfazed Erin seemed by such a big project.

"Aren't you nervous working on that?"

"I've had a couple of consults with his wife and first assistant to give me a good idea of their tastes. They have five children under the age of nineteen, so the yacht also has to accommodate plenty of space for family entertainment. I'm building in platforms on the upper deck to house Jet Skis, wakeboards and hoverboards, and of course there will be the basic recreational spaces like a gym, a spa, a pool and a beach club-like bar area, designed to integrate the internal and external living areas."

"Basics, huh?" Celia whistled through her teeth.

"Yes." Erin laughed. "We might consider ourselves to be wealthy, but when people's worth goes into billions, their demands can be eye-wateringly extravagant." She pulled a couple of small swatches from her pocket and put them on the table. "I've been carrying these around with me for the past two days; it enables me to visualize the interior. Cream gloss-coated sustainable pufferfish skin, reclaimed pitch pine, cream carpets, camel colored suede, burnt orange and royal blue fabrics, and duck egg blue high gloss accents that will look fresh in the natural light channeled throughout."

"Pufferfish skin?" Celia ran her finger over the swatch. "I've never heard of that."

Erin shrugged. "That's the point. It's unique and a way of giving them something beautiful that no one else has. Pufferfish are eaten and the skin is disposed of, so it's also a creative way of lifting waste to a luxury material."

"Clever. It must be nice to do something you're passionate about. You get so excited when you talk about design and materials."

"Of course. I love what I do and feeling inspired every day is important to me."

Celia felt Erin's eyes burning into her and she knew exactly what she was thinking. "You must find it strange that I do something so random for a living. And you're right to think that. I like running my company, but I don't love it; it just pays the bills." She paused. "I've never found something I'm truly passionate about."

"But you love art," Erin said. "Dieter told me you've accompanied him on many of his trips, and that you used to visit museums and exhibitions together when you were in Switzerland over your summer vacations."

"That's true. I do love art, but I don't have the eye for spotting new talent I'd need to make it my living. It's something I always wanted to do when I was younger, but I guess I've come to the conclusion that it's not for me."

"Dieter seems to disagree with that," Erin said. "He told me you'd make an excellent successor."

"He said that? That sounds a little daunting; I don't think I'd dare step into his shoes." Celia frowned, wondering why her uncle was so adamant she should continue running his business. Sure, she had some intuition and she'd studied art history, but they often disagreed on what they liked, and she couldn't even begin to understand some of the things he'd purchased over the years. Her preferences were more classical, safer perhaps. "I had no idea..."

"I think he wanted to leave you with the option after his death, so you wouldn't feel pressured into doing anything you didn't want to do. That's why he hasn't discussed it with you."

"Hmm…" Celia needed time to process that, as even considering taking over his business was something that would turn her whole life upside down. "I don't know what to say to that."

"You don't need to say anything. I just thought you should know." Erin hesitated. "There's actually something I wanted to ask you."

"What is it?"

"Well, I'll need art for my new project. Would that be something you'd be interested in helping me with? Their budget is huge, and they seem quite easy going so far."

"Me?" Celia narrowed her eyes. "I'm not sure if I'd be able to do that."

"It's low risk," Erin argued. "They want expensive decorative items, not investment pieces. Just paintings and sculptures that will look good with the yacht's interior. I usually hire consultants for that. Dieter has helped me a couple of times too, but his taste can be a little eclectic and his selections aren't always the best choice for a conservative customer." She gave Celia a reassuring smile. "No pressure. Have a think about it, there's no rush. If you don't want to do it, there will be plenty other people out there who can help me."

Celia nodded slowly as a whole new world of possibilities started opening up to her. She felt a flutter of excitement at the idea, but she'd never done anything like it before, and really wanted to talk to her uncle about this first. "Where is Uncle Dieter?" she asked, noting she hadn't seen him around in the past couple of hours.

"He's in his room with Andy. He wasn't feeling too well."

Celia's expression turned serious as she leaned back, crossed her arms and looked at Erin pensively. "He's getting worse, isn't he?"

"I think so," Erin said. "He wants to rest so he'll be able to enjoy Bermuda."

"I know." Celia pursed her lips. "Do you think that's a good idea? Him staying in Bermuda for a week? How are the hospitals there in case he deteriorates rapidly? It's possible..." She paused. "I feel like he might be better off flying straight back to Switzerland, with the healthcare there being top-notch and all...."

"He doesn't want to spend his last weeks in a hospital bed." Erin said. "That's why he didn't want any more treatment in the first place. Dieter wants to do exactly this, what he's doing right now, and although it's hard to see him decline, we have to respect that."

"You're right; I need to change my mindset. It's just so hard..." Celia felt despair return and sensing she was struggling, Erin got up, put her arms around her from behind and kissed her temple.

"It's hard now, and it's going to be a lot harder. But I'm here for you, okay?" Erin took a tighter hold of her. "I'm right here, and I'm not going anywhere."

"Thank you." Closing her eyes and leaning into her touch, Celia relaxed a little. "What are we going to do?" she whispered. "After all this..."

"We'll figure something out." Erin's voice was soothing, and Celia believed her. "I want to make you happy."

61

───────

"That doesn't look good." Erin narrowed her eyes as she looked at the sky through the binoculars, then handed them back to Eddie. In the distance, rain was falling from dark, low hanging clouds, blurring the horizon. The weather forecast had been good for this week, and the unexpected eerie view worried her. She was glad Eddie was in command. Building yachts was her specialty, not sailing them, and although she had years of experience with long-distance journeys, she'd never been in an emergency situation before.

"No, it doesn't look good," Eddie agreed. "I'm classing this as heavy weather and I'll warn the crew. Donald is already aware; he's making the necessary preparations."

Erin nodded. "Can we try to sail around it?"

"I don't think so, it's moving in too fast. There has been no tornado or storm warning but as you know, it's possible for a mild storm to spontaneously manifest over open water." Eddie pressed a button and leaned in to speak through the radio that was connected to his crew members' headset.

"Attention to all crew. Heavy weather moving in. Clear decks immediately. I repeat, clear decks immediately."

"Copy that," Ming answered. "I'll bring everyone inside." There was a creaking noise as Ming contacted her team over the same system. "Josh, heavy weather warning. Batten down all hatches immediately."

"Copy that," Josh said.

"Desirée, Ming here. Please close the bar and store away all loose objects from the decks, then come help me inside ASAP."

"Copy that." Desirée paused. "How long do we have?"

Erin looked at Eddie, who took a moment before he answered. "Ten minutes. I want everything cleared within ten minutes." She was thoroughly impressed by how calm everyone stayed. Although she knew the protocol and was trained for heavy weather warnings, she wasn't sure if she'd have been as efficient and prepared herself. There were no further questions, just another order from Ming.

"Marcus, Louise, heavy weather warning. Shut down and clear the galley."

"Copy that. Already on it," Marcus, who had been listening in, said.

"What do you need from me?" Erin asked Eddie, who was now adjusting their speed and taking necessary precautions to prepare the yacht for heavy winds.

"It would be great if you could help the crew downstairs and check if Donald's got everything under control before you come back up here."

"You got it." Erin rushed downstairs where Celia, Andy and Dieter had already been ushered inside. Celia was helping Ming close all cabinets and store away loose objects such as vases and decorative items. Outside, she could see the wind had already picked up by the way Desirée's strawberry blonde hair was blowing wildly around her face as she locked the lower deck's storage space where she'd put the lounge chairs, cushions and anything else that had been lying around outside. As soon as Desirée was back inside, Erin pressed the button to close the main hatch that covered the glass doors. It was made of thick shatterproof glass, allowing them to still see outside, and it was strange how it suddenly eliminated all the noise from the wind.

"It's so quiet suddenly," Andy said in a whisper. "Do we need life vests or something?"

"No, not until we go into code red, which is highly unlikely. But I can get you one if it makes you feel safer." Erin gave him a reassuring smile and continued when Andy shook his head. "Don't be afraid. It's not a serious storm but it will get rough." She noticed Dieter, who was sitting back on the couch, didn't seem phased, and neither did Celia. She was working fast and methodical, now securing the chairs to the dining table with large cable ties that Ming had given her. "From now on, no more glassware. Only plastic cups and plates. You can stay here, or you can go to your rooms. The swaying will be more subtle there."

"I don't think I want to be under the water level during a storm," Andy said in a squeaky voice.

"Then let's stay here. Play a game of Scrabble," Dieter suggested. "It will take your mind off things. From the look on your face, I take it reenacting *Titanic* is not on your wish-list anymore," he added in a humorous tone.

"No, I've changed my mind about that. And since you're a cheater, playing Scrabble isn't either." Andy let out a dramatic sigh. "But I suppose some distraction wouldn't hurt, so I'll get the board out."

Erin couldn't help but laugh at their exchange. "Just make sure not to move around too much. I don't want anyone to fall and hurt them—" She stopped herself mid-sentence when a wave hit them, making the yacht sway. Andy lost his balance and tumbled over, only just catching himself on Celia, who was bent over on the floor, aligning the chair leg with the table.

"Are you okay, Andy?" she asked.

"Physically, yes," Andy said, now with more panic ringing through his voice. "But if it gets any worse than this, I'm not sure if my fragile nerves will survive."

Erin glanced outside and noted that the dark skies hadn't even reached them yet. "As I said, we're going to be fine. It's not a heavy storm and *The Barracuda* is big and built to withstand bad weather. Ming, will you get them some buckets?"

"Buckets? Will we be scooping water?" Andy's eyes widened.

"No. You'll need the buckets in case you're sick. There are plenty of bathrooms onboard, but you might not get there on time. I suggest you take one of those sea sickness pills I gave you in case of emergency." Erin gave them an apologetic shrug. "I'm sorry. No bad weather was predicted, but this happens sometimes. As I said, be careful not to move around too much. I'll join you guys once the weather's calmed down."

"Where are you going?" Celia pulled the last cable tie and walked over to her, holding her arms out to balance herself.

"I'll be with Eddie on the bridge." Erin took her face in her hands and kissed her. "It's going to be okay; I promise."

"I know." Celia gave her a smile and ran a hand through her hair. "I'll see you on the other side. Let me know if there's anything else I can do to help."

62

"How are we doing?" A frown appeared between Erin's brows as she looked around the lounge area. "Oh, boy." Andy was sitting perched on the couch, hunched over a bucket and Celia was next to him, holding a bottle of water and a paper bag. The Scrabble board and its tiles were scattered across the floor next to a vomit stain on the carpet which she suspected was Andy's, but other than that everything was still in place. She rushed over to them and gave Celia a kiss on the top of her head while she stroked her hair. "Are you okay, babe?"

"I've been better; not sure if I can move yet," Celia joked, blinking her bloodshot eyes as she closed the bag and moved it away from them. "To be honest with you, I've never felt so sick in my life." She pointed to Andy, who had his eyes closed. "Dieter took a sleeping pill and went to bed, but Andy was afraid to be under water level, so I stayed up here with him."

"Let me get you some fresh air, that might help." Erin pressed the button to lift the main hatch just as Josh came in to open the other hatches. She closed her eyes and took a deep breath, feeling nauseous herself. It had been rough, and she'd been a little worried, but after four hours, they were finally in calmer waters. The heavy rain had turned into a drizzle and the low sun was poking its way through the clouds.

"You okay, boss?" Josh asked.

"I'm good. You?"

Josh shot her a grin. "Desirée locked herself in the toilet three hours ago and hasn't come out since, but the rest of the crew is fine." He shrugged. "This wasn't our first rodeo."

"I know. You guys did a great job." She held out her hand to help Celia up. "Want to come in the pool with me? I know it's raining a little, but it will help you stabilize."

"I'm willing to try anything at this point." Celia followed her outside with Andy on her heel. It was the first time she'd been in the rain since boarding *The Barracuda* in France, and the lukewarm droplets felt refreshing.

"I'll get us some Cokes. It contains phosphoric acid which helps control vomiting. I must admit; I've felt better myself." Erin waited for Josh to open the bar and grabbed three cans from the fridge.

"Don't you dare be sick in the water," Celia joked, shooting a warning look at Andy. She dropped her kaftan to the deck, lowered herself into the pool and drifted on her back, taking deep breaths in an attempt to get her nausea under control.

"I can't promise you that, so I think I'll just sit here with my bucket for a while." He took the Coke from Erin. "Is it me, or are we still swaying heavily?"

"It will calm down soon." Erin took off her clothes and joined Celia in the pool. "Better?" she asked as she closed the distance between them.

"I think my stomach's settling." Celia wrapped her arms

around Erin and nuzzled her face in her neck as she stood on her tiptoes on the pool floor. "How are you? Were you scared?"

"I'm fine." Erin kissed her temple as she ran a hand up and down Celia's back. "It wasn't as bad as I expected it to be. But I was worried about you, even though you seemed totally fine."

"Normally, I think I would have panicked being at open sea in a storm," Celia said. "But these weeks have been strange and I'm learning to take things as they come, just to get on with it, you know? It is what it is, I suppose, and I'm grateful for every day I get to spend in the company of friends and loved ones."

"That's a beautiful way of looking at it."

Celia smiled against her skin. "I was always afraid to take risks, worried I would fail, and I was afraid to let people in, terrified they might betray me. But looking back, that wasn't really living. My life was just a string of carefully planned events that kept me entertained enough not to get bored but didn't challenge me enough to stay engaged. And that's not what I want anymore."

"It sounds like you've been doing a lot of thinking."

"Yeah. You got me thinking, and then my uncle, of course. You're both very inspiring to me, and being here with you, especially now that times are very difficult, has made me realize that I don't always have to do everything on my own. That it's okay to be vulnerable because you give me strength and comfort."

Erin ran a hand over Celia's cheek as she let her words sink in. "I'm glad I can be here for you. But I need you to know that you're a huge comfort to me too."

"Really?"

"Yes." Erin said. "I think we're good for each other."

63

"You guys go ahead; my housekeeper should be there to welcome you." Erin stood up in the tender and pointed straight ahead. Eddie had dropped Celia, Dieter, Andy and the crew off at the pier in the tender after leaving the yacht at Erin's mooring space in Hamilton. "Take that path, then you'll see signs that say, *'Beautiful Dead End'*. Just follow them."

"Beautiful Dead End?" Celia quirked a brow as she took one of the suitcases.

"Yup. That's my address. Anyway, the crew knows where it is. I think you'll find that the name does itself justice when you get there." Erin blew her a kiss. "I'll be ten minutes."

"Okay, we'll see you there. Thank you so much, Eddie!" As Celia said goodbye to Eddie for the third time, she realized she'd grown close to the team during their time at sea. Even though they hadn't interacted that much apart from when they'd celebrated Ming's birthday, they'd been the first people she'd seen in the morning and the last ones she said goodnight to. Ming and Marcus were walking ahead, side by side. They were still nothing but professional, but she had a feeling that would change the second they were alone.

"Erin told me you've been here before," she said as they followed the steep path that wove between a parking lot and a long bed full of beautiful cacti. It was surreal to walk on steady ground again. Her legs felt weak somehow and wouldn't cooperate right away, resulting in a light sway to the left. When she looked behind her, she saw that Andy and Dieter—who had insisted he didn't need the wheel-chair for the short walk—had the same problem. Her uncle veered to the right and Andy to the left, which resulted in them clashing into each other every few steps.

"Yes, we've been to Erin's house before." Ming took in a deep breath and tilted her head toward the sun. "It's gorgeous here. I wish I didn't have to fly back home tomorrow."

"Are you staying in a hotel tonight?" Celia asked.

"Yes, Erin usually books the airport hotel for me. It's always so anti-climactic after a beautiful trip."

"You can stay with me for a couple of nights," Marcus suggested. "Your ticket is flexible and it's not too late to change it. I'll show you around the island."

Celia smiled at the exchange and shot Andy, who had caught up with them a warning look before he had a chance to comment. "Leave them," she whispered. "They don't want anyone to know."

"What? I didn't say anything." Andy's feigned innocent expression made Dieter laugh as he let Andy help him up the slope.

"It's never about what you say, it's what you're about to say," Dieter shot back at him. He stopped for a moment to catch his breath, then looked up at the small, pastel blue house that was perched on the cliff ahead, quite literally at the tip of the island. "Don't be fooled by the size; it's a very special place."

"I can see it's special." Celia studied the one-story rectangular building that resembled a bunker. It was nothing like she'd expected it to be, and the fact that Erin's yacht was way bigger than her house amused her. Despite the design being ultramodern, the pink bougainvillea growing up against the walls made it look sweet and pretty. The whole ocean-facing wall was made of glass, no doubt giving a spectacular view from inside, and the entrance was on the garden side of the house, where two long, horizontal windows spanned the length of the wall to either side of the door.

'Beautiful Dead End' certainly lived up to its name. In fact, it couldn't have been more fitting. Sun blanched cobble-stone steps led down to a small private beach where a speedboat was docked, the golden sand now only a thin strip as the tide was high. The sound of seagulls filled the air, and on the lawn next to the path, chickens were roaming freely between sleek rattan garden furniture placed around a big firepit.

"Welcome!" A woman opened the door and rushed outside to help them with their luggage. "Dieter, it's good to see you again."

"Likewise, Nene." Dieter patted Andy's shoulder. "This is Andy, my partner."

Nene greeted Andy, then turned to Celia. "And you must be Celia; it's lovely to meet you. I've been told to bring your things to Erin's room." Although it was a statement, it sounded more like a question, and going on the woman's curious expression, Celia had a feeling Erin didn't regularly have women over.

"It's very nice to meet you," she said, shaking Nene's hand. "Yes, I'll be staying with her."

Nene gave her a smile before leading the way through the open living space that had a surprisingly warm vibe to it, considering the minimalist interior. Two sleek white leather couches and a long, wooden coffee table formed a seating area next to a freestanding wood burning stove. On the other end of the space was an all-white modern open kitchen and there was also a reading area in the corner by the glass wall overlooking the ocean, consisting of two cozy off-white chairs, another coffee table and a bookcase. A huge, Aztec inspired carpet covered most of the floor and an abundance of plants in heavy artisanal pots were scattered throughout the space. The modern art on the walls injected a hint of color, tying in with the orange tones in the carpet.

"It's so stylish." Celia lingered in the middle of the space for a moment. The view really was spectacular, and it felt as if the house was at one with the ocean. She wasn't sure why it was such a big deal to be in Erin's home for the first time. Perhaps because she knew there was a good chance that she might be spending more time here in the future.

"Yes, it's a lovely place," Nene agreed. "I could never live so close to the ocean though, not with all the hurricanes we get here." She looked at Celia with interest once more as she let her into the master bedroom. "Forgive me if I'm overstepping but you must be one special lady. Erin never invites over female company."

"We're close, and Erin is very special to me too," Celia said, looking away to hide her blush as she put her suitcase in the corner of the room. The glass doors led out to a terraced patio that overlooked the ocean to the rear of the house, and the room was flooded with natural light and the scent of the sea. Again, the bedroom was simple but cozy. A wooden king-size bed with built-in nightstands stood against the wall opposite the glass doors, spaciously placed between a couch and a row of built-in closets.

This was the home of a designer, for sure. It was so perfectly balanced that it almost felt intimidating, and Celia wondered what Erin would think of her apartment that consisted of boring basic furniture, bought in a hurry without even considering how it would work together. The only things dear to her in her apartment were her various pieces of art, but the walls just didn't do them justice.

"What's that?" she asked, walking over to a narrow spiral staircase in the far corner of the room. It led up to the roof, which made sense as she imagined Erin having a nice seating area up there, but it also spiraled down into a small closed off space, she noticed as she looked over the railing.

"I'll let Erin show you what's down there as I don't have the key," Nene said, then opened the closets. "You can use these; there's plenty of space on the left side for your clothes and there's an en suite bathroom through that door."

"Thank you, that's great." Celia tried to imagine Erin sleeping here, living her life in this beautiful part of the world. Then she imagined them here together, but swiftly told herself to stop dreaming. Their time on *The Barracuda* had been intense in the best and worst of ways and life was still a whirlwind. Even though it felt like she'd been with Erin for a lifetime, the reality was that it had only been three weeks. In her world, in her New York world, that equaled three dates—one each Saturday night. Normally, she would have general conversations and if she liked the woman in question, maybe flirt a little on the first date. She'd sleep with her on the second date and by the third, she'd usually come to the conclusion that it wasn't going to work out.

Within the past three weeks though, she'd gotten to

know Erin inside out. She'd learned about her passions, her dreams, her strengths and her insecurities. She'd seen Erin's caring side, her loyal side, and she'd even seen her with her grandmother. At the same time, she'd opened up and let Erin in too. It was madness how three weeks could make such an impact on a relationship, but it was true. She couldn't imagine a life without her now.

64

"That was fun." Celia closed the bedroom door behind her after Erin's crew members had left. They'd had a barbecue in the front yard with plenty of food, beers, wine and music, and now that the crew wasn't on duty anymore, they'd been fun and free in their interaction, almost as if they'd flipped a switch that turned them into different people entirely. Real people with quirky personalities, surprising talents and strong opinions. Marcus was a great banjo player, Desirée was an amazing singer, and Ming had made them laugh with her arsenal of different accents that she could replicate almost fluently. Josh, Donald and Louise had helped Celia and Erin with the food, insisting Marcus needed a break, and she'd really enjoyed chatting to them in the kitchen.

"Yes, it's good to let off some steam together after a long journey," Erin said. "Most of them live on the island so they're only a short taxi ride home, and I've booked a hotel close to the airport for Louise and Ming, who live in the US." She smiled. "They're good people. I'm very lucky to have them."

"You are. I see why you're so close to them now. Even I felt a little sad saying goodbye." When their eyes met, Celia felt a flash of arousal course through her. Seeing Erin in her own bedroom now, it made perfect sense that she lived here. With her white linen shirt, faded jeans and fresh, no-nonsense appearance, she fitted in seamlessly with the natural feel of the house.

"So, you like my place?"

"I love it," Celia said, giving her a flirty smile. "It's very cool."

"Good. I want you to feel at home if you're planning on being here for a while. Dieter said he'd like to stay for at least two weeks if he feels well enough."

"Whatever Uncle Dieter wants." Celia smiled. "I'll fly back to Switzerland with him and Andy; I don't want to be in New York while he's so ill. Work seems to be under control so thankfully I'll be able to do that…"

"Great. Then make yourself at home." Erin followed Celia's gaze as her eyes flicked to the staircase.

"What's that? Nene was being all mysterious about it and then I got so distracted with the barbecue tonight that I forgot to ask."

"Aha." Erin smiled widely as she put her arms around Celia and pulled her in. "That, right there, is the reason I bought the land." She lowered her hands to Celia's behind and squeezed it.

"The land? Did you build this house?"

"Yes. No one in their right mind would even consider building a house here, with the hurricanes we get, but I'm sure you've noticed it looks pretty sturdy from the outside. The whole ocean-facing glass front has a stormproof shutter that can be lowered, and the windows have the same auto-mated protection system" Erin gestured to the room around them. "Since I'm experienced with building storm breaker yachts, I decided to build a hurricane-resistant house on this very special spot. It's withstood many storms so far, so I'm not even worried about staying at home during a hurricane anymore." She let go of Celia, took a key out of her nightstand, flipped the light switch above the staircase and walked down, holding onto the railing with both hands. "Be careful; it can get a little slippery on the bottom steps."

"You have me seriously curious now. I imagine there's an awesome wine cellar down there, or some James Bond-like secret tunnel that leads to the beach." Celia followed her, holding on tight too. It was steep and deep and a little scary to go so far underground in a narrow space, and she was relieved to finally reach the last step. "Or a sex dungeon," she added with a chuckle.

"I'm sorry to disappoint you but there's no sex dungeon here." Erin flipped another light switch, then unlocked the door that looked more like a vault entrance. "It's very well insulated, otherwise the damp would cause mold to spread in the bedroom." She took Celia's hand and led them toward a metal floating bridge.

The lights in the dark space came on one by one, and Celia could hardly believe what she saw. Beneath them was water so brightly turquoise that it didn't seem real. Industrial spotlights lit the water from underneath, exposing an other-worldly wonderland of stalagmites in white, orange and every shade in between. The cave's ceiling was covered in low-hanging stalactites, the icicle-shaped mineral formations shimmering in the light. It looked like a fantasy world so perfect that it was hard to imagine this had been created by nature. "What is this?" she whispered.

"It's a hidden cave."

"Incredible..." Celia kneeled down to run her hand

through the water. "It's surprisingly warm, considering it's so chilly in here."

"Yeah. I was surprised about that too when I first came down here. It's the Atlantic, of course, so it makes sense that it's more or less the same temperature."

"Do you swim here?" Celia found herself whispering as their surroundings were so spiritual in their natural beauty that it didn't feel right to make noise, but even her low voice echoed off the walls.

"Yes, I swim here sometimes." Erin pointed to the steps at the end of the walkway. "Your uncle loved it when he last visited, but other than him, I've only brought my parents here. There are other bigger caves in Bermuda, way more impressive than this one. Those were formed during the Ice Age and are off-limits for swimming. This one isn't as old and since it's generally just me here and I'm very careful, I'm not disturbing the ecosystem. I know it doesn't look like it, but the water is actually forty feet deep."

"Wow..." Celia's gaze turned to the cave walls, where alien shapes had formed among the wax-like drips. "You have your own cave. That's seriously impressive."

Erin beamed with pride as she pulled Celia along to the end of the bridge. "Yes, I have my own cave. Sometimes it's hard to grasp. It's not always as serene as today; I've given permission to a team of scientists to do research here for three months of the year, so when they're here, it feels more like a lab. They're not coming back until October though, so we have it all to ourselves." She winked. "Do you want to go for a swim?"

"I do." Celia watched Erin undress and she followed suit, stripping off her navy and white polka dot summer dress. It felt completely surreal to be naked in a cave with Erin, but then again, the past three weeks had been nothing but surreal.

Erin's eyes raked over her and she looked at Erin in return. The water reflecting off her skin made her look ghostly, but her touch was nothing but real and Celia shivered as her hand traced her hips and her waist.

"I've dreamed of having you here, you know?" Erin whispered. "But I never imagined it would actually happen."

"Well, I'm here and there's nowhere I'd rather be." Celia moaned softly at the sensation of Erin's warm skin as their bodies came together, and she closed her eyes as they kissed. Every time still felt like the first, even though she must have kissed her a million times by now.

The corners of Erin's mouth tugged up as she pulled back. "Don't tempt me because I won't be able to stop if we start now." She stepped onto the ladder and climbed down, then held out her hand to help Celia in.

The water was refreshing and still, the only ripples caused by their movement. "There are no sharks here, right?" Celia asked with a grimace.

"No, nothing at all, actually. There's no food here for fish so they don't survive. It's hard for them to get in as it is, and the unlucky ones who do, usually die if I'm not here to help them out and throw them back into the ocean."

"Poor fish... but that does make me feel better." Celia wrapped her arms and legs around Erin, who held onto the ladder. "This is incredible." She gave her a sad smile. "And despite my uncle being sick, this whole trip with you has blown my mind."

"It's been amazing for me too." Erin looked at her intently. "You're very special to me, and I'm not letting you go. I meant what I said." She paused. "How do you see your future? Or is that question too much too soon?"

Celia shook her head and ran her hand through Erin's hair. "No, it's not too soon. I've thought about that a lot lately." She bit her lip as she hesitated. "I don't really know what I want from my future, but I know I want you in it." A shy smile played across her face and she averted her gaze, baffled that she'd just said those words out loud. "But you have your business and your life here and long distance isn't exactly—"

"Shh... No 'buts'." Erin's eyes welled up, and she swallowed hard. "If that's what you want—and you have no idea how happy you've made me by saying that—then we'll be fine. You can come here, I can visit you, whether you're in New York or in Switzerland, and we can always meet up somewhere in the middle until we've got it figured out."

"Okay, I like that plan but for now how about you join me in the shower and we forget about everything else." Celia smiled as she kissed the corners of Erin's eyes, tasting the salt on her skin. Erin was right; they would figure it out. They were here together now and she would make every second count.

65

"Good morning. How are you holding up, kiddo?" Dieter joined Celia at the beach where for the past hour, she'd been sitting on a towel, absently wiping clean a white, heart-shaped shell she'd found.

"I'm okay. I was up early, and I like it down here." She gave him a brave smile and rubbed his shoulder, noting the bags under his eyes were getting darker. "How are you feeling?"

Dieter shrugged. "Physically, I've been better, but I'm glad to still be here. Every day is a blessing; don't you ever forget that. Especially when you get to spend it with loved ones." He hesitated, dipping his head as he studied her. "Have you and Erin decided what you're going to do?"

"Not yet," Celia said. "But personally, I've been thinking about selling my business and starting something new. Something I'm more passionate about. These past weeks have made me realize life is short and that I've been wasting mine away by not living it to the fullest."

Dieter clapped his hands together. "Finally. I'm so excited to hear that."

"I thought you might be." Celia chuckled. "Erin has asked me to procure the interior art for a hybrid superyacht she's building. It sounds like a fun project and there's no rush or pressure as the build will take at least a year, so I'll have plenty of time to look around." She hesitated. "But it's still daunting. I've never done anything like that before and the budget shocked me."

"Big budget?" Dieter's eyes lit up. "But sweetie, that's every art dealer's dream. You should be delighted to have plenty to play with."

"I know... I guess I just need a confidence boost, that's all."

Dieter nodded as he turned to face the ocean. "Do you remember that Riviera Clairmonte I bought, several years ago?"

"Yes... the one I loved. I saw you still had it last time I was in your library."

"Exactly. I bought it because you loved it so much. That wasn't my pick, it was yours and frankly, I thought seventeen thousand euros was a bit much for someone who wasn't that established yet. But I wanted to have it so I could leave it to you one day. And guess what?"

"Well?"

"Its value has skyrocketed and it's worth at least ten times what I paid for it."

Celia was quiet as she narrowed her eyes. "Are you sure?"

"Yes. I know you haven't paid much attention to the art world over the past decade, but she really took off shortly after I purchased that painting. "And the Marco Bellani that we went to see in Florence together..."

"You bought that one too? But you said—"

"I know what I said—it was too delicate, too feminine, it

didn't have enough impact to leave a lasting impression," Dieter interrupted her with a grin. "But you're my favorite niece, so I took a chance and bought it a week after we got back. Six months later, I sold it and made a great profit. You have an eye for it, Celia, so stop doubting yourself. No knowledge can compete with instinct. It's the most powerful tool when it comes to buying art and you have it."

"Why did you never tell me about this?" Celia asked.

"I was waiting for you to come to me—for you to be ready. You suddenly quit university before you graduated, and I never understood why. I had a feeling something bad had happened to you back then, since it was so unlike you." He paused. "You used to tell me everything, and I like to think that you still do, but when I asked you why you'd dropped out, you kept saying that it just wasn't for you anymore, and that you didn't want to talk about it. So, I decided to wait for you to tell me the real reason and now seems as good a time as any."

Celia nodded. Looking back, leaving her dream behind had been a reckless thing to do and she was slowly starting to understand what had happened. "I just lost my confidence," she said, deciding to leave it at that. There was no trauma, and she'd had no bad experience. Just bad advice, and she'd been stupid enough to listen to it.

Her uncle waited for her to continue, and when she didn't, he pressed on. "You want to do this, I know it." He paused. "Look, I don't want you to think I expect you to automatically take up the reins. I can simply terminate the business and the pieces that I'm not attached to can be sold off. But if you're interested, I will give you all my contacts, and spend my last days boring you with tips and the tricks of the trade. You already have the family name on your side; being a Krügerner does help."

"Yes, I suppose you're right." Celia pondered over that. "How would I even start?"

"I think doing this project for Erin is the perfect way to start. Re-familiarize yourself with the market and put together a collection that both you and the customer are happy with. They will refer you to other clients; that's just how it works. And then, while you visit artists and galleries for your projects, you simply wait until one day you fall in love with a particular piece, and that one will be just for you. Don't go out looking for it; it will come to you. The first one is special, so hold onto it for a while and appreciate it."

"I'd be very careful; I wouldn't waste money like my brother."

"I know you wouldn't, but you also have to be realistic and know that it's a high-risk business. When you win, you really win. And apart from re-investing, you could do something good with part of the profit, once you get going. I'd like you to continue running my foundation once I'm gone. As you know, I've supported many struggling up-and-coming artists over the years."

"You'd trust me with that?" Celia was starting to see the enormity of running her uncle's affairs.

"Yes. You know I don't like to brag but my foundation has changed the lives of countless artists. I've rented studios for a couple of sculptors who needed a big workspace, and I've sent talented young people to good art colleges. It's been fun to see them blossom into the artists they are today." He shrugged. "On the other hand, dealing in art still has its downside. When you lose, you lose, but that's the nature of the game and you have to accept that and move on."

"You haven't lost much, though, have you?"

Dieter laughed and slapped his thigh. "That's a myth. I've made some terrible decisions throughout my career."

"You have?" Celia laughed too. "Care to share?"

A mischievous smile played around her uncle's mouth as he considered that. "I had a crush on this painter..."

"Let me guess; you bought one of his pieces just to get into his pants?"

"Yes." Dieter buried his face in his hands and shook his head. "I swear, my gaydar is never off. I genuinely thought he was flirting with me, but it turned out that he was straight."

66

"Thank you for dinner," Erin said as they were heading back from her favorite harborside restaurant in Port St. George. It was a warm evening, and the many hills they were conquering had her a little out of breath, but the walk was a beautiful one and she wanted Celia to experience the calm vibe of the island that she loved so much.

"You're welcome, it was the least I could do." Celia gave her hand a squeeze. "It's so pretty here. The pastel-colored houses and their flower-filled yards..." She directed her gaze toward the ocean. "And that coastline..." She smiled. "Do you have permanent residency here?"

"Semi-permanent. I'm an American citizen but as long as I have my business and my house here, I'm good. I still go to L.A. every two months to see my parents."

"Do they ever visit you here?"

"Sometimes. They prefer me to come to their house; my mother likes to be in her own kitchen," Erin said with a chuckle. "She doesn't understand why I have a housekeeper; that's just unthinkable to her."

"Right." Celia laughed. "To my mother, it would be

unthinkable if she didn't have one. She even has someone who opens her post for her. I think the person's title is PA 3, and I doubt she even knows his name." She waved at one of the locals who greeted them from his front yard.

"I bet she'd be far from delighted if she knew we were dating."

"Yeah, well, I've never cared much about what she thought of the women I've dated." Celia turned to her. "Have you ever brought a woman home?"

"No. It's never been serious enough for that and besides, with my parents, it's a little more complicated."

"Would you ever consider introducing a woman to them, though?"

Erin turned to her and stalled. "You mean would I ever consider bringing *you* home to meet them? Because you're the only woman in my life and it will stay that way for as long as you'll let me." She tilted her head and smiled at the adorable blush that crept onto Celia's cheeks. "Yes, I would introduce you to them. I can't promise it will be fun; I expect the situation to be highly uncomfortable at first, but you're amazing and they'd see how happy you make me eventually. My parents have had years and years to prepare themselves, so it won't come as a complete shock if I tell them I have a girlfriend." She put an arm around Celia as they continued their stroll.

"Well, you've already met my mother and it can't get any worse than that."

"I can't say I actually formally met her; she kind of dodged me, but I'm sure she has some good qualities to her," Erin said carefully. "What was she like when you were younger?"

"She was standoffish but caring, I suppose. My father and I were very close, and I always sensed that she felt she was competing with me, if that makes sense. When he died, she wasn't there for me as she was busy numbing her pain with a string of younger boyfriends, so we just grew farther apart. Maybe she couldn't handle his death, or maybe she held some kind of grudge against me; she always liked to put me down."

"Put you down?" Erin narrowed her eyes and tried to suppress the wave of anger she felt. She couldn't imagine anyone putting the kind and caring Celia down, especially not her own mother. "What do you mean?"

"Well, I've had a lot of time to think lately and..." Celia hesitated. "I studied art history, as you know, and I wanted to be Uncle Dieter's apprentice after I graduated."

"Okay... So, what happened?"

"I told my mother I was planning on asking him and she said that was a silly idea, that I could never do what he did, and that I was running the risk of making a fool of myself."

Erin saw Celia flinch, as if the penny had only just dropped—that she'd finally realized what had happened.

"My mother took my confidence away," she continued. "She made me believe I wasn't good enough to be an art dealer or a curator or anything I was truly passionate about. Part of me thinks that she just wanted to make me feel small, and she managed." She let out a long sigh. "I wasted so many years just because I thought I wasn't good enough."

"That was a terrible thing to do," Erin said. "Even if you had no talent whatsoever, that was for you to find out yourself, not for her to tell you."

"Yes, I see that now. I remember vividly how my fellow students were always blindly supported by their parents. They were there at every presentation, bragging about how great their kids were, no matter what their grades were. And the way they looked at them so proudly... that was always a painful mystery to me because I never got that look from my mother."

"I'm so sorry to hear that." Erin's voice trembled with compassion for Celia. This woman was an incredible human being, and she hadn't even felt appreciated by her own mother. Life wasn't fair that way. "My parents didn't accept me for who I was initially, but they got over it, and now they're very proud of what I've achieved. Their approval is actually important to me and it must be hard for you not to have that." She took a tighter hold of Celia's hand as they continued up the path toward the house. Andy's high-pitched voice rang through the night air, shouting something about a Scrabble related word. Any other time it would have been funny but tonight, she ignored it. "It makes me so angry to think she wasn't there to encourage you and support you. You must have felt so alone."

"I was fine; it was a moment in time and I'm over it. I've learned to live without my mother's approval, I just wish it hadn't taken me so long to realize she wasn't always right." Celia shrugged. "Despite her shortcomings, I know that deep down she loves me, but she'll always put herself first and I used to be okay with that because I had my father, and later, Uncle Dieter in my life." She fell silent for a moment, contemplating that soon, she would only have her mother left. "I know things are going to change," she said quietly. "When she finds out that I've inherited Uncle Dieter's fortune she'll be the nicest mother in the world. I just have to remember that it won't be real. At least most of it."

67

"Here we are." Erin tied the small speedboat to the private dock, then held out her hand to help Celia out. "It's probably not what you expected; we only work on two vessels at a time, so it's less industrial than most shipyards."

"Looks pretty spectacular to me," Celia said as she looked around. Next to two building berths, a huge slipway sloped down into the water. "And how wonderful that you're able to take the speedboat to the office instead of driving."

"Yes, that part is very nice. Being on the water every morning gives me a great start to the day because it connects me to what I do." Erin waved at the security guard who was sitting in a small building at the end of the dock, then pointed to the berths. "This is where everything is welded and fitted together. After that, the ships are floated to the fitting-out basin. The interior is made to order in factories and workshops all over the world and delivered just before it's fitted. The other buildings are storage units holding basic interior and building materials."

"I'm a little overwhelmed." Celia stared at the enormous

steel carcass in the first berth and tried to imagine what it would look like when it was finished. "You said you designed yachts, but this feels more like architecture to me. That thing is larger than my mother's summerhouse."

"Of course; it is architecture. Maritime architecture to be precise, but I prefer to use the term design. It has more feeling to it and encompasses the process from beginning to end. I have very talented designers and construction experts on my team to help me through every step of the way but ultimately, I'm involved in all aspects of the build."

It wasn't until then that Celia understood how much Erin's work defined her, how she lived and breathed construction and design, and she admired her passion and courage to take on such significant projects. Although she'd spent a couple of hours a day on her laptop and she'd worked while she was on duty during their trip, she didn't come across as a workaholic. No, Erin simply did what she loved the most, and she'd managed to find a balance that allowed her to have a life too.

Next to the small parking lot, a staircase led up to a modern L-shaped office building that was built on a high concrete base. "And this is my studio," Erin continued, leading the way up the stairs. "It's Sunday, so no one is here today. It's normally quite noisy, but you'll get the idea and I'll introduce you to my team next time you visit."

Celia smiled at the idea of 'next time' while she waited for Erin to unlock the door. She'd been curious to see where Erin spent most of her time, and when she'd offered to show her around the shipyard that morning, she'd been really excited. "Swanky," she said, taking in the slick, white interior. The roof held a skylight that followed the L-shape of the office, ensuring all the desks sitting underneath had natural light. One wall was covered in detailed floor plans, another was adorned with mood boards containing fabric swatches, paint and material samples alongside inspirational imagery. "Is that your workspace?" she asked, gesturing to a big rectangular table in the corner that held a computer with a big screen and piles of rendered imagery.

"No, that's our rendering specialist's table. She needs a lot of space to lay out her proposals." Erin walked over to a high standing desk that only contained a closed laptop, a notebook and a pot with stationary. "This is my desk."

"Hmm... doesn't look like a 'boss' desk to me," Celia teased, arching a brow at her. "And how can you stand all day? Isn't that super tiring?"

"I never get tired, and it's a boss desk, all right." Erin returned her flirty look and wedged Celia between the desk and herself. "In fact, the boss thinks you should lie down on it right now. It seems like the perfect height to—"

"Hey, what are you doing?" Celia giggled as Erin lifted her up onto the high table.

"What do you think I'm doing?" Erin pulled off Celia's panties, hiked up her dress and flung her legs over her shoulders. "Good thing you're wearing a dress. Makes it so much easier to do this."

"Fuck!" Celia threw her head back as Erin pulled her forward by her hips, leaned in and ran her tongue over her center. She steadied herself on her elbows and closed her eyes while Erin's mouth attacked her, determined to make her come hard and fast. Erin knew exactly how to push her buttons and being taken in her office was beyond arousing. The feeling of her tongue running up and down her folds was exquisite, and the way she pulled her tighter against her almost made her come right there and then. Needing more, Celia shifted toward the edge and wrapped her legs around

Erin's neck, then leaned back as Erin's mouth worked its magic.

"Yes..." Celia panted, moaning and wiggling in her grip. She fought to keep her eyes open as she'd never witnessed anything as erotic as what Erin was doing to her right now. The way she licked and sucked at her like it was her one and only mission to make her come hard and fast, her fingers digging into the skin of her thighs while she brought her to the brink of an almighty orgasm.

Suddenly, Erin pulled away and stared at her from between her legs.

"What are you doing, boss?" she asked in a husky voice, her breath heavy as she reached out to run a hand through Erin's hair.

"Nothing. I just wanted to look at you for a moment. You're so sexy when you let go." Erin licked her lips before she delved back in, making Celia moan loudly.

"That's... Oh my God." Celia's breath hitched, and she bucked her hips while she gave into the delicious throbbing pulse in her clit. She watched her lover bring her to the edge again, and this time, she didn't stop. The sight of Erin feasting on her was so sexy that she was unable to look away, even when her eyes were threatening to shut tight.

"Good?" Erin flicked her tongue over her clit, causing the tightening in Celia's core to intensify, and she shuddered against her mouth. The echoes of her loud cry bounced off the walls, no doubt reaching beyond the office on the quiet premises.

"Yes! Yes, yes, yes..." Her voice trailed away as she fell back, covering her face in her hands.

Erin moved up and kissed her belly with a big grin on her face. "I've always wanted to christen this desk. But never in my wildest dreams did I think I'd have Celia Krügerner on it."

"Well you've certainly fulfilled your fantasy and Celia Krügerner wants to get underneath your desk now." Celia shot her a mischievous look as she sat up and jumped off, then walked around to the other side of Erin's standing desk. "Open your laptop," she said. "And do what you would normally do first thing in the morning."

Erin looked puzzled, but she complied and opened her laptop. "Why?" Typing in her password, she waited for her emails to load.

"Because I've always wanted to do *this*." Celia got down on her knees and crawled toward Erin underneath her desk to unbuckle her belt.

68

"What was my parents' relationship like?" Celia crushed a cracker in her fist and threw the crumbles onto the lawn. Immediately, the chickens came running over, feasting on the treat. She liked having them around. They were entertaining and very tame; some even let her pet them. "I remember them together, but at the same time I don't. I suppose they were rarely in one room together the last years before my father died."

Dieter leaned forward, and steadied himself on his knees, then joined in with feeding the chickens. "They were happy at first," he said. A deep frown appeared between his brows. "Your mother still worked as a model back then. I vividly remember the day he told me he'd met her. He phoned me after he came back from a business trip in L.A. She was doing a photoshoot there and they got talking at the bar after her shoot. He said he'd met this beautiful and mysterious woman who he couldn't get out of his mind. Your mother was beautiful indeed, but he hadn't exaggerated about the mysterious part either. I don't think anyone really got close enough to learn about her background, not even your father. Now and then, he'd picked up clues after she'd made a casual comment but in general, she didn't like to talk about her family in Texas, and he never met them."

"She never talked to me about her life before Dad either," Celia said. "I sometimes asked her about my grand-parents, but she always brushed it off, made me feel like it was a no-go topic, so I stopped enquiring."

"Yes, your father did the same. Saying that, I do believe she genuinely loved him, and he loved her. She moved in with him in New York and they were happy together for a couple of years, but your mother was very difficult to live with. He told me once he thought she had deep-rooted abandonment issues, but she refused to seek help. She was very mistrustful and paranoid, and since your father trav-eled a lot for work, they argued a lot." Dieter paused and pursed his lips, hesitating before he continued. "Your father came to see me at the castle for a couple of weeks one summer. He came alone, said he needed to get away as their situation was getting toxic and he wasn't sure if he could continue to live with her. I suppose being his older brother, I was his confidant and he wanted my advice. Although he was madly in love with her, life was just becoming too stressful." He shrugged. "I didn't want to meddle in their relationship and told him I couldn't come between him and your mother. That week, she called to tell him she was preg-nant with you."

"So they stayed together because of me?" Celia asked.

"I believe so. The wedding was rushed as your mother didn't want to have a baby bump in her dress."

"Typical." Celia chuckled. "Appearance has always been hugely important to her."

"Yes. I suppose being a model and not having an education... Add to that the fact that her family was not in the picture, perhaps it was all she had to hold onto."

"Was she happy to have me?"

"Yes, I believe so. But she never really knew how to be a mother when you were very young. I think she wanted to, but I could see her struggle when they visited. Your father on the other hand, was a natural parent, so she left a lot of it to him. He was the one who played with you and put you to bed when he was home, whereas your mother was more reliant on your nanny to keep you entertained." Dieter crumbled up another cracker and threw it between Celia's bare feet, laughing when the chickens started roaming between her legs and nipping at her toes.

Celia chuckled and pulled her feet up underneath her. "You never liked her, did you?"

Dieter shook his head. "It wasn't that. I just never understood her because she never opened up. And I felt sorry for her. She got what she always wanted; a wealthy husband, a family, a stable home and still, she wasn't truly happy. Material things made her happy short-term, though. A gift, a lavish vacation, or a shopping trip. And she loved visiting the castle. For someone who always wants more, I guess having a castle is the ultimate fantasy."

"Do you think she loves me?" Celia asked.

"Yes. She may be selfish, but I know she loves you. She just doesn't know how to express it." Dieter looked at her pensively. "Your mother was never able to really connect to people on a deeper level—not even your father—and seeing how close you were to your father frustrated her, I suppose. The fact that she didn't have that special relationship made it hard for her to witness the strong bond between the two of you." He paused. "Then, seven years later your brother was born, and she showered him with affection. It was like she felt she had a second chance to do better."

"Maybe that's why they're so close."

"Perhaps. Or maybe they're more alike and therefore understand each other better. You're your father's daughter. You have his morals, his generosity, his character, his dark hair, his smile, even his laugh. And Fabian is more like your mother both in appearance and in character. Blond, blue eyed, reserved, materialistic..."

"Hmm..." Celia absently emptied the remains of the cracker box on the lawn and stroked one of the chickens. "Do you know if Dad ever tried to track down her parents?"

"No. He thought about it later on in their marriage; we talked about it. He hoped it would give him a better understanding of who his wife was but at the same time, he knew it would ruin their marriage if he did. But then he got sick and he never went through with it."

Celia took a deep breath and tried to push the memory of her father's death to the back of her mind. She'd never talked about him much, but she felt that now was her only chance to learn more about him, as her uncle was the one person in her life who had been close to him.

"I wasn't there when he died," she whispered. "I wasn't allowed into the hospital room."

"He didn't want you to see him like that." Dieter patted the rattan couch he was sitting on and Celia got up from her chair, walked around the table and sat down next to him. She leaned in as he put an arm around her. "But I was there," he said. "And your mother was. It was the only time I've ever seen her cry."

"My mother cried?" Celia buried her head in the crook of his neck as she tried to imagine her mother emotional. She often got upset, but it never involved crying. Tantrums were more her thing. "I wasn't sure if she cared at the time. She wasted no time finding herself a younger boyfriend."

"I'm sorry she wasn't there for you. But I hope I was able to make a difference."

"You did." Celia let out a long sigh. "When Fabian and I came to stay with you the following summer, I could finally breathe again. Just having your support and not feeling like I had to be strong for Fabian all the time really helped. Roderick was great with us too."

"Yes. He always wanted children. We even spoke about adopting for a while, but then he...." Dieter's voice trailed away. "Well, it wasn't meant to be." He smiled. "But I had you and Fabian. He was a good boy when he was younger. I think he just lost his way a little and that's not strange considering his father died when he was much younger than you. Your mother did the best she could with him."

"Yeah. I worry about him sometimes, but he's got Mom." She closed her eyes, cherishing her uncle's familiar smell of cigars and red wine. "And I'm very lucky to have had you. Thank you for everything you've done for me."

"That's all right, kiddo, but I'm not gone yet." He kissed her cheek and ran a hand through her hair. "When I'm gone, I want you to talk to your mother. I think all the attention-grabbing behavior is a way of trying to get close to you. She creates this unnecessary drama because she has no idea how to just ask you outright if you care. Trust me; she knows she hasn't been a great mother and I'm certain she has many regrets."

Celia was silent as she considered that. "Okay," she finally whispered. "I'll talk to her."

69

G loom settled in the pit of Celia's stomach as she closed her last suitcase. They were flying home today and that not only meant the end of her time with Erin for now, but it also meant the end of her adventure with her uncle. He was deteriorating and although she was relieved that he'd soon be in the care of his own private doctor in Switzerland, she also knew her worst fear was about to come true.

They'd spent days playing Scrabble by the ocean together while Erin was at work. They'd named all the chickens as they could tell them apart by now and they'd had endless conversations about her parents, his past and his career. He'd stayed strong, laughed and participated as much as he could, but she'd not seen the normally ever-present sparkle in his eyes for days. He was tired, and he was giving up.

Wiping away the tear that rolled down her cheek, she took a deep breath and told herself to get a grip. She was tired too. She was tired of feeling emotional, tired of pretending, and she was tired of holding back her tears. *Stay strong.*

"Hey, babe." Erin came up behind her, brushed her hair to the side and gently kissed her neck.

"Hey. How was work?" Celia closed her eyes, cherishing the feel of Erin's soft lips on her skin.

"It was busy. Sorry I'm late; there were some things I had to take care of because I'm coming with you."

"What?" Celia turned to her and felt a lump rise to her throat at seeing Erin's earnest expression. "But you're super busy and—"

"There's nothing that can't wait." Erin pulled her in and wrapped her arms tightly around her. "We've started this journey together, and I want to be there for you and Dieter until the end; I've already discussed it with him."

"Thank you." Celia buried her face against Erin's neck and inhaled her scent. It brought her comfort, it always did. As they stood there and held each other, the jumble of emotions that coursed through her brought her to tears, but she swallowed them away and closed her eyes tight, adamant that she wasn't going to break down. Not yet.

Her phone rang on the bed, pulling them out of the moment, and she sighed deeply when she saw it was her mother. "I'd better get this; I haven't spoken to her in a while." She grabbed it and went outside to take the call, hoping the ocean breeze might keep her calm as she always got a little anxious when talking to her mother. As her uncle hadn't spoken to the family yet, Celia had been avoiding her, only sending short messages to let her know where she was. "Hey, Mom."

"Celia?" There was a pause. "Why haven't you answered my calls? Is everything okay?"

If Celia wasn't mistaken, she'd think her mother was worried about her, and she appreciated that. "Yes, everything is fine. I'm in Bermuda with Uncle Dieter, Andy and Erin. We've had a great trip and we're flying back to Switzerland tomorrow morning."

"Switzerland? Why on earth would you all go back there again? Don't you have work? Doesn't that woman have a life?"

Here we go again. As always, the hint of affection she felt for her mother was short-lived. "Her name is Erin," Celia said sharply, rolling her eyes toward the sky. "And yes, she has a wonderful life which I'm going to be a part of. We're together and I love her." She stalled and covered her mouth with her hand, shocked by the words that had just left her lips. Did she really love Erin, or had she just said that to wind her mother up? It was a huge statement for anyone to make, and for her, it was almost unthinkable.

"You what? Did you just say you love her? Celia, listen to me, that's just straight-out nonsense. You've only just met, you don't even know her and..." Babette Krügerner continued her rant but her words didn't register anymore. Glancing through the open doors at Erin, who was packing her suitcase in the room, Celia felt a surge of warmth, and she knew it was true. This woman had swept through her stable life like a tornado and turned everything upside down, and at the same time, she'd been her rock, keeping her sane and safe. She trusted her.

"Mom, I'm going to pass you onto Uncle Dieter now," she said when she saw her uncle standing at the edge of the cliff. "He'd really like to talk to you." Dieter grimaced and shook his head, but she ignored it and pressed her phone into his hand. "Tell her," she whispered. She could still hear her mother's protests as she walked back into the bedroom and closed the door behind her.

"Everything okay?" Erin asked.

"Yeah..." Celia took Erin's face in her hands, marveling at her handsome smile for a beat before she kissed her softly. It felt different this time, and the touch of her lips engulfed her like a warm blanket as she allowed herself to feel things she'd never felt for another woman before. Yes, she loved Erin, and although it had come as a shock, she wasn't afraid to love.

Sensing a shift in her, Erin pulled back to study her. "Are you sure you're okay?"

Celia nodded as she locked her eyes with Erin's. "Maybe this is too much, too soon, but..." Her voice trailed off, and she was suddenly anxious to say it out loud.

"Hey, that's my line," Erin joked, easing the tension. "What is it? Come on, you can tell me anything; you know that."

"I, ehm..." Celia hesitated as she ran her hands through Erin's hair. "I love you."

The silence that followed lasted so long that Celia panicked for a moment. Erin raised her head, opened her mouth to speak, then closed it again. "I'm sorry; I shouldn't have said that. I get it if you don't feel the same or if it's too soon."

"Shhh..." Erin hushed her. Her smile widened, and the swell of emotion in her eyes told Celia she was immensely touched by her words as she pulled her closer. She leaned in and pressed her forehead against Celia's. "I love you too."

70

Despite the cheery greetings echoing off the walls in Krügerner Castle, there was a tension in the dining room that anyone would have picked up on. A family gathering was rare unless there was a reason for celebration, but no reason had been given for this Saturday afternoon summoning. Hopeful and overly friendly stares were directed at Dieter, who was sitting at the head of the table, waiting for the food to arrive before he would make his announcement and use the rest of the afternoon to say his farewells to everyone.

After they'd returned to Switzerland, he'd been in bed most days, only venturing downstairs or outside for a couple of hours in the afternoon when he felt strong enough, and Celia, Erin and Andy had spent many hours playing Scrabble and watching old movies with him in his bedroom. The four of them had grown so close that there were no more secrets between them, and by now there was no doubt that Andy would always be in her life, just like Erin would always be by her side.

Celia glanced at her mother. She was wearing all black

—a color she only ever reserved for dramatic funeral appearances. They hadn't spoken yet as she'd arrived fashionably late with her brother in tow, but Celia suspected that they weren't the only ones who knew about her uncle's illness. Her Great-Aunt Margareth, her Great-Uncle Fredrick and their two daughters were also dressed in black, and so were her second cousins Peter and Bertrand, who had undoubtedly only shown up in the hope of inheriting part of his fortune.

Her uncle didn't seem to care about the somber crowd as he joked and made small talk with everyone. Unlike his guests, he stood out in the room and was wearing a pink suit Celia had never seen before. It matched Andy's, and she'd heard them laugh as they got dressed together. She'd been highly amused as her uncle never wore bright colors and it made him look like a campy seventies' TV presenter, with his white shirt, pink silk tie and tiger print shoes.

Plates with his favorite foods—schnitzel, sauerkraut, mashed potato and heaps of gravy—were brought in and placed in front of his guests before the staff topped up the red wine. In their circles, the dishes being served were considered totally inappropriate, but just like his suit, Celia knew it was a 'fuck you' to everyone who had criticized him for being so flamboyant and eccentric throughout his life.

Erin was sitting next to her, and that had also attracted curious glances. Celia didn't know her relatives that well; most of them weren't close family and although she'd met them many times at the castle, she'd felt no desire to keep in touch with them. Her mother kept telling people her sexuality was a phase, and so the party seemed surprised that she'd brought Erin to an official luncheon.

To an outsider, the view over the room must have looked a little comical. Dieter and Andy wearing pink, Celia and

Erin dressed mostly in white, and various other relatives who looked like they were going to a funeral. Celia took pity on them as she imagined the situation being highly confusing. What do you wear to someone's final family meal? What do you say to a man who is about to die? Even if they didn't care all that much about him, it must have been difficult coming here.

"Dieter, you look sensational in pink," her mother lied. "Have you lost weight?" She shot him a wide smile as she looked him up and down.

Celia could hardly believe what she was hearing. Her mother had never been very subtle, but this was a whole new level. She glared at her, then almost felt sorry for her when she looked down at her plate shamefully. Clearly, she had no idea what to say either.

"Yes, Babette. For all the wrong reasons but nevertheless, thank you for the compliment." He loosened his tie, then tapped his spoon against his crystal wineglass and addressed the table. Immediately, the room fell silent.

"Dear beloved family. Thank you so much for coming here today and at such short notice. As most of you know—in fact, I believe all of you know by now—I don't have much longer to live." Dieter cleared his throat and paused for a moment. Andy stood, too, and took his hand while he continued. "I'm grateful to have this opportunity to see you all one last time, and to tell you how wonderful it's been to have known you. Family is important, whether it's family by bloodline or chosen family." He smiled as he turned to Andy and Erin. "And because family is so important, I wanted to make a couple of announcements while everyone is here, so there will be no..." Pausing, he chose his words carefully. "Confusion about my will."

Celia took in a quick breath as she saw him glance at her

mother for a split second, and it suddenly clicked that he'd arranged this meeting not for himself, but for her. Following her father's death, their family had fallen apart after her mother had contested his will, and it had taken a good five years for most of them to be in the same room again. Will or no will, this way, there would be no ambiguity over what her uncle really wanted.

"As my primary beneficiary, Celia will have full ownership of Krügerner Castle, my art collection and all my personal belongings. I trust her to keep the castle in her name for as long as she's able to. I have arranged to be buried here, so if you should ever visit after my death, please stop by my mausoleum in the back yard and say hi," he joked. There was no laughter at his black humor as all attention had shifted to Celia now. "Celia will run the castle in a way that best suits her lifestyle. I'm aware the upkeep in relation to this fabulous piece of medieval architecture and its staff is not cheap, so she may have to commercialize it. That means you won't always have the opportunity to vacation at the castle anymore, and in fact, this may be your last time here."

Dieter took a sip of his wine while absorbing the silent tension in the room. "Celia has also expressed the desire to take over my business and with that, she will gain ownership of my business account of which the balance will not be revealed. I'm immensely proud to say that she's just accepted her first project, procuring the art for one of the biggest superyachts ever built. She has raw talent and I know she will do very well for herself." He rested his eyes on Babette again and paused for a moment, making sure she'd heard him loud and clear.

"Now, onto my cash capital. My accountant told me I have a little short of fifty million euros across private accounts and funds, which I must admit, is not bad for someone who started off with the generous but far smaller family capital of one point two million at the tender age of twenty-one, when my father died." He smiled and paused again as everyone held their breath. "Now since most of you are very lucky already, I've decided I want to help those who are less fortunate. Therefore, of the fifty million, twenty million will be put into my foundation to send talented kids from a poor background to art college." Ignoring the exasperated gasps in the room, he continued. "Another twenty million will be divided between six different charities related to planet conservation and LGBTQ youth. Due to lack of support and understanding, I struggled with my sexuality when I was younger and I know how hard it can be here, let alone in underdeveloped countries."

The latter was a dig against at least three people in the room, for sure. Celia saw her mother and brother's faces go paler than milk as it sunk in that they would get very little, if anything from Dieter's will, but there was nothing they could do. Causing a commotion would expose them as greedy vultures among the rest of the family, so their only option at this stage was to say nothing.

"Finally, seven million will go into a fund to pay for castle renovations, property taxes and so forth, and that leaves three million," he said in an exceptionally chirpy tone for someone in his situation as the faces before him dropped with disappointment. "And as you will be pleased to learn, that will be split between all of you, and that includes my dear Andy."

A sudden strange noise sliced through the room as everyone exhaled, already mentally calculating how much they'd take home. It disgusted Celia, and she wondered how many discussions had taken place over the years, speculating when her uncle would finally kick the bucket and how much they would inherit.

Dieter walked over to Erin and put a hand on her shoulder. "I've appointed my dear friend Erin here as the executer of my will. She's not family and therefore impartial, but above all, I trust her with my life." He winked as he turned to Celia. "And I can't begin to tell you how happy it makes me that Celia and Erin have found each other. Because what's more beautiful than love, right?"

Murmurs rose from the older and more conservative family members, and Erin looked slightly uncomfortable as she gave everyone a wave. Celia expected dirty looks but instead, fake smiles were cast in their direction. Even her mother managed a semi-motherly smile, knowing Celia would soon be the lady of the castle.

Dieter walked back to his place at the table and sat down with a deep sigh. "I think that was all I had to say. Let's eat and mingle with a drink together afterward. I can only function for a maximum of three hours a day and I'd like to take this opportunity to say goodbye to all of you."

71

"It's time," Dieter mumbled. He glanced from Celia to Erin and Andy as he took Celia's hand. His eyes were tired, half closed, and he didn't seem aware of the dribble that ran from the corner of his mouth.

They were standing around his bed after his live-in doctor had been called to his room in the middle of the night. He'd been confused, drowsy and in a lot of pain for a while, but since his latest dose of morphine, he'd started speaking again. The lights were dimmed, and they'd moved Dieter's bed to the back wall that had floor to ceiling windows, so he could look out over the lake.

"I'm very grateful you're here. You're my chosen family and you're all that matters." He paused, catching his breath to continue. "Celia, you're my angel, you always have been. Before your father passed away, I promised him I would take care of you. Your brother was a little younger, and although he loved him just as much, he was mostly worried about you because you were so much like him; kind, generous, loving, but that also made you vulnerable, unlike the rest of our family." Even on his death bed, Dieter still managed a sarcastic chuckle. "Anyway, I hope I made good on that promise. I believe I did the best that I could."

Celia nodded and squeezed his hand, trying her hardest not to cry. "You've always been there, through everything. You're the only one I trusted, and I hope you know how much that meant to me." Keeping her emotions under control had become more manageable after three months with him. Maybe she'd made peace with the fact that he was dying, maybe deep down she wanted him to go so he wouldn't suffer anymore, or maybe she'd simply run out of tears. She suspected it was a combination of all three.

"May I?" The doctor squeezed through, wearing one of the castle robes. His eyes were puffy, his shoulder-length gray hair a tangled mess, and he looked nothing like a doctor while he took Dieter's pulse in his opulent bedroom. Seeing him take care of her uncle in the past two weeks, though, Celia knew he couldn't have been in better hands.

"Anything we can do to make you more comfortable, Mr. Krügerner?" he asked. "Water? More pillows?"

"No, thank you, Bernard. It's been a nice ride, but I'm done with this."

"You might feel better tomorrow..." Celia realized her words made no sense as she placed a cool cloth on his forehead and wiped his mouth with a napkin. There was little hope he would make it until the morning, especially if he had no desire to live anymore. Her uncle had been reasonably okay for quite a while, but since returning to the castle, he'd deteriorated quickly and now he was pale and skinny, only a shell of the man he used to be.

She'd never been able to imagine him as skinny, despite the extensive cleanses and diets he did from time to time in a fruitless attempt to lose weight because his doctor had told him he was at risk of a heart attack. They'd never worked, or maybe he'd never really tried; he was a hedonist after all and had always enjoyed the finer things in life, including food and wine. Not only had he lost a significant amount of weight now, but he was fragile and weak, his loose skin almost translucent, and it was incredibly hard to see him like this.

"I won't feel better tomorrow." Dieter gave Celia a small smile and squeezed her hand. "You know that too." He let out a long sigh, his body relaxing a little after the morphine. "This is it; I can feel it. Strange, isn't it? That one can know when the time has come. And I want you to know that I'm okay. My life has been full of love and fun and wonder. Even the loss of my dear brother and Roderick have not stopped me from enjoying it, and I want you to do the same, after I'm gone."

Celia was unable to fight back her tears any longer as she sat down on the bed next to him. "I love you," she whispered, her bottom lip trembling. He looked so fragile, as if a gentle nudge would break him into a million pieces.

"I know, sweetheart. I love you too. More than you will ever know." Dieter groaned quietly as he slowly turned his head to Erin and Andy. "And I love you both too. Very much." He raised a brow at Erin, who was in floods of quiet tears. "You've been here for me through all of this and you have no idea how much it has helped me, to not be alone in the fight. But you need to pull yourself together, my friend, because you need to stay strong for Celia. She's going to need you." Then he focused his eyes on Andy. "And Andy, my love, you are very, special and talented. You just need a little push of confidence to help you in life, so I hope you're ready to become my property manager for the coming year."

Andy's eyes widened, and he shook his head. "Hey, that's

not fair, we haven't even discussed this and I'm not capable of..."

"You'll be fine," Dieter mumbled. "There's nothing you can't do if you believe in yourself, and I believe in you. I've discussed it with Celia. She's more than happy for you to help her."

"I don't want a job, I want you," Andy whispered.

"Life is life, Andy. Panta Rei; everything flows..." Dieter's voice trailed away as his eyes fluttered shut.

"Wait, don't go. Please." Andy got on the bed and wrapped an arm around Dieter's chest. "I need you." Tears were streaming down his cheek and his whole body was shaking as he pushed his forehead against Dieter's.

Celia cried too as she watched her uncle slip away. Away from them, away from the room and away from his body. The corners of his mouth tugged up into a tiny smile as he let out a long breath. At that moment, she would have given anything to know what he experienced. She waited for the next breath, but it never came. Then she felt Erin's arms around her. He was gone.

72

"I can't believe he left us with this impossible task," Erin said as she closed the file Dieter's notary had sent over to Celia. "We discussed the formal part of his funeral, but we never went into this much detail. Frankly, I think it's a little naughty of him that he kept all of this from me." She sank farther down in Dieter's office chair and rubbed her face.

"This is exactly why he kept it from us," Celia said with a humorous smile. "First, he has you sailing halfway around the world and now he wants us to arrange a funeral that would put a Cirque du Soleil show to shame." She glanced over the list that was endless and full of detail. "A biodegradable papier-mâché coffin with hand-written messages from every single artist he's ever worked with, an all-white celebration of his life for three-hundred and fifty guests with a gospel choir, a pagan ceremony and seven white horses pulling the carriage with the coffin around the castle grounds? And what's this thing about Andy?" Sitting back with a sigh, her eyes met Erin's and they couldn't help but chuckle at the absurdity of the situation.

"Did I hear my name?" Andy asked as he let himself into the office. He looked tired but there was also a sense of relief about him after having been at Dieter's bedside for days on end. "Do you need my help with anything?"

"Yes!" Celia and Erin both said in unison, then laughed out loud. It felt really good to laugh again, and Celia had no doubt that her uncle's over-the-top demands were put together just to keep them busy and quite possibly even entertained in the weeks after his death. Erin had been amazing in the past three days, consoling her, but also giving her space when she needed it. This morning, she'd dragged herself out of bed, knowing she had responsibilities and would have to get on with things. Thirty-five family members were due to arrive at the castle next week for a three-day get-together before his funeral. She'd also briefed the staff this morning, discussing room arrangements and menus with them. The hectic schedule had been good for her, as the endless enquiries had kept her busy and distracted to the point where she hadn't had a moment to herself. And then there was the funeral, of course—something she'd just learned would be far from straightforward.

"What's so funny?" Andy took the file, his eyes widening as he scanned Dieter's final wishes. "What the fuck? And I thought I was the diva in our relationship. I hope he had good insurance because this won't be cheap."

"Clearly you weren't the biggest diva." Erin rolled her eyes. "And yes, he had very good insurance. It looks like what started with a lavish celebration will end with a lavish celebration. Did you see the thing about the all-male ballet performance over dinner?"

"I can't say I mind that part," Andy mumbled, looking intrigued as he kept reading. "And oh my God, I get to ride in a carriage and lead the procession."

"It seems like you're getting your ultimate *Andy show*," Celia joked. She felt her mood lifting just a little, and she was happy to see a hint of enthusiasm from Andy's side too after he'd locked himself in Dieter's room for days on end.

"It's the *Andy show* all right. I told him a while back I've always wanted to ride in a carriage pulled by white horses, dressed in white, and I can't believe he remembered that. But playing the lead in this kind of gig was never part of my show-girl dreams." Andy let out a deep sigh. "Why did Dieter do this?"

"He just wanted to distract you, I think." Celia paused as the corners of her mouth curled up. "And perhaps piss off Great-Aunt Margareth and Great-Uncle Fredrick. They always put him down for being gay and a little different when he was younger; I can only imagine their faces when they show up for the funeral. But all of that aside, I think it will be beautiful and reflect Uncle Dieter's personality. It's just unusual, that's all." She stood behind Erin and put her hands on her shoulders. "Honey, I know you don't have time for this, so Andy and I can put a team together. Are you okay with that, Andy?"

"Of course. I'll do anything I can, and I'm sure the castle staff would be happy to help. Lina has been very upset; I think it would be good for her."

"My mother and brother are staying here until the funeral, so they might as well make themselves useful." Celia kissed Erin's cheek. "You can use his office to work; we'll move the funeral preparations into the parlor."

"Are you kidding me?" Erin shook her head. "I love a challenge, and this is about as challenging as it gets. I'll check in with work tonight; the time difference is kind of a blessing right now. I used to work sixty hours a week and I'll do it again if I have to, so don't worry about me."

"Very well." Andy walked over to the big filing cabinet in the corner of the room. I'll get Dieter's Filofax, see if I can track down all those artist's numbers. I noticed there were only twenty contacts in his phone; he's always been old-fashioned like that." He sighed. "If all artists email us a message, a picture or whatever they want within the next three days, we'll have them in time to have the coffin made." He glanced around the room. "Do we even have a printer?"

"No, I don't think so." Erin scrolled through her phone. "I'll order one now, make sure it gets delivered tomorrow with plenty of ink and whatever type of paper we need to make this work. There's a company in Zurich that makes those coffins, so I'll call them today."

"Great, that would be helpful. Then I'll try to find those white horses," Celia said, sitting down on Erin's lap as she produced her own phone from her pocket.

"And I'll get onto the pagan minister after I've tracked down those artists." Andy pursed his lips. "I imagine they're just as rare as unicorns around here."

73

Celia shot her mother a smile as she passed her in the corridor. They hadn't spoken much as they'd been busy with the funeral preparations and that was just as well. It had been years since they'd been around each other for this long and their interaction was rusty to say the least.

"Good morning, dear."

"Good morning, Mom." She expected her mother to walk on so they wouldn't have to engage in small talk but instead, she stalled and lingered.

"How are you holding up?"

"I'm fine." For a moment, Celia didn't know what else to say, but her mother still made no effort to leave, so she continued. "It's been very hard."

"I figured as much." Babette's expression softened and she took Celia's hand. "I'm sorry, honey. I know you loved him very much. It must feel like you're losing your father all over again."

"Yes." Celia swallowed hard, unsure if her sudden swell of emotion was caused by the mention of her uncle or her mother's rare display of affection. "I miss him."

"I understand. I still miss your father every day." The statement came as a complete and utter shock. Celia had never heard her say anything that sounded so authentic, and clearly her mother hadn't seen it coming either as she bit her lip and frowned. "I'm..." She hesitated. "I'm sorry I wasn't there for you when your father passed away. I know you hate me and you're—"

"Mom, I don't hate you."

Babette stared at her and Celia would have given anything to know what she was thinking. Even though her behavior was as predictable as the weather most of the time, the woman was still a mystery to her. "You don't hate me..."

"No. You're my mother. I still love you, despite everything."

Babette's eyes welled up, and she averted her gaze, staring down at her pumps as if searching for a reply. The obvious answer would be 'I love you too', but this was Babette Krügerner, and she was a little more complicated than that. "You do?" As she raised her gaze back up at Celia, confusion passed over her features. "But I've been a terrible mother; I've done everything wrong. I'm still doing everything wrong."

Celia felt for her, because she had immense trouble expressing herself as her mouth opened and closed while her hands balled into fists. She couldn't help her though, not in this instance.

"I love you too," Babette finally whispered in a shaky voice. "What I did to you was unforgiveable, but you have to understand that..." Taking deep breaths, she tried to regain control over her emotions. "Our marriage wasn't great. I was always afraid your father might leave me. And then when you came along, you and your father were so close that I felt like I didn't fit into my own world anymore." She shot a shifty look at one of the staff members who passed them.

"Do you want to go and sit somewhere private with me?" Celia asked. Now that she had her, there was no way she was going to let this conversation end unfinished. Without waiting for an answer, she placed a hand on her mother's back and led her outside to one of the benches in the back yard. "Is this okay?"

"Yes, here is fine." From the way she acted, it was clear her mother was totally out of her comfort zone and that wasn't strange as serious conversations didn't come naturally to her. The silence that followed wasn't uncomfortable, but Celia knew she'd have to be the one to take charge or this would end right here and now.

"Why was it so hard to be a mother? Did you regret having me?"

Babette shook her head. "I admit that getting pregnant was a means for me to save our relationship at the time but no, I never regretted having you. My only regret is that I was a bad mother, and I wish I'd done things differently. I just didn't have maternal instincts the way every single other woman in this world seems to have. Years later, I tried again with Fabian and it was a little more natural with him but even so, it was still a struggle." She shrugged. "Truth be told, I didn't have the best example myself."

"What do you mean by that?" You never talk about your side of the family."

"No." Babette tensed up, her body and brain immediately switching into fight or flight mode. "We're not going to go there; I shouldn't have brought this up." She paused. "Maybe one day, but not now. This week is hard enough as it is, I don't want to burden you with my past."

"It's not a burden. I'm here if you want to talk," Celia said, placing a hand on her knee.

Babette looked down at her leg as if an alien object had just landed on it, but she reached out and placed her own trembling hand on top. "Thank you, but maybe it's time that I see a professional first. It's long overdue."

It was the most intimate they'd ever been, and Celia wanted to hug her, really hug her. Not like the polite greetings they usually exchanged, but one that expressed love, which she assumed her mother had never received from her own parents.

"I envied you," her mother said. "I still do. You always had your father's unconditional love, and you grew into a real person, a good person. God only knows how you managed to turn out like that. It was your father's influence, I suppose. He was a good man." She sniffed, and for the first time, Celia saw a tear trickle down her cheek. "And you were beautiful and talented and everything I never was. You still are, despite..." her voice trailed away, and she let out a long sigh.

Celia had no idea how to reply. She wasn't going to tell her mother that she had put her down time after time; she already knew that. "It's not too late. We can still have some sort of a relationship," she said instead. "A better one, I mean."

"Would you be open to that?"

"Yeah. We're talking. This is a start, isn't it?" She gave her mother a small smile. "It's more than we've ever had." Celia saw something new in her mother's eyes. Hope.

"If you let me, I promise you that I'll do the best that I can. I know I can't make the past go away, but I would love nothing more than to have another chance with you."

"Okay. Let's take it one step at a time. Maybe we could

meet up for lunch, just you and me when I'm back in New York?" Celia looked up when she saw Erin walking around the castle. She stalled when she spotted Celia and her mother and was about to walk back, but Celia called her over. "But first I want you to make an effort with Erin. She's the love of my life."

Babette nodded and gave her hand a squeeze, then raised her hand to give Erin a clumsy wave. "I don't ever think we've formally introduced ourselves," she said, getting up. "My name is Babette Krügerner, Celia's mother."

74

"Dieter Krügerner was a free spirit," Erin said, looking over the crowd of people gathered around the mausoleum, then to the coffin that, along with Roderick's remains, would be placed inside a marble sarcophagus and laid to rest inside the tomb. Every guest had placed a single white rose on top of it, filling the air with the scent of late summer. She was the last speaker and was adamant to get her message across. "I like to think that he still is. He was the only person I've met who truly lived life to its fullest, right to the very end. No regrets." She cleared her throat and put a hand on Celia's back. Celia had kept herself together during her own speech, and she would do the same. With three-hundred and fifty pairs of eyes on her, she was not going to cry, she told herself. "I believe that we were meant to meet that night, at Mark and Djuna's house," she continued, briefly smiling at the couple. "And that he came into my life for many reasons. He gave me joy, wisdom, laughter, inspiration, support, strength and love. Love, he always said, was the greatest gift of all." Taking a deep breath, she leaned into Celia as her hand curled around her waist. "So, let's remember Dieter with love in our hearts and a smile on our faces. It's what he wanted." Swallowing hard, she looked at his coffin and bowed her head as she threw the last rose inside. "I'm going to miss you, my friend."

Soft murmurs rose in the yard as a violin quartet started playing *'Adagio'* by Albinoni, and a shiver ran through her when she pulled Celia into a hug. She felt not just her own relief, but Celia's relief too.

"Thank you, that was beautiful," Celia whispered. She squeezed her tight and held her like she had no intention of ever letting go. "You did so well," she whispered, and kissed her cheek.

"So did you. Just a couple more hours, then we'll have the place to ourselves."

"Good. I can't wait. I'm just going to check on the cellist and—"

"Already done," Erin interrupted her.

"Oh." Celia squeezed her hand. "Then I'll—"

"Hey, stop. You can sit down with me for dinner. Trust me; the event planner's on top of everything and you really need to eat something substantial."

Celia nodded. "Okay. I hope she put me next to you. Did she? I haven't even checked..."

"Of course. And Andy's at our table too, I've asked the staff to bring breakfast to our room tomorrow. Besides food, you also need sleep and I want to ensure you don't leave the bed all day."

"Thank you. That sounds really, really nice." Celia straightened her long, white cowl-neck dress before they walked into the opulent dining space where some of the guests were already looking for their tables. "Are you ready to endure my family for the last three hours of the day?"

"I am. I made small talk with your brother and your mother has actually been quite nice to me today."

When they stepped away from the mausoleum so people could pay their final respects, Erin saw that not only were the guests focused on the one-of-a-kind blue pearl granite building, but also the white horses. In their rush to get everything organized, they hadn't thought about what they were going to do with them after the procession, and Celia had asked the owner to leave them there as her uncle would have appreciated it. She walked up to one of them to stroke its neck.

"They seemed so fitting here today, right?" Andy said as he joined them. He looked immaculate in his white suit and top hat.

"They do. How are you holding up?" Celia asked.

"Hanging in there. I'm just glad the hard part is over." Andy shrugged. "It may have seemed over-the-top a week ago but that really was a beautiful service."

"Yes, it was, and you did well." Celia gave him a hug. "I think my uncle would have been proud."

"I think so too." Andy swallowed hard, avoiding her gaze. "Well, I'd better go and get myself a drink. I really need one by now."

Celia nodded and patted his back. "You go do that. We'll be there shortly."

Erin took a couple of deep breaths, centering herself. Tired and drained after the funeral preparations, it felt good to finally be able to relax a little, but with that also came the grief and the realization that he really was gone. Just like Celia, she would remember Dieter as he was. Loud, cheerful, chubby, and always smiling. And yes, she agreed that he would have loved the funeral. The mausoleum near the lake at the end of the back yard truly was a piece of art. The gardener had planted rose bushes around it and placed candles on the ridge, and with all guests dressed in white, it had been a sight to behold. As she looked back at it one more time, she saw that two doves had landed on the roof, and that made her smile.

As they sat down at the head of the longest table, Celia reflected once again on how much her life had changed since she was last at the castle with Erin. Just over three months ago, Erin had grabbed her wrist when she was on her way to the restrooms. At the time, whilst flirting with her, she'd been blissfully ignorant—oblivious and unprepared for the roller coaster that was about to turn everything she knew to be true about her life upside down. She'd travelled the world, seen extraordinary things. She'd made beautiful memories that she would cherish forever, and she'd felt great joy and immense sadness. While sailing, she'd reflected on her life and had become inspired to make changes to her career as well as her personal life, and she'd regained confidence in herself and her abilities. She'd lost the person closest to her but had been fortunate to spend his final months by his side, learning from him and living those precious moments to the fullest. She'd made a friend for life in Andy—a man who had perhaps seemed a little shallow at first—but whom she knew to be one of the most decent people she'd ever met. And she'd found love. What had started as pure passion had turned into something deep, meaningful and lasting. Erin was the one for her, and Celia had no doubt Erin felt the same.

Her heart swelled when she saw genuine concern in Erin's eyes. She had no idea what she would have done without her. Erin had helped her through a very difficult week, and she'd been instrumental in coordinating the complex funeral preparations. She looked tired too.

"Thank you for being here for me," she whispered. Erin's white suit looked incredibly sexy on her and despite the sad day, she longed to touch her. "I'm going to miss you when I'm back in New York."

"I'll miss you too, but it won't be forever." Erin leaned in and inhaled against Celia's hair before kissing her neck, then retracted as people joined them at their table.

"No. As soon as I've taken care of things, I'll come visit you in Bermuda. I'm hoping to have everything wrapped up before Christmas." Celia patted Erin's thigh, then turned to her Great-Aunt Margareth sitting next to her. She didn't like the woman one bit, but she reminded herself that her uncle had always welcomed every family member with open arms, and she would do the same.

EPILOGUE

"Hurry up, babe. We're going to miss the flight." Erin glanced at her watch while she waited by the front door of the castle with suitcase in hand.

"No, we won't. The airport is only a twenty-minute drive, so stop pressurizing me," Celia said, then turned to Andy. "Andy, call me if you have any questions, okay?"

"Will do. Now get your cute ass going." He slapped her behind and gestured to the door. "Erin's right; you need to leave."

They'd spent three weeks in Switzerland, so Celia could help Andy prepare a series of events. The castle had been booked for four huge weddings in May, then there would be another wedding and the annual summer ball in June, which Celia and Andy would throw in Dieter's honor, and she'd also organized a networking event to which she'd invited all Dieter's contacts, alongside ten up-and-coming artists who would have their work displayed in the ballroom during the event. While also working on Erin's new project, she'd been super busy, but now things were about to calm down a little.

Celia had rented out her apartment in New York, and her assistant was in the process of buying herself into her business so she could take a step back and be a silent shareholder. New York seemed like a lifetime away since Krügerner Castle had become her business hub and her second home. After her uncle's death, she'd spent most of her time with Erin in Bermuda, though. They both travelled a lot; sometimes together, sometimes apart. Their evenings by the beach at *The Beautiful Dead End* were incredibly precious to her, and she was looking forward to the coming weeks, in which they'd have more time for each other. She'd work from home while Erin went into the shipyard, and she planned to visit the office to discuss the art she had in mind for the spaces that had now been signed off on Erin's new project. They'd have many beautiful and peaceful mornings and nights in bed together and Celia needed that, because the past weeks had been stressful, and she could feel a growing tension between them today. They only ever quarreled about one thing; Erin was a stickler for time, and she was the opposite.

"It's fine; it's Sunday so the traffic will be light."

"We still have to take the rental car back, though. Seriously, you need to hurry up." Erin was pacing now, irritation written all over her face. "I never missed a flight in my life until I met you, but this year it's happened twice already."

"Quit riding my ass! I can't think when you do that." Celia sighed and scrolled through her phone, checking off the list of things she'd have to bring back with her. "I can't find my phone charger."

"We'll buy a new charger at the airport."

"I don't want a new charger; I want my own. It's got a really long cable and a built-in LED light, so I can use it in the dark. They're really hard to find."

"Yes, the pink one. You packed it. I'm sure of that." Erin groaned and held her hands up in defeat. "You know what? I'll put my stuff in the car. Meet me outside in five minutes. I can't watch you pull everything out of your suitcase for the second time." She walked over to the sideboard under the hallway mirror where they always kept the keys. "Where are…" Rummaging through her pockets, she turned to Celia. "Do you have the car keys?"

"No, they're under the mirror. I saw them like five minutes ago." Celia lay down her suitcase to open it, then huffed in frustration when the zipper got stuck.

"Well, they're not. Are you sure you don't have them?"

"Yes, I told you, I…" Celia's voice trailed off as a strange feeling overcame her. It wasn't physical or mental, but something in between and it made her heart race. She stopped fidgeting with the zipper and stood up to look around the grand hallway. Holding her breath, her eyes darted up the staircase, then to the ceiling.

Andy and Erin were suddenly quiet too.

"It can't be…" Andy followed her gaze, but there was nothing but an eerie silence.

"Uncle Dieter, is that you?" Celia felt a little silly as she said it out loud, but Erin and Andy kept quiet as if waiting for an answer.

"If this is you, it's not funny," Erin added. She sounded equally unsure of herself, but Celia could tell by the goose bumps on her arms that she'd felt it too. "Celia and I have a flight to catch and this is no time for games."

They stood nailed to the ground for long moments, waiting for something, anything to happen.

"I'm not sure what to think of this," Andy whispered, rubbing his arms.

"Me either." She turned back to Erin and as she looked

at her, a moment of total clarity came over her. Her heart swelled as their eyes locked, and she closed the distance between them and wrapped her arms around her waist. "You know what? It's only a stupid charger. I don't need it." She smiled and rested her forehead against Erin's. "I love you so much, and I don't want to bicker."

"I love you too." Erin took her face in her hands and the emotion reflected in her eyes brought a lump to Celia's throat. Erin kissed her softly, as if she suddenly had all the time in the world to do just that.

"I love you too," Andy repeated in a sickening tone, rolling his eyes at them. "Come on, lovebirds, I'll drive you. If the keys have magically reappeared by the time I get home," he continued, raising his voice as he glanced around the hallway, "I'll take your rental back for you. If not, you'll just have to pay to have it picked up."

"Again," Erin added with a sigh.

Celia laughed and gave Andy a long hug. "Thanks, Andy. You're a peach." She took Erin's hand, picked up her suitcase and followed by Andy, they went outside. Just before Andy closed the door behind them, she could have sworn she heard the jingling of keys.

Andy held up a finger to hush them. "Did you hear that too?" When Erin and Celia nodded, he opened the door again to check the hall, but there was no one there and there were still no keys under the mirror. "Am I losing it? Please tell me if I am..."

"If you're losing it, then we all are." Celia glanced at the mausoleum at the end of the yard. "Wait. There's just one more thing I need to do before we leave." She expected protest from Erin, but instead, Erin took her hand and went with her. They picked some wildflowers from the edge of the lawn and put them at the base of the stone mausoleum.

"I miss you, my friend," Erin said.

"We both miss you very much," Celia whispered, squeezing Erin's hand. "We'll be back soon." She nodded at Erin, letting her know she was ready to go.

Erin put an arm around her and as they walked to the car, Celia leaned into her, feeling blessed to have found true happiness with the woman she loved.

A love lost; a love gained. It was bittersweet, but she took comfort in the hope that maybe her uncle was watching her. And she would make him proud.

AFTERWORD

I hope you've loved reading *Blue* as much as I've loved writing it. If you've enjoyed this book, would you consider rating it and reviewing it on www.amazon.com? Reviews are very important to authors and I'd be really grateful!

ACKNOWLEDGMENTS

Writing 'Blue' over the pandemic was challenging, and I couldn't have done it without the lovely people who have supported me throughout the process.

Niki (Wonder Woman), thanks for your encouragement, kind words, and for giving me a peaceful space to write. I hope I can return the favour one day when I have my own oasis in the sun.

Claire Jarrett, thank you for being patient, supportive and always honest about my writing. You've not only been a fantastic editor, but also a good friend, and I really value our working relationship as well as our personal relationship. I also appreciate the title suggestion as I was really stuck on that one :)

I also want to thank my proof/beta reading team. Laure Dherbécourt, I always enjoy working with you and I wish you all the best in this new chapter in your life. DJ - you are so efficient, and Alistair Grant, it's been a real pleasure!

ABOUT THE AUTHOR

Lise Gold is an author of lesbian romance. Her romantic attitude, enthusiasm for travel and love for feel good stories form the heartland of her writing. Born in London to a Norwegian mother and English father, and growing up between the UK, Norway, Zambia and the Netherlands, she feels at home pretty much everywhere and has an unending curiosity for new destinations. She goes by 'write what you know' and is often found in exotic locations doing research or getting inspired for her next novel.

Working as a designer for fifteen years and singing semi-professionally, Lise has always been a creative at heart. Her novels are the result of a quest for a new passion after resigning from her design job in 2018. Since the launch of Lily's Fire in 2017, she has written several romantic novels and also writes erotica under the pen name Madeleine Taylor.

When not writing from her kitchen table, Lise can be found cooking, at the gym or singing her heart out some-where, preferably country or blues. She lives in London with her dogs El Comandante and Bubba.

ALSO BY LISE GOLD

Lily's Fire

Beyond the Skyline

The Cruise

French Summer

Fireflies

Northern Lights

Southern Roots

Eastern Nights

Western Shores

Northern Vows

Living

The Scent of Rome

Under the pen name Madeleine Taylor

The Good Girl

Online

Masquerade

Santa's Favorite

Printed in Great Britain
by Amazon